OUTLAW JUSTICE

OUTLAW JUSTICE is the fourth story to feature potter's daughter, Mathilda of Twyford, and the Folville brothers; criminals from the fourteenth century nobility.

Book One - The Outlaw's Ransom
Book Two - The Winter Outlaw
Book Three - Edward's Outlaw

The Outlaw's Ransom can also be found within the timeslip contemporary fiction novel, Romancing Robin Hood, written under Jennifer's romantic fiction pen name, Jenny Kane.

JENNIFER ASH

OUTLAW JUSTICE

Littwitz
PRESS

COPYRIGHT

Littwitz Press
Dahl House, Brookside Crescent
Exeter EX4 8NE

Copyright © Jennifer Ash 2020
Jennifer Ash has asserted her rights to be identified
as the author of this work in accordance with the
Copyright, Designs and Patents Act 1988.

First published in Great Britain by Littwitz Press in 2020

www.littwitzpress.com

A CIP catalogue record for this book is available
from the British Library.

ISBN: 978-1-9993501-3-0

Dedication

To my amazing children.
Loved always.

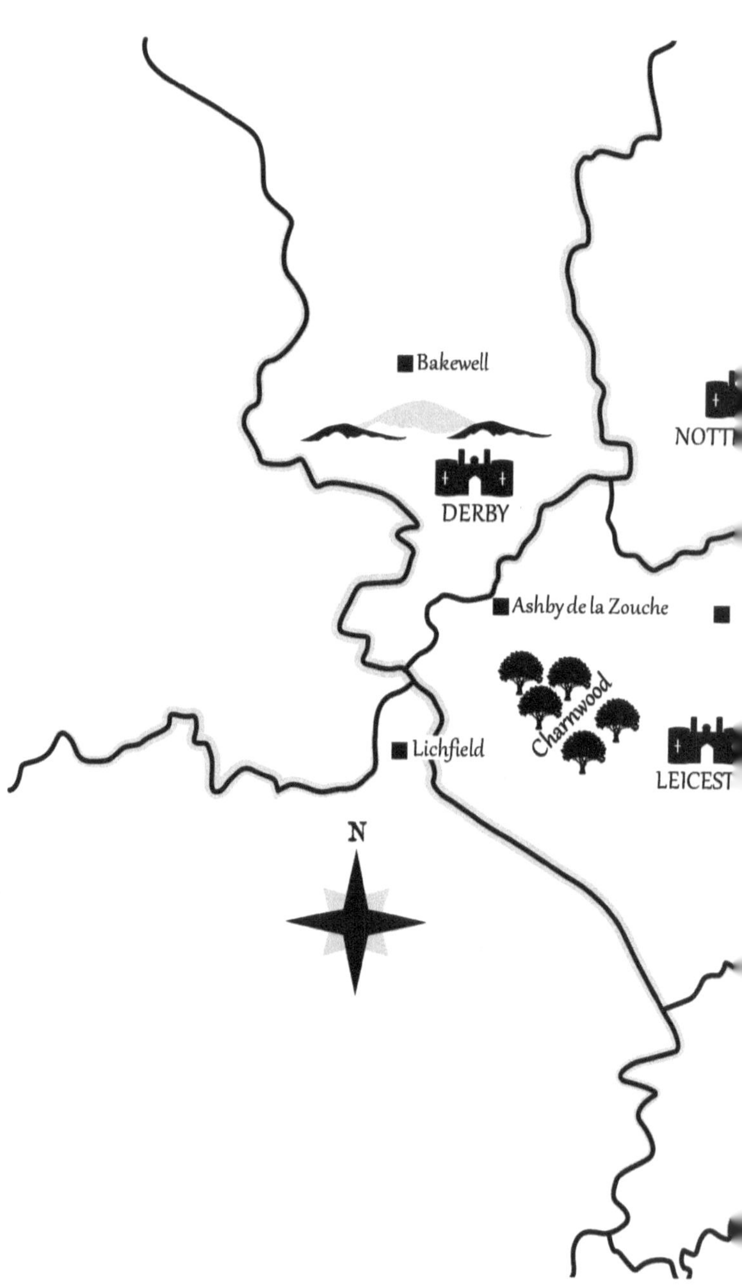

Bakewell
NOTT
DERBY
Ashby de la Zouche
Charnwood
Lichfield
LEICEST
N

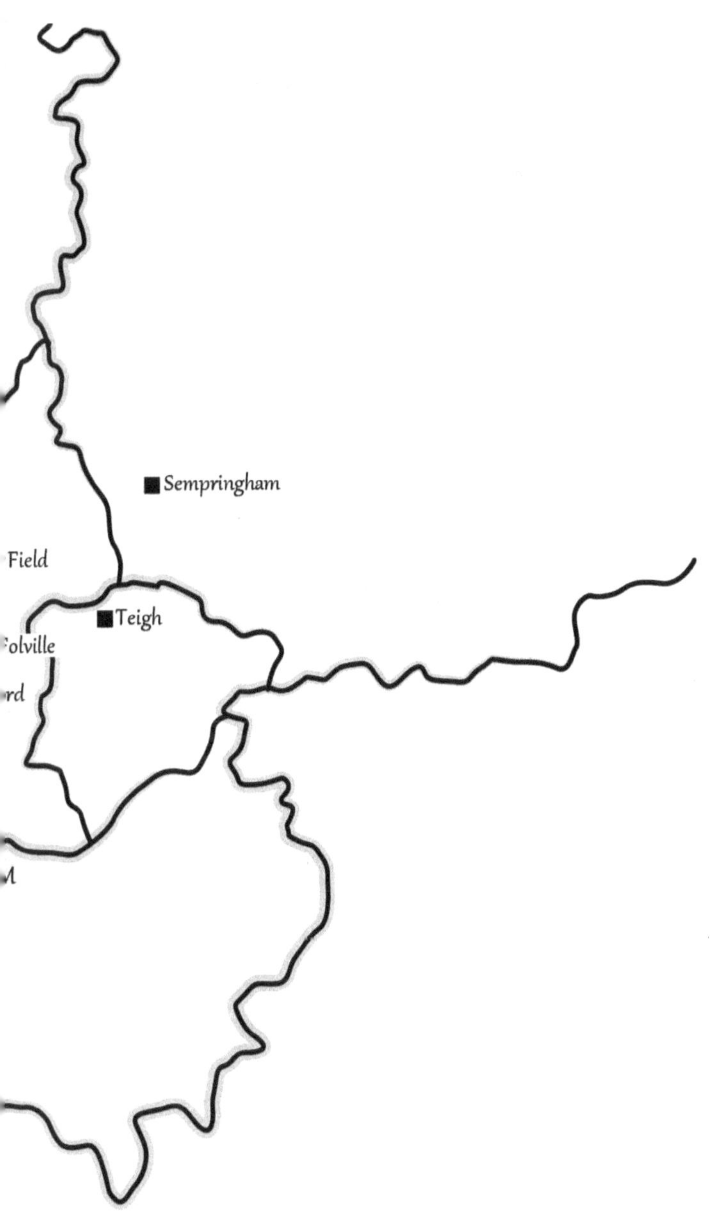

Sempringham
Field
Teigh
Folville
rd
Λ

"And some to ride and some to recover what unrightfuly was won;"
"He instructed men to win it back again through strength of hands"
"And to fetch if from false men with Folvilles Laws"

Langland, Piers Plowman

The Coterels poached, ambushed, had a spy in Nottingham, ill-treated clerics, were pursued by bounty hunters and the sheriff, operated in Sherwood, entered royal service, had as an ally a member of the gentry who had lost his inheritance, were retained at one time by a local magnate and wore his livery.

Bellamy, J. G., Crime and public order in England in the later Middle Ages (1973)

~ *Prologue* ~

30th November 1331

'Lady Isabel is safe, my Lord?'

'I've seen her escorted to her mother in Lincolnshire by trusted friends. Her ravings these past few months have become intolerable. It's not good for the children. I increasingly fear for her sanity.'

Keeping his countenance neutral, Bennett removed his master's cloak. 'May I be of assistance, my Lord? A drink after your journey perhaps?'

'You may be of assistance by saying nothing of this to anyone. If King Edward were to hear of my wife's shameful state, he might deem me unworthy of the office he so recently bestowed upon me.'

Bennett dipped his head respectfully and withdrew into the kitchen. He'd worked for Sir Richard de Willoughby long enough to know when to keep his mouth shut.

Damping down the kitchen fire for the night, absorbed in thought, the steward headed towards Lady Willoughby's chamber. He'd seen no signs of mental instability. He'd heard no ravings. He had, however, heard a row between her and her husband earlier that day. The one and only time in her whole miserable marriage she'd stood up to her lord.

Pushing his mistress's door open, Bennett surveyed the scene. Lady Isabel's travelling cloak hung over the back of a chair by the window. Her hairbrush sat on her side table, and her riding boots waited patiently by the door.

A furrow formed on the steward's forehead as he closed the chamber door, locking it securely behind him.

~ *Chapter One* ~

2nd December 1331

Eustace de Folville shook the parchment in his fist. 'The king has made him Justice to the Court of the King's Bench! As if his arrogant head wasn't swollen enough with power. We need to act. Now!'

Not one of his brothers argued.

Glaring at the crumpled missive, Eustace slammed a palm against the oak table which took centre stage in Ashby Folville manor's hall. 'We can delay no longer. Our removal of that leech, Roger Belers, was a bold step towards curbing the corruption that plagues this land. But that particular Baron of the Exchequer was nothing compared to this scourge on society. This... Justice!

'He steals lands and chattels, using the law to cover his tracks; doing anything to improve his estate's assets. An estate everyone knows only exists because both he and his father married well; although I pity any woman who has to share his marriage bed and '

'Justice!' Walter de Folville spat into the fire, sending angry orange sparks dancing. 'The fact Willoughby has the right not to mention the cheek to call himself a justice...'

Robert de Folville cut across his kin's escalating outrage, pushing two flagons of ale in their direction. 'Perhaps you could tell us what the missive actually says, brother?'

Grunting, Eustace glared at the parchment as if it was responsible for the coming storm. 'It's from Nicholas Coterel. Word has reached his family in Bakewell that, as of yesterday, the first of December, Sir Richard de Willoughby, Chief Justice, has been commissioned to arrest Nicholas, James, and John Coterel, and as many of their associates, protectors, and supporters as he can. On the word of a vicar!'

The eyes of Robert, Laurence, Thomas, and Walter de Folville moved as one; their gazes landing squarely on their reverend brother, Richard, Rector of Teigh.

With his usual righteous indignation, the churchman blustered, 'You look at me, but you know I wouldn't do this. Nor could I have done.'

'For once, this evil does not fall at your door, Richard, but you need to decide. Now. Are you with this family or against it? Your deeds in recent years have made your loyalties questionable to say the least.'

'I will not dignify that with an answer, beyond stating that I am a Folville. Anything I may have done is nothing compared to the deeds of Willoughby.'

Robert's eyes narrowed. The suffering his clerical brother had caused him and his wife, Mathilda, was far from trifling. 'Willoughby's excesses have gone on too long. He rigs court cases, pockets fines, and changes the rules as he goes along. The Coterel brothers have always agreed that action must be taken against this man, and now they are under direct attack from him; as are we by association.'

'As were you personally, Robert,' Thomas de Folville stared into the flames, 'along with Eustace and Walter, last January when Willoughby ordered you to be detained over the alleged theft of a horse and some cattle. We heard of the order, but nothing happened. Why is he acting now, but did nothing then, I wonder?'

'Whatever his reason,' Robert mused, 'it'll be for personal gain. This isn't just about protecting our own people anymore, not like it was with Belers. Willoughby's range has stretched from his home in Nottinghamshire, across Leicestershire, Warwickshire, Derbyshire, and Lincolnshire.'

'And the Crown will never stop his excesses,' Thomas growled. 'Young King Edward continues to be happily blind to the corruption left in his mother's wake.'

'Then maybe,' Robert frowned, 'we should use this opportunity to show the Crown what its chosen man is doing? Send messages to London that would make the king sit up and take notice of the ambitions of Willoughby?'

Thomas smiled. 'Fine words, Robert, but this isn't a Robyn Hode story, and if James Coterel couldn't convince the king of Willoughby's misdeeds when he was the queen's bailiff, then how can we convince Edward now?'

'It will take some thinking about.'

'It takes no thinking about!' Eustace slammed his hand against the table for a second time. 'The world is better off without Richard de Willoughby. It's obvious. The man has to die.'

Robert grimaced. 'Many nobles in the region will aid us. Feelings run high on this matter.' He gestured towards the parchment. 'If the Coterels are concerned enough to alert us to Willoughby's orders, we can't delay any longer.'

'What say you, Rector?' Eustace's eyes locked onto those of his clerical brother. 'You are remarkably quiet for one so opinionated.'

Richard gave a calculating smile. 'I was just wondering what the fair Mathilda will say when she learns that we intend to wipe a second of the king's most empowered officials from the face of the earth?'

'He has a point, Robert.' Eustace narrowed his eyes. 'Don't speak of this to your wife. Better she knows nothing until the deed is done.'

'What if the situation could be used to change things?' Mathilda put away the pretence of doing embroidery. In truth, she'd been doing little more than stabbing at the cloth with a needle while her husband shared the details of the meeting he'd had with his brothers, omitting their plans for Willoughby's ultimate disposal.

'I had the same notion,' Robert unbuckled his belt, letting his sword drop to the bed. 'But change things how?'

'To make King Edward take notice. To make him confront how bad the corruption within his justice system has become.'

Repeating the point Eustace had made earlier, Robert shrugged. 'But if James Coterel couldn't make the king see sense while he was bailiff to Queen Philippa, what can we do bar taking more direct action?'

'Direct action doesn't have to mean murder.'

Robert held his wife's gaze. He hadn't mentioned killing Willoughby; but she'd been a Folville long enough to know what the brothers considered a failsafe solution to the biggest problems.

'James Coterel proved he was not to be trusted with his bid to take control of Rockingham Castle. It is little wonder King Edward wasn't swayed by his plea. Why would the Crown believe a word he says?' Mathilda paused, her fingers traced over her stitches. 'You've never told me the details of Roger Belers' death.'

Robert's eyebrows rose. 'But you do know of it. The man was a ruthless tyrant. We had to take action.'

Mathilda's eyes returned to her sewing. It would all need unpicking before Sarah, their housekeeper, saw it and tutted at her lack of wifeliness. 'I know why his death happened. I do not know *how* it happened or who delivered the killing blow.'

Robert took his wife's hands in his. 'Does that matter now?'

'Of course it matters.' Mathilda, used to her new family's reputation, had never been able to square Robert's gentle nature with the act of murder. The people called the brothers' actions "Folvilles' Law", taking the necessary steps that the judicial system was unwilling to make towards a fairer England. But it was still murder, however pure the motives. 'What can be learnt from your actions all those years ago? Can we apply those lessons now?'

Robert kissed her hand. 'You're plotting something.'

'I am thinking something through.'

Suddenly, Robert was suspicious. 'Eustace and my brothers bade me not to speak to you about our plans for Willoughby, and yet, despite that, you seem to have ideas ready on your lips?'

Undaunted, Mathilda smiled. 'I have been your wife for nigh on three years. Did you think I wouldn't learn how to listen through walls so I can keep track of this family's ventures? I am aware you only tell me the bare minimum out of courtesy. It is in my interests to make sure my husband isn't too reckless. I have a strange desire for you to come home alive and whole from your enterprises.'

Robert couldn't help but laugh. 'Tell me about the musings resulting from your spying, wife.'

'There might be a way, but Eustace won't like it. You

might not like it either, and it would mean disruption to us all if it works. And worse if it doesn't.'

'Doesn't everything we do?'

'True.' Mathilda stroked a hand over the butterfly girdle she wore at her waist, 'But my idea would leave Willough-by alive.'

'My brothers won't like that.'

'Even though it could save all your lives?'

'Willoughby is a blight on society.'

'But he isn't the only one, is he? How many of them do you need to expunge from England before the king notices that the problem isn't you and the Coterels, but the majority of our legal officials?'

'By fighting these justices we are branded the problem, not them.'

'Exactly! Don't you get tired of them using you as an excuse for their underhand activities? They pursue their se-cret crimes, committing increasingly worse atrocities, while telling the Crown of *your* misdeeds; using them to mask their own.'

Robert raked a hand through his hair. He knew Mathilda was right, but persuading Eustace not to charge in and kill Willoughby wouldn't be easy. 'I confess I'd be happier with his complete removal from God's good earth.'

Mathilda turned her palm around and slipped it into his, enjoying its comforting weight. 'Better, surely, to have Wil-loughby humiliated and his power curbed?'

Robert levered his wife from her seat by the fire and steered her towards the bed. 'Taking away his power would be immensely satisfying.'

'It wouldn't just be his power either. All the country's justices' entitlements could potentially be curbed.' Wrap-ping her arms around his neck, Mathilda whispered, 'You need to tell me everything. Then, should the others agree, we'll plan a way of steering things. If we're clever, we might even be able to ensure Willoughby talks himself into a noose all on his own.'

~ *Chapter Two* ~

2nd December 1331

Sarah rested her hands against the edge of the table, laying down the knife she'd been using to peel a pile of apples. 'On the word of a vicar?'

Adam nodded, pouring his wife a mug of weak ale before turning his attention to building up the kitchen fire. 'Not even a recent incident, apparently. Something that has been left to simmer for years until it's become useful.'

'The Church lowers itself further in my estimation with every new day.'

'Shh!' Adam looked over his shoulder in case any of the family should hear her. 'You don't want to be saying things like that too loud.'

Snorting, Sarah took a swig of her drink. 'The Folvilles would agree with me if you asked them.'

'Even Richard?' Adam struggled not to snarl when he spoke the name of the clerical Folville. He hated that he and his wife had to sleep under the same roof as the man, albeit only when the rector of Teigh visited the family manor. He had treated Sarah appallingly in the past, blaming her bitterly for many of his own failings. Every time Adam laid eyes on him, it was an effort not to pull the knife from his belt.

'He has less belief than any of his kin.' Sarah flexed her right arm, which was given to stiffening since she'd been stabbed a couple of years earlier. 'You're right though, I shouldn't say such things. If young Bettrys heard me, she'd be scandalised. The maid has fitted in well, and learnt much since she arrived here, but she clings to the teachings of the Church as if they're a lifeline.'

'Understandable.' Adam reached across the oak table and gave Sarah's hand a quick squeeze. 'The girl was badly shaken by her life at Rockingham Castle. It is not so strange she moved closer to the church rather than away from it.'

Sarah conceded the point. 'The vicar of Bakewell; you were going to tell me what complaint he'd laid at the Coterels' door.'

The steward allowed himself a seat at the kitchen table. 'According to Lord Robert, back in August of 1328, Lords James, John, and Nicholas Coterel, with the help of Roger Savage… do you know him?'

'Of him, certainly. Savage has been an ally to the family on occasion. Go on.'

'Well, this vicar, Walter Can, claimed he was evicted from his church by Savage and the Coterels, who then stole ten shillings from the collection plate. Possible, do you think?'

'Not just possible. It happened.' Sarah retrieved her knife and sliced through an apple as if it were thin air. 'If memory serves, it was a commission the Coterels received from Robert Bernard of Lichfield Cathedral. The Reverend Can had been getting rather free with his services.'

'When you say services, you aren't referring to the religious kind, are you.'

'Bernard was convinced Walter Can was stealing church funds. There were also rumours about the demands he made in the name of "friendliness" on some of the women of the parish.'

'Hypocrite!'

'The ten shillings the Coterels took back was a fraction of what Can stole. It was more a warning than a robbery.'

The sound of booted feet heading towards the kitchen sent Adam to his feet as he asked his wife, 'Why now, though?'

'Perhaps Willoughby has Can in his pocket.'

Eustace de Folville snorted as he strode into the housekeeper's domain. 'Does nothing miss your ears, woman?'

'Very little, my Lord.'

'Then you'll have worked out that the Coterels' blow against the misdeeds of Can is nothing but a convenient excuse. A cover for the real motive behind Willoughby's long-held need for revenge.'

'Certainly I have.' Sarah lifted a jug of ale. 'May I offer you some refreshment, my Lord?'

'A flask of ale for my journey would be welcome.'

Adam picked up an empty skin flask for Sarah to fill. 'You are leaving us, Lord Eustace?'

A half-smile played at the corner of the Folville's lips. 'Perhaps you'd see to the horses. Thomas, Walter, and Laurence will ride out shortly too.'

Sarah opened her mouth to ask a question, and then shut it so abruptly that Eustace burst out laughing. 'What's this, Mistress Calvin? No comment on the briefness of our stay at the family home?'

'I'm sure you know your business best, my Lord.'

'I'm quite sure you know our business too.'

The housekeeper's cheeks flushed. 'I was not listening in on your meeting, my Lord. Nor would I presume to.'

Eustace saw Adam grin as he left the kitchen for the stables. 'I would never suggest such a thing. I merely stated how astute you are.'

Sarah grunted, but her eyes shone with amusement. Eustace de Folville might be one of the most ruthless men in England, but she remembered him and his brothers as tearaway children who ran her ragged while their parents' toured Britain. 'Behave, Master Eustace, or you'll get no supper.'

Barking with delight, the second eldest Folville brother's humour quietened. 'It's been many a year since anyone called me Master Eustace. If you'd told me back then, Sarah, what state our England would be in now…' He shook his head. 'You'd think mankind would learn from his mistakes, yet he seems doomed to repeat them.'

The housekeeper's heart lightened to catch a glimpse of the compassion kept hidden so deeply within a man with so much blood on his hands. 'That, my Lord, is why mankind is balanced by womankind.'

'You're a good soul, Sarah.' He pinched a slice of bread from the table. 'And the best cook in the world, but it's going to take more than female thinking to sort the Willoughby situation out.'

Wisely resisting the urge to remind Eustace that, if it hadn't been for female thinking, half his family would be dead by now, Sarah moved the last few chunks of bread out of his reach. 'Whatever you do, my Lord, do it carefully. I need my chicks safe. All of them.'

'It was 19th January two years before we met.'

Mathilda laid a hand on Robert's naked thigh, resting her head on his shoulder. '1326?'

Gently twirling a lock of her hair through his fingers, he asked, 'Are you sure you want to hear this?'

'No, but I'm sure I need to hear this.'

'The law will tell you that the attack on Roger Belers was unprovoked. It wasn't. Belers had threatened our family on more than one occasion, and he'd physically injured two of our followers.'

'He attacked them personally?'

'No. He would never consider getting his own hands dirty,' Robert growled. 'Belers stood close, watching as two of our men-at-arms, good men, were beaten with cudgels by more guards than they could have fought off. I was not there, but I'm told the baron laughed as they suffered.'

'Were they badly hurt?'

'Their wits were knocked from them, bones were broken. One of them, Ackerley his name was, never really recovered. He died of fever the following winter.'

'Weakened by the onslaught and unable to fight the malady?'

'Yes.' Caught in the memory, Robert went on, 'In Leicestershire in particular, Belers was intensely unpopular, even before he began to openly abuse his power.'

'I remember my father and brothers muttering about him in the pottery. It wasn't hard to work out that Belers was a man others were wary of.'

'He was a turncoat!' Robert smacked a hand against the side of their bed. 'One-time follower of Thomas of Lancaster, he made a fortune out of deserting his cause and backing the hated Despenser. After that, even if he'd become purity itself, it would have made no difference. The people were against him.'

'You're saying he'd proved he couldn't be trusted, and rather than try and regain that trust he capitalised on his unpopularity, using it as an excuse to be cruel and greedy.'

'Exactly.'

Pulling the bedcovers higher, Mathilda tried to think.

'Belers was a Baron of the Exchequer, wasn't he?'

'He was. And as rotten and corrupt as they come.'

'But he wasn't a justice like Sir Richard de Willoughby?'

'No. Willoughby's is a fairly new position which came out of the chaos of Isabella and Mortimer's rule.' Robert grunted, 'As, I suppose, did our salvation after Belers' death.'

'What do you mean?'

'I told you before we married that I'd been outlawed for Belers' murder. If the country hadn't erupted into confusion with the deposition of King Edward's father, I have no doubt our family would have been pursued until arrest. But suddenly Queen Isabella had overruled her husband and the country had bigger worries. Not long after that, we were pardoned of our past offences. All of them. The slate was wiped clean. An act helped, not insignificantly, by Eustace paying a fortune for that beautiful stained glass window in Ashby Folville's church.'

Mathilda considered, before asking, 'Do you think, and speak honestly, husband, that the county benefited from Belers' death, and that the risks you took in securing his removal were worth it?'

'I don't need to think. I can answer yes without hesitation. It's said that King Edward himself was privately grateful for our actions.'

A trickle of fear coursed through Mathilda's slight frame. She lived with the knowledge that she could lose her husband to the law every day; but she'd never come to terms with the fact he chose to live in the shadow of the noose.

'Are you alright?' Robert wrapped an arm around her shoulders. 'You've gone cold.'

'Sometimes, the possibility of losing you... '

'I have no intension of going anywhere.'

'Yes, but…'

'If we don't act against him, Mathilda, no one else will, and he'll get worse. Willoughby's greed increases by the day. He already has lands in this county, Derbyshire, Warwickshire, and Lincolnshire. He married well to secure Wollaton Hall, where he resides in Nottinghamshire, and we've had word that he hopes to take more ground in the south.'

'I know of his ambitions. I know he needs stopping before he defrauds more people of their money and their livelihoods.' Mathilda placed a finger over Robert's lips. 'But sometimes I fear you forget you're not Robyn Hode, you are not Gamelyn, nor are you Adam Bell.'

'I don't pretend to be.'

'Yet you aspire to their values, and sometimes… Sometimes I wonder if those values will kill you.'

'Values I believe in.'

'As do I.' Matilda closed her eyes. 'Do you remember the first time I met your brothers?'

Thrown by the apparent change of subject, Robert nodded.

'I stood in the hall here and listened, as Eustace asked you to recite a piece from the *Tale of Gamelyn*.'

'Come from the seat of justice: all too oft
Hast thou polluted law's clear stream with wrong;
Too oft hast taken reward against the poor;
Too oft hast lent thine aid to villainy,
And given judgment 'gainst the innocent.
Come down and meet thine own meed at the bar,
While I, in thy place, give more rightful doom
And see that justice dwells in law for once.'

Robert stroked his wife's hair as her recital came to an end. 'A suitable passage for today, as well as back then. Words that Gamelyn declared to the justice at his false trial.'

A scratchy dryness formed at the back of Mathilda's throat as she forced herself not to cry. 'Do you also recall giving me a message, a sign of entry, to deliver at the Coterel manor gate to prove myself when you first sent me out as your spy?'

Robert exhaled a long, drawn-out breath. 'I asked you to say the names De Herdwyk and La Zouche, to prove you were from me.'

'And those men were involved in the plotting of Belers' murder, were they not?'

Robert said nothing, his eyes clouding with regret at how Mathilda had been treated on her arrival at the manor.

'I think now, all this time later, you owe me an explanation as to the true nature of your own involvement in that baron's removal.'

Seeing her husband's expression change from sorrow to concern, Mathilda was determined not to let him evade the subject. 'I need to know how Belers meet his end. Who was it, Robert, who organised the assault and dealt the final blow?'

After a lengthy silence, Robert spoke. 'A lot of planning took place before Belers fell at Brokesby. I was involved in that planning.' He lifted his hands up, holding his open palms out to his wife, 'But these hands did not kill him.'

Mathilda's shoulders sagged with relief. 'So who was it? If I am to help you now, I require the truth of then.'

~ *Chapter Three* ~

3rd December 1331

Despite the solidness of the wood, the main door to Wollaton Manor trembled in its frame as Lord Willoughby slammed it behind him.

Lady Marjory de Willoughby tensed. Her father had a way of announcing his presence so that everyone within the manor, and probably in the nearby church and village, knew he was in residence. Keeping her eyes cast down, she smoothed out the sewing which rested on her lap. Knowing it was unlikely he would acknowledge her presence as he joined her in the hall, his eldest daughter muttered, 'Greetings, Father,' anyway.

She couldn't help reflecting on how different her mother was from her father. Quiet, refined and kind, Marjory often wondered if Lady Isabel resented having been thrust into a marriage which was no more than a bid to secure land for the Willoughby estates. If she did, she'd never said. Marjory tried not to shudder when she considered what match her father might arrange for her. She sent a private prayer of thanks to Our Lady that she was the third of five children. With two older brothers who, thankfully, monopolised most of her father's distracted attention, she was frequently glad she was more or less invisible to him.

Rubbing the back of a hand over her tired eyes, Marjory listened as Lord Willoughby muttered to himself. She couldn't make out the words, but they'd be a complaint of some sort. It was all he seemed to do. Nothing was ever good enough and no one could come close to pleasing him. Marjory had long since given up trying to, as incurring her father's wrath was not a task for the faint-hearted. But today, she'd promised herself, she was going to talk to him.

Her hand slipped and the prick of the needle sent a brief sharp pain through her fingertip. Sucking her finger, checking no blood had damaged the cloth; Marjory risked a second glance in her father's direction, wondering how to start a conversation she didn't want to have.

No one had commented on the fact that Lady Isabel de Willoughby hadn't been seen for almost a week. No one seemed to have noticed apart from her, but then, no one seemed to notice her either. Carefully laying down her work, Marjory curled her palms into fists, and took a steadying breath. She would ask her father if he was well. Then she would enquire if her mother was well, for she hadn't seen her of late.

No sooner had Marjory parted her lips to speak, when her eldest brother, also Richard, walked briskly into the hall.

Half relieved that she hadn't risked igniting her father's ever ready anger and half annoyed that she'd screwed up her courage for no reason, Lady Marjory picked her sewing back up and covertly observed her brother.

Richard was already fussing around their father as if he was the king come to stay. Marjory stitched faster, jabbing at the linen, taking out the frustration of her existence as she listened.

'I passed the very place yesterday. Brokesby Field,' Willoughby growled at his eldest son as he scowled into his goblet. 'The very spot Belers was hacked to death by those monsters.'

Richard's eyes narrowed. 'What took you towards Melton Mowbray, Father?'

'That is no business of yours!' Taking a draught of wine, Lord Willoughby relented in a way he never would for anyone else. 'Forgive me, son, we live in trying times; felony has infected our noble households to the point of contagion.'

Marjory closed her eyes as she stifled a sigh. Her father was about to moan about the influence of the Folvilles again. All he did was gripe, but not act. He'd had the chance to arrest some, if not all, of the brothers on a number of occasions, but he hadn't taken it. As she picked a fleck of dust off the gown she was mending, a notion came to Marjory that caused her to peer in her father's direction once again.

He's afraid of them.

The idea shocked her, all the more because she instinctively knew it to be true as her father continued to complain.

'Years have passed, and no one has been tried for Belers' death, although everyone knows who's responsible!' He shouted across the vast hall. 'The only punishment the Folvilles received was to have their lands at Reresby taken from them. There were no arrests, nothing. A token outlawry was issued and nothing more. It was a half-hearted gesture towards justice. If I'd been in charge then, so many things would have been different!'

He slammed his goblet against the table. 'Well, I have the power now, and I'm going to do what should have been done years ago. The king is particularly anxious to curb the influence of the Coterel brothers in Derbyshire, and by lucky happenstance, they are close associates of the Folvilles. I will take great delight in teaching them that they should choose their friends more carefully.'

Lowering her gaze from her father's sharp-featured, clean-shaven face, Marjory let the words she'd heard so many times before wash over her. She wondered if her mother had finally had enough of her master's belly-aching and run away. But if she had, why hadn't she taken Marjory and her younger sister, Joan, with her?

Another thought, one that had recently taken shape   a thought she didn't want   loomed larger in her mind as she heard Richard offer to refill his father's goblet.

What if Mother has been removed from this house by force? Or even... from this world?

'You are troubled, Father, may I be of service?' Richard poured himself a drink and sat opposite his sire. He didn't offer refreshment to his sister, although she sat at the end of the same table.

'I have spoken to you of the murder of Roger Belers.'

'Often, Father. He died at the hands of the Folvilles.'

'He did.' Willoughby shifted his chair closer to the fireplace. 'They orchestrated the outrage and many of them were present at his death.'

Marjory's ears pricked up as her brother asked with undisguised surprise, 'I was given to believe they killed him. Did they not?'

'What difference does it make? They ordered his death!' The justice's palm hit the edge of the table so hard, his wine cup toppled to the side. Bouncing across the length of the wooden surface, it sent a stream of red liquid shooting across the hall, missing the men entirely, but splashing Marjory's needlepoint; spattering the pale blue linen she held in her hands.

Leaping backwards, Marjory cried out in dismay at the ruined gown.

'Daughter! Cease that self-pitying display!' Willough-by's shout echoed around the silent hall. No one moved. 'It is no one's fault but your own if you can't take care of your possessions.'

Tears welled in her eyes, not for the ruined dress, but at the injustice of her father's claim when he was solely responsible for the damage. Screwing up the material, she got up, spun on her heels, and marched from the hall without a backward glance.

Her father's voice floated across the hall after her. 'I see you've learnt your manners from your mother. She never had the good grace to ask for permission to leave my presence either.'

Unsure what was giving her the courage to keep walking, from not turning and pleading with her father to forgive her lack of politeness, Marjory found her mind latching on to one word her father had just said.

'She never *had* the good grace…'

Had. Past tense. As if, perhaps, she wouldn't ever disappoint her husband again.

Bettrys smoothed out the bed linen in Lord Eustace's rooms. Since Lady Mathilda had rescued her from her life as a castle servant at Rockingham, giving her the chance to train as a housekeeper under Sarah's careful tutoring, she'd never been so happy. A light blush formed on her cheeks. The friendship she'd developed with Daniel, the household's general servant, was rather nice too.

Kneeling to sweep the dust from under the bed, Bettrys speculated about her future. She'd always assumed she'd remain alone, with just servants for company. But now, when she looked at Sarah, so content with Adam, her husband of only eighteen months, she dared to dream that maybe, one day, Daniel would ask her to be his wife.

'Bettrys?'

The maid clambered to her feet, brushing dust from the skirt of her tunic as she replied to the housekeeper's enquiry, 'I'm in Lord Eustace's room, Sarah.'

That was something else she'd had trouble getting used to. Using names. At the castle, Cook had insisted on everyone being referred to via their title. Here, apart from the family, everyone used Christian names.

One glimpse at the anxious expression on Sarah's usually calm face evaporated some of Bettrys' joy. 'Are you alright? Have I made a mistake?'

The housekeeper shifted the weight of the pile of linen she carried from one arm to the other. 'Not at all. You shouldn't be so quick to assume yourself in error whenever I call you.'

Bettrys blushed. 'Sorry, Sarah.'

'There's nothing for you to be sorry for.' Sarah tutted, but not at her companion. 'If I'd ever had the chance to lay my hands on that cook from Rockingham, I'd have given her what for! Fancy making you feel responsible for every fault and error.'

'Thank you, Sarah.'

'You have a good heart, Bettrys. I hope you don't lose that.' Sarah's countenance creased back into concern. 'Before you came here, Lady Mathilda told you how this family worked. The good and the bad.'

'She was very honest with me.'

'Well, since you've been here, although there have obviously been, let's call them interesting episodes, there's been nothing to cause much concern.'

'But now there is?' Bettrys' palms prickled. Daniel had told her about the incidents the Folvilles had been involved with in the past. That lives of people he'd loved had been lost. That even working for the family put them in danger. He'd wanted her to leave. It had been the closest he'd come to telling her he cared.

'You've been a blessing to both me and this family, Bettrys. But trouble is fast on our heels. So, I am giving you a chance, now, today, to leave if you wish to.'

'Leave?' The word came out as a terrified whisper. 'I don't want to leave, have I…?'

Sarah raised a quietening hand. 'You have made no errors, you've done no wrong. That is why, if you wish to, you should have the chance to go now, before the storm hits.'

'But what is it that's happening? Can I help? Could I be useful to you?'

Sarah sagged. 'Of course you could, but I've lost so many people I care about. I don't want to lose you too.'

Taking the linen from Sarah's arms, Bettrys hoped the shake starting in her shoulders wasn't visible. 'Whatever it is that's about to happen, I'm staying. Lady Mathilda and Lord Robert have shown me nothing but kindness. I cannot abandon them.'

Relieved, but knowing her conscience would prick her if she didn't give her at least one more chance to flee, Sarah pointed to the linen. 'Could you take those covers to the store for me?'

'Certainly.'

'And while you're there, please, for me, think hard about everything I'm sure Daniel has told you of the deaths of our friends, and of what Mathilda has suffered in the past. I fear that all that has gone before is nothing to what is on its way.'

'He told me.' Bettrys' ruddy face paled as she saw the sincerity in her friend's face. 'But, Sarah, *what* is coming?'

'Death and justice, child.' Sarah muttered as she headed

back to her kitchen. 'Death and justice.'

~ *Chapter Four* ~

3rd December 1331

The question, 'How long will you be gone?' formed itself on Mathilda's lips, but didn't escape. It was a pointless enquiry. Checking he had enough food in his saddle roll, she passed Robert his cloak. 'Give my best wishes to Nicholas and his brothers.'

Robert's countenance darkened. 'Why Nicholas before the others?'

Rolling her eyes, Mathilda looped her arms around his waist. 'Because he is the only Coterel I know well enough to address by name.' She kissed Robert's cheek, 'Forget any simmering jealousy, husband of mine. It is but a foolish waste of energy when you need to preserve all you have.'

Running his hands over her girdle, his fingers tracing the butterfly latticework, Robert shrugged. 'Can I help it, that I am wary of someone snatching you away from me?'

'Others have tried and failed, my Lord.' Mathilda pushed his scrip into his hands. 'Now go, before Lord Eustace leaves without you.'

Bowing, a half-smile on his lips, Robert's gaze flicked across the bed they'd just vacated. 'I'd rather be staying with you.'

'Good. Consider the amusements we'll enjoy on your return. Unless you reconsider and take me with you.'

Robert, unwilling to relive the argument of the night before, when Mathilda had offered her services as a calm voice amongst so much hot air, shook his head. 'I have to put your safety before all. If you come, you'll end up in danger again.'

'You don't think danger will come knocking on the manor door anyway?' She titled her head to one side, her eyes tired after a night of little rest. 'I could help, I could –'

'Could get killed.' Robert placed a finger on her lips. 'Stay here and care for our friends and our home.'

'As you wish.' Mathilda paused, 'At least try to keep a rein on your brothers' impetuousness for me.'

'You might as well ask me to catch a rainbow in my hands.'

For five minutes Sarah's domain was a hive of bustle as the brothers scooped up every vestige of bread they could lay their hands on, a couple of apples apiece, and a flask of ale. Then the chaos migrated to the stables before, in a scurry of stamping, circling horses, they were gone. An unreal silence, only punctuated by the crackle of the fire, fell across the kitchen.

With an exaggerated sigh, Sarah picked up a large mixing bowl from the side table. 'Daniel, could you fetch me some flour from the store, please. The masters have left us to starve again.'

Mathilda took a cloth from the water bucket by the fire and wiped up the spilled ale which spotted the table in sticky puddles. 'They are like underfed hounds when they get together.'

Sarah watched Mathilda set to the household tasks in

the same way she had when she'd been a hostage at the manor, before marrying Lord Robert. 'May I ask a question, Mathilda?'

'Of course. I can't guarantee an answer. I haven't asked where they've gone.'

'You know though.'

'I can guess. But I may be wrong.'

Sarah laughed. 'And I may be the Queen of England!'

'And a wise queen you'd be.' Mathilda pulled a knife towards her. 'I'll prepare tonight's stew while you get that bread started.'

As Daniel came in with the flour, Mathilda asked, 'Could you fetch a couple of cabbages and an onion or two as well? And have you seen Bettrys? I'd like to talk to everyone.'

Daniel blushed at the suggestion that he should know where the maid was. 'I saw Bettrys earlier, but I don't know where she is now.'

'I have a confession…' Sarah coughed. 'I gave her the option to leave. I know it wasn't my place, but she's a good girl. Bettrys doesn't deserve…'

Mathilda brushed away Sarah's concerns. 'You did right. I was going to offer her the same option.'

'But ' Daniel stopped speaking as soon as he started.

'But you care for her.' Mathilda spoke gently, 'and so do we. She deserves to know what may be about to happen. And so do you.'

'I've already heard about the warrant against the Lords Coterel. My Lord Eustace shouts so loud but that's all I know.'

Mathilda took a seat at the table. 'Perhaps, once you've fetched the vegetables, you could find Adam for me and bring him in. We'll look for Bettrys. We can prepare supper together as we talk. I have no idea how long the men will be, but I do know that when they come back, every single one of them will act as if food as never passed their lips before.'

'I didn't say sending a messenger to issue Willoughby a warning against the consequences of his foolish court was a bad idea, Eustace, I was just saying that I do not wish my wife to be the messenger!'

'We heard you, Lord Robert.' Nicholas Coterel lowered his goblet to the table and turned to Eustace. 'But I don't think Lady Mathilda would like it if we trusted such a mission to anyone else. She ought to be part of it.'

'Part of it?' Anger swelled in Robert's stomach. 'I have fought too hard to keep her safe to '

Nicholas cut across Robert for a second time, addressing the entire assembly rather than just Mathilda's husband. 'Think about it for a minute. The woman is brave and clever, that has been proven on many occasions. Would it not be better to send her into Wollaton with a warning than one of us, or a hired stranger?'

'Absolutely not!' Robert leapt to his feet, 'How could you even think of putting her in danger after all she's been through in the past? She's your friend, though Our Lady knows why!'

'And your wife! Although Our Lady knows why!'

The atmosphere around the table, which was already tight with tension, now tasted of ice. Eustace, who'd suspected his brother had a rival for Mathilda's affections but hadn't been sure until now, struggled not to laugh. 'What is it about that woman?'

No one answered. The question had no answer. Instead, Robert and Nicholas stopped glaring at each other as Walter de Folville interceded, 'Do you think Mathilda would deliver our message if asked?'

'I'm not asking her.'

'If you don't, I will.' Eustace leaned closer. 'Nicholas is correct. Mathilda is good at being invisible, and she's good at getting on with people when she wants to be seen. And let's not forget, she's an expert at information-gathering. Not only does Mathilda have more chance of getting into Willoughby's domain than any of us, but she might learn about what he's planning for this travelling court of his.'

Robert gripped his beaker so hard it was a miracle the vessel didn't shatter into a thousand tiny shards. 'She isn't our spy anymore. She's my wife.'

Thomas de Folville peered up from where he'd been staring into his empty cup. 'And a fine wife too. But she's also a Folville, Robert.'

Seeing he had the attention of the room, Thomas went on, 'I understand your desire to keep her safe, Robert, but it baffles me as to why she isn't with us right now. We are here to plan what to do and how to do it. Of all our families and associates, Lady Mathilda is the best at that, whether she plays a part in the plan's execution or not.

'I was with her in Rockingham, remember. I saw her in action, her mind doing the work of a dozen swords. I do not say this out of shallow flattery for another's wife.' His eyes met those of Nicholas Coterel, before moving on to Robert's. 'I say this because it is true.'

Sarah's heart sank when she saw the little cot. The blanket was folded into a neat square and the floor beneath had been swept.

'Poor Daniel.' The housekeeper whispered under her breath. The boy was sixteen. Old enough to suffer heartbreak. Sitting on the abandoned bunk, Sarah wished she hadn't spoken to the girl, but at the same time was glad

Bettrys was safe and away. 'But away, where?'

It hadn't been part of the plan for Bettrys to just up and leave. Sarah would have seen her safe into service elsewhere.

'Sarah?'

The housekeeper looked up in surprise. 'I thought you'd gone.'

Bettrys' eyes fell to the neatly folded bedclothes. 'Where would I go?'

'But you almost went?'

'I needed to think. I clean when I think. It helps.'

Sarah smiled. 'That is a sentiment I understand. Nothing helps focus the mind like being busy.' She brushed her hands down her apron in a manner designed to hide her relief. 'Lady Mathilda wishes to address us in the kitchen. I have already informed her that I gave you the option to leave. She may well offer you the same chance.'

'I'm staying.' The girl spoke with a finality that brooked no argument.

Adam lifted the cooking pot closer to the fire, ready for the vegetables that Sarah, Bettrys, and Mathilda were peeling and chopping with a speed that would have made a warrior's eyes water.

Consigning an onion to diced cubes, Mathilda pushed it towards Daniel, who dropped it into the bubbling stock. 'Now then,' she reached for a second onion, the sting of its aroma pricking at the corners of her eyes, 'Bettrys, what do you know of Roger Belers?'

The maid flushed as she worked. 'I have heard the name uttered often in relation to this family, my Lady, but I don't know what it means.'

'Until this morning, I was unaware of the finer details

myself.' Mathilda laid down her knife as she addressed her friends. 'My husband has agreed that I should inform you, as best I can, of the events which may or may not be about to overtake us.'

Adam's eyes narrowed. 'How is the murder of Belers relevant, my Lady? That was five years ago.'

Mathilda sat down with an unladylike thump. 'As I understand it, Roger Belers, former Baron of the Exchequer, was a dangerous man. He bled the area dry of money and his acts of cruelty were legion. I am, it must be stated, repeating my husband's words at this point. I am not speaking from knowledge. Robert may have exaggerated.'

'There was no exaggeration.' Sarah paused in her work. 'He was a curse on society.'

Watching his wife pound the bread dough hard in the bowl, Adam added, 'Even in Nottinghamshire we heard tales of Belers' greed. My old master, Lord Markham, detested the man.'

'Forgive me,' Daniel frowned as he stirred the cooking pot. 'What has all this got to do with now?'

'The murder of Roger Belers is important now because he was a close friend to Justice Richard de Willoughby; and it is this man who has been ordered to capture the Coterel brothers. Apparently Willoughby has been waiting for the chance to get revenge on our family for years. Now he has the legal power to back up his actions, he is grabbing the opportunity to act against us with both hands.'

'You said the Coterels, my Lady?' Bettrys' brow wrinkled, 'The family from Bakewell in Derbyshire? The ones who tried to take Rockingham Castle from my former master, Lord de Vere?'

'The very same.'

'But you stopped them. You stopped Lord James Coterel

getting hold of Rockingham. Why would the Folvilles help the Coterels now, when they worked against him then?'

Understanding the girl's confusion, Mathilda smiled. 'Because this time it is in our families' interests to work together. Last time, it was in our interests to stop an increase in the Coterels' hold over territory so near to us.'

'Oh. So, this justice hates the Folvilles, but is getting revenge on them by chasing the Coterels?' Bettrys wasn't sure she understood.

'I know it seems backwards, but Willoughby knows the families work together. Go after one, and you implicate the other.'

Sarah nodded. 'It seems Willoughby came across an old crime by the vicar of Bakewell which the Coterels resolved in an unlawful way. He's pounced on that as an excuse to act.'

Bettrys' frown deepened. 'This Lord Willoughby has annoyed both families like Belers did?'

'It is more that the Folvilles and Coterels feel his removal, like Belers' before him, is essential   not just for their continued liberty, but for the good of the whole region.' Picking the knife back up, Mathilda ploughed on. 'As of this morning, I discovered that it was not a member of this family who killed Belers on the ground at Brokesby Field. The Folvilles arranged the crime, but it was Roger la Zouche who dealt the blow.'

'The former sheriff,' Sarah confirmed, 'was more active in those days. Although he wasn't sheriff at the time of course. That came later.'

Daniel was shocked. 'So the Folvilles didn't kill Belers after all?'

'No, they didn't, but for the good of Leicestershire, they made sure he died.' Mathilda met Sarah's eyes, foreboding filling them both. 'It nearly cost them everything. This time, unless I can think of a way to convince them that killing Willoughby is not the answer, the price they'll have to pay will be much higher.'

Leicester Abbey's high ceiling echoed with murmurs as the Folville and Coterel brothers discussed and agreed a list of potential accomplices to help them prevent Willough-by's travelling court ever taking place. In the brief silence that followed, as each nobleman took a drink, the sound of stone-distanced voices, united in religious song, floated through the air.

Breaking the rare moment of accord, Eustace addressed the group. 'So, messages are to be sent to Robert Lovet, Roger la Zouche, Roger Savage, Robert Helewell, and Alan of Baston.'

John Coterel nodded. 'We should add Geoffrey de Max-eye to that list. He'll be an asset should we have trouble extracting financial remuneration from Willoughby.'

'You trust him?' James Coterel sounded surprised. 'The man's a notorious thief.'

'To carry out the task allotted him, yes. But I am aware he'll inevitably attempt to steal something extra for his trouble. In this case his skills will outweigh his greed.'

A resigned murmuring of agreement accompanied Eustace as he continued to recount the reel of potential helpers. 'How about Sir Robert de Jort, Sheriff of Nottinghamshire and Derbyshire? Where do we stand with securing his allegiance, Lord Coterel?' Eustace turned to James as he added, 'Our own sheriff, Sir Robert Aylesbury, is a man with a title but no interest in the region, so is of no consequence. Jort however would be a useful ally if he can be persuaded.'

The elder Coterel swigged his ale as he shrugged, 'As

yet the man is a ghost. We have attempted an audience, but like Aylesbury, he's rarely on hand, preferring to live out of the area. I've heard he's a good man, which could bode ill or well for us. I will continue to investigate the possibilities there.'

'Well, don't take too long about it.' Eustace snapped, impatient to begin their campaign. 'So, is the initial plan at least agreed? As you, my Lords James, John, and Nicholas, are Willoughby's prime targets, it will fall to my family to orchestrate pruning this specimen from our soil.'

'Take care, Eustace,' James Coterel growled, 'You make it sound as though you believe you are doing us a favour. We are capable of sorting out our own problems.'

Robert, who'd braced himself, expecting Eustace's usual rage to burst forth, was relieved when his elder sibling reined in his usual emotion. 'You are. Forgive me, my Lord. I am keen to rid the world of this justice. This isn't about you or us, but the region and England as a whole. I feel you should go into hiding while you have time to safely do so.'

The Coterel brothers exchanged stunned looks, but said nothing as Eustace continued, 'Robert and I will co-ordinate events and make sure everyone is kept informed of progress. Trusted messengers will visit each of the afore-mentioned potential helpers to secure their assistance over the next few weeks. We will meet at Lichfield Cathedral in one month's time.

'Initially, we will send a messenger, possibly the Lady Mathilda, to give Willoughby the chance to cancel his court. He will, of course, decline to use common sense. After that, we'll agree on a time and location to kill Willoughby. Rich-ard,' he gestured to his reverend brother, who sat, smug as ever, at the end of the table, 'has been chosen to carry out the actual dispatching of our target. He is, after all, the most practised in the art.'

'You flatter me, brother, with claims to my skill, but I am not fooled. You pick me for this task because you see me as disposable if it goes wrong.'

'True.' Eustace's expression didn't even flicker, 'And because we know you'll relish delivering the killer blow.'

'There, I am unable to argue.'

Nicholas Coterel stared up at the vaulted ceiling of their Christian hideaway as he sniggered into his ale. 'A holy man declining from argument! Perhaps there are such things as miracles.'

~ *Chapter Five* ~

14th December 1331

It had been sixteen days since she'd last seen her mother. Lady Marjory counted them off in her head as she watched as her younger sister, Joan, giggle delightedly. Hoisted onto her new palfrey by the groom, the ten-year-old was already in love with her early Christmas gift.

Their father had said Mother had sent it, but Marjory wasn't so sure. There'd been something about his voice… or maybe it had been the flint-like glint in his eyes… The words had sounded honest, but they'd felt like a lie.

Marjory's brother Richard had told her Lady Isabel had gone to stay with her family in Lincolnshire. That their father was worried for his wife's health and believed a change of scene and the comforts of her own mother would ease her mind.

Nothing about the situation was right. Lady Isabel, as far as Marjory recalled, had never been ill in her life. She was a doting parent, who would never leave her children without saying goodbye.

When she'd mentioned such concerns to Richard, he'd sneered, 'What do you know of the hidden mysteries of a woman's health, sister?'

The implication had been plain. Their father had planted the seed of doubt as to their mother's sanity into Richard's head, and the seed had taken root. Marjory felt sick whenever she thought of it.

An inconvenience to be removed. Was her much-loved parent really with her grandmother, Lady Mortain, or was she locked up somewhere? If so, why? She wasn't ill, Marjory was sure of that.

Lady Joan's chuckles as she bounced around on the back of her new mount broke through Marjory's concentration. Her sister's joy was clear as her little hands gripped the dark grey mane, and her legs hugged the patient pony's sides.

If the horse isn't from Mother, where did it come from?

It had crossed Marjory's mind to ask to be sent to join her mother. That if Isabel de Willoughby really was ill, perhaps the helping hands and company of her eldest daughter would be a welcome distraction from her suffering. But her father had barely been home to ask, and if she just left, making her own way to her mother, who would care for her younger sibling?

Am I supposed to be mother to Joan now?

Leaning against the wall of the stable block, Marjory mumbled into the hooded cloak that protected her from the winter air, 'And even if I got to Mortain Manor, who's to say Mother would be there when I arrived?'

The emissary had come and gone. Mathilda had recognised him as one of Eustace's most trusted mercenaries, but had no name with which to address him. He'd asked to speak to Lord Robert alone. Whatever it was he'd had to say, it had been brief and left her husband pensive.

There had been many such messengers over the past week, but Robert had been resolutely taciturn about what they'd said. Mathilda wasn't used to her husband not sharing family business with her, and his brooding left her at a loss for what to do or say. After Robert's visit to Leicester Abbey, Mathilda had expected something to happen straight away, but none of the other brothers had been back to the manor since then. Nor had rumours reached Ashby Folville of felonies or incidents which could be attributed to her kin. There'd been nothing but messengers, some of whom left Robert with an expression of grim determination, and others who galloped from the courtyard leaving her husband fuming or frustrated.

Mathilda decided not to waste her breath asking Robert what the situation with Justice Willoughby was, but headed to the kitchen instead.

'Good morning, Sarah.' She gestured in delight to the collection of pastries laid out on the kitchen table. 'My favourites! They smell delicious.'

The housekeeper pointed to the sweet treats nearest her mistress. 'I thought you needed cheering up, and it was a good excuse to practise my baking skills before the Christmas and Solstice celebrations.'

The mouthful of warm, melting, honey-flavoured pastry filled Mathilda with gratitude for her friend. 'Neither "divine" nor "delicious" does the taste of these marvels justice, Sarah, and talking of justice,' she picked up a second morsel, this one dotted with flakes of almond, 'I think it's high time I stopped waiting for Robert, and discovered what's going on for myself.' She took a third pastry. 'I thought they'd jump into action in their usual unthinking way, but the days drag on, and with every new messenger that arrives Robert becomes more withdrawn. There have been no rumours about the town concerning what's going to happen. Nothing at all.'

Sarah frowned. 'Now you come to mention it, it has been oddly peaceful. I've just been content to have everyone safe for a while.'

'But it isn't safe. The very air hangs with the weight of the task that hasn't been done.'

Running her eye over the sweetmeats and other delicacies her deft fingers had created, Sarah sighed. 'I knew I was foolish to wish the situation away, but as the guard outside had not been increased, I hoped...'

'That they'd changed their minds?'

'I wondered if Lord Robert's simmering anger came from the cancelling of the mission to cull the justice. I know he hates Willoughby. How couldn't he after the man attacked him personally?'

Mathilda's hand stopped moving on its journey towards her mouth. 'Attacked him personally?'

Sarah paled. 'You didn't know?'

'I did not.'

Wishing she'd kept her mouth shut, the housekeeper explained, 'It wasn't long before you came to us. Lord Willoughby remained beside himself with anger at the murder of his friend, Belers.'

'But why attack Robert and not Eustace, or one of the others involved?'

'I don't know.' Sarah looked awkward. 'Convenience of timing perhaps? I never asked.' Sarah reached a hand out to Mathilda, 'I have survived here a long time by never asking questions I might not want answers to.'

Mathilda nodded as she inhaled the scent of cinnamon and mixed spices, laying her pastry back on the table.

Sarah shifted uneasily. 'What are you going to do, my Lady?'

The sudden use of her title wasn't lost on Mathilda. 'I'm

going to get some answers.'

Leaving the hopeful aroma of pre-Christmas cookery behind her, Mathilda tightened her cloak around her shoulders and went out to the courtyard.

She hadn't taken more than a few steps when Robert waved at her from the stables. It had been so long since she'd seen him smile that it took her by surprise.

'It's good to see you in better spirits. I've been worried about you, my Lord.'

Robert chuckled. 'And frustrated as hell that I haven't told you what's going on.'

'Have I bothered to deny it?' A grin crept across Mathilda's face. 'Can I assume, from your improved demeanour, that a plan of action has been decided upon?'

'No, you can assume that I've realised what a fool I've been, thanks to Adam here.' Robert acknowledged the quiet presence of the steward. 'He has talked some sense into me.'

'About not sharing what's happening between you, your brothers, and the Coterels, with me?' Unable to keep the hope from her voice, Mathilda was disappointed when Robert brushed her question away with a flourish of his hand.

'No, for letting events stop me from enjoying the company of my beautiful wife.' Taking Mathilda's arm, he escorted her to where Adam was bringing out their horses. 'I thought we'd go and see your father. It's been ages since you visited his pottery in Twyford.'

Mathilda stood still, her mouth opening and closing as a variety of questions tried to form on her tongue all at once. 'My father?'

'Yes.' Robert was getting more enthusiastic by the minute. 'After all, the festive season will soon be upon us. We should go and extend an invitation for dinner at the manor.

I'm sure Bertred, Matthew, and Oswin would take pleasure in sampling Sarah's winter cooking.'

Oswin!

Suddenly Mathilda understood. Perhaps Robert wanted to talk to her younger brother, Oswin. He'd been in service with the Coterels in the past. Maybe he was needed to help with the Willoughby campaign in some way?

A smile crossed her face. 'Thank you, Robert, I'd love to visit Twyford, we could invite my family here for the Solstice, so we can raise a glass to our marriage with them. Or maybe for Christmas?'

Mathilda was about to allow Robert to assist her into the saddle, when she recalled Sarah's cooking. 'Why don't we take a few morsels for the journey? Sarah is working magic in the kitchen.'

Without waiting for a response, Mathilda ran to the kitchen. Explaining that she and Robert were going to Twyford, she helped the housekeeper wrap up some food for them to share with her family. Sarah was so relieved that Mathilda wasn't dashing headlong into a search for information about Willoughby that she added in some extra treats she'd previously earmarked for Adam.

'Do you need anything from the pottery, Sarah?'

The housekeeper gave her domain a brief but critical examination. 'Perhaps an additional eight beakers. The brothers have drunk the life out of many of these, and with Christmas coming, you never know how many visitors we'll have through the doors.'

'I'll get those ordered for you.'

'Mathilda?' Sarah studied her mistress's face. 'Whatever it is you're up to, please be careful.'

'Whatever makes you think I'm up to something?'

Sarah raised her eyes to Heaven, but said nothing as

the mistress of the manor swept up the parcels of food and headed into the courtyard.

~ *Chapter Six* ~

14th December 1331

'Mathilda! Lord Robert!'

Grabbing the nearest clean rag, Bertred of Twyford wiped the clay he'd been working from his fingers, before engulfing his daughter in a hug.

'It's so good to see you, Father.' Mathilda beamed. He was looking well and happy. A stark contrast to the man from whom she'd been stolen over three years ago, when the Folvilles' had kidnapped her as a ransom to his debts.

'And you, my child.' Bertred broke away from his daughter and gave her husband a courteous bow. 'My Lord Robert, it's good to see you too. You must forgive Matthew's absence. He is tending to the lands you so graciously bestowed upon us after the former Sheriff de Cressy, um...'

'Decided to let them go?'

'As you say, my Lord, he let them go.'

Mathilda shivered at the thought of the man who'd caused her so much trouble, and almost her death. 'I can't say I mourn that particular sheriff.'

'I can't imagine anyone does.' Robert's eyes narrowed, 'De Cressy's death was a relief to many. I trust the lands are proving profitable to you, Bertred?'

'More than I could have hoped for.' He smiled. 'Matthew is often there rather than here. The associated orchard and field are producing fruit and crops, and the house on the edge of the site will prove an excellent home for him and his future wife.'

'Future wife?' Mathilda's face lit up. 'He has hopes of someone, Father?'

'He does. The daughter of a silk merchant in Leicester. A good match for the likes of us.'

'Her name, Father?'

'Alice, daughter of Master Leon de Picardy.'

Robert's eyebrows rose. 'Picardy? Well now, there is a coincidence.'

'There is?' Mathilda turned to her father, who merely shrugged.

'When my family came to England at the beginning of the twelfth century, it was from Picardy that they came.'

'Each day I learn more about the family into which I've married. I wonder if Alice is a distant relative.'

'Unlikely, but possible, I suppose. If you enjoy coincidences, then I should also tell you that Alice was my mother's name.'

'So it was.' Mathilda smiled. 'I remember Sarah telling me. Lady Alice favoured travelling with your father, rather than being a content wife at home.'

Robert laughed. 'I clearly have similar taste in womenfolk to my sire.' He turned to Bertred. 'Is a date set for their marriage?'

'Spring. Alice's father is abroad sourcing new silks. They'll wed when he returns.'

'Please give Matthew our warmest congratulations. This is wonderful news indeed.'

'Gladly, I will.' Bertred gestured towards the house.

'Come inside. You must be in want of refreshment.'

'A drink would be most welcome, Father. It would go well with the pastries I've brought from Sarah.'

'In that case you'd better call Oswin from the pottery. He's selecting ware to take to Leicester market tomorrow. He'd never forgive us if he missed out on sampling some of Sarah's cooking.'

Sarah's food had been consumed and local news shared, when Oswin reluctantly got to his feet.

'It's been a pleasure, Lord Folville, sister, but I must return to the pottery or we'll not be ready for tomorrow's market.'

'It's been good to see you.' Mathilda embraced her youngest brother. 'It has been so long since I helped at the market, I miss the camaraderie of it all sometimes.'

Robert gave his wife a look that could have been either approval or suspicion, she wasn't entirely sure. 'There is no reason why you shouldn't go with your brother tomorrow, unless Oswin feels he'd be better off without you.'

Oswin laughed. 'Far from it, my Lord. Mathilda was always the best at selling. Even her singing along to the balladeers didn't put people off our stall, and if you've heard her sing, you'll understand just how good a saleswoman she is!'

'Cheek!' Mathilda gave her brother a playful shove. 'I don't think I've heard ballads sung since our wedding feast.'

'Nor I. And we do so love listening to them.' Robert regarded Bertred. 'Could Mathilda go with Oswin, or do you think her presence would cause hindrance now she's married to a Folville? Speak honestly, no offence will be taken. I am not so blind as to miss the pluses and minuses of our association.'

'As far as I'm concerned, she'd be welcome at every single market and fair. This decision however has to be Oswin's. I am working in the pottery tomorrow. With the festive season almost upon us, the demand for new plates, beakers, and cooking pots has been more than steady.'

'That reminds me!' Mathilda gathered up the wrappings that had protected the hastily consumed morsels from Ashby. 'Sarah asked me for eight new beakers. Do you have any, Father, or should I send Daniel to collect some next week?'

'I suspect I could see my way to letting you have eight.' Bertred winked. 'Oswin, could you help Mathilda choose some for Sarah?'

'Certainly.' A beam crossed his happy round face. 'I'd love your company, if his Lordship can spare you?'

Mathilda looked beseechingly at Robert. 'May I?'

'Who am I to come between brother and sister?' He kissed Mathilda's hand. 'As long as you keep her safe, Oswin. I'll come and collect you, from here, the day after tomorrow.'

'I'm happy to bring her to Ashby Folville after the market, my Lord.' Oswin was delighted at the prospect of his sister's company.

'You'll be tired, Oswin, and I'm sure Bertred would rest easier in his bed for knowing his children, and the day's takings, are safely back here after the market.' He gave a smile that Mathilda sensed wasn't completely genuine. 'It'll also give your father the chance to make Sarah some more beakers so he doesn't have to pillage his market stock.'

Robert was ready to take his leave from Twyford with only a fraction more politeness than haste. Leaving her father and Oswin in the pottery, Mathilda followed Robert to the stables.

'Is there anything you wish me to acquire from Leicester market, my Lord? Or in Leicester itself, perhaps?'

'I don't think so. Sarah and Adam seem to have us well equipped at the moment. Although if you see a treat for yourself you should get it. I don't present you with enough trinkets.'

'Trinkets?' Mathilda felt the unease that had stirred in her earlier increase, 'Since when have we required trinkets as proof of our love?'

'I simply meant that, were I coming with you, I would find a gift for you.'

'Why don't you stay and come with us?' Mathilda hoped she didn't sound too inquisitive. 'You could call upon those of your brothers residing in Leicester, and I'm sure Lord Ingram would welcome a visit.'

Robert kissed her forehead. 'Stay safe with Oswin and enjoy the minstrels. I hope you get to hear a Robyn Hode tune or two.'

Mathilda said nothing else as she watched her husband circle his horse and canter into the distance.

15th December 1331

Even the need to start work before dawn didn't dampen Mathilda's spirits as she helped Oswin load the plates, pots, and beakers into the straw placed in the cart to protect them from the rigours of a bumpy ride to Leicester.

Relishing the prospect of a day with her brother, Mathilda also looked forward to the hubbub of one of the region's liveliest markets. She'd also resolved to keep her eyes and ears open. Where better to hear the whispers on the wind than at a busy market, where ale flowed and the gossips' tongues were loosened to the scandal of the hour.

Keeping silent her thoughts about Willoughby, and the trouble that she could sense waiting around an unseen corner like a spectre preparing to pounce, Mathilda shared news with her brother about the growth of the garden, the last harvest, and the improved fortunes of their father as they travelled.

Holding her breath to keep her nostrils closed to Leicester's ditches, which stank of debris and dung, Mathilda followed Oswin's lead into the city. Increasing her palfrey's pace from a walk to a trot as they approached the market square, she then slowed to queue the last few yards for their pitch.

The friendly banter, the calls of surprise from fellow traders as they saw Mathilda with her brother for the first time in years, and the challenge of displaying the pots on the wooden dais at the front of the wooden stall that her father had hired for the day, was immensely satisfying. For a few precious hours, Mathilda was so engrossed in the hard work that she forgot her worries, until she chanced to hear a voice in the crowd muttering the words, 'Isabel de Willoughby.'

Matilda looked up so sharply from where she was serving someone with a new pot, that Oswin enquired, 'Are you alright, sister?'

'Yes, sorry.' She gave the servant girl, who was waiting for her change and her master's new pot, an apologetic smile.

As Mathilda worked her mind raced. Who was Isabel de Willoughby? She'd heard so much about Sir Richard de Willoughby, about what a corrupt and malicious man he was, that she hadn't given a thought to the family who'd had to deal with the consequences of his misbehaviour.

The whisper she'd overheard had evaporated into the crowd before she'd caught its context. With her ears more alert to future conversations, Mathilda continued to work, but she wasn't so focused on the task in hand, and was glad when custom tailed off from a scrum of buyers to a trickle.

Oswin, who hadn't missed his sister's preoccupation, took his chance as soon as there was a lull in trade. 'What did you overhear?'

'How did you know?'

'I have known you as a sister and a Folville. There is a reason you fit in well in that family. You heard something that has pricked either your concern or your curiosity.'

'Both.'

'Can you tell me?' Oswin knew well that some notions could not be safely shared.

'No one has told me I cannot, but in truth, I'm not exactly sure what I have to tell.'

Making sure the passing shoppers were intent only on their quest for new possessions and food rather than listening to them, Oswin said, 'Go on?'

Lowering her tone in case Oswin's surveillance hadn't been thorough, Mathilda said, 'Have you heard any rumours concerning my family, a Justice Willoughby, or your former employers?'

'The Coterels?' Oswin's eyes searched the crowds with more diligence than before.

'Any whispers on the breeze?'

'Of the Coterel brothers, no.' He rubbed a large palm across his forehead. 'But as I didn't know you wished me to be listening out, I was only paying attention to our customers.'

'As you should have been.' Mathilda sighed, 'I wasn't

thinking of just today. Something is coming, something bad.'

'And you think you can stop it?'

'No.' She plunged her cold hands in to the folds of her cloak. 'But I may be able to lessen the blows that will follow.'

Oswin pulled out two stools that had been tucked under the counter of their market stall. 'From the beginning, sister, if you please?'

It took but a few minutes for Mathilda to detail the information she had. That Justice Willoughby, after years of corruption and avarice, had tipped the balance of local hate so firmly in his direction by targeting the Coterel brothers directly, that the Folvilles and Coterels were drawn to act against him. She explained how enraged everyone had been but then there had been nothing. In fact, the only evidence that the matter was still in hand was the arrival and departure of Eustace's men as they despatched messages between the two families and their accomplices, and the air of disquiet that hung over the manor.

Quiet for a second, Oswin spoke slowly. 'Willoughby I have heard of. Lord Nicholas was always complaining about his greed. My masters were grateful to the Folvilles for removing his friend, Belers.'

'And now this justice has the power to get his revenge.' Mathilda struggled not to disguise the concern in her voice as a young man approached the stall, his arms laden with goods.

Oswin greeted the newcomer. He was serving him with a pitcher when Mathilda announced that, if her brother could spare her, she'd like to take a turn around the fair.

She wanted to find the minstrels.

~ *Chapter Seven* ~

15th December 1331

As soon as she saw the balladeers positioned at the far end of the market square, Mathilda's smile widened. Had Robert known that these men in particular would be here for her to find?

Her pleasure at the freedom of being alone in a familiar place grew as she wove her way through the market. Few women were as lucky as she was, but then few women lived amongst the Folvilles.

The three minstrels, one singing his heart out, the other two accompanying him on vielle and flute, didn't notice her at first. Mathilda deliberately hung back from the crowd so they wouldn't break off the tale on seeing her. It was a saga her mother had sung her as a child. Mathilda's palms suddenly itched; as if she was on the cusp of understanding something just out of her reach.

Isabel de Willoughby.

The way the name had been spoken, hushed, as if dangerous to utter, yet full of curiosity, came back to her with startling clarity as the balladeer sang 'Robyn Hode and the Potter' into the crisp midday air.

"Robyn Hode was the yemans name,

That was boyt corteys and fre;
For the loffe of owre ladey,
All wemen werschepyd he ... ”

As the tale faded into applause, the crowd moved away and Mathilda stepped forward.

'Lady Mathilda! We are honoured to have you amongst our audience. How time has flown since your wedding day.' The minstrel looked around in concern. 'No Lord Robert, my Lady? No escort? Do you need our assistance to get you safely home?'

'You are kind, Aldus, but I'm safe enough. I'm assisting my brother on our father's pottery stall today.'

'Still a woman of the people, Lady Folville.' The minstrel spoke with approval. 'You wish to know something though, I think?'

'I wish to know two things.' She appreciated Aldus's direct manner, and knew it was one of the reasons her husband favoured him as a singer in their home when they were entertaining. 'We would love it if you, Dicun, and Noll would spend the Christmas and Solstice period with us, if you are not otherwise engaged.'

'Even if we were, we would become unengaged in a trice. No minstrel would be such a dolt as to turn down a summons from a Folville.'

Mathilda's smile remained, but a sense of unease trickled through her. 'I wouldn't want you to cancel an assignment because we're Folvilles.'

Aldus bowed. 'I know, my Lady, but it has to be admitted, only an unwise man or a rich man would go against your family's requests.'

Unable to argue, Mathilda said, 'If you are free, we'd welcome you. If you aren't, I will pretend I have not seen you to ask, and you can honour your previous arrangements.'

'We are free, and we'd be delighted.' Dicun laid his vielle down with all the reverence of a man who knows his next meal depends upon the safety of his musical instrument.

'You said there were two things,' Aldus prompted as Noll joined them.

'I'm after some information about a man called Sir Richard de Willoughby. Have you encountered him?'

Aldus barked out a humourless laugh. 'I'd say we've encountered him!'

'Every balladeer and mummer in the region has heard of him, and most are wise enough to give him a wide berth.' Dicun grimaced. 'Once you've played for Lord Willoughby in Wollaton, you hope that you're never asked back. You'd have to be desperate for food or shelter to return.'

Mathilda frowned. The impression Dicun gave was in line with other people's reaction to the mention of the justice, but he wasn't the only person that lived at Wollaton. 'Did his family not appreciate your music?'

'The family of Lord Willoughby appreciate precisely what he tells them to.' Aldus picked up his cup of ale and lowered his voice lest he be overheard. 'Only his elder son, also Richard, receives any level of respect from the man, and even then he can be scathing.'

'I see.' Mathilda nodded. 'The character of the man fits with what I've heard before, but I am always wary of the truth of hearsay. He has a wife, a daughter?'

'Both. Two daughters and three sons, I think, although it's been two seasons since we were there, so...'

Mathilda, caught in thought, missed the end of Aldus's sentence as she asked, 'Isabel de Willoughby? His mother, wife, or child?'

'His wife.' Aldus cleared his throat nervously, 'My Lady

Folville, forgive me, but why do you ask about that particular family?'

Giving her minstrel friend a reassuring smile, Mathilda passed Aldus three pennies. 'You have nothing to fear. I have no intention of compromising your trusted reputation.'

'The pennies are welcome, but what are they for?' Dicun and Noll exchanged glances as Aldus shared the unexpected pay between them.

'For your beautiful voices, for making my day better whenever I hear you sing my favourite songs, and for answering one more question.'

Aldus laughed. 'Which is, my Lady?'

'Have you heard any rumours about the aforementioned justice pursuing a vendetta against the Coterels of Bakewell and, by association, the Folvilles?'

'Did you enjoy the ballads, sister?'

'I did. Aldus and his friends are at the other end of the market; they've agreed to play for us at the manor for Christmas. You'll come too, won't you?

'I, um, I'd like to, but...' Oswin paused, uncertain. 'Father and I are to go to Matthew, now he has a house and a wife-to-be. I confess I'd rather not, sister, but it's what's expected of me.'

Mathilda concealed a stab of disappointment as she realised he was right: in future years, Matthew, as the eldest brother, would probably always expect Oswin and their father to go to him. 'Alice and Matthew do not wed until April at least, I'm sorry you're not spared the whim of convention for this year at least.'

Telling herself her family might well be safer away from Ashby Folville this festive season anyway; Mathilda surveyed the depleted market-goers. Most servants had come and gone, grabbing their household's requirements early so they had majority of the day in which to complete their daily chores. A few revellers, rather too full of the nearest inn's ale, were lounging against the side of the spice merchant's stall. Wafts of barley interspersed with puffs of cinnamon, reminding Mathilda of just how close the festive season and her wedding anniversary were.

'Oswin, can I ask a favour of you?'

'Of course.'

'I'd like to by some cinnamon for Sarah. Her pastries are so delicious, and I know her stocks are low.'

'But you don't relish the idea of a stroll through the knaves who prop against Davidson's stand as if it would topple without their support?'

'I've faced worse, but if I don't have to squeeze past them, then I'd rather not.'

Oswin laughed as Mathilda handed him some coins. 'A single serving or more?'

'Two, please.' She hugged him tightly. 'Thank you, little brother.'

'Little?' Oswin rolled his eyes playfully as his giant frame strode across the market.

Watching him go, Mathilda sat on the stool that came with the stand and considered what the minstrels had told her. The more she thought, the more she was convinced Robert had intended her to speak to them. He had encouraged her to go and listen to them after all. Why else would he have let her go off alone with Oswin so easily?

Aldus had laughed, understanding all too well why Mathilda had taken the precaution of paying them for the information she was after. Even if they'd heard nothing, just being party to the question, knowing the reputation of the justice, was dangerous.

'We've heard little, but for the fact the lord in question has summoned a travelling court to hear cases in this area early next year. The focus of his concerns is to stop the influence of the Coterel family growing further. I have heard no mention of your family, my Lady, but where the Coterels are mentioned it is not beyond the imagination to conclude the Folvilles will be considered part of that influence.'

Dicun had kept watch while Aldus spoke, then Noll had broken his preferred silence. 'You mentioned Lady Willoughby. The rumours there are wilder, for the wife of Wollaton has not been seen for some weeks. No one knows where she's gone.'

Mathilda's pondering of the rumours the minstrels had shared came to an abrupt end as Oswin waved his spicy purchases towards his sister.

'Thank you. Sarah will be delighted.'

'I'm delighted too. It means I'll get to eat more of her food.' Oswin regarded the few remaining pots with satisfaction. 'A good day's selling. Thanks largely to the thrill of being served by a noblewoman no doubt.'

'Due to the skill of the potter, more likely.'

'Let's pack up. Then you can tell me what you've been thinking about. I heard your determined musings from across the way there.'

Mathilda laughed. 'I spoke not a single word while you shopped for me.'

'And yet your thoughts were loud indeed. Pass me those dishes to wrap in straw while you tell me why you really wanted to come to the market.'

'I came to see and help you.'

'And?'

Mathilda sighed. 'To see if I could learn anything about the situation my family find themselves embroiled in.'

'This would be the situation where the Justice Willoughby is on the Coterels' tail?'

Mathilda opened her mouth in surprise. 'You know of this?'

'I know that my former employers have been targeted for arrest. I know that will impact on you, sister, and that you'll try and do something about it. Probably something dangerous and foolish.'

Ignoring the accuracy of her brother's remarks, Mathilda said, 'Do you know more? Do you have details?'

'Only rumour and gossip.' Oswin lifted the only pitcher that hadn't sold into the cart and buried it in the straw. 'Willoughby blames the Folvilles for Belers' death. He blames Lord Robert.'

'But he didn't…'

'I know he didn't, but that doesn't matter. He approved the death. They all did. They made sure it happened.'

'And the country benefited as a result. Even the king was relieved to see the back of Roger Belers.'

'Makes no difference to Willoughby.'

Mathilda closed her eyes for a second, trying to think. 'His wife is missing, Lady Isabel. Have you heard anything about that?'

'Nothing.'

Opening her eyes again, Mathilda caught the concern on her brother's face. 'I won't do anything rash, don't worry.'

'If you think I'm going to believe that, then you take me for a fool.' Oswin was suddenly serious. 'I wondered if I would receive a summons from Nicholas Coterel for my help. Each day I expect the request to come, but there's been no word.'

'I too am living every day as if some trap is about to spring.' She lowered her voice to a whisper, 'They wish to kill Willoughby. I had hoped to curb that plan, but Robert refuses to talk about it. Every enquiry meets a wall of silence.'

Becoming increasingly grave, Oswin ran a large palm through his matted hair. 'Then they must be really worried. Lord Robert values your counsel. As do the others; if they would but swallow their pride and admit it.'

Mathilda stood stock still. An icy chill shot through her as she gripped the side of the cart. 'Robert wasn't hoping I'd learn something by allowing me to stay here. He was getting me out of the way.'

'What?'

'That's why he was so eager for me to come here with you today.' Mathilda worked faster. 'I have to get back to the manor. Now. Before I'm expected.'

'But, sister…'

'The Folville brothers are up to something.' She fastened her cloak around her shoulders. 'Forgive me, Oswin, but I must leave you to return to Twyford alone.'

'I will take you to Ashby Folville.'

'There is no need.'

'There is every need. Lady Willoughby is already missing. The last thing any of us need is for you to go missing as well.'

~ *Chapter Eight* ~

15th December 1331

From Leicester, through Charnwood Forest, they had trundled as fast as the unwieldy nature of the almost empty cart and the uneven road surface would allow. Reaching the border of Ashby Folville after, what to Mathilda, felt like a frustratingly long ride, but was in fact only a couple of hours, they paused in the shelter of the trees. Once they broke cover, it would be but a short walk to the manor's entrance. It was only now they were at a standstill that Oswin asked his sister of her intentions.

'What will you do?'

'Go home, of course.'

Oswin stretched a hand from his cart across to Mathilda and held her palm in his. 'You know what I mean. Robert more or less insisted you stay at Twyford tonight. What reason will you give for disobeying him?'

'I thought I'd try the truth. Robert knew who he was marrying, as much as I knew what sort of family I was marrying into.'

The tilt of her chin and the straightness of her back would have fooled anyone else of her haughtiness, but not her brother. 'Then why do you quake on the inside at the prospect of what you might be walking into?'

Giving Oswin a weak smile, Mathilda sagged in her saddle. 'I have to find out what's going on. You said it yourself; they value my advice, even if they'd be at the point of death before admitting it.'

'Which is an improvement on before. A year ago I think they'd have died first.'

Mathilda laughed at her brother's truth. 'It's important that you go home. I don't want you implicated here.'

'But Lord Robert would have my hide if I let you ride from Leicester alone.'

'I will tell him I bid you farewell here, in this very spot. It is the truth. You have to get home to Father with the day's takings. It is not safe to roam abroad with so much money in these dangerous times.'

Seeing it was pointless to argue further, Oswin made to turn the horse and cart around. 'Very well, but I intend to stay here until I've judged you've walked through the manor gates.'

'You can't see them from here.'

'I shall wait nonetheless. Then, if you need to flee on seeing what awaits you, I'll be here.'

Grateful for her brother's wisdom, realising just how much he'd learnt while he was in the Coterels' service, Mathilda thanked him. 'No more than ten minutes, or you'll draw the sort of attention to yourself you do not need.'

'Ten minutes, my Lady Folville.' Oswin bowed. 'Stay safe, sister.'

Bringing her palfrey to a halt in the lee of the gate, Mathilda examined the scene before her. There were many horses tethered in the courtyard's stalls, but she recognised most of them.

The Folvilles were all here. Even Lord John, and so, if her memory for horseflesh served her well, was Sir Robert Ingram, the former sheriff. There was one further animal, which she judged would probably belong to Ingram's steward or personal guard.

Ignoring the nerves that raced up her throat, Mathilda considered the situation. Neither Adam nor Daniel were in sight, which meant the horses had already been seen to. Wondering what they'd planned in her absence; schemes they clearly didn't want her to know about, Mathilda dismounted and led the palfrey into the stalls. The fact neither Daniel nor Ulric had come out to see who'd arrived meant they were either busy in the hall, or that her arrival at the manor had been drowned out by the arguments of the brothers within.

Even after reasoning the lack of welcome party through her mind, it still felt odd that no one had heard her. It was the time of day when Bettrys should be helping Sarah in the kitchen, readying a meal for the family's evening feast. The kitchen backed onto the courtyard, and it was hard not to notice when someone arrived on the premises. It wasn't beyond reason that the housekeeper would be in the hall attending to the needs of the men, but it was unlikely they'd want the maid hearing their discussion.

She stroked the palfrey's mane faster. 'If they are keeping things from me, then Sarah won't be with them either. She always confided in me. Robert knows that.' A shadow clouded Mathilda's face. 'Unless he is secretly counting on Sarah sharing all she hears with me.'

An increased sense of foreboding quivered through her. Mathilda wished she'd allowed Oswin to come with her after all, but the ten minutes had gone. He'd already be on his way to Twyford.

'Come on. This is your home.' Pulling her shoulders back, Mathilda tucked her cold hands beneath her cloak and walked to the kitchen door.

The second she pushed it open the sound of shouting hit her. In fact it was a marvel that she hadn't heard Eustace de Folville's angry tones ringing through the courtyard, he was so enraged. There was no sign of Sarah, Adam, Daniel, or Bettrys.

Mathilda leant against the closed kitchen door and listened. Eustace was livid to the point of incoherence. She could picture him scoring his knife through the wood of the dining table as he growled out his protests.

The silence of the other brothers spoke volumes. If no one was trying to shout Eustace down, it was because they either agreed with him, or had previously tried to stem his protests and failed. Were they just riding out the tide of his angst until such a time as it was safe to speak?

Picking up a jug of ale, assuming that any refreshments in the hall would have been consumed long since, Mathilda strode towards the door. She was about to lever it open when Robert's voice echoed from within. His words stopped her in her tracks.

'You can huff and puff as loudly as you like, Eustace, but I've been telling you for weeks that I do not like the idea of using my wife as a messenger, and nothing is going to change that.'

Mathilda licked her dry lips as she listened. *Me as a messenger? A messenger for what?*

'Yet you concede she is suited to the role. You said so yourself!'

There was a loud slap. Mathilda was sure either Robert or Eustace had banged a palm down onto the long suffering oak table.

Is this why there's been no progress? They've been arguing over my role in their plan for almost a month! She closed her eyes as she listened.

'And that's the problem!' Robert's shout subsided into a frustrated calm. 'I know Mathilda is more than capable, but I hate the idea of sending her into that place. Hasn't my wife been through enough?' He paused before saying, 'Look, Eustace, if even the minstrels refuse to go there, then '

The minstrels? Wollaton? Robert must know Aldus hates going there.

' then why on God's good earth would I send my wife there?'

'Because,' Lord John de Folville cut through the conversation, exasperation ringing from every syllable, 'Lady Mathilda has skills. Skills that have kept her alive through horrors I wish she had not been subjected to, but nonetheless she has, and she survived.'

Mathilda swallowed. The hand holding the jug of ale quivered as she listened to the Lord of the Manor. She knew what was going to be said next.

'What she experienced at the hands of Rowan Leigh must never be repeated.' Lord John spoke with a finality that suggested she'd never have to face worse. Mathilda wanted to believe that, but knew she didn't. One horror remained to stalk her nightmares, and she was very afraid that Lord Richard de Willoughby was the one to make her fear into a reality.

Robert responded to his eldest brother. 'And yet, we don't know what awaits anyone who goes into Wollaton. And with the news of Lady Isabel's disappearance '

Walter's gravel voice cut across his brother. 'That could be no more than rumour.'

'And it may not be.' Robert rounded. 'I'm not prepared

to take that chance.'

Mathilda pressed her ear closer to the door. She could hear the men speaking, the faint blaze of the fire, but she couldn't hear anyone moving around. No servant's foot-steps. No pouring of ale. The oak door kept out a certain amount of sound, but she'd eavesdropped through it often enough to know its limitations.

If Adam, Sarah, and the others aren't in the hall, then where are they?

Eustace was clearly biting back his anger now. 'You have no choice, Robert. We have made the connections we needed to make. Got the help we require in place. It's time to act, and as much as I'd like to dispense with the formality of a warning, I do not wish to lower myself to Willoughby's level. A chance to halt this folly of a travelling court before it begins must be offered.'

The curling sneer of a different voice filled the hall. Mathilda's skin crawled as Richard, the Rector of Teigh, took over the conversation.

'We are all known to Willoughby. Your wench is not, little brother. We need a messenger to deliver Willoughby's one chance to change his mind; she has a proven ability as a gossip collector and a spy. It has to be her.'

Mathilda knew Robert was going to curse his clerical kin before the words had even left his mouth. It took stern shouts from both John and Eustace to curb his protests at his wife being called a gossip. Mathilda wondered if anyone had been obliged to hold her husband back from knocking Richard's teeth down his throat.

Whatever was happening inside, she had a choice to make. Now. This minute. Did she creep away, ride to Twy-ford, and pretend she'd never been there, or did she push her way into the hall and demand to know what unpleasant, but necessary, task had been lined up for her this time? She'd survived being kidnapped, frozen, assaulted, and, most recently, she'd resolved a murderous scandal within Rockingham Castle but his time it wasn't her survival that worried her. Willoughby hated her husband. Mathilda could withstand anything happening to her. But to lose Robert…

With a sharp cough, Lord John gathered the meeting back to something resembling order. 'This is not a time to indulge in your petty grievances, Rector, nor do we question Lady Mathilda's honour. The problem of Willoughby remains; and it becomes more pressing every day. He has been a thorn in the side of the region for years; now he threatens us directly by his proposed actions towards the Coterels.

'Now we have secured help from many of our mutual associates, almost all the players are in position. The time to meet the Coterels in Lichfield approaches. If we find they are in agreement with our proposed course of action, then we need to be prepared for the consequences. These may be severe. It is inevitable that, whether we act or not, we'll find ourselves on this rogue justice's arrest list.'

'May I make a suggestion, my Lord?' Sir Robert Ingram leant forward, his hands steepled together beneath his chin as if in thought, or perhaps prayer.

'Please do, Sir Robert.'

'The Lady Mathilda is, as we've agreed many times before, clever and quick-witted.' The former sheriff gestured an arm towards the hall door through which Mathilda had silently appeared. 'Why don't you ask her what she thinks you should do?'

~ *Chapter Nine* ~

15th December 1331

'Mathilda!'

Robert's expression wrestled between anger, surprise and relief as his wife stood before them, a jug of ale in her hand and a furrow creasing her forehead.

'Husband.' She greeted him with a curtsey as she took in the other residents of the hall.

Bettrys and Daniel stood next to each other at the far end of the long table. Their eyes wide, their mouths firmly closed. There was no sign of Sarah or Adam.

Lord John rose from his position at the head of the table. 'My Lady, we were given to understand you were residing in Twyford tonight.'

'That was the plan, my Lord, but a situation arose which hastened me here.'

'A situation?' Robert addressed his wife directly.

Striding forward, placing the jug on the table with an exaggerated thud, Mathilda fixed her gaze on her husband. 'I came to believe that my family were keeping secrets from me.' She surveyed the room, 'Secrets that would affect my welfare. It appears I was correct.'

'You forget yourself, woman! What right do you have

to…?'

Mathilda ignored the outburst from the Rector of Teigh, turning instead to the head of the household. 'Lord John, forgive my intrusion. I am aware it is not usual for a wife to be so disobedient, but I am a Folville wife. Would you expect me to be any other way? Especially when I sense trouble for my kin.'

John's reluctant smile was echoed by stifled laughter from Thomas and a grunt from Eustace. 'I would not.'

Robert Ingram's eyes shone his approval as he spoke for the group. 'Lady Mathilda, I imagine you know more of this matter than your family has assumed; perhaps you would share your information?'

'Certainly, my Lord, but first, please could someone tell me where Sarah and Adam are?'

Robert gestured his wife towards the empty chair next to him. 'They are having a day off. They've barely had a chance to be alone since they wed.'

'And you didn't want Sarah eavesdropping on your conversation and telling me what had been discussed here, whereas young Daniel and Bettrys will keep their mouths closed when told to?'

Her husband had the good grace to look sheepish. 'That too.'

'May I also enquire as to why no one is watching the courtyard? I arrived without notice. Is that wise in the current climate?'

'It is being watched.' Lord Eustace growled. 'My man Pykehose is out there with three guards. He had instructions only to reveal himself if he didn't recognise any visitors.'

Mathilda felt reassured. John Pykehose was amongst Eustace's most trusted men. 'One more question before I share what I've learned. There is a horse I do not recognise in the stables. My Lord Ingram is clearly here alone, so the mount cannot belong to a companion of his. Who does the horse belong to?'

Robert cleared his throat, as if the words he was about to say were choking him. 'It's yours.'

'Mine? But I have a horse. What purpose do I have for another, especially one that would be more suited to a male rider?'

Even as she'd asked the question, Mathilda wasn't sure she wanted to hear the answer.

'Lord Willoughby has a son. In fact he has many children, but his eldest child, also Richard, is a known appreciator of fine horses.' Robert licked his lips, meeting his wife's eyes properly for the first time since her unexpected arrival. 'He is not so good, we are given to believe, at memorising people. If he has seen you before, it is unlikely he paid you much regard, but there is a good chance he'd recall the fine nature of your palfrey, and therefore link you to us.'

'I see.'

'Do you?' Lord Thomas studied his sister-in-law shrewdly. Out of all of the brothers, beyond Robert, he knew her best. 'You see what that means?'

'That this is about Justice Willoughby, yes. And that you wish to send me as a messenger or spy into Wollaton; that much I overheard. As to the horse   clearly I am to ride it while acting as that missive, as it is vital no one there knows who I am, and therefore, who I'm married to. Although, to my knowledge, I have never set eyes on a single member of the Willoughby family, nor anyone associated with the justice.'

Thomas nodded, but his face was etched with concern. 'I knew you'd see it.'

Robert placed a protective hand over his wife's. 'I hate

the idea of sending you there.'

'I know. Presumably, that's why you've refused to talk about it for weeks.'

'I was hoping to find another way.'

Mathilda hoped her anxious gulp went unnoticed as she addressed the servants. 'Bettrys, Daniel, I'm sure their lordships will be hungry soon. Perhaps, with Lord John's permission, you would return to the kitchen to prepare some food.'

A nod from the eldest Folville sent Bettrys and Daniel scurrying away with noticeable relief, before Lord John said, 'I'd like you to tell us what you've discovered before my patience wears thin, Lady Mathilda.'

Observing the combined brothers carefully, Mathilda repeated what Aldus and his colleagues had told her about not wanting to work at Wollaton again and how they'd heard that Lady Willoughby hadn't been seen for some weeks. Judging from their expressions, so far she wasn't telling them anything they didn't know.

Pouring herself some ale, Mathilda levelled her gaze at Lord Eustace. 'Justice Willoughby has called for the travelling court to visit various locations in Lincolnshire, Leicestershire, Derbyshire, and the surrounds in January. The New Year is to see it begin.'

Suddenly every brother was locked on to what Mathilda was saying. The air in the hall froze around her as she kept talking.

'The underlying plan of this court is to capture and convict as many people, man or woman, whatever their status, who have supported the Coterel brothers at any time, past or present.'

The crackle of the fire seemed abnormally loud, until Eustace, with an eye to his older brother, finally spoke.

'You heard that as general gossip in Leicester market, Lady Mathilda?'

'No, my Lord. I heard this from Aldus the minstrel. He did not say where he'd heard the news. The only connected rumour amongst the market-goers was that, as I said, Lady Willoughby has not been seen for some time. A whisper Noll confirmed to have been gathering credence.'

'I see.' Eustace was curt. 'If the minstrels have heard about the travelling court, then others will know.'

'My brother Oswin knew. He's been half expecting word from Lord Nicholas Coterel, requesting his help.'

Laurence angrily catapulted a lump of bread into the fire. 'Then all hope of all this being mere tactics to frighten us into recklessness can be forgotten.'

'That was never likely.' Robert grumbled as he looked at Mathilda. 'Anything else?'

She exhaled slowly. 'Only that Lord Willoughby holds you, Robert, personally responsible for the death of his friend Roger Belers. I believe he once had you assaulted in retribution?'

Silence re-cloaked the hall.

Mathilda was the one who broke it. 'I know you didn't kill Belers, Robert, but it makes no difference to the law which man actually did the deed. What matters is who is believed to be responsible. So,' she brushed her hands down her front and removed her travelling cloak, 'perhaps you would like to tell me why you were arguing in my absence about me being a messenger? After that, I'd appreciate being told the nature of that message and what you think it might achieve. You speak as if time is passing like flour through a sieve, yet you waste so much of it.'

Glancing at Lord John, who shrugged in resigned agreement, Robert replied to his wife. 'We have had word from

James Coterel. As you know, he is no longer held in high esteem by the Crown after his plan to take over Rockingham Castle came to light, thanks to you. Anyway, James has sent his brothers into hiding. A state in which he is soon to join them.'

'Hiding?' Mathilda sat up straighter. 'Are they within Lichfield Abbey? I know they've hidden out there for brief periods of trouble in the past.'

'The Peaks. They are sleeping in the forests and shelters of nature. Although we should be meeting them, all being well, at Lichfield in three days' time.'

This news shook Mathilda. Her encounters with the Coterel brothers had left her with the impression that they were untouchable. She took her time to frame her next sentence.

'The fact you have already purchased a horse for me, despite my husband's reservations, so I can act as messenger to Wollaton speaks volumes as to the urgency of this mission. However, as I said, I have never seen any member of the Willoughby family. Why would I want to undertake such a task on a horse I am unfamiliar with, especially while travelling a road I don't know?'

Eustace replied. 'The new horse will gallop faster than your palfrey. You'd reach Wollaton in less time and, should a hasty exit be required, you'd achieve that quickly. This particular steed is used to making hasty turnarounds.'

Surprised, and disquieted by Eustace's concern for her safety, Mathilda asked, 'The horse is known to you, my Lord?'

'Lady Joan la Zouche supplied it for you.'

Mathilda's eyebrow rose in surprise. Lady Joan's father, Roger la Zouche, the real killer of Belers, was a man of considerable influence. Currently he represented the county of Leicestershire at Parliament in London. 'And you are sure that the younger Willoughby will not recognise it from her stable?'

Eustace shook his head. 'The horse is relatively new to Lady Joan.'

Mathilda dipped her head in gratitude for the information. 'So Her Ladyship was made aware of what I'm being instructed to do before I was?'

'Your safety needed assuring.' Lord John tilted his head to one side, his expression unmoving.

'In that case, would it not be prudent to explain all that is expected of me? What is the situation exactly, Robert?' Mathilda faced her husband, not caring if she was impudent.

'We intend to prevent Willoughby from holding this foolish court. In the first instance we will give him a chance to withdraw his plans, so that he does not lose face before the Crown.'

'Are you saying that is all you have come up with in a month?'

'On the contrary, as we said, we have secured all the help we need for after the message fails to persuade Willoughby to change his mind. Which it will   fail, I mean.'

Mathilda tilted her chin up, hoping the shake in her shoulders would hold off for a few more minutes as she spoke out, 'So you have condemned Willoughby to death already?'

Eustace glared at Robert while snapping at Mathilda, 'There is no other way!'

Thomas leant forward, his words beseeching. 'We are sending a message to prove we are not as bad as Willoughby. We need to give him a chance, but we know he won't take it, Lady Mathilda. I wish it were otherwise. And for that chance to be offered, we need a messenger.'

'And that messenger would be me.'

'We need someone we can trust,' Eustace answered.

Mathilda nodded. That at least made sense. 'And if Lord Willoughby is set on his plan to see as many of the Coterels' supporters rounded up as possible, how soon before you intend to send him to join his friend Belers?'

'Our plans are made. It is safer you do not know of them.'

'Is that so?' Mathilda held Lord Eustace's gaze. Taking a deep breath, she filled the hush that had descended on the hall. 'Murder may not be the most rewarding solution, my Lords.'

Eustace's face flashed red. 'You do not know the man!'

'No, I don't, but could we not use him rather than kill him?'

Robert held a hand out to Eustace to stop his protesting. 'Mathilda, this false justice is a user of men, not a man you can use. Whatever happens next, we will try and persuade Willoughby to give up this quest before it goes any further. A peaceful solution all round.'

'Sensible. And what manner of message will achieve that, do you think?'

Eustace barked without hesitation, 'A blackmail note, of course.'

~ *Chapter Ten* ~

15th December 1331

Robert wrapped an arm around Mathilda's shoulders and pulled her closer, propping up the bolster that protected their heads from the wooden bedstead.

Their moment's escape from reality already forgotten, his words lay heavy with regret. 'I wish there was another way. But with the Coterels gone to ground, it's too late. We all know the warning won't work. It's merely a gesture to show we are fairer in our operations than Willoughby is.'

'Which makes the gesture an important one.' Mathilda kissed her husband's cheek. 'But the manner in which they want me to go to Wollaton worries me.'

'You won't be sent alone.'

Mathilda hadn't thought she would be, but as yet hadn't considered who might escort her. 'None of the family can come with me, and Adam and Daniel are needed here. I can't ask Oswin, as his association with the Coterels puts him in jeopardy, and my brother Matthew is away tending to the lands you granted my family on our wedding day.'

'Eustace has assured me you will not go alone.'

Mathilda knew she should feel reassured by this news. Eustace only employed the best mercenaries, and they betrayed him at their peril, yet she couldn't rest easy at the prospect of her reception at Wollaton when she handed over what would basically be a threat.

'Can I ask why one of Eustace's men can't deliver the message?'

Robert ran his fingers through the red hair that swathed his wife's shoulders. 'That's what I wanted to happen, but my brothers said it was too confrontational to send someone who was obviously a hired thug.'

'I suppose that would make the whole idea of the peaceful solution pointless.' Mathilda muttered. 'Whereas a woman's touch…'

Mathilda's words trailed away as Robert snarled, 'My reverend brother suggested we sent Sarah.'

'I bet he did! He'll be hoping she's captured and killed. He's never forgiven Sarah for his being sent into the Church, even though it was not her choice.'

Robert shrugged. 'Some wounds go so deep they lose logic.'

'Like Justice Willoughby's loss of his friend, perhaps?'

'Perhaps.' Robert ruffled a hand through his hair. 'We had no choice with Belers. His death solved so many problems and saved lives.'

'I know. But…' Mathilda paused, unsure how to continue.

'But what?'

'I can't help thinking that solving the problem of Willoughby's corruption in the same manner, killing him to rid the world of his influence, will eventually end up with this situation happening all over again. With one of his friends seeking revenge. Revenge they can legally sanction. How many men of law will our family have to murder to make everything alright? How long before you have to sacrifice your life over the death of a power-hungry official?' Mathilda voice cracked into little more than a whisper as she spoke her fears. 'The idea I may lose you to this enterprise… I couldn't bear it.'

Caressing his wife's frightened face, Robert kissed her. He didn't speak, there was nothing to say. They both knew the price for how they lived.

Mathilda had slept a little; her night littered with bad dreams and wakeful periods of worry. She knew Robert was awake, even though it was not yet dawn. 'Who will write the message I am to deliver?'

'Eustace. His hand is the clearest.'

'Is that wise?'

'Probably not, but I will attempt to make sure his hot head does not take over as he writes.'

Rolling onto her side so she was face to face with her husband, Mathilda asked, 'I know I will be accompanied to the hall, but how will I find my way about once I get there? It isn't as if I can expect a warm welcome at Wollaton Hall. There is nothing to stop Justice Willoughby calling our bluff and keeping me as a hostage.'

'Willoughby is greedy and corrupt, but he is not stupid. Besides, he'll want you to deliver a reply.'

'He could send someone else with a reply and hold me prisoner.'

'If he did that, he knows we would raid his home and take his children.'

'If he does not worry over a missing wife, why would he care for the removal of his children?'

Robert sighed. 'I don't know, Mathilda. But I'm sure you'll be safe.'

'No you aren't.' She kissed his nose. 'But thank you for

lying to me for my peace of mind.'

He laughed. 'You're too clever by half.'

'So I'm told.'

'You've been lying there thinking of ways out of this mess, haven't you?'

'Yes, but I'm not sure I've succeeded.'

'Tell me.' Robert lifted himself up on one elbow.

'The minstrels know the layout of most of Wollaton Hall because they've played there in the past. Aldus told me that only balladeers desperate for work go there, so it is unlikely that Lord Willoughby will have engaged any for the festive season. Especially if his wife is not at home to make such arrangements. But we do. We have minstrels engaged for the festive season'

Robert's eyebrows rose. 'Do we?'

'You sent me to the market on purpose, didn't you? In the hope I'd encounter Aldus and learn from him?'

'There is little the minstrels don't see or hear. Why they are believed to be blind and deaf to the world around them just because they are singing, I've never understood.' Robert kissed her slowly, before pulling away. 'You engaged them for Christmas.'

'Yes.' Mathilda eased herself up onto an elbow and grinned at her husband's surprised face. 'I have employed Aldus, Noll, and Dicun for the season, so they will have to sing where we tell them to. Could they not, therefore, deliver our message?'

Robert beamed. 'You are devious, wife of mine.'

Mathilda looked uncomfortable. 'I know. Yet I can't help wishing I wasn't. Aldus and his men are good people. It feels cruel to put them into the lion's den.'

Robert thought. 'If we could get them to go   I'd pay them to go, rather than order them   then they could leave the message lying around somewhere a couple of days *after* their arrival. They'd be no reason for anyone to know they were the bearers of the message.'

'The safer they are the better.'

Robert frowned. 'It would be better if they were invited to Wollaton in the first place by someone from the household, but that's too much to hope for.'

'Not if they were in the area.' Mathilda tried not to picture Aldus's dismayed face as they asked him to act for them. 'They could go and ask at the kitchen door. It isn't unusual for minstrels to come calling at a manor house to ask for shelter in return for work over the winter months. Although, Aldus made it clear they never intended to go to Lord Willoughby's home again, however desperate they were.'

'I can't blame them for that.'

Mathilda was solemn. 'It won't be long after the court starts before they come here will it? I can't imagine why it's the Coterels' name on that arrest warrant and not ours.'

'They are the excuse to get to us. No more than that.' Robert gripped her hands in his. 'Which is why we must act. This isn't a case of us moving in unthinking haste, Mathilda, as I know we are prone to do. This is my family trying to protect its friends.'

'And itself.'

'And itself.'

Lady Marjory twisted and turned beneath the bed linen, but sleep continued to elude her. How could her father brush off her mother's disappearance so easily?

She'd tried to talk to him again the previous evening, but he'd dismissed her to her chamber before the words were fully out of her mouth. He'd claimed he was too busy with court matters to worry about 'mere trivialities'.

Trivialities! Her mother!

A shudder ran through Marjory. She pulled the covers up over her head like she used to when she was a little girl, afraid of monsters in the dark. Now she was afraid that the monsters were real, and that one of them was her father.

No one would talk to Marjory about her mother. The servants just looked frightened when she mentioned Lady Isabel, and her brother Richard dismissed her as foolish. Their father had told them her mother was away with family, and so that was the matter closed as far as the younger Richard de Willoughby was concerned.

'Mother is staying away for her own sake,' Richard had told her that she was, 'disloyal to think such unworthy thoughts concerning their father.' His outburst had worried Marjory more than ever, for she hadn't mentioned any such theory about her father having removed their mother in an underhand way. That must mean Richard had doubts of his own, but was simply too sensible, or too afraid, to voice them.

It was just over a week until Christmas. Her mother loved the festive season. They'd always gone out together to deliver alms to the poor and listen to the church services, while privately admitting to each other they were quite dull, and looking forward to Cook's feast of sweetmeats and pastries. It was inconceivable that Lady Isabel would not be home to share her favourite time of year with her children.

The last time Marjory remembered seeing her mother felt so long ago now. The anxiety of the long weeks of waiting for her to walk into the hall, holding some embroidery and using the smile she kept entirely for her children, was beginning to make her eldest daughter sick with worry.

Now she thought about it, Marjory couldn't recall ever

seeing her mother look fondly in her father's direction.

As she huddled beneath the covers, there was only one thing Marjory could think of doing. She'd go to her grandmother's home in Lincolnshire. At least, she'd get to share Christmas with a family who liked her. She sighed into her pillow. No one here would notice if she'd gone anyway.

Giving up on sleep, Marjory grabbed her chemise, sliding it on before getting out of bed and stepping into the chill of the room. It was too early for her maid to come and attend her, so Marjory pulled her clothing on alone before covering herself with her travelling cloak to guard against the cold. Her fire had all but gone out, and she didn't know how to encourage its flames higher.

Marjory sagged onto the end of the bed. 'I can't even light a fire. What chance would I have of surviving the winter air, searching for my mother on a road I don't know, on my own?'

~ Chapter Eleven ~

16th December 1331

Lady Marjory had expected Wollaton's main hall to be quiet but for servants preparing the space for the day ahead. The sight that met her however, as she slipped through the main door, was of her father in full campaign mode. She couldn't help thinking he looked like a knight going into battle rather than a justice preparing for a court.

Keeping to the shadows, positive her arrival would do nothing but annoy her father for its potential to slow his progress, Marjory listened as he issued instructions to Bennett, before pulling his eldest child to one side.

'This trailbaston, this vital court, when it begins in January, will be the most important of my career, Richard. Possibly the most important in English history.'

Marjory felt queasy as she saw her father's puffed-up demeanour and self-satisfied expression.

'Our Midland counties have been ruled too long by criminals. Conceited families who believe themselves better than those of a rank so much higher than their own…'

As she listened, Marjory remembered an argument between her parents. It was the only time she'd heard her mother stick up for herself. Come to think of it, it hadn't been long before she'd last seen her.

Lady Isabel, her voice calm but firm, had told her husband that he was only as powerful as he was because of the Mortain lands, and money that marriage had brought the Willoughby name. Her father hadn't liked that. The implication that he couldn't be powerful without his wife had made him spit like he'd been forced to drink bile.

His face contorted in a similar manner now as he continued to speak to his son. 'My information tells me that the Coterels have over one hundred and fifty supporters! People bringing them food, hiding them, helping them with their evil crimes! So many have strayed from the path of the law, and it is my job… my pleasure… to punish them for disloyalty to their Crown and country and our Lord God.'

Marjory could see her brother nodding his agreement, wise enough to hold his tongue as their father moved on, as they knew he would, to his hatred of the Folville family.

'And should I catch the Folvilles trying to aid their allies, which I will, then the counties of Leicestershire and Derbyshire will forever be in my debt.'

The younger Richard had opened his mouth then. Whether it had been to agree with his father, to wish him luck, or to advise caution, she'd never know, for her father hadn't finished his outburst.

'Rumour even has it that the most cursed Folville of all, Lord Robert,' he almost spat as he spoke, 'the killer of my friend, has wed a woman of peasant stock who dares to call herself a lady! And, moreover, this chit has a taste for sticking her nose in where it isn't wanted. She's even been known to detect killers.'

'Killers, Father?' Surprise broke through the Willoughby heir's dutiful silence.

'*Lady* Mathilda de Folville, a mere potter's daughter

from Twyford, discovered who killed a maid at Rocking-ham Castle. As if that was important! She will have to go alongside the rest of them.'

Lady Mathilda. Marjory wrapped her arms around her chest with a shiver; already afraid for a woman she'd never met who, it seemed, cared far more about the people than her father did.

Her stomach rumbled, but Marjory was too consumed with the desperate need to act to consider eating. Her father was about to leave Wollaton to consult his fellow officials as to where and when to begin trying the men he hoped the bailiffs of the region were already rounding up. It was the perfect time to start searching for her mother. But how?

Bettrys hadn't slept well. Her eyes blurred as she tried to spark some life into the hall fire for a third time.

Sitting back on her haunches, she poked at the log formation in the hope that, if she moved the grate Daniel had laid in readiness the night before, then the flames would take.

Lady Mathilda had warned her. So had Sarah, Adam, and Daniel. Each of them had individually told her that some of the things the Folville brothers did would challenge her ideas of right and wrong. Bettrys had listened, but realised that, until now, she hadn't believed them.

Muttering a prayer into the unlit hearth, Bettrys wondered if she should leave after all. They'd told her she could. Mathilda had said if she was ever worried or scared and didn't want the life being associated with the Folville family brought, she could go. But go where in the heart of winter?

An image of Daniel flashed through her mind. He'd never leave. He'd been here since he was a child. He was now a young man of sixteen, and Bettrys couldn't imagine him anywhere else. Would she want to leave without him?

Bettrys tried to light the fire again. This time it caught, and as she gently blew the fledgling flames into life, she thought over all she'd heard in that very room the day before.

They'd talked of a bad man called Willoughby, a justice of England. Bettrys' head ached as she remembered a song her former master, the Constable of Rockingham Castle, had sung about justice being turned on its head, and the outlaw being more honourable than the sheriffs. She hummed the tune, as she tried to fish the words from the back of her mind, only to stop abruptly as soft footsteps entered the room.

'The Outlaw's Song of Trailbaston.' Sarah's eyebrows rose, 'I didn't know you knew such tunes, Bettrys. Lord and Lady Folville would most certainly approve, especially in the current situation.'

Getting up from the floor, Bettrys brushed smuts from her skirts. 'Lord de Vere used to sing it. It just came into my head.'

'Indeed.' The housekeeper noted the maid's pale demeanour. 'You are worried about the current situation.'

'A little.' Bettrys admitted shyly, before attempting to change the subject 'I hope you and Adam had a nice day yesterday.'

'We did, thank you.' Sarah threw the wet cloth she'd been carrying against the oak table, rubbing it in firm circular motions across the surface. 'Could you tell me what the brothers have cooked up in our absence?'

Bettrys went paler still. 'I… I'm not supposed to say what I heard.'

'Of course you aren't, but it would be a good idea if you

did. Safer all round.'

'Safer?'

'Oh yes.' Sarah didn't look up, but kept up the rhythmical cleaning motion. 'The longer you're here, Bettrys, the more you'll realise that the brothers are often in too much of a hurry to act, to think as clearly as they ought to. Lady Mathilda and I do our best to curb their enthusiasm, but to do that, we need all the facts.'

Remembering Mathilda saying something very similar, the maid said, 'But we're just servants, what can we do?'

'Influence things.' As the girl started to light the candles around the room using a spark of flame from the fire, Sarah explained, 'The way this family works is complicated, but it is important to remember that we must always let the brothers think they are the decision makers, while we check they are good decisions, and do our best to steer them onto the right path when they aren't.'

'How?'

'By making sure we know everything that's going on.' Sarah smiled. 'They rely on us to think things through for them, even if they haven't all worked that out yet. I promise you won't get into trouble for talking to me.'

'Promise?'

'Absolutely.' Understanding the girl's unease, Sarah said, 'I tell you what. Ask Daniel if he thinks you should tell me and Adam what we missed. If he says not to, then don't say a word, but if he agrees you should, then come and find me in the kitchen. We have another hour at least before the Lords Eustace and Robert stir. The others have already gone.'

Lighting the last candle, Bettrys headed towards the stables to ask Daniel's opinion. She was almost at the door, when she realised she was wasting her time. Of course he'd encourage her to tell Sarah. He was probably outside telling Adam all they'd heard already. Sarah would never have given her the option of speaking to Daniel first if she wasn't confident of the answer.

Bettrys turned and went back to the table. 'I'll go and start the bread.' The maid gave a nervous smile. 'I'll tell you all I can remember while we knead the dough.'

'I was wrong, Robert.' Pulling her knees up under her chin, Mathilda hugged them against her chest.

'Wrong how?'

'About using the minstrels. We can't send them into Wollaton.'

'But why not? It would save you having to…'

She was shaking her head hard now, her red hair swiping at her shoulders, 'If anything happened to them I'd never forgive myself and, more importantly, we need a reply to the message. An instant one. The minstrels would hardly be able to turn up, deliver the paper, and then leave. Their reputations would be ruined for one thing, and they might be prevented from departing for another.'

Robert sighed. 'Willoughby would certainly make sure they never played locally again.'

'It has to be me.'

'I wish it didn't.'

'I know.' She kissed him gently on the lips, before saying, 'But it does not have to be murder. Even once he's said no.'

'Which he will. Without a doubt.'

Mathilda wrapped her arms around herself as she walked from her chamber to the kitchen. The winter had been mild so far, but overnight the temperature had dropped, capturing the cool air between the stone corridors of the manor.

On entering the kitchen, Mathilda warmed herself by the fire as Sarah and Bettrys threw newly created batches of dough onto thick wooden boards.

'Good morning, my Lady.' Sarah curtsied as her friend and mistress came in.

Mathilda smiled. 'Excellent, I was beginning to think I'd have to waste time telling you about the brothers meeting, but Bettrys has clearly been good enough to save me the trouble.'

The maid blanched in concerned confusion. 'My Lady, I…'

The housekeeper placed a gentle had over her maid's and gave it a reassuring squeeze. 'Lady Mathilda and I have a way of letting each other know that we know things. It's alright.'

Relieved that she wasn't in trouble for sharing what she knew with Sarah, Bettrys listened as her mistress sat near the fire and began to speak.

'As you'll know, the situation is serious, and I fear that what the men folk have planned will only work in the short term.'

'You think it will work though?' Sarah washed dough from her fingers. 'Killing the justice would bring him to an end, but to do it without it being obvious as to whom the culprit is…'

'Exactly.' Mathilda frowned. 'The deed would bring an instant end to the problem, but it wouldn't make it go away for long.'

'Another justice would come.' Bettrys picked at her fingers, 'I remember at Rockingham, there was always another one, ready to make money out of the criminals, or the people they'd decided were criminals.'

Mathilda nodded. 'You are right to see they're not always the same thing.' She poured herself a drink. 'Even if his death could be achieved without suspicion being cast our way, which would be hard enough, I don't see how it could do any more than delay the whole situation starting again in a year or so, just like it did before.'

Sarah groaned. 'You mean they killed Belers, Willoughby came along, so kill him too, and in time another will come who is as bad, or even worse.'

'And so it would go on and on. Nothing would change. But if we could use things to prompt the Crown into changing how the justices worked… If we could manoeuvre the situation to show the king how corrupt his officials can get, how they are often more criminal than the criminals…' Mathilda sighed. 'I tried to discuss this with the brothers, but they were closed to my thoughts, hell bent on retribution.'

The housekeeper regarded her mistress. 'You want the Lords Folville to make an example of Willoughby in the hope it improves the entire system.'

'It would be better, surely, than another death being laid at our door?'

'And how on earth,' Eustace pushed the kitchen door open wide, his expression creased into disapproval, but his voice unusually level, 'do you propose we do that, Lady Mathilda?'

'Do you really want to know, my Lord?'

'I don't know. That depends on what you have to tell me.'

~ *Chapter Twelve* ~

16th December 1331

'He didn't shout at you?'

'No.' Mathilda passed her husband some ale. Robert appeared to be in shock.

'And he listened to what you had to say without interrupting?'

'He did.'

'Eustace? The one with a temper so short it's frayed? He didn't shout when he discovered that the maid and housekeeper were in discussion with you about the Willoughby matter, and that you were thinking about ways to succeed in this venture that did not include killing a man he hates?'

'Hard to believe, I know, but that's what happened. Or didn't happen.' Mathilda had been confused too, but not as much as Robert. 'I did wonder if Lady Joan la Zouche may have influenced his manner of late.'

'Lady Joan?' Robert raised his eyebrows.

'You can't have missed the liking between them. If she has suggested that he curb his tongue on occasion, and perhaps even likes the idea of murder not always being the answer, then Eustace might be prepared to listen for once.'

'She's a married woman.'

'To a man working hundreds of miles away as the Sheriff of Yorkshire. She views him with complete indifference; and vice versa. Lady Joan doesn't even use his name unless he's around; preferring to use La Zouche, like her father.'

Neither commenting, nor wasting time speculating on what his second brother may or may not be doing with the daughter of one of their most powerful friends, Robert looked at his wife with friendly suspicion. 'And why would Lady Joan, who has not been privy to our conversations, have exactly the same idea as you?'

'Because I suspect she is as up-to-date as Eustace with events and because she is very clever.'

'And because you've spoken to her?'

Mathilda tilted her head to one side, 'And when would I have done that?'

'When you were supposed to be selling pots with Oswin.'

'And just how do you imagine I got to Lady Joan at Lubbersthorpe, back to Leicester to engage the minstrels for Christmas, and then returned to Ashby Folville in such a short time?' She spoke pointedly, picking up her travelling cloak as she did so.

'Fair enough.' Robert remained suspicious. 'Seems a huge coincidence though.'

'In truth, Lady Joan may have nothing to do with it. Lord Eustace may have simply appreciated the logic of what I was saying.' Mathilda packed some bread and water into their saddle packs. 'Are you ready to go?'

'Are you ready to try and convince everyone of the wisdom of your plan? I can't say how you'll be received in Leicester. They won't want to linger either. We're to ride to Lichfield to consult with the Coterels straight after we've gathered at Ingram's favoured inn.'

Mathilda passed Robert his cloak. 'If they don't like

what I say, at least I'll have tried to save you all from the noose.'

Adam was ready and waiting in the courtyard with Robert's horse and the new beast Lady Joan had presented for Mathilda.

'I'd rather have my own horse.'

'You need to get used to riding him, my Lady.'

Mathilda examined the mount. It was three full hands taller than her usual ride, and the glint to the beast's eye showed he lacked the docile nature she was used to. Before coming to live at Ashby Folville, she'd done very little riding. Her favoured palfrey had been a gift from Robert, a gentle horse so she could get used to riding safely. This beautiful but imposing black beast did not feel gentle.

'But Adam, if I'm seen on this horse with the family, won't that defeat the object of me being able to ride him, should I have to go to Wollaton at a later date?'

'I couldn't say, my Lady.' Adam stroked the animal's nose with respect. 'His name is Jep.'

'Hello, Jep.' Patting the horse's jet black neck with fake confidence, Mathilda allowed Adam to help her into the saddle. 'Are you coming too?'

'I am. Lord Eustace has assured me that Master Pykehose and his men will be on guard, so the manor will be safe.'

'Good.' Mathilda walked Jep in wide circles around the courtyard to try and get used to his stride. She quickly realised Jep lacked the lightness of touch she was used to. To do what she wanted, she'd have to be prepared to nudge him hard. Then she'd have to work out how to stop him again.

The ride to Leicester hadn't been as bad as Mathilda feared.

Placed between Eustace and Robert, with Adam riding directly behind her, she felt that Jep was suitably penned in, so if he'd bolted, at least the horsemanship of her companions would ensure she was kept pace with until he slowed again.

Conversation was minimal, each consumed with their own thoughts while they rode towards the inn where Lord Ingram conducted his off-duty business. Mathilda couldn't help but wonder how they'd react to her proposal. She'd mulled over the wording of what she wanted to say with each fresh step. How she started her plea was vital. Mess up the first sentence, and they'd dismiss listening to her, and maybe even remove her from the room altogether. After all, convinced Willoughby would take no heed of their warning to stop the court, they believed they were meeting to discuss the safest manner of achieving Willoughby's death, prior to visiting Lichfield. It wouldn't have occurred to them that a new idea might be coming their way.

As she dismounted in the tavern's stable block, Mathilda's eyes landed on a fine grey palfrey. Lady Joan?

She flicked her gaze to Robert to see if he'd noticed the horse tethered up with many others, but he was in conversation with Adam about the care of their own mounts while they were within.

Lord Eustace had seen it. Mathilda watched as his eyes hovered over the mare. He didn't look surprised to see it there. Had he asked her Ladyship to attend this meeting to represent her father? Mathilda felt a ray of hope. Perhaps she wasn't going to be alone in persuading the brothers to change their plans?

Mathilda curtseyed low to Lady Joan, whispering, 'I am more than a little delighted to see you, Lady Joan.' Unheeded by the brothers she bowed in quick reverence to the Lady la Zouche, before they settled themselves around the fire near the already seated Ingram.

'And I you.' Lady Joan gave the barest flicker of a smile, but Mathilda saw it and understood. Whatever Joan was doing there, it was in the hope of the enterprise keeping as many people alive at the end as possible. Whether that included Willoughby, only time would tell.

'Lady Folville.' Ingram got to his feet as he saw Mathilda, 'I am pleased you could come.'

'Was my presence in doubt?' She bobbed politely before the former sheriff.

'It was suggested to me,' Ingram flicked his eyes towards Richard de Folville, 'that it was unlikely you'd be invited.'

'In that my reverend brother-in-law is correct. I was not invited. And yet I'm here.'

She could feel her husband's eyes on her as Ingram took her cloak and pulled out a seat for her next to Lady Joan.

Perhaps I have more allies here than I thought.

Mathilda's confidence rose for a second, only to be overtaken by a new thought. One that made her palms perspire. What if they'd expected this? What if Ingram, and possibly Lord Thomas and Lady Joan, expect me to think of another way a better, safer, way to end this business?

In the past she'd solved murders and escaped a kidnapper, but this was different. This wasn't fighting to stay alive or avenge the death of an innocent girl. This was plotting the downfall of one of the most influential men in England. This could get every single one of them hanged.

The glint in Thomas de Folville's eyes as he glanced in her direction confirmed Mathilda's fears. They had known she'd come. Half of the assembled group were relying on her to come up with an alternative to their scheme.

Suddenly Mathilda wasn't sure who she was most wary

of, the men who could see nothing but a vision of Lord Willoughby's fallen body, or the people who had taken it for granted that she'd stop that from happening.

'Sarah?' Bettrys heard the door behind her squeak as she wrestled a clean sheet onto Robert and Mathilda's bed.

'Yes, it's me.' The housekeeper used an elbow to nudge open the lid to the heavy linen chest, before levering it wider with her foot and depositing the armful of blankets inside. 'Have you already done Lord Eustace's room?'

Bettrys nodded, too breathless from lifting the heavy mattress to speak.

'Good girl.' Sarah rested her hands on her hips in satisfaction. 'Now, I think we've earned a sit down.'

Bettrys was surprised. 'But we haven't swept or laid the fires yet?'

Sarah wrapped a protective arm around the young maid's shoulders. 'When Lady Mathilda employed you, it was on the understanding that I taught you the skills of being a housekeeper, so that one day you can take over from me.'

Bettrys' mouth opened, but no more than a squeak came out.

'In order to teach you, I need to talk to you, and as we get precious little time to do that, we should grab the chances we get. It isn't often that the whole household is absent at once, so I don't see why we shouldn't take the chance to discuss the future.'

Shocked that Sarah was talking about a future with her as housekeeper, Bettrys obediently followed. Lady Mathilda had once mentioned that she should be trained as a housekeeper to help Sarah as she got older, but it hadn't occurred to her that the promise would be kept.

Sarah pointed to the seat that ran the opposite side of the

kitchen table to where she stood. 'Take a seat and I'll show you how to make Lady Mathilda's favourite honey drink.'

Relaxing a little as she realised Sarah was about to teach her something, Bettrys paid close attention as Sarah poured a little honey into a pottery cup and took a pinch of cinnamon from her precious spice store.

'The trick is to add the right amount of hot water. Only a drop or two is required, or the honey will be over-diluted and loose its sweetness and smooth consistency. This is a short drink with plenty of flavour and comfort, rather than a thin drink to quench the thirst.'

Bettrys watched, knowing how important it was not to waste either the honey or the spice. An aroma of sweetness filled the air, and she could see how this drink would make you feel better.

As Sarah stirred the thick honey and water, Bettrys saw the golden paste separate and dissolve into the mix.

'Here you go.' Sarah took a tiny sip of the mixture, before pushing the finished drink towards the maid. 'It's excellent. Drink up. It's best while it's warm.'

'For me?'

'You need to know what it tastes like, otherwise how will you know if you have the measure right?'

Lifting the shallow cup to her lips, Bettrys inhaled slowly. 'It smells heavenly. Like Christmas.'

Sarah beamed, and gestured for her to take a sip.

Letting the thick liquid roll around her tongue, Bettrys savoured the taste before allowing it to slip down her throat. 'Wow!'

Sarah laughed. 'I'll take that as a compliment.'

'It's delicious.'

'Come on then.' The housekeeper passed the stone honey pot towards Bettrys. 'Your turn.'

Concentration etched itself on the maid's face as she diligently followed the steps that Sarah had just taken. Then, with a nervous hand, she spooned up a tiny bit to try.

'How is it?' Sarah asked, watching the girl with pride as she tasted the mixture.

'It's a little weaker than yours, but it tastes good.'

Sarah took her spoon, and sampled a liquid. 'A tiny bit too much water, but a perfectly acceptable drink. Do you think Daniel would like it?'

Bettrys blushed. 'He might. I expect he's cold out in the stables.'

'Then why don't you call him in. He's probably ready for a rest, and what I have to say to you concerns him too.'

~ *Chapter Thirteen* ~

16th December 1331

Cupping the honey drink, praising Bettrys for her skill in making it, Daniel asked, 'You wanted to talk to us, Sarah?'

'Yes.' The housekeeper took a deep breath. 'Lady Mathilda has left a task for us. Well, for you two.'

Daniel placed the cup onto the table. 'A task?'

With her best reassuring smile, Sarah gestured for the lad to sit as she explained. 'Lady Mathilda has proposed an alternative plan to Lord Eustace concerning the curbing of, rather than the disposal of, the Justice Willoughby.'

The two servants shifted uneasily on the wooden bench, but said nothing.

'Bettrys, if you are truly to learn what it means to become a housekeeper here within this household your skills will need to develop beyond your ability to run this manor, to feed the family and make sure they are clothed, clean, and comfortable.' Sarah tried not to notice that the girl had gone pale. 'You need to be able think on your feet and cope with anything their lordships throw at you.'

Daniel, either unconscious of what he was doing, or uncaring if Sarah saw, placed a hand over the maid's. 'Bettrys is brave and clever.'

'Aye, she is.' Sarah noticed the girl in question self-consciously wrap her palm around Daniel's, in what, she suspected, was the first open display of affection they'd shared. 'Bettrys, if you wish to progress in this particular household, you will need to prove you can cope with the additional tasks that will come your way.'

'Like with whatever it is that Lady Mathilda has left for Daniel and me to do?'

'Precisely.'

The young couple looked at each other. No words were spoken, but Sarah could feel the communication occurring anyway. For a moment she regretted having met Adam so late in life, but then shrugged the feeling off. She knew herself well enough to understand that if Adam Calvin had entered her life when she was sixteen, she'd have had no interest in him. She was acting mother to a growing family of Folville boys even then, and outsiders had had no place in her busy life.

Breaking the hush that had fallen over the kitchen, Daniel asked, 'And the task is?'

'To go to Willoughby-on-the-Wolds. As its name suggests, the village is under the ownership of Justice Willoughby.'

'And when we get there?'

'Listen. Pay attention to the conversations around you.' Sarah watched the flames of the kitchen fire dance in the draught from the door. 'Lady Isabel Willoughby has gone missing. Rumour had reached Leicester market, so it must have reached Willoughby-on-the-Wolds. Lady Mathilda wishes to know the local theories as to the lady's whereabouts.'

Daniel regarded Sarah shrewdly. He knew what was being asked of them was more dangerous than it sounded.

'You are to do nothing but listen. Any danger, if you sense you're being watched, or if you see anyone that may know you as part of this household, then you come back here. Immediately.'

Licking her drying lips, Bettrys gripped her empty cup. 'And how do we listen? I mean, won't we stand out as strangers, especially in the village? What reason do we give for being there?'

'Lady Mathilda had a suggestion, but it is up to you if you follow it.'

'Which is?' Daniel was cautious, and Sarah couldn't blame him.

'To be a couple of runaway servants searching for better a life.'

Bettrys opened her mouth to claim they weren't a couple, but then looked at the hand that was warming hers. They hadn't held hands before. In another situation it would have felt good it did feel good but she hadn't imagined that the first time they touched would be at the kitchen table while receiving instructions that could place them in danger.

On hearing no rejection of the plan, in fact, on hearing no word from her companions at all, Sarah went on. 'Lady Mathilda suggested you say you'd run away from Rocking-ham.'

'That would be believable at least,' Bettrys muttered, 'its reputation for receiving criminals is well known.' As she stared at her cup, the memory of her life at the castle came back to her. She'd survived living there so she could survive this. Sitting up straighter, Bettrys withdrew her hand from Daniel's grasp. 'Where is Willoughby-on-the-Wolds? Is it a long journey?'

Daniel recognised the resolve forming on the maid's face. 'North of Leicester. One day's ride from here.'

'A whole day just to get there!' Bettrys paled, 'But won't you need me here, Sarah? There's so much to do with the brothers coming and going and Christmas getting closer.'

The housekeeper held up a hand. 'I'll be busy, but Lady Mathilda will help me, and if Daniel were to go alone, it would arouse suspicion.'

'Why?' Daniel asked bluntly. 'Could I not be a messenger working for my master?'

Bettrys answered before Sarah did. 'If you were alone, tongues that might otherwise flap would be more guarded. With a female in your company, you would not look like a man with a master who might find overheard conversations useful. If we pretend to be without a station in life, then we'll be invisible. Unworthy of consideration.'

Sarah smiled proudly at the maid. 'Being in female company makes you less of a threat, Daniel.'

The lad considered, before asking, 'Once we've heard news of interest in Willoughby-on-the-Wold, do we stay on in the hope of learning more, or are we to return here?'

'Return home.'

'How long do we stay if we hear nothing of interest?'

'Two days. Longer would arouse suspicion as to how you could afford to pay your way.'

Bettrys' hands shook, but she sat straight and proud. 'We will have to pretend we stole the money.' The maid blushed as she asked, 'Why news of Lady Isabel rather than the Willoughby court in general? What can she do to help our plight? Does she have influence with her husband, in the manner of Lady Mathilda and Lord Robert?' she asked hopefully.

'No lady has influence over her husband like our Mathilda,' Sarah laughed, before becoming instantly sober. 'Lady Mathilda is good at solving puzzles, and she wondered if, should we should discover what's become of Lady Isabel, it could help our cause. Although should you hear anything of general interest, then that would be good too.'

Bettrys went to the kitchen door and peeped outside. The morning frost had gone, and although the winter had been relatively kind, the tang of snow hung unmistakeably in the air. 'If we are to go, we should go early tomorrow morning, before the weather turns against us.'

Sarah passed a small pouch, taken from her pocket, across the table. 'Lady Mathilda bid you take this. It's enough to pay for shelter until you return. Aim for the inn at Willoughby-on-the-Wolds itself, and then the inn at Ragdale if you need to break on the way home. Lord Eustace has arrangements with the innkeeper. Although he doesn't know you, should trouble come your way, a discreet mention of Lord Eustace's name and he'll aid you if necessary.'

Bettrys turned to Daniel, her tone determined. 'If you see to your clothing, I'll fetch some supplies.' Then she stuttered, as if remembering herself, 'B-but I can't ride!'

Sarah and Daniel exchanged glances, before he spoke up. 'You won't need to. Servants on the run from their master only tend to risk stealing one horse.'

Although Mathilda wasn't surprised to have a representative from the Coterels present, she hadn't expected to see the man who walked into the inn's back room, late and breathless from his ride.

Roger Wennesley eased himself into the already cramped space with obvious caution, and stood next to Walter and Laurence de Folville.

When Mathilda had last seen Roger, in Rockingham Castle, he'd been up to his neck in deceit. That he'd secretly been a spy for the Coterels had been a surprise at the time;

now it seemed he had a more visible, and more dangerous, role. As she recalled, Wennesley owed the Coterels his freedom and they would expect considerable payback. It was a miracle they hadn't killed him.

He leered at her now. Not in the contemptuous way that the Rector of Teigh did, but with the clear opinion that this room was no place for a woman. Although he didn't pay Lady Joan the same lack of regard. Perhaps he knew of Eustace's interest there? Wennesley was an unpleasant man, but he was not a fool.

Calling the room to order, Robert Ingram asked Mathilda to explain her presence, adding that he assumed she had some thoughts on the matter in hand.

The hush that fell was almost unnatural as she spoke; highlighting her fear that if they did resort to murder, then history would simply repeat itself, and that, should they all escape the Crown's justice, the same situation would soon present itself and they'd be meeting to discuss the dispatching of yet another corrupt official. Mathilda had never known the Folvilles to pay so much attention to her before. As she went on, suggesting that there might be a way to use the situation to encourage the king to make changes to the law, rather than just to kill a corrupt man, unease tripped through her; although she wasn't sure why. The brothers were listening, paying attention. Not even the rector was sneering at her. She should have been pleased. Instead Mathilda was suspicious

It was Lady Joan who spoke first once Mathilda's speech had faded into silence. 'Use Justice Willoughby as an example, you say?'

'Yes.'

'It won't work.' Wennesley was blunt, as if the subject was already closed.

'Perhaps not.' Lady Joan tapped the back of her hand against the table, knocking her rich collection of jewelled rings against the wood, 'And if that is so, then Willoughby's lifespan could still be shortened. But if it did work, the advantages to us all, and to the region, would be more than worth it.'

Roger frowned. 'My masters are in hiding, and they do not like it. This isn't lying low for a few weeks in Lichfield Abbey. This is nights in the open forest or cold caves. Bands of men-at-arms are sweeping Derbyshire. Bakewell itself is subject to regular patrols. Villagers known to be sympathetic to my masters have already been taken into custody. A speedy end to this is not requested, it is demanded.'

Eustace responded before Mathilda or Lady Joan could. 'They may demand it, but we are not their men to demand anything of. We are helping them because it is in our interest to do so. That is all. We have common interests, but don't fall into the trap of thinking the Coterel brothers are our friends.'

'Lord Nicholas is Lady Mathilda's friend.' The words shot from the Rector of Teigh's mouth with so much relish that every set of eyes in the room stared at him with either disapproval or scorn.

'We can always rely on you to say something helpful, Richard.' Thomas glared at the rector. He knew Richard would be enjoying riling Robert, who had never been comfortable with how fond Nicholas Coterel was of his wife.

Lady Mathilda laid a hand on her husband's leg, silently urging him not to rise to the bait as she responded to Wennesley, 'Do you know where your masters are?'

'I can't say where they are; not because I've been told not to say, but because I don't know. However, I do know they'll be heading to your meeting at Lichfield.' Wennesley chewed on the inside of his cheek. 'They are unlikely to be pleased to hear you are considering letting Willoughby live.'

There were general murmurings of agreement from the Folville brothers as Wennesley asked, 'I need to get word to Lord Nicholas prior to the meeting so they know when exactly to expect you. He is bound to ask how your plans progress. What do you want me to tell him? That the killing is off? Can you imagine how that news will be received?'

Eustace stopped playing his dagger through his fingers. 'Wennesley asks a valid question; and one I'd also like an answer to, Lady Mathilda. Your idea is noble. Robyn Hode-like even. But how do you intend this notion of yours to work?'

'Robyn Hode-like… of course!' Mathilda, who'd been wondering how to orchestrate her suggestion, looked straight into her husband's eyes. 'We'll do what he'd do.'

Robert's eyes widened and a smile curled the corners of his lips. 'A ransom?'

'A kidnap and a ransom.'

Lady Joan caught Eustace's eye. 'My Lord, I believe I see where this is heading. You are suggesting Lord Willoughby is humiliated, made an example of, and then forced to pay for his freedom.'

'Like many a traveller through Robyn Hode's forest. Yes.'

'Oh, for God's sake!' The Rector of Teigh threw his hands up in mock prayer. 'The man has money to burn. How will that hurt him?'

Mathilda ignored the cleric and turned to Lord John and Eustace. 'You know him, my Lords. What do you think the first thing he'd do, once he'd paid the ransom and we freed him, would be?'

'Free him!' Walter interrupted. Voicing what others were clearly thinking. They'd never imagined letting him go.

Lord John tilted his head to one side. 'He'd report his humiliation to the king.'

Mathilda smiled. 'Precisely.'

~ *Chapter Fourteen* ~

16th December 1331

'Let me see if I understand what you're saying, Lady Mathilda.' Ingram, steepled his palms together in front of his face as he always did while thinking. 'You *want* word to get to the king? You *want* King Edward to know we have done this?'

'I'd rather he did not know that it was us specifically, although I don't see how that can be avoided.' The heat of the overcrowded room engulfed Mathilda. Every set of eyes was focused in her direction. 'That it has been done, yes. Most important of all, it must be known *why* it was done. That piece of information must wing its way to London before Willoughby has so much as cried out in rage at his treatment.'

Robert began to understand what his wife was saying. 'This all hangs on offending Willoughby's dignity and using that, plus his past corruption, to show the Crown why he was targeted rather than any of the other officials around here.'

Mathilda nodded. 'His crimes would need to be known and be provable. Do we have proof? Not hearsay, but actual proof?'

'Of course we don't! Everyone knows of them; but proof... you're living in a dream world, woman.' The rector had had enough. 'This is such a waste of time. I say we should just '

Eustace got to his feet, pushing his face so close to his clerical brother that only a fly could have come between them. 'You can just listen for once in your miserable life!' He drew back and turned to Mathilda. 'Evidence or not, what would you have us do with Willoughby once we have him? He'll be able to afford the ransom, however high it is.'

'We let him go.'

'What? I thought you were joking!' This time it wasn't just Richard who objected. The room erupted into a clatter of banged goblets and angry bellows.

Shouting above the din, Mathilda yelled, 'We have to keep our word. If we don't, we are no better than him!'

'But what's to stop him going straight back to chasing my masters?' Wennesley was looking increasingly uncomfortable about passing this information on to the Coterels.

'Nothing. Although, putting the fear of God into Willoughby while he's in our custody might tarnish his enthusiasm for hunting felons for a while.'

Mathilda swallowed. This was the part of the plan that she didn't like. The part where it could all go wrong; where they could lose everything. 'We'd have to join the Coterels on the run for a while. Strength in numbers.'

Lady Joan spoke before uproar overtook the room again. Her tone was practical, as if she was choosing between eating chicken or pork for supper. 'You are condemning the family to outlawry rather than death.'

'If we murder Willoughby, we are all dead. All of us. If we humiliate him and make a lot of noise as to why we're doing what we're doing, then we have a chance.' Mathilda ran her hands over her belt. 'The alternative is to do nothing; letting the Coterels take their chances, and their followers continue to be rounded up and removed.'

'We're damned either way then,' the rector scoffed.

'We're already damned, Richard,' Robert glared at his brother. 'We might as well add another good reason to the list for going to Hell.'

'Do you think they'll agree?'

Robert shrugged as he tightened the girth of his horse's saddle. 'Your guess is as good as mine.' He checked they weren't been watched, before kissing his wife fiercely on the lips. 'You'll be careful at the manor, won't you? Eustace has left an invisible guard, but…'

'I will be careful. I am more concerned about you. I wish I could come to Lichfield. I'm not good at waiting while others act.'

'Help Sarah prepare for our wedding anniversary celebration.'

'Your brothers and the Coterels may still want to kill Willoughby.'

'I can guarantee they will. But that doesn't mean they'll do it. I have no doubt we'll frighten the life out of him though. Your plan is less risky to both families and, although it will cause more discomfort to us in the short term, better to be outlawed and buy back our freedom later, than being sent to a noose with no way out.'

'Robert?' Mathilda wrapped her arms around him. 'You don't really think we'll go to Hell, do you?'

He kissed the top of her head, but didn't look at her as he spoke into the straw dust that danced around the stable. 'Of course I don't.'

Mathilda sighed. 'I wish we weren't relying on guesswork. If we knew more about Willoughby it would be easier to work out exactly how he'll react. We have nothing to work on apart from his greed.'

'Isn't that enough?'

'No. We don't know his weakness. If we did, we could use it against him.'

Robert titled his wife's chin up so he could see her eyes. 'I'm going to be away for four, maybe five days, by the time we've got to Lichfield and back. You promise you'll stay safe, that you won't do anything rash?'

'Says the man who has just discussed the kidnap of one of the most powerful men in the country.'

'Mathilda, I mean it. I can't concentrate on keeping myself out of harm's way if I'm worrying about you.'

'You would have me sit on my hands and wait at home like a dutiful wife?'

He smiled despite himself. 'No, Mathilda, I'd have you stay safe at home working out what Willoughby's weakness might be, in case we need extra leverage.'

The sound of the brothers leaving the inn, and heading in a flurry of thudding boots in their direction, made Robert hurry. 'I have to go. Wennesley is to head straight to Lichfield, but we plan to get as far as the inn at Desford tonight, and then stop at Polesworth Abbey tomorrow night. The monks of Lichfield Cathedral, all being well, will greet us the day after that.' He ran a hand over her belt. 'You must return to Ashby before night closes in any further. Adam will escort you. Stay to the trees, move fast, and don't stop for anyone.' He kissed her hand and then turned to his horse, leaping into the saddle without a backwards glance as their steward arrived at Mathilda's side.

'My Lady, are you ready to go home?'

'Lady Isabel...'

The steward's countenance darkened. 'My Lady?'

'His weakness.' Mathilda strode through the brothers,

paying no attention to them as she reached her horse. 'I'll tell you once we're home, Adam. But we need to leave now. Tomorrow is going to be a very long day.'

17th December 1331

Bettrys hadn't known where to put her hands. She'd never been so physically close to a man before, let alone one she had hopes of. Yet as Sarah's calls of goodbye faded, and Daniel turned his horse away from the manor and towards the road north, Bettrys found herself wrapping her arms around his waist and holding on for dear life. The ground below felt a long way down.

Squeezing her eyes shut, Bettrys opened them again as nausea raced up her throat. The romantic image she'd allowed herself the night before, of being cuddled up to Daniel, chatting companionably as they rode, was shattered by the reality of her fear of falling and the rushing sensation of the wind in her ears, as they moved further away from the relative safety of the manor.

Offering up a silent prayer to Our Lady, Bettrys realised there was a very real possibility that her first task for the family beyond the house would begin with her being sick all down Daniel's back.

Sarah and Adam exchanged glances as they watched Lady Mathilda add a second flask of ale to her travelling roll.

'Are you sure this is a good idea?' Sarah passed her mistress a couple of apples. 'Shouldn't you wait for Lord Robert to come home before you venture to Wollaton? What if Lord Eustace sends someone telling you to go back to the original plan and take a message there anyway? After all, we don't know how the Coterel brothers will react to your idea.'

'I promised my husband I would work out Lord Willoughby's weakness. That weakness is Lady Isabel, I'm sure of it.'

'And you may well be right.' Sarah rubbed at her arm as she spoke, 'But why do you have to go to Wollaton? The woman is missing, presumably she isn't in Wollaton or someone would have found her by now.'

Adam was uneasy. 'You think he's got rid of her, my Lady?'

'I think he has knowledge he isn't sharing about her whereabouts. Otherwise wouldn't Willoughby, a man with the command of armed officials at his fingertips, be yelling all hell for people to find his wife?' Mathilda paused and took in her friends' worried faces. 'If I can find out why she has disappeared, or been removed from sight, then we'll have something on Willoughby beyond the crimes his official position can evaporate.'

'And if she's dead?'

Mathilda bit her bottom lip. 'Then the sheriff will be informed. I won't investigate, I'll come home.'

Not believing a word of it, knowing full well that if Mathilda stumbled across a body she'd want to find out who had hurried it to an early grave, Sarah peered out of the window. It was almost light. 'Bettrys and Daniel will be a good hour's ride from here by now.'

'They were alright about going?' Mathilda spoke more gently as she realised that Sarah was already worried about two of her flock, and now she was intending to leave the manor too.

'They were. I think Daniel was more nervous about looking after Bettrys than the task in hand.'

Mathilda sat down. 'I shouldn't have sent them. If anything happens… it just feels so important that we know as much as we can about Isabel. I'm sure the key to our success lies there.'

'I wish I could be so certain.' Sarah sat next to her friend. 'You promise you will go to Wollaton, stay just one night, and then return? If you discover nothing in that time, you'll come back? If you go to the manor, you may never get out again should they discover who you are.'

'I have no intention of approaching the manor. Ulric is coming with me.' Mathilda got back to her feet and pulled her cloak tight around her shoulders. 'He'll keep me safe.'

'The boy is not going with you. I am.' Adam spoke sternly, as if addressing an errant daughter rather than the mistress of the house. 'Ulric will stay with Sarah.'

Sarah folded her arms in satisfaction, making Mathilda wonder if they'd been cooking up plans of their own during the few hours of sleep afforded to them since they returned from Leicester.

Adam took the water flask Sarah passed him. 'There is an inn at Ruddington. I know the landlord. He was kind to me when I was on the run from West Markham. It will be a hard day's ride to get there, but once we are, it is but a two-hour ride onto Wollaton the following morning.'

'I had planned to get to Wollaton today.'

'And stay where?'

'An inn.' Mathilda shifted uneasily as she admitted, 'I hadn't thought beyond getting to the town and back before Robert gets home.'

Sarah pulled herself to her feet. 'We suspected you'd never be able to sit here and wait for your husband to come home.'

Adam bowed to Mathilda. 'Your palfrey is saddled, my

horse is ready, and my pack roll is in place. There is a market in Wollaton tomorrow. If we stay at Ruddington, then we'll blend in at Wollaton all the better for an overnight delay. Shall we go?'

~ *Chapter Fifteen* ~

17th December 1331

Daniel had taken hold of Bettrys' hand the moment they'd left the horse in the inn's stable, and hadn't yet let it go. 'We made it! We have shelter for the night, and we have food.'

'He thinks we're married, doesn't he.' Bettrys peered around the inn's tiny room, taking in the narrow cot in the far corner of the room.

'It doesn't matter if he believes we are wed or not. We didn't lie to him. He just assumed.'

A few minutes ago, all Bettrys had wanted was to be allowed to lie down until the world stopped spinning after the ride, now she was glad that there was enough of the day left to begin their assignment, and start to move amongst the villagers.

'Where should we begin?' She rubbed her palms down her cloak, wiping away the nervous perspiration that dotted her skin.

Squeezing her hand tighter, hoping she'd understand how brave he thought she was without him having to say so, Daniel hid the purse of money Mathilda had given them under the blankets and pointed to the door. 'How about we go for a walk? Get used to the layout of the village.'

'Won't people think that odd? It isn't normal to see folk just walking with no apparent purpose.'

'I know.' He ran a hand through is hair, reminding Bettrys of Lord Robert when he was unsure of himself, 'But we have to start somewhere. Remember what Sarah said, we're two servants hunting for work.'

'What if we're offered it though? We don't really want a job.'

'We'll say we are on the way north, but would welcome a day's paid employment to cover food and shelter.'

Bettrys nodded. 'It would be easier to learn things if we're seen to be useful, but…'

'But?'

'We'd be split up. No one will want my help with any labour you might be offered, nor are you likely to be asked to sweep a house or bake pies.'

Knowing there was a lot of sense in what Bettrys said, Daniel paused, his hand on the door. 'We'd learn more, wouldn't we, if we worked separately?'

'I suppose so.' Bettrys started to feel nauseous again, 'But even if we found employment in the same house, it's unlikely we'd be wanted just for the day. We'd have to run away after we'd learnt what we wanted to know.'

'Risky.' Daniel grimaced.

'It's all risky. The only place that might be happy to employ us for a brief time is this inn, but it didn't look like they needed help when we walked through the room downstairs or the stable courtyard.'

Daniel opened the door to their room. 'We're new to the area. What could be more natural than us taking a stroll?'

'Well, if you put it like that…'

Beyond the inn, Willoughby-on-the-Wolds stretched out towards the Church of St Mary's and All Saints. Lined with woods to one side of the road, a spattering of houses and workshops joined together to form a hum of activity as the Folville servants walked along.

'We aren't far from Nottingham,' Daniel said as they moved, 'The ancient Fosse Way road goes past here. I remember Lord Robert telling me once that it connects much of England.'

'Are we in Leicestershire or Nottinghamshire?'

'On the border. Just within Nottinghamshire, I think. I'm not sure. Adam would know.'

'Let's head to the church. It'll appear as if we have a purpose.' Bettrys felt eyes on her as they walked. Everyone they passed was too engaged upon their purpose to stop working, but she knew they'd all noticed the two strangers wandering the street mid-afternoon. Minds were racing, even if tongues weren't yet wagging.

'We're being watched.' Bettrys hoped she was speaking quietly enough not to be overheard by anyone other than Daniel.

'We were bound to be.' He lifted his head higher, as if in defiance of the thoughts passing through the villager's heads. 'But if we don't get noticed then we can't talk to people. We wouldn't learn anything, and all this will have been pointless.'

Wondering how Lady Mathilda would act if she were there, Bettrys asked, 'Justice Willoughby is the lord here?'

'He controls a lot of the land around here. His treatment of his people has not impressed Lord Robert for a long time.'

Bettrys took a step closer to Daniel as she mumbled, 'Is that why Lord Eustace is careful to keep connections at the inn, so he can keep an eye on the place?'

Daniel stopped in his tracks. 'Lord Eustace! It's so obvious.'

'What is?' Bettrys urgently gestured for them to keep walking so they didn't draw even more attention to themselves.

'The inn. We *could* work there.'

Bettrys spotted the gate to the churchyard, 'But we just agreed they didn't need help there.'

They walked through the lych-gate, and into the graveyard as Daniel replied, 'If I told the keeper that we were on important business from his Lordship, and needed to blend in for the day, he wouldn't dare refuse.'

Bettrys was uneasy at the idea. 'Shouldn't we keep it secret though, the reason we're here I mean?'

'Maybe.' Daniel could see men and women working in the strips of land beyond the church. When he turned to look back the way they'd come, he felt the occasional glance of the workers as they went about their business.

'Shall we go inside?' Bettrys felt the need for the sanctuary of the church. 'Some time away from curious eyes might help clear our minds.'

'Good idea.'

The scent of fresh plaster hit their senses as they pushed the wooden door open and reverentially stepped inside. Bettrys didn't stop to examine her surroundings before moving to the nearest pew and dropping to her knees to offer up a prayer for guidance.

Daniel, more accustomed to caution, surveyed the small space. He took in the tomb on the right-hand side, and supposed it contained a long-dead relative of the man his masters were hunting. The altar before him looked as bleak and unwelcoming as any he'd seen. Daniel had never liked churches. He could feel the very walls judging him. Just being within a church triggered a sense of guilt for everything he'd ever done.

He glanced at Bettrys as, her head bent, her lips moving at speed, she beseeched the Almighty for help. He couldn't help wonder if, should they be spared, Bettrys would be quite so keen to kneel on Holy ground and ask for help once she'd worked for the Folvilles for a while.

The maid was lost in contemplation when the door to the church opened. Rushing to Bettrys' side, Daniel fell to his knees beside her as two people, who, he sensed, had been in conversation for some time, paused in the open doorway. He wasn't sure if they'd seen him. They probably had, but that was alright, surely? He was on his knees in a church, praying for his soul… well, Bettrys was, and he looked as if he was, so that was fine.

Listening intently, Daniel made out the distinct tones of a man and a woman. The man was speaking in the hushed manner of one who doesn't want to be overheard, but the female was talking as if she was unaware of how much sound travelled in a church.

'Father, they say she's mad, but that can't be true, can it?'

'It can happen. Women, forgiving your presence, can be tempestuous creatures. The balance of their minds uneven.'

Daniel smiled. He couldn't stop himself from imagining how Sarah or Lady Mathilda would react to such a statement from a man of the cloth or any man, come to think of it. He imagined the cleric would be limping by now as his toe was greeted by a heavily proffered boot.

Bettrys was beginning to stir next to him. Daniel placed a warning hand on her knee, before removing it again as if he was scalded when she looked up at him. He knew shouldn't be touching her at all, let alone in a church, but he needed her to know that they were not alone. She'd been so intent upon her purpose, he wasn't sure she'd heard the arrival of the newcomers, who remained on the cusp of the entrance.

With an urgent flick of his eyes from Bettrys to the door, Daniel saw her bob her head in understanding, and freeze into position next to him as they heard the woman speak.

'You may be right, Father, but her Ladyship is not one for outbursts of temper or emotion. A more placid creature I've yet to meet.'

'I will pray for her. Wherever she may be, you may be assured that God will have his eye on her.'

'Thank you, Father.' There was a shuffling of feet as if the woman was preparing to depart. 'I must get back to Wollaton. There is much to do before his Lordship departs.'

'God go with you, my blessings to Lord Richard.'

'Thank you, Father.'

Bettrys opened her mouth to speak, but an urgent flash of the eyes from Daniel, stopped her. The cleric was walking down the aisle towards the altar. He'd realise he was not alone any second now.

Deciding not to wait until they were discovered, Daniel got to his feet. 'Father, forgive us if we startled you. We are new here, and wanted to thank God for our safe deliverance thus far on our journey.'

The clergyman appeared surprised for a second, but soon had control over his wizened features. Daniel had the impression it would take a lot to shock him. It would also take a lot to change his mind once he'd made it up.

'You are welcome. You are on a journey, you say?'

Bettrys got to her feet and curtseyed. 'Yes, Father.' Feeling awkward, she added, 'This is a beautiful church.'

'It is.' He looked around, as if seeing his place of work clearly for the first time in years. 'The village is lucky to have such a place. Will you be staying long?'

'One night, perhaps two, if some brief employment can be found to help pay our way.'

'You head far north?'

Not sure why he said it, Daniel replied, 'To West Markham. We've heard Lord John Markham has a need for servants.'

'Have you indeed.' The cleric peered down his unusually long nose. 'Then I wish you safe travels.'

Feeling that this was a dismissal, the would-be travellers made for the door, each repeating the words they'd heard the female from Wollaton had uttered as she'd left St Mary's and All Saints. 'Thank you, Father.'

Walking rather faster than was seemly through a churchyard, Bettrys peered about her as they went. 'Which way do you think she went?'

'I've no idea.' Daniel joined in the surveillance. 'If she was from Wollaton, then she'd have had a horse, and probably an escort.'

'But why come here? And why talk to the Father here? There must be a church in Wollaton.'

'It wouldn't be so unusual for Lord and Lady Willoughby to worship here sometimes. They own the land after all. Perhaps the woman assumed the rector would know something, or at least would have an opinion on the rumour...' Bettrys paused, 'it was Lady Isabel they were talking about, wasn't it?'

'I suspect so, but we can't be sure. No name was mentioned. It could be a coincidence.'

'It wasn't.' Bettrys was sure she was right. 'And that means that someone else isn't convinced Lady Willoughby has gone away of her own accord.'

The afternoon light was beginning to fail. 'We should head back to the inn. I know it isn't late, but we don't know this place. It wouldn't be a good idea to linger.'

Bettrys glanced around, concern on her face. 'You think we're in danger?'

'Not if we're sensible.' He took her hand, 'The innkeeper thinks we're married. It might be a good idea to maintain that notion.' Daniel turned the little palm in his hand. 'Unless you don't want to. I mean, I'd never assume that…'

A pink flush spread over Bettrys' complexion so fast that heat rushed to her head. 'Of course I want to,' she blustered as they walked back towards the inn, 'as long as you don't mind that I want to.'

'I don't want to let you go. Not ever.' A warm glow rose inside Daniel as he saw the light in Bettrys' eyes. 'Let's see if the ale at the inn has loosened any tongues.'

~ *Chapter Sixteen* ~

17th December 1331

The inn at Ruddington hadn't had any rooms free until Adam had discreetly muttered into the landlord's ear just who it was he was escorting, and why it would be a very good idea if knowledge of Lady Folville's stay should remain a secret.

Mathilda experienced a twinge of guilt as she settled into the pile of blankets in what she suspected was the landlord's personal room. A second wave of guilt hit as she pictured Adam sleeping in the hayloft above the horses. He'd told her not to worry, that he was used to far worse. That didn't make her feel better about being warm and comfortable when he was in a draughty wooden building, where people came and went all night, and horses stirred with each new footfall.

As much as she'd wanted to get all the way to Wollaton that day, Mathilda was grateful for Adam and Sarah's common sense. The winter nights were drawing in faster with each passing day, and after the rigours of her trip to and from Leicester, Mathilda was sleepier than she'd realised.

Images of Robert and his brothers, of Lady Joan and Lord Ingram, staring at her as if she held all the answers to

Heaven and Hell weighed heavily on her mind. She'd been convinced that not killing Willoughby was the best plan. But what if she was wrong?

Daniel hesitated as his hand went to the door handle to their room. 'I could sleep in the stables. No one would question me wanting to keep an eye on our horse.'

Bettrys peered at her feet. She should agree with him, send him to sleep in the straw, keep her virtue intact. But she didn't want to.

'You're exhausted, you need to sleep. I had no idea working in an inn was such hard work.'

'But we're not…'

Taking his hand, Bettrys found herself whispering under her breath, lest the occupants of the other rooms should hear her. 'We both need to rest before tomorrow. If we roll up a blanket, lay it down the middle of the cot, and lie head to toe, then we'll be able to talk to each other, knowing we are safe together, not have to worry about each other, and we'll get some sleep. The Lord above knows we've done no wrong in here; what others think is their problem.'

Pushing open the door, Daniel grinned. 'Lady Mathilda is having a good effect on you.'

A few awkward minutes later, they lay facing a pile of blankets and each others' feet. It was freezing.

'I'm glad you told the innkeeper about our connection to Lord Eustace, but I do wish it had been a quieter night. I've never washed so many beakers in my life.' Bettrys blew out the candle and held her water-chapped hands together under the covers. 'Did you hear anything much from the people using the stables?'

'That the tanner in Nottingham short-changes people was the main gripe.' Daniel stared up at the ceiling. His whole being was acutely aware that Bettrys was very close to him, and that they were alone. It was making thinking straight extremely difficult.

'It's possible that he does.' Bettrys spoke into the dark. 'I heard that complaint while I was serving ale. He's a clever man by all accounts, and it's so easy to claim a price is different from what a customer believes it to be, when you're wealthy.'

Smiling into his straw pillow, Daniel asked, 'And of Lord Willoughby or his wife, did you hear anything there?'

'Oh, yes.' Bettrys sat up; drawing the cloak she still wore over her fully clad chest, in an automatic act of self consciousness. 'What we heard in the church is the talk of the village's womenfolk apparently. There were two men in the inn's far corner, rather worse for ale, they were each complaining to the other that their wives spent too long gossiping and not enough time working in their homes.'

'And the gossip in question concerned Lady Isabel?'

'They didn't mention a name, but they said Her Ladyship and that she was said to be mad. "Raving" was the word one of them used.'

Daniel sat up so he could see the maid's face. 'You don't think it's true, do you?'

'I have no idea, but whoever came to the church had heard the same rumour and they didn't believe it either. I got the impression that woman was from Wollaton and was there specifically to ask the Father his opinion on the matter.'

Nodding, Daniel said, 'He didn't dismiss the idea though, did he.'

'He is in the pay of Lord Willoughby. Would he dare commit an opinion one way or the other?'

Daniel frowned. 'What do you mean?'

Bettrys spoke eagerly now. The idea that something un-just had happened to Lady Isabel refused to leave now that it had arrived in her head. 'What if Lady Willoughby isn't mad, but has simply disappeared? What if it suits his Lord-ship to have people think her insane?'

'Bettrys, are you suggesting Lord Willoughby has re-moved his wife and is seeing this rumour spread to cover his tracks?'

'It wouldn't be the first time such an act has happened.' She shrugged, 'Then again, perhaps Lady Isabel simply got tired of being bullied and ran away?' Bettrys could hear Daniel breathing, and had to force herself not to reach out a hand in his direction. 'I've been thinking about the voice in the church. It belonged to a female, but not a noblewoman; the cleric didn't address her as my Lady. But she wasn't dis-missed as being unimportant either. I got the sense that the rector was a man who wouldn't listen to anyone he didn't deem worthy of talking to.'

'He certainly got rid of us fast enough.' Daniel agreed, 'but if he is Lord Willoughby's rector here, then he'd have to listen to anyone attached to the household, whether they're servants or family, surely?'

'Maybe,' Bettrys shivered, 'Perhaps she was attached to the manor in some way. Do you think we've heard enough to head home yet?'

Daniel sighed. 'Not until we're sure it's Lady Willough-by they're talking about.'

'I was afraid you'd say that.' Bettrys snuggled under the one blanket left after they'd created their security barrier down the bed. 'At least we can work here tomorrow. It's nice and warm downstairs.'

'The stables are warm too. Horses tend to give off more heat that you'd like, even in the coldest of weathers.'

'Good. I didn't want you to be cold.'

They lapsed into silence for a while, before Daniel said, 'Are you cold now?'

'A bit.'

'Me too,'

18th December 1331

'So that's Wollaton Manor.'

Mathilda reined her horse in next to Adam's as they took in the scene before them. The house was bigger than the manor at Ashby Folville, but not as ostentatious as she'd imagined it would be. It sat quietly on the edge of the town, the church of St Leonard's in sight, the manor's gates closed, but with no visible guard on the door.

'We'd better not get any nearer, my Lady.' Adam shifted in his saddle, 'The heart of Wollaton runs that way.'

Mathilda followed the point of his arm off to the right and turned her palfrey in that direction. 'Is the market here large?'

'Not like Leicester, but yes, it's generally well-attended. I visited it once or twice for Lord Markham when he wanted something specific from the town.'

Keeping her eyes on the road ahead, Mathilda asked, 'Are you likely to be recognised?'

'No.' Adam scanned the trees to their left as they rode; the faint sounds of market activity grew louder in the foreground. 'It was over ten years ago, and Fletcher was an old man even then. He had no children as I recall, so unless he took an apprentice, his skill at arrow-making will be no more.'

'Lord Markham got his arrows here?'

'Nottinghamshire is famous for its fletchers.' Adam slowed his horse, 'We aren't far away now. What is it we are looking for?'

'Word of Lady Willoughby and anything pertaining to our family or the Coterels.'

'I meant, we are going to a market, we should be seen to be intending to purchase something or we'll stick out even more than we will already, my Lady.'

Mathilda smiled. 'Forgive me, Adam, I was so preoccupied with our aim, I was forgetting the obvious.' She could hear the bustle ahead growing louder now, and a sense of apprehension stole through her. 'Let's just look around. If the sounds floating on the breeze are anything to go by, it's busy. We shouldn't be viewed as anything more than what we are, a woman and her faithful steward, in town for the day.'

Adam laughed, and quickly stopped. 'Sorry, my Lady.'

'You find the idea of us being a typical mistress and steward amusing?'

'I don't think, my Lady, that you have ever been a typical anything.'

'That's what my husband says, he... Husband. Of course!'

'My Lady?'

'A betrothal gift.'

'For Lord Robert?'

'For my brother.'

Adam's eyebrows rose. 'Oswin is to marry?'

'My other brother, Matthew. With all that's been happening I hadn't got round to saying. He is to marry in the spring. A gift to show our pleasure at the news would not be so unusual.'

'Nor would a gift at Christmas, my Lady.'

Mathilda shook her head. 'What is the matter with me? I keep missing the obvious. Christmas gifts would be just the things to purchase at a market.'

'I'm glad I bought a half-empty pack-roll, my Lady.'

The horse was of quality, and Daniel took pleasure in grooming its sleek mane. It stood placid and calm, but he could tell from the well-formed muscles of its flanks that when called into service, it would move with a speed and power that would be the envy of any horseman. Daniel wondered who it belonged to as he made a final sweep of the brush down its side, before moving on to the smaller, less honed mount next to it. Less patient, it shuffled its back hooves, its grey coat spattered with mud suggesting a hasty ride.

Daniel could see the inn's regular groom in conversation with the landlord. They'd clearly worked together for years, and fell easily into each other's company. The groom, a large and gentle man, was grateful of his temporary helper, and had been kind to Daniel, but if he'd hoped to learn much about the visitors who passed through the inn from the groom, he was destined to be disappointed, for the man was accustomed to holding his tongue in public.

He was less discreet however with his friend, whose voice, so used to shouting over the internal din of a busy inn, was unnaturally loud over the quiet of the morning calm.

'Lincolnshire, you say?'

Daniel stopped moving the brush as the groom replied to the innkeeper, his tone quieter, and harder to hear.

'His Lordship has a lot of ground between Lincolnshire and here. Between Lincolnshire and Leicester for that matter.'

'His messenger tells me,' the landlord gestured to the horse Daniel had just finished grooming, 'that his master will expect a room here when his travelling court arrives in Willoughby, but he gave no date beyond the "around the turn of the year". Without a care that I may have others visiting who'll pay for the service. He takes for granted the room with be his for the using.'

Daniel's palms prickled as he watched the groom ruffle a hand through his shaggy beard. 'He's a tough master, that's for sure, but you'd be wise to keep that room free once the current occupant has gone. If the court takes less time in Grantham than Lord Willoughby thinks, he could be here earlier than the dawn of January.'

'Or it could take weeks longer, and I'll have an empty room, earning us no money, for a month or more.'

'I'd best reserve some space for his horse, and those of his men. He'll not thank me if they are not properly sheltered in the heart of winter.'

'You're wise, my friend.' The innkeeper slapped the groom heartily on the back, 'I'd best get on. Bettrys is a good girl, but she'll be on her way soon, I'll warrant, and I'd like to get as much work out of her as I can before she flees to wherever they're heading.'

'The lad's good too. Shame they are bent on travelling north, I could use a good pair of hands like his. Knows his horses, does young Daniel.'

Resuming his brushing, Daniel flushed with relief that the innkeeper had not shared with his friend his knowledge of their real employers. He worked faster. He needed to talk to Bettrys.

Daniel had hoped to hear more about Lady Isabel, but instead he'd discovered where Lord Willoughby was going to be as the year turned, as the travelling court wound its way slowly closer to home. It was time to leave.

~ *Chapter Seventeen* ~

18th December 1331

The market was smaller than she was used to, but Mathilda was impressed nonetheless. What it lacked in numbers of stalls, it more than made up for in its variety of goods. She was having no trouble in pretending to be enthusiastic about the wares, for she found herself immersed in gift shopping with a fervour never previously experienced.

It was while Mathilda was examining a fine roll of blue silk, with her mind on a gift to thank Lady Joan for her quiet support, that she was sharply reminded of the reason for her presence in Wollaton.

'Lady Marjory, please, we have all we need. We should return to the manor.'

Mathilda caught Adam's eye as the plaintive female voice cut through the bustle of people behind them. Slowly putting down the bolt of material with a polite, 'This is most fine, I will return shortly,' Mathilda backed away from the crowded stall. She turned to see a well-dressed young woman, of about Bettrys' age, on a black pony, being led by a groomsman. A tired-looking woman, her arms full of purchases, stood next to the girl's mount. Her outfit was good, but not as rich as her charge's. She had a lady's maid's air about her.

'I tell you, Anne, Mother would like that silk. I will take it for her Christmas gift.' The tone of the young girl was defiant, but it held a depth of sadness that Mathilda felt hanging in the air around her.

'But, Lady Marjory, your mother is unwell; you'll not see her. Your father left strict instructions and '

'And you're afraid of him!'

The words had come out faster and louder than Mathilda suspected the girl had intended them to, and she was not surprised to see a number of fellow market-goers twist to face the small company.

'Please, my Lady, I have my orders.'

The young woman's jaw was set, her face pale. Mathilda could see how hard she was trying not to cry. Her heart melted for the girl, who was surely one of Lord Willoughby's children.

'Adam, follow my lead.' Without giving her steward time to work out what that lead might be, Mathilda strode towards the noble party, her wide. 'Why, Lady Marjory, how good it is to see you. It's been so long, I hardly recognised you.'

The young woman's mouth opened, but no words came out as her maid curtseyed with a polite greeting. 'My Lady, forgive me, I do not recognise you.'

'There is nothing to forgive. Did I hear Lady Marjory call you Anne? I am an old friend of Lady Isabel's, but marriage moved me away. I've not been back here for far too long. Would you do me the honour of allowing me to buy you some refreshment, Lady Marjory? You seem flustered.'

Anne looked more panicked than ever, while the taciturn groom had spied Adam's set expression, and wisely kept his mouth shut.

'I don't know that we should. No offence meant, my Lady, but I had orders to bring the young Lady Willoughby to buy gifts for her siblings and father, and then return. I don't have leave for more, I'm sorry.'

Giving her maid a pointed stare, Lady Marjory smiled at Mathilda. 'Take no heed of Anne. You are very kind. I don't often get to meet friends of my mother's. I would be delighted to take refreshment with you, but, pray, what's your name?'

Trying not to panic, Mathilda mentally dashed through all the high-born ladies she could pretend to be. She was about to claim to be Lady Joan la Zouche, until she reasoned the child might know the name Zouche all too well from her father's vendetta against her family after Belers.

'I'm Lady Ingram. Mathilda Ingram.'

The maid's head shot up. 'Lord Robert Ingram's wife?' She curtseyed. 'We're honoured, my Lady, but we must forego your kind invitation, for time is against us. His Lordship leaves on business tomorrow, and we are having an early winter celebration. I'm sure you'll understand.'

'But of course, I must let you go in the circumstances.' Matilda turned back to Lady Marjory. 'I'm so glad to have seen what a fine young woman you've grown into. I'm sure your parents are so proud. Give my best to your mother.'

A single tear trickled down Lady Marjory's face as she opened her mouth to thank the unexpected bearer of kindness, but her throat had closed over in grief, and she knew if she uttered a single word, then her composure would break and the tears would flow in earnest.

Sensing what was about to happen, Lady Mathilda smiled brightly at Anne. 'Lady Marjory seems fatigued after the ride and the bustle of the market; allow me and my steward to help escort you through the crowds. You're Wollaton bound, I presume?'

Without waiting for a reply, Lady Mathilda signalled for Adam to go the other side of Marjory, and take the bridle, so that she had two male guides through the openly curious onlookers.

As soon as they were out of earshot of the market-goers, keeping pace with the pony, Lady Mathilda asked, her voice lowered, 'You're distressed, my Lady, is your mother unwell?'

'They say she is.' The venom of the answer was fired at Anne, but Mathilda got the impression that the 'they' in question was more general than that. 'They say she's...' The young woman paused and ran a sleeve over her nose, making her maid tut at the unladylike behaviour.

'She's what, Lady Marjory?'

'That she's gone away because she's gone mad. But she hasn't gone mad I mean. Never was there a sweeter woman, and she'd never leave us, not me and my brothers and little Joan. She wouldn't, she '

'That's quite enough, my Lady!' Anne appeared more frightened than cross. 'What would your father say if he heard you speaking against him like this?'

Matilda glanced at Adam, who said nothing, but was obviously thinking plenty. 'Forgive me, I meant to help, not cause distress. You have no fear of gossip from me or my steward. We know how to keep our counsel.'

Anne dipped her head curtly, but Mathilda was sure she didn't believe her.

'Your mother has gone away for the good of her health?'

'Father says she is raving, but I don't believe a word of it. Mother never raved in her life. She only ever argued with Father once, and now...'

'They argued? When? Do you know why?'

Anne gasped at the audacity of the question. 'Lady Ingram, I really don't think you should ask questions about a private matter.'

Mathilda was about to apologise, but Lady Marjory cut in. 'Mother said that the only land Father had acquired legally had arrived with her. I didn't hear the rest, but she was distressed and fearful as well as angry.' The young lady wiped a tear from where it had escaped, 'Father did not like the reminder that Mother is from a better family than he is.'

'And you haven't seen Lady Isabel since?'

'Not once.'

As Lady Marjory shook her head, the road to Wollaton stretched before them now, and Mathilda could think of no more reason to hold the company to her side, nor of what to say about the girl's estranged parents.

'I must leave you, my Lady, but it has been good to meet you.' Lady Mathilda bowed her head. 'I will pray for your mother.'

Lady Marjory, as if suddenly remembering her position, stood a little straighter, her chin tilted proudly. 'Thank you, Lady Ingram. May I ask something of you before we take our leave?'

'Certainly.'

'If your husband comes across news of my mother, will you get word to me?' She ignored the gasp from Anne as she went on, 'A former sheriff of the shire must hear a great deal that he'd rather not know.'

'I promise.' Mathilda said nothing more as Anne and the groom pulled the pony from Adam's grip, and led the eldest daughter of Willoughby back to the manor.

Waiting until the party was out of earshot, Mathilda and Adam strode back to the market.

'What do you want to do now, my Lady?' Adam was relieved to see the shoppers had lost interest in them, now it was clear there wasn't going to be a fight or even a mild argument between members of the nobility to entertain them.

'We need to go home.' Mathilda had the urge to run towards the inn to fetch her horse, but knew it would draw attention to them. 'Not only have we learnt that Lady Isabel has been sent away under false pretences, but that Willoughby is due to leave the manor tomorrow. That can only be to commence his travelling court.'

Adam kept pace with his mistress, 'It seems odd that he'd start out now, so near to the festive season.'

'If Robert is to be believed, he is a man possessed. Lord Willoughby will be chafing at the bit to try as many Coterels and their followers as his men have rounded up.'

'An early Christmas present for him.' Adam remained vigilant as they reached the edge of the market. 'Did you want to buy the material for Lady Joan before we go?'

'I would. She's been kind to me.' Mathilda wrapped her cloak closer around her chest, 'Then we'll fetch the horses. We might not get as far as Ashby Folville today, but if we can return to Ruddington, then we'll be that bit closer in the morning.'

'When do you expect Lord Robert back, my Lady?'

'In three or four days. Assuming all goes well.'

Adam grimaced. 'Lord Willoughby will have started his court tour by then.'

'Indeed.' Mathilda looked up at her friend. 'We could send Ulric with word to Lichfield, but there is no saying he'd find his masters before they came back. There are so many places he could miss them on the road. We have no choice but to wait it out.'

'At least we'll have news for them once they do get

back.' Adam gestured to the market stall. 'The blue silk you admired is still there, would you like me to fetch it?'

'Thank you, Adam, but I'll go. If you could wait here for me.'

The steward watched as his mistress walked sedately through the depleted group of buyers. The height of the market day was over, and it was only a matter of minutes before he saw Mathilda instruct the stall holder as to her requirements.

'Thank you, Adam.' Mathilda passed the roll of material to her steward. 'It still feels odd to pass the burden of carriage to another after so many years of working on market stalls myself.'

'You are very welcome. It is an honour to work for someone who thinks to thank her staff.'

Grinning, Mathilda plastered a more seemly poise upon her face and headed to the inn. 'Do you think they will have room for us at Ruddington?'

'It will always have room for you, my Lady. Lord Eustace chooses his informants well.'

'Then we'll leave now, while there's an hour's light to travel in.'

~ *Chapter Eighteen* ~

18th December 1331

The journey back to Ashby Folville seemed to take no time at all, a stark contrast to the trip they'd taken in the opposite direction. Bettrys clutched at Daniel's waist with less self-consciousness than before. She felt safe, a sensation at odds with the situation that awaited them.

Bettrys wondered if Sarah would know just by looking at them that they'd been as close as two people could be. She felt as if she was giving off some kind of tell-tale glow.

As Daniel steered their horse into the manor's courtyard, he spoke under his breath, 'Are you alright, my love?'

'I am. Are you?' Bettrys flushed at hearing his affectionate address.

'More than I've ever been.'

Leaping to the ground, Daniel helped her dismount. 'It will be difficult keeping this a secret.'

'I know. Especially as I feel like telling the world.'

'Me too.' Daniel checked to make sure no one was watching, before sweeping a stray hair from the maid's face. 'Once this business is over, we'll tell them.'

Straightening her cloak after the ride, Bettrys' smile was nudged aside by concern. 'It's very quiet. Where's Adam?'

No sooner had she asked the question, when Sarah rushed out, with Ulric on her heels. 'You're back! How wonderful. Do you have news?'

'We do.' Bettrys embraced her friend, 'But where's Adam? And Lady Mathilda's horse is missing.'

Ushering her companions in like chicks to a henhouse, Sarah bid Ulric tend to their horse. 'Come inside and tell me everything, then I'll tell you what your mistress is up to this time.'

Nicolas Coterel had been quiet for a long time. Robert had been watching him out of the corner of his eye as Mathilda's plan was discussed. He'd expected Nicholas to agree, simply because it was his wife who'd come up with the alternative to murdering the justice. So far however, Nicholas had held his peace while his elder brother, James, asked the questions.

'You have considered, I'm sure, that this may not work, and we might have to kill Willoughby anyway.'

'We have.' Eustace spoke for the Folvilles. Robert was amazed that his patience was holding. They'd been over the same ground many times now. It dawned on Robert that Mathilda could be right; Lady Joan was known for her aloof calm. Perhaps she was more of an influence upon his tempestuous brother than he'd realised.

James Coterel, his usual neat attire muddied and torn, his face drawn, looked to his brothers and then back at Eustace. 'Would you give us a moment to discuss Lady Mathilda's proposal in private?'

Eustace got up from the cold wooden pew upon which his bulky frame had been perched. He watched as the three hunted men moved to the far end of Lichfield Cathedral's Lady Chapel.

'What do you think, Robert?'

'I think they're glad to be in the safety of the cathedral for a while. They make light of it, but their supporters are clearly not providing the safe havens they were banking on.'

'Fear of arrest for helping the Coterels. Fear is a powerful weapon, Robert; I've used its strength enough times to know that.' Eustace toyed with the empty sheath where his knife would have been, if he hadn't handed it to the monks as a gesture of respect on their arrival. 'Willoughby has been clever and swift in his movement of soldiers into the area. As we heard from John Coterel, at least twenty of their local associates have already been taken and await Willoughby's arrival to hear their fate.'

'A waste of time. He'll have condemned them in his mind before he's even left Wollaton,' Robert glanced at his brother, 'but if we kill Willoughby, such hostages are likely to be treated even more harshly than if we merely inconvenience him.'

'It might appear that they incited his death, you mean?' Eustace scowled.

'Exactly.' Robert watched the Coterels huddled together in heated discussion. 'You have come around to Mathilda's way of thinking, Eustace?'

Feeling the eyes of his other brothers upon him, Eustace grunted noncommittally. 'It would be a bold achievement, would it not, to curb the power of every justice in England?'

Robert smiled. It was the closest he was going to get to a yes. 'But will the Coterels agree?'

From his place leaning against a stone pillar, Thomas shrugged, 'If they don't, the only reason will be because they want this over quickly. Lady Mathilda's plan is a far longer game to play.'

'Then maybe they will say yes,' Walter chipped in. 'The

Coterels like playing games with people.'

'They do. The problem is they can be inclined to change the rules without telling you first.' Robert sneered as he saw the eldest Coterel get to his feet. 'You have made a decision, Lord James.'

'We agree to the plan. With two conditions.'

'Which are?'

Nicholas levelled his flinty gaze directly at Robert. 'That we forego the warning message. The kidnap itself is the warning.'

A general grunt of agreement came from the Folvilles, as Robert asked, 'And the second condition?'

'That Lady Mathilda herself is consulted every step of the way, and should it be decreed that someone has to visit Wollaton at some point for Willoughby to be overthrown from his position – it should be her.'

'What!' Robert's yell erupted across the chapel, and echoed down the nave, shattering any chance they'd hoped of keeping their meeting quiet.

Unmoved by the outburst, Nicholas went on, 'She is reliable. We know she'll make sure any communications that are needed with be faithfully delivered and, should she be taken prisoner, as a valuable piece in the game she will be tended, rather than hacked to death in an instant.'

'You can't possibly know that!'

'I can't, but it is likely. Remember, Willoughby himself won't be there. It is to his eldest son that any potential missive would be delivered.'

'But it'll still put my wife in danger!'

James Coterel cut in irritably, 'It is what we want to happen. Besides, this condition may well not be needed. But, if it is, not a soul knows Lady Mathilda at Wollaton. She can pretend to be there under threat. That you forced her to come or her husband would be killed; or some such excuse.'

The silence in the air after Robert's outburst hung heavy with menace as the allies regarded each other suspiciously. They all knew this was a fragile relationship, but they also knew they needed it to work   for everyone's sake.

Before Robert could protest further, Thomas Folville said, 'I imagine that Lady Mathilda would insist on taking any message that may be needed anyway.'

Eustace grunted. 'I can hear her saying so.'

Nicholas Coterel inclined his head. 'She is a brave woman, who deserves so much more.'

'And you can offer that, can you?' Robert yelled across the pews. 'Look at yourself, man! Covered in mud, hungry, on the run!'

Thomas hurriedly drew Robert away from the Coterels before the monks' precaution, of removing their weapons before allowing them to meet, was deemed pointless in the face of his brother's jealousy and Nicholas's gleeful goading.

'We should leave.' Eustace drew back. 'You have someone we can use to get word to you of our progress?'

'Wennesley is at your disposal. If you need another then I'm sure Oswin of Twyford will help us.' John Coterel glared at Nicholas, hoping he didn't feel the need to make a dig about Mathilda's brother.

'Do you have a place of safety for tonight?' Thomas studied the haggard faces of the three men before him. They were usually pristine, wearing the latest fashions, so in control; already they had the dishevelled air of hunted wolves.

'We are staying here. The monks have been good enough to offer us food and shelter this one night. Then we'll return to the Peaks. We must be close to our people should they need us.'

'Then go safely.' Eustace gestured for his kin to prepare to take their leave. 'We will get word to you as best we can, but surely rumour will inform you once the deed is done.'

'We look forward to it.' James gestured for his brothers to head towards the north choir aisle and the door that led to the chapterhouse. 'Oh, and whatever you do, make that man suffer.'

Eustace bowed. 'My Lord Coterel, it will be a pleasure.'

~ *Chapter Nineteen* ~

19th December 1331

Sarah had half expected Adam to return alone. It would not have surprised the housekeeper if her mistress had defied Lord Robert and gone into Wollaton Hall in search of the missing Lady Isabel. Her relief at seeing both her husband and Mathilda ride in, each huddled in a travelling cloak, made her exhale loudly.

Mathilda waved at her housekeeper as she hailed the stable lad, who was immediately at her side. 'Daniel, it's so good to see that you're home. Is Bettrys also returned? She is safe?'

Raising a calming hand, Sarah reached out to help Mathilda from her palfrey. 'She is here too and she is whole.'

'But did they discover anything worthwhile?' Adam jumped to the ground, placing a comforting palm on his wife's shoulder.

'They did.' Sarah ushered them inside. 'Daniel, could you find Ulric and ask him to deal with your horses? I'm anxious for Lady Mathilda to hear your news. I will find Bettrys. I'm sure their Lordships will want to know of your findings without delay.'

'We too have information for my husband.' Mathilda followed Sarah into the kitchen. 'If our findings tally, then no one will be able to argue that the risks we took in travelling into the lion's nearest dens weren't worthwhile.'

'You fear Lord Robert will be less than impressed?' Adam threw an extra log on the fire, warming his hands against the flare of fresh heat.

'He asked me to find Justice Willoughby's weakness, and I have done so. He did not say how I might achieve this, but I doubt he'll be thrilled by my absence from Ashby Folville.'

Following them into the kitchen, Bettrys went to sit next to Daniel, without being conscious that she was openly seeking him out.

'My Lady, it's so good to see you.'

'And you, Bettrys. You are very brave for undertaking the task I set. I'm thankful to you and Daniel.'

Bettrys blushed as Daniel said, 'In truth, my Lady, we were never in danger. The innkeeper helped us a great deal, and our timings were fortunate.'

'Timings?' Mathilda gratefully took a honey drink from Sarah.

'Yes, my Lady.' Bettrys turned to Daniel, who encouraged her to tell their story. 'When we got there, we decided to walk to the church. We didn't really know where else to start.'

'A sensible beginning.' Mathilda was impressed, 'There is always much to learn from the hub of those twin communities, the church and the inn.'

Bolstered by Mathilda's enthusiasm, Daniel explained, 'We overheard a woman talking to the Rector of St Mary's and All Saints. Whoever she was, the reason for her visit was plain. She spoke of a lady. Someone she'd been told was mad. But she didn't believe that. She confided in the cleric, sought his opinion. He, however, was clearly Lord Willoughby's man, and presumed the lady in question to be afflicted.'

'Lady Isabel?' Mathilda frowned.

'We suspect so, but we can't be sure.' Bettrys looked to Daniel as she added, 'However, I took work in the inn. There was gossip concerning Lady Willoughby and her impaired senses whispered there.' The womenfolk exchanged significant glances, before Mathilda said, 'It is beginning to sound like Lord Willoughby has labelled his wife mad for his own convenience.'

'You can't know that though, my Lady,' Bettrys peeped shyly through the fringe that had escaped its line. 'Although... the woman in the church... we thought she must be connected to the house in some way because, although she wasn't high-born, the rector did not dismiss her as a tattle-tale.'

'And he sounded the type who would.' Daniel leant forward, 'We have more news. Not about Lady Isabel, but about Lord Willoughby and his travelling court.'

'Tell me.' Mathilda found herself leaning forward in turn, as if being closer to her servants would bring the information to her ears faster.

'We discovered from the innkeeper and the groom,' Daniel paused, 'well, I overheard them while I saw to the horses,' he shifted uncomfortably on his chair, 'that Lord Willoughby will start his court in Lincolnshire, and that he'll be finishing and heading towards Leicestershire, on the Grantham Road, soon after the turn of the year.'

Adam's mouth opened and closed. He was on his feet, anticipating the order from Lady Mathilda to ride to Lichfield. 'They'll need to know this, my Lady.'

Mathilda's mind raced ahead to Eustace's reaction when he discovered where they could find and intercept their target, even if they didn't know exactly when.

'Combined with what we found out in Wollaton, this is vital information, but I wonder… Are we better waiting for my husband and his brothers to get back here? It is already too late to share our findings with the Coterel brothers. And for that matter, we don't yet know if they have agreed to my idea.'

Sarah sighed with relief. She hadn't just been reunited with her man to watch him fly off again so soon. 'Could you at least tell us what you and Lady Mathilda discovered, husband, before you exhaust your horse further?'

Mathilda frowned as she considered where Robert could be. He, assuming all had gone to plan, should be on his way back to Polesworth Abbey. He might even have travelled further. Either way, the earliest he could be home was late the following day.

'Sarah's right. We should wait. Tempting as it is to race off, thanks to Daniel and Bettrys, we now know have time on our side. If we don't need to act against Willoughby until after Christmas, although…'

'My Lady?' Bettrys took a sip of her drink, glad of the warm liquid as a winter draught licked beneath the kitchen door.

'I was thinking of the Coterel brothers. It's getting colder with every passing day, and it's going to get worse as the year draws to a close. I'm not sure Nicholas, John, or James will be happy to wait until the New Year to strike against the justice; especially if they have to do so in hiding, and out in the open at that.'

'Surely they have followers who would shelter them?' Sarah got to her feet and reached for her peeling knife and a pile of apples.

'They did, and a great many of them. But Willoughby has been swift and clever in his actions, and only a brave few will risk harbouring them now.'

'Could they not come here?' Bettrys asked quietly.

Mathilda gave a weak grin. 'As they're relying on us to undo this mess, then they could certainly use our boltholes. The problem is, they have to get across a great deal of land to reach them, and Ashby Folville itself is too dangerous to shelter even one Coterel at the moment, let alone all three. It is a miracle to me that this house has not been searched by Willoughby's soldiers already.'

Bettrys stared at the door, as if expecting a horde of armed men to burst through it. 'What did you learn, my Lady? Did you hear the same rumours we did concerning Lady Willoughby?'

Mathilda glanced up from her drink. 'The woman you overheard in the church, how old would you say she was?'

'I couldn't see her, so I couldn't rightly say.' Daniel ran a finger around the top of his beaker. 'Not old certainly, nor a girl.' He shrugged. 'That's not helpful, I know, but as I said, we got the feeling she was from the Willoughby household, but not a lowly servant. The rector was respectful, even if he was at odds with the woman about her query as to whether Lady Willoughby was ill or not.'

'And you definitely got the sense that she didn't believe it?'

'Either that,' Daniel said, 'or she didn't want to believe it.'

Mathilda turned to Adam. 'I wonder if it was Anne?'

'Anne?' Sarah asked as she sliced an apple into quarters.

'We met Lady Marjory Willoughby and her maid, Anne, in the market.'

Sarah was astounded. 'You met one of Willoughby's children! Did you talk to her? Was that wise?'

Mathilda couldn't help but laugh. 'You ask if I spoke to

the girl, while already assuming I did   and then you question my wisdom!'

'Well, I am getting to know you, my Lady.'

'Wise or not, we spoke to her, and Anne. They had a groom with them too, but he didn't speak.'

Adam passed a wooden bowl to his wife. 'They do not know of our connection with this household. Lady Mathilda was taken to be Robert Ingram's wife, and we didn't correct the error.'

'The former sheriff's wife!'

Mathilda smiled, 'I didn't say who I was exactly, and they didn't ask. It's rather that Anne made an assumption as to my marital status. The point is, I wonder whether Anne was the woman that Daniel and Bettrys heard in the church the day before we met them.'

'Is that possible?' Adam wasn't sure. 'She seemed adamant on the issue to me.'

Mathilda thought fast. 'She was frightened of her master; Lady Marjory accused her of as much. And if she was the one who spoke to the rector at Willoughby-on-the-Wolds, and he confirmed that Lady Isabel must be mad because her husband said so, then maybe she'd been convinced into believing it.'

Adam inclined his head as he listened. 'Lady Marjory certainly doesn't believe it though, does she?'

'She does not.' Mathilda pinched a slice of apple off Sarah's pile and took a bite. 'She asked, if the former sheriff would listen out for news of her mother.'

A short silence descended on the table before Bettrys cleared her throat, 'What would you have us do now, my Lady?'

'In truth, I'm unsure.'

'I'm not.' Sarah pointedly pulled the diced apples away

from her mistress. 'We have a family celebration ahead, do we not? In two days' time it's the Solstice; the anniversary of your wedding. That means there are only two things that need doing with any haste.'

'Which are?' Mathilda smiled fondly at her housekeeper.

'Cooking and cleaning, my Lady. Nothing better for keeping the mind straight and the feet on the ground.'

~ *Chapter Twenty* ~

20th December 1331

The door opened with a stealth that Mathilda recognised as someone trying to enter the chamber without letting the old wood creak. An impossible task, no matter how much candle wax Adam had applied to the door's hinges.

'Robert?'

'I didn't mean to wake you.'

'You didn't.' Leaping from the warmth of their bed onto the stone cold floor and into her husband's equally travel-chilled arms, Mathilda's teeth chattered as she spoke. 'I couldn't sleep for wondering where you were.'

'Snow's falling on the other side of Charnwood Forest. We'd out-ridden it by the time we reached Leicester, but it's coming this way. I'd be surprised if we weren't blanketed in white by dawn.'

'No wonder it's so cold.' She snuggled closer to his chest. 'Are you alone? Your brothers?'

'Thomas is here. Sarah is bustling him into a room with so many extra blankets in her arms you'd think she was intending to smother the man. The others stopped in Leicester. I wanted to get back to you.'

She rested her head on his shoulder, ignoring the damp

of the night air that clung to his cloak. 'I'm glad you did.'

'I didn't want you to worry, and I didn't want to risk the weather cutting me off from you with the Solstice approaching. The dawn of the day we wed is only hours from now.'

Kneeling to undo his boots as Robert unbuckled his cloak and shrugged it to the floor, Mathilda smiled. 'You wouldn't want to miss the minstrels' arrival either.' She tugged at his right boot, 'assuming Aldus and his men can get here by morning.'

Stroking her hair as he wriggled his foot free, Robert laughed, 'I wouldn't want to miss a Robyn Hode tune, but in truth I hadn't thought of that. I wanted to make sure you were here, wife of mine, and hadn't taken it in to your head to go off on an adventure of your own.'

Rising to her feet she kissed his cheek. 'As if I would.'

'Umm.' Throwing the rest of his travel-stained clothing to the ground, he pulled Mathilda into the bed with him, savouring the lingering heat of where her body had been only seconds before.

'The Coterels, did they agree?'

'They did.'

'And how did they react when '

'Not now, Mathilda.' Robert pushed her loosened hair from her shoulders, 'There is much to say, but for now, let's rest. I will confess to being weary of the whole matter as well as the journey.'

Mathilda kissed his shoulder. 'Then we will rest.'

She'd just closed her eyes, when Robert poked her softly in the stomach. 'When I said rest, I didn't actually mean rest…'

'Indeed, my Lord.' Mathilda gave a slow grin. 'Perhaps you'd like to show me exactly what you did mean, then?'

21st December 1331

The sounds of Sarah and Bettrys moving around the kitchen echoed along the corridor and played at the corner of Mathilda's mind as she sat in the hall with Robert and Thomas. Having been told about the Coterels' reaction to their plan, she was torn between staying to discuss what might happen next, and going to help prepare for the feast planned for that evening, Mathilda felt unsettled in a way she couldn't explain.

The snow Robert had predicted started in earnest not long after they'd heard the church bells chime nine. It had loomed in the sky since before she'd risen, like a blanket of grey gloom patiently waiting to fall from the heavens. Mathilda wasn't sure if her brothers-in-law or her family from Twyford would make it to Ashby Folville that afternoon or not. Part of her hoped they wouldn't.

Although she'd miss her father and brothers if they couldn't make it to the planned Solstice feast, an evening off from contemplating what lay in store once the New Year came appealed.

Pulled out of her thoughts by a loud crackle from the fire as a log dropped to the back of the grate, Mathilda was suddenly aware that someone was talking to her. Thomas was looking across the table at her expectantly.

'Did you hear me, Lady Mathilda?'

'I'm sorry, Lord Thomas, I was considering the preparations for the evening meal. Forgive me.' Mathilda scolded herself, 'I shouldn't be dwelling on our festivities when others are in danger and discomfort. I hope the Coterels have found shelter from the snow.'

'When we left,' Robert picked up the ale jug to refill his cup, 'James was sweet-talking the Abbot of Lichfield

Cathedral into letting them stay in shelter until the snow had passed.'

'I hope he succeeded,' Mathilda was fervent, 'even if it is only for a few days' respite from the winter, it would be good.'

'It wouldn't be for any longer than that, whatever the conditions outside.' Thomas looked grave. 'The abbot is a kind man, but not a stupid one. He has no wish to incur the wrath of Willoughby, nor would it do his position any good should King Edward hear of his divided loyalties.'

'How do you think Lord Eustace will react when he hears about what Daniel and Bettrys learned concerning Willoughby's planned route?' Mathilda asked.

Robert grunted into his ale. 'Satisfaction and frustration. He'll be pleased to have a time frame to work with, and frustrated as all hell that we have to wait so long to intercept the justice on safe ground.'

'Safe ground?'

'We know the Grantham road well. Don't forget, our family has land in Huntingdon. Lincolnshire is not strange to us, but the closer the justice gets to Leicestershire and Nottinghamshire, the more we're on surer ground to both take him and hide him without unnecessary risks being taken.' Robert took a draught of ale. 'The Grantham road should work very well for us as a… Shall we call it a collection point? It's a track we know; wooded on both sides; it leads to a wide variety of locations.'

'Providing the snow has passed, it should be perfect for the job in hand,' Thomas added.

Mathilda considered the situation. 'Because of leaving tracks in the snow which could be followed to wherever you chose to take Willoughby once he has been collected?'

'And because of how the cold and damp will affect the

concentration of those watching his movements. We'll need to post sentries on the road for several days from the minute the year turns. We can't risk missing the window of opportunity open to us.' Robert paused. 'At least, I'm sure that's what John and Eustace will say.'

Thomas dragged a hand through his hair in the same manner as Robert did, making Mathilda think how much of a household trait that was. 'Eustace employs able men, but even his chief mercenary, Borin, might have his wits dulled by weeks of waiting, unseen, unmoving, in the depths of winter.'

'Should I have sent Ulric to Eustace as soon as I heard?' Mathilda looked up to a window, too high to see out of, but clearly spattered with snowflakes. 'If this snow banks, we might not be able to get word to him or Lord John for days. If we miss the chance because I made the wrong decision...'

Robert dismissed Mathilda's fears. 'You made the right decision. The chances of the lad finding Eustace, or any of us, travelling back from Lichfield was slim. Ulric might still be out there now, on a fool's errand, as we rode unawares in the opposite direction.'

'I suppose so.' Mathilda got to her feet. Until Eustace arrived, there was nothing more to discuss. She hoped their anniversary feast wouldn't turn into a kidnap-planning meeting. At least, she reasoned, it wasn't going to be murder-planning. 'If you'll excuse me, my Lords, I will go and see how Sarah and Bettrys are faring with the preparations.'

Robert got to his feet as Mathilda made to leave the hall. 'I don't think it would be a good idea to mention your trip to Wollaton to Eustace, or to any of the others. Thomas and I have discussed it, and we agree that he'd not be sympathetic to your views on Lady Isabel.'

'But surely that is to our advantage?' Mathilda sat down

again, 'You said to find his weakness. Lady Isabel is that weakness. She is missing. The rumour of her madness has spread fast, but it is a false rumour. A gossip of convenience spread by the justice himself.'

Thomas gave her a kind smile, which annoyed Mathilda intensely. 'With respect, my Lady, you have only guessed at that. We can't know it isn't true.'

'It isn't true.' Mathilda couldn't explain why she was so sure of this, without having any evidence to back up her theory. 'Her own daughter, Lady Marjory, who is almost a woman herself, doesn't believe it. And before you even consider telling me that the word of a daughter cannot be trusted, I'd warn you that I'm not to be shifted on my conviction of Isabel's slighting by her husband.'

'Because?' Robert spoke levelly, but she could tell he was biting his tongue against raising his voice.

'Because, not only was Lady Marjory convinced of her mother's full health, her maid didn't believe it either. However, Anne that's the maid was obviously too afraid to say otherwise. This all ties in with what Daniel and Bettrys heard. Lady Isabel is missing and rumours are rife, but the gossip of her ill-health appears more of a surprise to everyone than her disappearance does.'

'But why would Willoughby do this? I can't see what advantage this carries for him.' Robert glanced towards the open doorway as an abrupt draught shot along the corridor and into the hall, making the fire flicker. 'Someone's arrived.'

As they all rose to see who their visitor was, Mathilda replied, 'Because Lady Marjory said he'd had a row with his wife about land. The only row she'd ever known them have.'

'About land?' Thomas eyebrow's rose in surprise. 'They

have plenty of land. More than most of the landed families in the region.'

'Lady Isabel reportedly told her husband, in anger, that the only land he had legally had arrived with her.'

Robert and Thomas exchanged glances, before Robert, with an abrupt change of heart, said, 'We need to find this woman. Let's hope she hates her husband as much as we do.'

~ *Chapter Twenty-one* ~

21st December 1331

Letting the men go on ahead, Mathilda remained in the hall, staring into the fire. Suddenly, it was so obvious what she'd missed.

Everything she'd been told about Justice Willoughby should have made it clear from the start. Yet, she was so used to the brothers exaggerating situations to justify their actions that she'd not seen the most obvious possibility. If the justice was as ruthless as everyone claimed, then Lady Isabel was very probably dead.

An image of Lady Marjory flitted through her head. She'd mentioned a sister, a younger girl called Joan. And there were other children, weren't there? An older brother, also called Richard, and two more… boys, she thought. They didn't know what had happened to their mother, and if Anne was anything to go by, the household servants were too afraid to speculate or ask their master questions.

'What if she is?'

'What if who is, what?' Sarah came into the hall with a tray laden with jugs and beakers.

'Oh, Sarah, I'm sorry. I ought to be helping you, I was just thinking aloud.'

'About?'

'Lady Isabel. I have a horrible feeling she's dead.'

'Do you indeed?' Eustace's gravelly tone was sharp as he strode into the hall.

Cursing inwardly, knowing she'd now have to go against Robert's wishes and tell Eustace she'd been to Wollaton, Mathilda curtsied. 'Forgive me, my Lord, I wasn't aware you'd made it through the snow. How is the terrain?'

'Slow, but passable. The snow has stopped, but the temperature is dropping fast. There's no ice yet, but I suspect tomorrow will be bad.'

'Did you arrive alone, my Lord?'

Eustace gave his sister-in-law a shrewd stare. 'I have Lady Joan with me, and Walter and Thomas are not far behind.'

Wisely not questioning the Lady la Zouche's ready appearance at his side, Mathilda said, 'Lady Joan's counsel is always welcome.'

'Her father was the main instigator of Belers' death. She naturally promised him she'd keep a close eye on events while he is in London.'

'Most sensible, my Lord'

Unmoved by Mathilda's feelings on his excuse for Joan's presence, Eustace leant against the edge of the table, he spoke bluntly. 'You mentioned Lady Willoughby's potential death. I think you should explain yourself.'

'My Lord, I '

'Not now. Once everyone is here to listen.'

Mathilda gave an inward groan. The notion was formless and too fresh to share. She needed to think further and talk to Robert. 'Certainly, my Lord. If you will allow me to assist Sarah, then the feast will begin all the sooner.'

Tilting her chin in the air in a manner she'd seen Lady

Joan adopt when she was determined not to be overruled on an issue, Mathilda swept from the hall, her heart hammering in her chest.

Glad to see Daniel in the kitchen refilling the log basket by the fire, Mathilda bid him find Robert. She could feel Sarah's questioning gaze levelling on her across the room.

'Do you really think Lady Willoughby has been killed?'

'It's a possibility that I should have thought of much earlier.' Mathilda piled some of Sarah's pastries onto a platter. 'Lady Isabel hit a man in a place where no woman should hit him.'

'Excuse me?'

'His pride, Sarah. In what Lady Marjory referred to as their only ever argument, Isabel accused Willoughby of greed, and of only having his lands because of her.'

'Dangerous talk at the best of times. Worse with a man like that.' Sarah brushed some flour off her hands and surveyed the rows of laden plates before her with satisfaction. 'Tis a shame to have to talk about such things today.'

Inhaling the sweet aromas of cinnamon and ginger, Mathilda gave her friend a brave smile. 'It seems we are not to be allowed a day off to celebrate the Solstice. Still, at least we are safe and warm, with your wonderful cooking and a roaring fire.'

Not missing the point, Sarah tilted her head towards the door to the courtyard. 'I don't envy the Coterels and their followers this day.'

'I keep thinking about them too.' Mathilda saw an image of Nicholas Coterel in her mind's eye. Cold, alone, and afraid. Three things she'd never normally associate with such a powerful and self-assured man. She wished Robert and he wouldn't bicker so much, especially over her. She was sure Lord Nicholas had no feelings in her direction whatsoever, but simply enjoyed baiting Robert who was always quick to bite where she was concerned. 'I know they are safe at Lichfield for today, but soon they'll be without shelter.'

'They'll have others who'll harbour them.'

'I'm not so sure they will this time, Sarah. The people are afraid. Justice Willoughby has stirred up an atmosphere of distrust and tension. Those willing to take in the brothers are less inclined to do so. For the first time they fear the law's retribution more than the Coterels' revenge.'

Sarah was spared answering by Daniel's return. His round face was flushed with cold. 'Lord Robert bids you to meet him in your chamber prior to heading to the hall.'

'Thank you, Daniel.' Mathilda turned to Sarah, 'Is there anything you'd like me to do before I go? I feel as if I've left you to cope alone too long already.'

'You're the lady of the manor. You shouldn't have to worry about helping me.' Sarah winked. 'Go to your husband and discuss what needs discussing before Lord Eustace questions you.'

'Apart from your food, it doesn't feel like the celebration we hoped for today.'

Sarah gave a sad shrug. 'Once Lord Robert has finished talking with you I'll send Bettrys along to help you change out of your gown. She can dress your hair as well. The celebration of the Solstice and your anniversary may have been overtaken by events, but there is no reason you can't look the part.'

'Thank you, Sarah.'

'Aldus, Noll, and Dicun are here.'

Robert bought Mathilda the welcome news of the minstrels' arrival as he swept into their chamber, brushing straw dust from his arms after helping in the stables.

'That's wonderful.' A genuine smile lit up her face. 'A lift to our spirits is just what we need.'

'Aldus promises some Robyn Hode ditties, but perhaps not the Geste. He says he clearly remembers Eustace's eyes clouding over with the length of the piece at our wedding celebration!'

'Did they now!' Mathilda rubbed her chilled hands together, 'That tempts me to request that very piece.'

Robert snorted. 'My brother has displeased you?'

'Lord Eustace arrived in the hall just as I was musing, rather too loudly for my own sake, on what may have happened to Lady Isabel. I am sorry to say it is unlikely I can keep my trip to Wollaton a secret.'

'Ah.' Robert frowned, as he held his wife's hands in his. 'You had better tell me your thinking.'

'That's just it. It is but thinking. An idea struck me, and now Eustace wants all my information and I can't back up my idea with anything beyond instinct. You can imagine how the Rector will respond to that.'

'In that you are at least fortunate. Richard is unlikely to join us; the snow was more challenging for his ride back to Teigh.'

'Small mercies.' Mathilda perched on the edge of their bed, trying to frame her thoughts about Lady Isabel's possible demise into some sort of logical argument. 'If I just had more time to think.'

Robert sat down next to her, 'Now that we know Willoughby won't be moving in this direction until January, thanks to the bravery of Bettrys and Daniel which I will ensure my brothers fully acknowledge we do have time on our side.'

'But Lady Isabel may not. In fact, I fear it may be too

late for her already.'

'You think she is dead.'

'I think she had become inconvenient to her husband at a delicate time in his career.'

Robert placed a finger under his wife's chin, raising her face to his. 'Soon, I'll leave you alone to think, to go through what you learnt in Wollaton and to decide what you know and what you think you know. I can't protect you from my brothers' questioning, but I am going to put a limit on it. If Eustace has not said all he needs to say, or learnt all he wants to learn, within one hour, then it can wait until tomorrow. Today is our day, and I'm not having our anniversary disintegrate into chaos the same way our wedding day did.'

Kissing him on the lips, Mathilda then rested her head on his shoulder and closed her eyes. 'What if I don't have the answers your brothers want? I can't always solve everything, you know.'

'I know, and they don't expect you to.'

'It feels as if they do.'

'Perhaps, but they aren't fools, Mathilda. Foolish on occasion, and certainly impulsive, but they don't believe in miracles from God, let alone from you.'

Holding her close for a second, Robert got to his feet. 'I have a gift for you'

'You do?' A smile wiped away the concerned creases that had lined her face.

Opening the wooden chest on his side of the room, Robert pulled out a pale green gown. Mathilda gasped as she saw it. The silk was the finest she'd ever seen, the lustre to the fabric shone in the candlelight.

Holding up to her face, Robert brushed the material against her cheek. 'It matches your eyes.'

'Oh, Robert, it's beautiful.'

'As are you, Mathilda.'

'Where did you get it? When?'

Robert laughed. 'Always with questions.' He brushed a stray coil of hair from her face. 'I had heard from your brother Matthew about his forthcoming nuptials prior to our visit to Twyford. Matthew was good enough to send word to me about his plans for the house he's taken, and his ideas for the land. He also told me of Alice of Picardy. This dress was made by her father. It's the finest Byzantine silk.'

'I love it.' Mathilda took it from his hands and laid it reverently on the bed. Its simplicity made it stunning. 'Matthew is certainly marrying well.'

'Will you wear it for me today?'

Noting the husky edge to his voice, Mathilda's eyes flashed with mischief. 'I would be glad to.'

'But for the love of God wear a cloak over the top during the meeting before the feast, or I'll never concentrate.'

'I'm flattered, my Lord,' Mathilda lifted the silk to the light, 'but if I didn't wear a cloak with it, I'd probably freeze to death, which, right now, would make Eustace very cross.'

Robert groaned. 'Is it wrong of me to wish them all a million miles away so we could just be on our own for once?'

'If it's wrong of you, it's wrong of me too.' Mathilda laid a palm on his thigh. 'When this is all over, then we'll have time enough.'

Holding her gaze for a split second, Robert stared at her dress. 'I hope so, Mathilda. I do hope so.'

As Aldus and his troupe got ready to play, the meeting finally over, Bettrys and Ulric started to serve food and ale.

Sat next to Robert, their backs to the fire, just as they had on the day they married, Mathilda looked around the smaller than planned gathering. Lord Eustace, in Lord John's absence, was at the head of the table, Lady Joan to his right-hand side. Next to Joan sat Thomas, Walter, and Laurence, while next to Eustace, Sir Robert Ingram took his position. Saddened that none of her family from Twyford had made it through the snow, Mathilda knew she should be grateful that they were at least safe at home.

Considering all that had been said, Mathilda felt proud of Daniel and Bettrys as they'd stood together and given a full account of their trip to Willoughby-on-the-Wolds. As predicted, Eustace had been more than pleased with their news, and soon he'd sent Ulric outside to fetch John Pyke-hose. Seconds later, with no heed to the perilous weather, Pykehose was on his way to summon Borin and a few of his most trusted men to Ashby Folville.

Her own account of her trip to Wollaton had been scru-tinised, but Eustace had declared the need to consider the Lady Isabel situation for longer, so he could work out how to use it to their best advantage. Mathilda had almost choked on her sweetmeat in surprise that he hadn't explod-ed on learning she'd visited Wollaton without consulting him first. Once again, Lord Eustace was thinking before he acted.

As the melody of 'Robyn Hode and the Monk' filled the hall, Mathilda sensed Lady Joan's gaze upon her. 'I trust the music and food is to your liking, my Lady.'

'Very much, Lady Mathilda.' She dipped her head with gentle grace, 'I have always shared your taste for stories of ballad heroes.' Her eyes passed over Eustace for the briefest second before returning to her hostess. 'Your dress is most becoming.'

'A present from my husband.'

'You are fortunate indeed. My own husband sent me pheasants for the pot for the festive season. By the time they reached Lubbersthorpe from Yorkshire, they were already high. How he imagines we could save them to eat in four more days from now, I cannot conceive.'

Unsure how to respond, Mathilda gestured to Sarah's food. 'We are lucky to have Sarah to feed our needs.'

'An excellent and diplomatic answer, Lady Mathilda.' Joan raised her glass in salute to her host just as the music paled to silence.

Aldus bowed to the splattering of applause, accepting a drink from Adam as he did so. 'My Lords, Ladies, do you have any requests?'

'I have one.' Lord Robert rose to his feet. 'I'd like you to care for my wife.'

Mathilda sat up with a start, 'My Lord?'

Aldus kept his face expressionless as he asked, 'We care very much for Lady Mathilda. The pleasure she takes in our art is always appreciated, as is your own, my Lord.'

'Robert,' Eustace's brows knitted together as he glowered at his brother, 'what are you proposing?'

'That Mathilda goes in search of Lady Isabel.'

~ *Chapter Twenty-two* ~

28th December 1331

Mathilda, Sarah, and Bettrys watched as Borin and his companions rode out of the courtyard and disappeared into the woodland that surrounded two-thirds of Ashby Folville manor.

'I'm sure they should have taken more food, my Lady.' Bettrys shivered as a cutting breeze shot through the courtyard.

'They had every chance to take more. We cannot be accused of offering less than required.' Sarah brushed flour from her palms. 'As it is, they've eaten nearly all the cabbage and onion I'd earmarked to last the entire winter. All seven Folville brothers couldn't get through as much as those three did in just five days!'

'They'll want to travel lightly.' Remembering the visitors coming and going from Rockingham Castle, travelling with just the bare essentials so they could keep their horses unburdened and swift, Bettrys retreated from the doorway into the warmth of the kitchen. 'I hope they'll be alright.'

'One thing I think we can be sure of is that Borin and his men will always be alright.'

'But we don't know how long they'll have to hide in the

open air, keeping watch over Lord Willoughby's court.' The maid busied herself by the fire, more to thaw out her numb hands than because the hearth needed sweeping.

Mathilda drew closer to the fire. 'It could be weeks before Justice Willoughby is ready to leave Lincolnshire. I swear the waiting is far worse than acting once the decision to act has been made.' Moving away, she pointed towards the door. 'I'll help you with the bed linen, Bettrys. After so many guests it'll be a job for two.'

Bettrys chewed at the inside of her cheek as she trailed after her mistress, unsure if she should ask what had been worrying her since the Solstice feast. 'My Lady, are you really going to travel to Wollaton in search of Lady Isabel?'

'Unless she reappears before Borin sends word that Lord Willoughby heads our way, then yes.'

Bettrys picked at the hem of her apron as she knelt on the floor, 'Will it… will it be like Rockingham?'

Mathilda peered into the fire's dancing orange flames. She understood Bettrys' fears on the matter. The girl had escaped a household where she had unwittingly served a murderer; now she was working for a family full of criminals. It was only the good intentions behind their motives for killing that marked the Folvilles apart from the rest.

'No, Bettrys, there'll be no killing on your doorstep.' Mathilda crossed her fingers, hoping she wasn't lying to the girl. 'Willoughby will, hopefully, just be frightened and taught a lesson. And he won't be at Wollaton when we're there.'

'I was thinking of Lady Isabel. What of her, my Lady?' Bettrys clambered to her feet, her eyes showing her troubled thoughts.

'Her Ladyship has already been missing for weeks, what if we're too late? I thought we'd be sent out as soon as Lord

Robert suggested you tried to find her. What if she is already dead, or is hidden away somewhere against her will? Or worse, is praying for an end to some torturous suffering!'

Taken aback by the strength of Bettrys' concern, Mathilda took the maid's hand and led her to the bench that ran along the kitchen table. 'I will be truthful, Bettrys, I share many of your fears, however to act too soon would be reckless. With each day that passes messengers come with news that more of Justice Willoughby's men are searching the area for those they suspect of harbouring felons. So far they are concentrating on land to the other side of Charnwood and the Peaks of Derbyshire. According to Lord Robert, we have lost word of where the Coterels are hiding. Uncertainty stalks the land beyond the safety of the manor walls. If we were to go abroad now, with no real idea of where to find her Ladyship, we'll cast suspicion upon ourselves and risk arrest simply for being out with no good reason.'

'But, my Lady, we are already clouded in suspicion as far as Lord Willoughby is concerned. You're a Folville and I work for you.'

Mathilda sighed. 'I know, Bettrys, I know.'

'Forgive my impudence, but I don't understand why we're waiting. If Lady Isabel's children are worried about her, if rumours are flying around… surely she deserves our help?'

'She does, and she will get it.'

Emboldened by her mistress' determined tone, Bettrys went on. 'I keep thinking about the rector Daniel and I met in Willoughby-on-the-Wolds church. I'm sure he was saying that Lady Isabel was out of her wits because he'd been told to.'

'You may well be right.' Mathilda straightened up, 'I promise you, as soon as the weather is calmer and we receive word from my husband that the plan to waylay the justice is in operation, I will go in search of Lady Isabel, or at least, endeavour to discover what has become of her.'

'With the minstrels?'

'They have agreed to travel with me as far as Wollaton.'

'With *us*, my Lady.' This time it was Bettrys who stood, her back straight, her jaw set. 'It would appear suspicious if you were to travel with three men and no maid. I am coming too.' Then, as if remembering herself, she added, 'If that's alright, my Lady.'

Resisting the urge to give her maid a hug, knowing it would disconcert her, Mathilda smiled. 'How can I disagree with such logic?'

'You mean I can come?'

'I was going to ask if you would like to,' Mathilda held up a hand before Bettrys could speak, 'but only if you wished to. It will be dangerous. Should you change your mind between now and then, I will ask Sarah to accompany me, and you can run the house.'

'Run the house!' Bettrys was stunned. 'Me, my Lady?'

'Of course. You are a fast learner; you care about your work.'

'But I'm not ready. What if I let Sarah down?'

Mathilda couldn't help but laugh. 'Bettrys, you are priceless. Between going out into a dangerous world to hunt for a missing woman and staying and running the manor, it's making a mistake and letting down Sarah that worries you.'

'I don't want to let her down.' Bettrys muttered, the familiar pink blush of embarrassment crossing her cheeks as she smoothed a clean blanket over the bed recently occupied by Lady Joan.

'You're a good woman, no wonder Daniel is so taken with you.'

The words had come out of Mathilda's mouth before she'd registered what she was saying. Seeing the maid's cheeks bloom from pink to bright red, she immediately apologised. 'I'm sorry, I didn't mean to pry, nor say anything. My tongue got ahead of my brain.'

'Is it obvious then?' Bettrys stared at her hands as she started to pick at her apron hem again.

'That you take pleasure in each other's company? Yes. That's a good thing. No need to be concerned. Lord Robert and I would not be against your union, should that be what you wanted.'

Tears glistened in Bettrys' eyes, although she smiled through them. 'You are so kind. It seems not a minute since I was in Rockingham, feeling all alone, and now I'm here... and then there's Sarah, and a future I could never have dreamed of. And now Daniel and I...' She broke into a snuffling sob, as if overwhelmed by good fortune.

Tapping the corner of the bed, indicating for Bettrys to sit down, Mathilda said, 'Why don't you take a minute. I'll be in the kitchen with Sarah. We can do the rest of the chambers later.'

Refraining from comment when Mathilda explained that Bettrys needed a moment, Sarah pointed to a pile of the parsnips and a single cabbage and onion. 'Ulric's been as efficient as ever, I see. Good lad, that.'

Mathilda nodded. 'He must have been to the store for them first thing. Either he was acting on an order from you last night, or he's hinting towards parsnip soup.'

'Both. He hinted towards his liking for it yesterday, so I told him if he wanted it, he'd have to dig the snow away from the food store and fetch what I needed to make it.'

Sniffing and rubbing her eyes dry, Bettrys appeared at

the door. 'Should I start chopping the cabbage, Sarah?'

'Please. It'll need a good wash.' Sarah sent her apprentice out into the cold to fill a bucket with water.

Taking the chance while Bettrys wasn't there, Mathilda spoke hurriedly, 'Bettrys has asked to come with me when I return to Wollaton.'

'Will you let her?'

'I think so. But will you be alright here without us?'

'It won't be the first time.' Sarah pulled an onion towards her. 'Just make sure you both come back again.'

'I will do my best.'

'You won't go to the hall though, will you?'

'No, it's too dangerous; especially as Lady Marjory's under the impression I'm Lady Ingram. We'll go to the town and stay at the inn. I'm glad Adam and I didn't end up staying there last time; at least we won't be known.'

'And the minstrels who are to escort you; what will they do once you're in place?'

'They'll go to the inn too, and try and get work singing there.'

'Which means they'll be close by if you need their help.' Sarah spoke with approval as she reduced the onion to tiny slices. 'I can see the logic of heading to Wollaton, but where will you begin your search for Lady Isabel? Even with a maid to accompany you, it would still appear odd for you to be roaming the area without a male escort. Especially if you decide to search the woodland. You'll be vulnerable from the moment you leave Ashby Folville.'

'I know.' Mathilda scooped up the discarded onion skin and dropped it into the scrap bucket by the back door. 'I've been thinking of little else but how to approach the problem. Everything I've considered so far has bars in its way.'

'You could take Daniel or Adam.'

'If they're not needed here, I may well, but until we know the situation fully, I can't presume their availability.'

'Yet you are convinced we need Lady Isabel to speak against her husband, or act as an incentive for him to change his ways?'

'If she's alive and willing to address King Edward about her husband, even if only privately, then our case to curb his powers will be stronger. If Willoughby has contributed to her death or her removal from public life however, then that evidence would also help our cause.'

An abrupt blast of noise from outside made both women stop what they were doing and turn to the door. Bettrys rushed inside, the pail of water for washing the vegetables splashing around her ankles in her haste.

Mathilda's jaw clenched as she heard hooves clatter across the courtyard and men shouting to each other reached her. Male voices were laughing at the maid's fear; commenting with no subtlety whatsoever about how much fun she'd be in the hay store. 'Bettrys?'

'Men... Rockingham. I recognise one of them. He's a very bad man.'

~ *Chapter Twenty-three* ~

28th December 1331

'Is Daniel out there?'

'Yes!' Bettrys looked frightened, 'And he's on his own!'

'How many men?' Matilda tugged a thick cloak over her shoulders.

'Three, my Lady.'

'Do you know their names?'

'Just the face of the one nearest the kitchen. He's a thief. A violent one.'

Mathilda spoke quickly. 'Go and fetch Lord Robert and Adam. Then go and change out of your wet clothes or you'll catch your death. Quickly now.'

As Bettrys flew from the kitchen into the heart of the manor, Mathilda strode towards the courtyard with Sarah at her heels.

'Were you expecting visitors, my Lady?' Sarah whispered.

'Not beyond the occasional messenger from Lord Eustace.' Mathilda threw the door open with a bravado she didn't feel. A blast of early morning frost prickled her face as she stepped outside, trying her hardest to look imposing. 'Daniel!'

'My Lady.' Daniel kept hold of the two horses he was holding, as his mistress approached. 'Visitors for Lord Eustace, my Lady.'

Relieved this wasn't the visit by Willoughby's mercenaries she'd been dreading, Mathilda viewed the three men who'd arrived in a noisy flurry of galloping hooves and banter.

'Visitors with no respect for others' property, and no sense of subtlety.' She spoke with deliberate clarity, so that the three unexpected guests would all turn to face her. Dismissing their dour expressions, assorted scars, and battle-hardened appearances, Mathilda adopted the 'lady of the manor' attitude Lady Joan had taught her when they'd first met. 'I can't imagine Lord Eustace will be impressed at your lack of finesse. I was under the impression he only employs the best. Clearly the best were busy. Who are you?'

Stung by the manner of greeting, the nearest visitor spat out a contemptuous response, 'Men who don't answer to the likes of you, child!'

'You'll answer to me though. And if you speak to my wife like that again, you'll answer with more than words.'

Mathilda hadn't heard Robert or Adam arrive, but now they seemed to fill the courtyard, her husband's presence quietening their visitors, but not wiping the scowls from their faces.

'You!' Robert pointed to the nearest man. 'Your name and the reason you're here.'

'Geoffrey de Maxeye.' He scuffed a weathered boot against the icy ground, adding, 'my Lord Folville,' as an afterthought.

Robert's hand rested on the pommel of his sword. 'I have heard of you and your reputation for dishonesty. My brother, Lord Eustace, does not trust you.'

The man barked a humourless laugh. 'Nor I him, my Lord. Yet he respects my skills and I his.'

'He sent you and these men to my home?'

The arrogant certainty slipped from Maxeye's face for a second. 'Me, yes; my companions he is, as yet, unaware of.'

Robert's expression darkened further. 'Then your companions will leave my property.'

'Lord Robert, I '

'Are you deaf as well as untrustworthy?' Robert signalled to Adam, 'Perhaps you'd find *one* space in the stalls for Maxeye's horse?'

As the steward snatched the reins from his hands, Maxeye twisted on his heels and grunted at his fellow travellers, who took back their bridles from Daniel with ill-concealed displeasure. Remounting, they stirred their horses from standing to a canter in seconds and disappeared into the woodland beyond the manor's walls.

'You'd better come in.' Robert turned from Maxeye to Mathilda. 'Could you ask Bettrys to prepare the least pleasant guest room?'

'I'll get her to add grit to the mattress.' Mathilda didn't trouble to lower her voice as she returned to the house, with Sarah scowling after her.

'Where is he?'

'I've locked him in the smallest bedroom, and I sent his henchmen away.'

'Locked Maxeye in? That's a first for him.' Eustace raised an eyebrow, more amused than cross as he regarded Robert and his wife. 'I wasn't expecting him to bring company. How many of them?'

'Two. They left soon enough.'

Eustace nodded. 'They won't have gone far. I'll let

Pykehose know.'

Mathilda looked up, 'Pykehose is watching the house?'

'Of course. I wouldn't trust anyone else to guard the family home in Borin's absence.'

Robert passed his brother a jug of ale across the hall table. 'Maxeye is a notorious thief, Eustace. Surely you could find another to help with Willoughby's kidnap?'

'I could have chosen many others, but if the justice is less than willing to cough up the money we'll demand of him, then Maxeye has the skills to go into Wollaton by stealth and take it for us. He's never been caught. Not once.'

'Until now.' Mathilda gestured in the direction of the locked chamber door. 'And when we have the ransom, by whatever means necessary, what do we do with it? If we keep it, then being in possession of the money could hang us all anyway.'

'The men helping us will need paying. Maxeye is demanding a hundred marks for his services, probably in the form of Willoughby's rings. The rest of the money will pay for shelter for the Coterels, and a refuge of our own, should we need to spend time away from our homes.'

Mathilda said nothing. Instead she regarded Robert as he acknowledged the point. 'You think that's a real possibility, Eustace?'

'Don't you, brother?'

'Sadly, yes, but better a short time running as an outlaw, than prison and then the noose.' Robert raked a hand through his hair. 'I hope the wait for news from Borin isn't too long. I dislike having Maxeye under our roof.'

Mathilda, who didn't like the idea of Maxeye's presence any more than her husband did, sat up straight as something Eustace had said echoed through her head. 'The rings off Willoughby's fingers.'

'Mathilda?' Robert stretched a hand out to his wife, but she didn't notice the offering of comfort as a trickle of apprehension flickered down her spine. She was beginning to see a way to learn about Lady Isabel; a way that would be much more effective than hiding out at the town's inn, hoping to overhear something of interest. But far more dangerous. 'You said Willoughby wears rings on his fingers. Is one of them likely to be a seal ring? Most men of importance to the king seem to wear them.'

Lord Eustace played his dagger though his proudly ringless fingers. 'I would be surprised if he didn't. It's not as if he has to worry about rings getting caught on daggers or while he works. He pays others to do his dirty work for him. Why do you ask, my Lady?'

'If I am to find out about Lady Isabel, the best place to start would be the manor. I'd like to talk to her servants and children. However, that is dangerous, unless I have his seal ring to prove I come from Willoughby himself. If I had that, they'll have reason to trust me.'

Eustace agreed. 'If you had the ring, or his seal if he doesn't wear his official stamp on his finger, it would look as if you were there on his say-so.'

Robert scowled. 'You can't really be suggesting you walk into Willoughby's home. Mathilda? If we are to stick to the plan we made with the Coterels, then once the ransom demand arrived, you'd be there   right in front of them directly in line for their anger and suspicion. No. It's too dangerous.'

'But if I could get into Wollaton safely, husband, using the ring as a signal from Lord Willoughby himself, maybe with a fiction about his concern for Lady Isabel on my lips...'

Eustace took a swig of ale. 'It might be worth a try.'

Robert waved a palm as if batting the idea away. 'Word of his capture would follow fast on your heels, Mathilda. Even if they initially believed you'd come honestly, how long before they realise you could have stolen his seal yourself? When the household discover their master has been captured, you'd be in trouble.'

'Then I'll have to act fast.' Mathilda had been expecting this argument and was already ahead of him. 'I'll claim to have seen His Lordship on the road some time before he was taken. Remember, the occupants of Wollaton don't know I'm a Folville. Thanks to Lady Marjory's assumption, they think I'm Sir Robert Ingram's wife.'

A rare grin spread over Eustace's face. 'Once word of the kidnap has reached the hall, you could even ask one of their servants to get word to your "husband" concerning where you'd seen Willoughby before the attack.' Eustace slipped his dagger away with a swipe of satisfaction. 'Lady Mathilda, you never cease to amaze me.'

'One thing though, my Lord. I mean no offence to Lady Joan after the generous loan of her horse, but I must take the palfrey.'

'But, Mathilda '

'Hear me out, husband. When Lady Marjory saw me in Wollaton, I had my own horse with me. To maintain my fiction, all must be as it was before.'

'So Adam must go with you too.'

Mathilda had been so busy pretending her palfrey had been seen, so she could avoid using Jep, that she hadn't thought about needing Adam with her to maintain their fiction. 'Unless he is vital to your plans.'

'Helpful, but not vital.' Robert sighed. 'You've already decided you're going to do this, haven't you?'

'I don't like the idea of Lady Isabel being cast out just

because she stood up to her husband.'

Eustace sniffed at the foolishness of female emotion as Mathilda went on, 'The minstrels could still escort us. We could say we met them on the road, and recognising them from a previous event, invited them to keep us company as our destination coincided. The more people who address me as Lady Ingram, the better.'

'Hang on,' Robert leant forward, 'you are going to ask Aldus, Noll, and Dicun to do the one thing they really didn't want to do after all　go into Wollaton manor itself?'

Mathilda felt uncomfortable. 'I don't like the idea of forcing anyone to do anything, but if they'd stay for one night, then they could act as additional eyes and ears. People forget minstrels can hear; they said as much to me when I saw them in Leicester. It's like they are invisible when they aren't singing or playing their music.'

Eustace sat quietly, sipping his ale as he stared into the fire. Mathilda glanced at her husband. She could see he wasn't happy with her plan, but she also knew he'd accepted it was going to happen anyway.

'We'll get Maxeye to remove the rings after Willoughby's hands have been tied behind his back, that way he won't know Mathilda has them.' Eustace got up, 'I'd better go and talk to our thief. He'll be spitting mad at being locked away.'

Robert held a hand up to stall his brother, 'And if Maxeye takes the rings and runs off with them before Mathilda gets the one she needs?'

'Let him keep the others.' Mathilda hugged her cloak around her chest to fend off the cold that had crept into her at the thought of what she was going to do.

'But they'll be worth a fortune! Far more than the hundred marks we owe. Maxeye is entitled to just one or two rings.' Eustace shook his head.

'But those rings will link the holder with the theft of Willoughby's goods.' Mathilda gripped the side of the table as she leant towards her brother-in-law. 'Do you really want that theft to be traced back to us, as well as the kidnap and ransom?'

'What difference will it make?'

'Perhaps none, but perhaps it would tip the balance against you. Making an example of the justice, humiliating him to bring the attention of the Crown to his corruption, is one thing. Robbery for personal gain, on the other hand, will not impress King Edward, and would act as a mark against our sincerity.'

Eustace snorted out a laugh. 'You're no fun, my Lady.'

'She's right though, Eustace.'

'Of course she is, Robert. She's always bloody right!'

Mathilda frowned. 'How will I get the seal ring though?'

'I'll send a messenger with it. To here or a pre-arranged place on the road to Wollaton, if you've already started your journey.' Eustace got up. 'I'll go and give Maxeye the good news. Then we'll need to talk to Sarah and Adam about the others.'

'What others?' Robert frowned.

'The men who'll help us carry out the kidnap, of course. Where else would they go while we wait for word from Borin?'

Mathilda jumped to her feet. 'How many men, my Lord?'

'Four. Maybe more.'

'And they'll be staying here, as well as the family, until we get word to act?'

'Yes.'

'But it could be weeks yet!'

Eustace wasn't pleased to be questioned, 'And it could

be tomorrow, Lady Mathilda, so I suggest you get this house in order and your own pack roll together so when the time comes you are ready to move!'

Robert was about to object to his wife being spoken to in such a fashion, but Mathilda got there first. She brushed down her cloak as she regarded her brother-in-law in a manner she'd never have dared adopt even a year ago. 'My Lord Eustace, I have told you I am willing to walk into the lion's den for this family. I have done so before, and I don't suppose this will be the last time.

'I will, if you'll excuse me, go and explain the situation to Sarah and Adam. Ulric can erect some beds around the side of the hall, and Daniel can arrange the stables for additional horses. I have no objection to doing any of these things. I do however object to being spoken to like a serf.'

She curtseyed to Robert and walked towards the kitchen. Sarah was not going to be happy about the forthcoming invasion.

~ *Chapter Twenty-four* ~

13th January1332

Mathilda lifted her pack-roll from where it had been stowed, ready for action since the day Maxeye had arrived in Ashby Folville. Her plan to go to Wollaton and find Lady Isabel, alive or dead, had been rehearsed so often in her mind that it had begun to feel like a story she was telling herself, rather than something she was going to do.

As the year had turned and no word had come from Lincolnshire, she'd started to think the day to take Willoughby would never come. Each morning Mathilda woke hoping the justice had changed his mind and would call his hounds from his vendetta against the Coterels and her family. But he hadn't, and now – finally the hour to act had struck.

Borin had arrived at Ashby Folville not long after Mathilda had gone to bed. Bundled in a cloak and wrapped in blankets to protect both her dignity and keep out the cold, she'd run with Robert to the hall. Eustace's man's expression had been as empty as ever, his voice sharp, his words to the point. Reporting directly to Lord Eustace, he'd explained that Willoughby would be travelling along the Grantham road, towards Melton Mowbray in Leicestershire, during the afternoon of the following day. Then, with no more than a dip of acknowledgement to his employer, and nodding a silent thank you to Sarah for the parcel of hot meat she'd wrapped for him, he'd gone; heading back to his post in Lincolnshire, over five hours' ride away.

Now, as the hour headed towards midnight, the need to return to bed was forgotten. Every occupant of the manor had flown into action. Mathilda had expected it to be noisy, as everyone rushed about, but they all moved with an economical silence which sent a shiver through her heart. Murmuring to Our Lady, Mathilda prayed her plan to kidnap and make an example of the justice was the right one, and then suffered a rash of guilt for what she was asking of the most blessed of all women.

As she slipped away from the hall to gather her own possessions, Mathilda wasn't sure if she was relieved the waiting was over or not. The manor had hung heavy with tense frustration for days. Those who'd volunteered to help, or had been paid to be part of Willoughby's kidnap, had passed the last fortnight with ever-growing impatience. Not one of them was the sort of man who relished being penned in for an hour, let alone days at a time.

All of the brothers were in residence, except for Lord John, who it was agreed should keep out of it. He held the bulk of the family's lands, and not one of them wanted to give King Edward any excuse to take those away. As well as the six remaining Folvilles, Robert Lovet, the parson of Ashwell in Rutland a man who had far too much in common with the Rector of Teigh for Mathilda's liking was sleeping in one for the guest rooms, along with another cleric, Robert Helewell.

Helewell took such delight in reminiscing about his involvement in the death of Belers that Bettrys had requested she be kept away from him, for his stories made her feel physically sick. Robert had warned the cleric if he didn't curb his tongue, it would be sliced off. Mathilda hadn't been as revolted as she should have by the threat, a fact which had been bothering her ever since.

Alan Baston, the Canon of Sempringham Priory, who'd harboured the Folville family from harm on many occasions, had been sound asleep when Borin came, and was still snoring loudly in the best guest room. Mathilda was glad it was Adam who'd been tasked to go and wake him once his horse was readied for action. So far Mathilda had refrained from commenting to her husband as to the largely clerical nature of the kidnap party. Her faith, already rocked from her experiences since she'd become a Folville wife, was never going to be the same again.

Maxeye had been allowed the run of the manor and a pallet bed at the side of the hall since the evening of his arrival. Eustace claimed he'd only double-cross them if they didn't give him some freedom. However, he'd taken the precaution of threatening to remove Maxeye's hands if anything went missing from the manor, a threat the thief wisely respected.

Maxeye shared the hall with the younger Folville brothers, the servants, and a man called Roger Savage, whose appearance matched his name. Mathilda hadn't asked her husband if Savage's name was given at birth or was one that he'd earned via means she'd rather not know about.

As Mathilda fastened her travelling cloak around her neck, her hands shaking more than she'd have liked, she looked at the bed she shared with Robert. Running a palm gently over the blankets she gave a sad smile. It was their place. Their safe haven from everyone and everything. Mathilda bit back the thought that they may never lay their together again, and picked up her pack, just as Bettrys, red-cheeked, with eyes puffy from either tears or lack of sleep, arrived in the doorway.

'Lord Eustace wishes to address everyone in the hall, my Lady.'

Cradling her pack in her arms, Mathilda stroked the butterfly belt that ran around her waist. For a second her words stuck in her throat, before she managed to say, 'Are you ready, Bettrys? It isn't too late for you to change your mind. Sarah would come and you could stay here.'

'I'll come. The waiting here, the not knowing if… It would be worse than going.'

'That is a sentiment I understand all too well.' Knowing the girl was worried about leaving Daniel at the manor, where he was to act as messenger and Sarah's helper, but was doing her best to put on a brave face, Mathilda passed her the pack. 'Far better to be busy and to keep the mind occupied. No point in dwelling on things. Now,' she brushed her hands down her cloak as she followed the maid from her chamber without a backwards glance, 'give that pack to Ulric, then hurry back to the hall. You should hear what Lord Eustace has to say as well.'

As Bettrys wove through the people that were making their way to the stables to ready their horses before Eustace's address, Mathilda went in search of Robert. She found him in the food store, helping Daniel divide a pile of apples into a heap of leather travelling pouches.

'Mathilda.' Robert gestured to the stable lad, who took the hint, and carried the bags to the kitchen for Sarah to add loaves and wraps of pork to. 'Come here.'

Allowing herself to be engulfed in his arms, Mathilda inhaled deeply. She had an acute desire to memorise how he smelt, how it felt to have his arms around her. Just in case. The lump she'd been trying to stop from forming in her throat arrived in full force, and Mathilda struggled not to cry as neither of them spoke.

Kissing the top of her head, Robert traced his hands over the butterfly belt, letting his fingertips dance over the lattice work. 'Aldus, Dicun, and Noll have left already. We thought it best they didn't set off with you and Adam. It would be more convincing, and truthful, if you can say you met them on the road and agreed to travel together for safety in numbers.'

Mathilda nodded, not yet trusting herself to speak.

'They'll intercept you at Melton Mowbray, near the inn I suspect.'

Again she nodded. She could feel time slipping through their fingers. Eustace would be restless and ready to leave. They ought to be heading to the hall.

'I wish we'd had time to sleep, but the journey ahead is long. If we don't leave soon then we'll miss our opportunity, then all of this planning would have been for nothing and you'd never get to Wollaton with time to learn about Lady Isabel.'

Mathilda licked her dry lips. 'You will take care, won't you?'

'And you will too.' Robert pulled her closer, 'I hate sending you to Wollaton like this. I should be with you all the way, protecting you and… You don't have to go, you know.'

'I do. If we have Lady Isabel on our side – or perhaps just some of her children   then it could make all the difference in the world.' She cut across his guilt. 'And you are protecting me, and everyone else in the region. If this works we'll all be better off.'

'You know the chances of King Edward taking any notice of us at all, even after all this, are slim, don't you.'

'Yes, but if he does…' She bit her lip, 'and if Willoughby

isn't killed, then at least we can't be labelled murderers of a Justice of the Crown.'

'Kidnap and ransom holds the same punishment as murder, Mathilda.'

'I know.' Now the tears came despite herself. 'But if you aren't caught, then…'

'He'll tell everyone it was us.'

'But he won't know for sure. Eustace said Willoughby will be blindfolded before anything happens; before he's seen anyone.'

'If you think he won't guess who's doing this, then '

Mathilda placed a finger over her husband's lips. 'I know.'

With a final hug, Robert eased her away. 'We need to go inside. Eustace will be champing at the bit to get going.'

Wiping her eyes, Mathilda shoved her shoulders back. 'Let's go, then.'

As they left the store, Robert slipped his hand into hers. 'Once you've found out what happened to Lady Isabel, if you do in the time you have, then you come home. Straight home. No hanging around to solve her murder if she's dead. Promise me, Mathilda.'

'I promise.'

14th January 1332

Eustace was pacing up and down in front of the fire. He was angry, which Mathilda knew meant he was restless and frustrated at having to wait for everyone else to prepare for the off.

Sitting next to Lord Thomas, Mathilda gave her favourite brother-in-law a grimacing smile as the hubbub of voices stilled in response to the bang of Eustace's palm against the hall table. He didn't waste time in getting to the point.

'Midnight has come and gone. My man Borin is an hour ahead of us. After years of waiting to avenge ourselves, the day to act against the scourge that is Sir Richard de Willoughby has come.' Eustace paced as he relayed the plan they'd heard before, one last time.

'Willoughby's court will leave Grantham after the noon bell today, or later if the matters of court take longer than planned. Borin's men have listened to the hearings so far, and it seems running over time is unlikely, for the justice is dispatching his verdicts with speed and a scant regard for the truth of any matter. All he is concerned with is acquiring as much land for himself as possible from the accused, whether they are guilty or not.'

Thomas grunted next to Mathilda. Eustace turned to the row of men lounging against the back wall of the hall, their expressions calculating and hungry. 'Lovet, Helewell, Baston, Maxeye, and Savage, you will travel to Waltham-on-the Wolds with me and my brothers, the Reverend Richard, Walter, and Laurence. We'll wait in the shelter of the woods and watch the road from Grantham for Willoughby's entourage. This, I'm assured, is small. Just the justice, three men-at-arms, and a clerk. He clearly believes his reputation will keep him safe from cutpurses and outlaws.'

There were murmurs of approval from the group as Eustace went on. 'Lovet and Helewell, as you have not encountered Willoughby before, you will hold up the group as if you're common outlaws. Walter and Laurence, you will provide protection for them from the cover of the trees   it is important you are not recognised. While you, Rector, will separate the justice from his party, execute the kidnap, and lead him towards your brothers.'

'You make it sound so easy, Eustace,' Richard de Folville sneered as he unfolded the hooded tunic he planned to wear to cover his face during the operation.

'And you will love very second of it, so don't play the troubled hero with me! Sarah, Daniel, and Ulric are to stay here. They will be joined by Lord Thomas, after he returns from accompanying Lady Mathilda and her party to Kesteven Forest. Once home, he will act as keeper of the manor and send out the lads as messengers as and when required.'

Eustace turned his attention to Mathilda. 'The minstrels will "accidentally" meet you near Melton, then, as a group you, Thomas, Adam, and Bettrys will wait within the forester's hut in the area of Kesteven known as Morkery Woods. That's where we will take the justice once we have him and deliver the seal ring to Mathilda.'

Thomas nodded. 'I know the one.'

'Meanwhile, Robert, you will travel alone to Leicester to inform Ingram of our status, before riding on to join me and our brothers. Keep to the depths of the woods and forests. You're to leave first, for your trip is longer.' Eustace stabbed the tip of his dagger into the hall table, 'Right then. Let's get going. The time for retribution is long overdue.'

~ *Chapter Twenty-five* ~

14th January 1332

Bettrys hadn't spoken for over an hour. Mathilda's heart went out to the girl as the horses moved from a trot to a canter, skirting the edge of woodland that lined the road. It was clear she still wasn't comfortable on a horse, and although she had been given a small pony, which was used to novice riders and long journeys, she was gripping both the reins and its mane for dear life.

Mathilda wondered if she was wishing that she and Daniel had had time for a private goodbye.

Glancing across at Adam, Mathilda noted his expression was as calm as ever, but she would have put money on his thoughts being with Sarah. In fact, she suspected they were all thinking the same thing. *Would everyone who went out this night come back, and would those at home in Ashby Folville, be there on their return?*

Although Robert had still wanted her to take Jep, as soon as he was gone, Mathilda had selected her palfrey to ride anyway. A minor rebellion - but she and her mount knew each other, and the comfort from the grey's presence felt reassuring as she glanced from left to right, peering into the gloom of the forest shadows. Each one might shield a desperate outlaw, a stag about to bolt, or a group of the king's foresters, determined to catch a night poacher and win praise from his lord. Or worse, there could be mercenaries hired by Willoughby lurking nearby. If they'd finished scouring Derbyshire, then it was only a matter of time before they headed into Leicestershire.

Gripping her reins tighter, Mathilda forced her mind to confront the task ahead. They'd been riding for almost two hours. Lord Eustace and his party of brothers and hired helpers had left just over an hour before them, travelling along a different road. At the last minute it had been decided that Walter and Laurence would travel separately, taking the middle path, but ultimately heading towards Eustace. If they rode a little apart, if something went wrong, they could act as messengers, one heading towards Mathilda's group, and one towards Robert to alert them of the change of plan.

Nothing will go wrong.

She repeated the words over and over to herself with each mile that separated them from Ashby Folville and took them into the unknown.

Maxeye would get the seal; he would bring it to her at Morkery Woods. Then she, Adam, and Bettrys would go to Wollaton. Meanwhile, their minstrel friends would go on to the inn, ready to offer assistance and company for the forward journey, and Lord Thomas would return to Ashby to care for her friends. After that it would all come down to just how convincing she could be. Would anyone at Wollaton believe that Lord Willoughby had had a sudden change of heart about his wife's well-being? She knew it wasn't in character for any official to part with his seal stamp unless his life depended on it.

The more she considered the issue, the less likely it seemed to be. But there had to be a way. There must be.

Thomas manoeuvred his horse closer to her as the track narrowed; he spoke softly, wary of how sound travelled in the dead of night. 'Are you alright?'

'Thinking about how to get through the doors at Wollaton. I'm not sure they'll believe me if I say Willoughby asked me to come.'

'If you make it sound like an order, then they'd believe it.'

'An order?'

'If you made it sound as if he'd given you no choice in the matter, then that would be in character. If you make Willoughby appear concerned for his wife, then you'll be subject to suspicion from the off.'

'And they'd never let me through the door, seal or not,' Mathilda muttered into the dark. 'I've been so concerned with how to act once I'm inside the manor that I forgot about being allowed in.'

'If they don't let you in, go to the inn as originally planned. Stay one night and then go home. No matter what. We'd rather have you safe and the plan fail, than...' Thomas paused, 'than the alternative.'

Mathilda glanced ahead to her maid, who was following so close to Adam's horse it was as if the beasts were roped together. Ducking as they rode beneath some low-hanging branches, Mathilda shuddered as cold drips of night frost trickled onto her gloved fingers, trailing up her sleeves and somehow finding a way to meet her skin despite the many layers she'd dressed in for the journey.

'An order.'

'Pardon?' Thomas whispered louder as their conversation became muffled by the denseness of the trees around them.

'Lord Willoughby, he could have ordered my husband

by which I mean Lord Ingram to put pressure on the current sheriff to look for his wife.'

'Why would he?'

'Because...' Mathilda thought fast as they negotiated another bend in the track, '...the king! He's the only one Willoughby would do this for. That's it!'

Bettrys turned towards her mistress, and Mathilda realised she'd been shouting. Hastily lowering her voice, she said, 'If King Edward had told Willoughby he is to be presented at court, and that Queen Philippa is keen to meet his wife...'

'Yes.' Thomas's expression broke into a beam. 'That would be believed. That would also explain why he'd given you his ring as proof you come from him. It might also buy you a little time after the kidnap. Although,' Thomas shook his head, spraying early dew from his hood as they rode, 'it doesn't explain why Lord Ingram sent you and not Sheriff Jort or one of his bailiffs.'

'Yes, it does. I'll say that Jort is concerned about the safety of Justice Willoughby, that he decreed all fighting men, including the former sheriff, to be detailed to protect him while on his court rounds. Ingram would have no choice but to send his wife and an entourage to represent him.'

'Without a single bailiff or '

'Adam.'

'Adam?' Thomas frowned.

'He could be one of Ingram's men. A steward now, but previously a trusted bailiff. Someone who Ingram has worked with before.'

'And therefore someone who'd be perfect for such a mission. Not too noisy, not obviously investigating. Someone subtle,' Thomas added. 'After all, Willoughby would want things to look as if he was concerned for his wife, but at the same time, not make a fuss or draw outside attention to the matter, especially if the disappearance really was of his own making.'

'It would also explain our interest in Lady Marjory when I visited Wollaton last time.' Feeling like a weight had been lifted from at least one of her shoulders, Mathilda concentrated on the track ahead, which was mercifully widening out again, the shadows to either side less menacing than they had been as the road into Melton Mowbray appeared in the distance before them.

The innkeeper at Melton Mowbray had been expecting them. Mathilda didn't ask how, but assumed Eustace had something to do with it. It was bliss to slide off her horse, even if only for a few minutes. While Adam found their beasts hay and water, she and Bettrys relieved themselves behind the inn as best they could.

As Mathilda flexed her legs, she led her tired maid inside and passed her a cup of warmed ale that had appeared from behind the bar, despite it being before dawn.

'Would you like to wait here until it's all over, Bettrys? I'd make sure you were cared for, although you might have to work to earn your stay.'

Rather than appear relieved, the girl looked as if she'd burst into tears. 'You think I'll let you down, my Lady?

Mathilda was stunned. 'Of course not, why ever would I think that of you?'

'What if I say the wrong thing? What if I call you Lady Folville by mistake, what if…?'

Reaching out a hand, Mathilda took the maid's palm in hers. 'You won't. I trust you, Bettrys. If I didn't I would not have invited you into my home, nor would you be here now.'

'Oh.' Her cheeks pinked into their usual state, bringing some much-needed colour to her pale, worried face.

'I know you're worried about Daniel. I would think it odd if you weren't.'

'We didn't even have the chance to say goodbye.' The words came out in an embarrassed rush; Bettrys aware with every syllable that maids and their mistresses didn't usually have conversations like this.

'I know, and I'm sorry.' She glanced across at Thomas, who was helping Adam with the horses. 'I didn't get to say a proper goodbye to my husband, but we'll see them again. Come on,' putting her beaker down, Mathilda started to walk towards the men, 'if we can find out what's happened to Lady Isabel, then we'll have played our part. Whatever happens, we'll know we tried our best and can hold our heads high. Consequences or no consequences.'

Downing the last of his ale as Adam finished checking their saddles, Thomas said, 'It seems the minstrels passed here not long before our arrival. They'll meet us on the road. They carry their instruments and possessions, so travel slower than us.'

Mathilda asked, 'Do you think your brothers are nearing their goal?'

'Assuming all is well, they'll be about halfway. Their journey is about an hour longer than ours, although the roads are clearer.'

'Right.' Mathilda allowed Adam to help her up into the saddle and adjusted her cloak so it fell around her legs, meaning as much of her was covered as possible.

'We could have several hours to wait once we reach Kesteven Forest.'

'I know, but at least we'd be there.'

'And not have to worry about not being in the wrong

place if everything happens earlier than planned, you mean?'

'You know your older brother; if Eustace has the chance to act sooner than expected, he'll take it.'

'I can't argue with that.' Thomas watched as Adam lifted Bettrys into the saddle and solicitously wrapped an extra blanket around her legs. He spoke so only Mathilda could hear, 'It's almost as if they're father and daughter.'

'That's how Sarah thinks of you all. Her boys, her children. They'd have made good parents if they'd met in their youth.'

Thomas smiled. 'And you, Mathilda, do you think you and Robert will make good parents?'

'I hope so.' A spark of hope flickered in her heart and then blew out. To even think about having a family when they were always only days away from either walking into a noose or outlawry for life was insane. They were Folvilles. How could they bring a child into that world? And yet…

'This will be over soon, and whether you are in Ashby Folville or an abandoned forester's hut in Kesteven Forest, I'm sure you'll have that family.' Thomas tucked a stray red hair into Mathilda's linen.

'And you'll teach our children the tales of Robyn Hode and show them how life ought to be.'

'Quite right.' Thomas kissed her hand. 'But first,' he sighed, 'the whole family will work on making the country a better place for when my future nephews and nieces are older. Are you ready?'

'Yes, my Lord.' Mathilda rounded her palfrey so it sat between Adam and Thomas, the hope that had become extinguished within her, daring to flame again.

~ *Chapter Twenty-six* ~

14th January 1332

Aldus and his friends had been waiting at the crossroads which took travellers either towards Nottingham or on to Lincoln. Although there was no one about to see, they'd been careful about the appearance of their loitering, acting as though Dicun's mount was potentially lame when the Folville party pulled up next to them.

Few words were exchanged between the two groups beyond offers of companionship on the road to Wollaton. As Mathilda listened to Thomas and the minstrels, she felt as if she was eavesdropping on the rehearsal of a play. And as the three balladeers fell in step behind them, she could see why they were so good at their jobs. If they hadn't been musicians, they could easily have been mummers.

With each passing mile, dawn steadily broke over the horizon, highlighting the silver silk of freshly spun cobwebs in the trees. The forest dew shone in the orange glow of a crisp new day. Thankful that there'd been no fresh snow, and that rain had held off, Mathilda flexed her numb fingers, trying hard not to think about Robert and if he was alright. She could hardly feel her hands as they gripped the leather reins. Forcing her mind to focus on the journey that lay ahead, not just to Morkery Woods, but the additional five-hour ride she faced to Wollaton Manor, Mathilda wondered how Eustace and his men were getting on. They'd be in place by now, surely if not they'd be close to the Grantham road. Then they'd have to wait. *But for how long?*

The sun was rising, but its weak rays did little to warm the air. Conversation, which had been muted and sparse, came to a complete halt for fear of alerting early risers to their presence. With Thomas in the lead, all six horses followed him as they ducked back off the main track, onto the narrow pathway that ran at the edge of the woods to their right. While they weren't hidden from view, Mathilda knew that, should danger come, they could disappear into the trees, and at least some of them would escape whoever was in pursuit. She didn't want to consider if they could escape any arrows that might be aimed at either them or their horses.

Stop it. You've seen no soldiers. There has been no hue and cry, no bailiff and his men. No force of arms of any sort has been seen since we left the manor. Willoughby's men are all still combing Derbyshire or are with him in Lincolnshire. Stop panicking and start thinking. They are all relying on you.

The words ran through Mathilda's head on a continuous loop. *They are all relying on you.*

The idea that Lady Isabel's testimony against her husband might make the difference between the Crown believing that the Folvilles were doing was for the good of the community, rather than personal gain or any ingrained criminal predilection, wouldn't shift from Mathilda's mind. Although the idea of presenting his official seal as a token of entry was a good one, she was uneasy about whether it would work. If Willoughby's son Richard was anything like his father, would he be willing to listen to her long enough to hear, let alone believe, that she'd been given the ring in the circumstances she was to claim?

If she could get Lady Marjory to trust her, Mathilda suspected she'd have a chance of at least discovering where her Ladyship was; but that depended on whether she was permitted to see Lady Marjory in the first place.

Just because I've stumbled across a few answers in the past.

The feeling that the mysteries she'd helped resolve in the past were more down to luck, and being in the right place at the right time, than any skill on her part, sent nausea swimming through Mathilda's stomach. The palms of her hands prickled within her gloves as she remembered Sarah's parting words. 'In the past you've found answers because you had to, because your life, or the life of others, depended on it. This is just the same. You'll succeed, as you have before, because you must.'

Leaning forward, Mathilda whispered into her horse's ear as she ruffled its mane. 'I will work out where Lady Isabel is. I will.'

Her horse whinnied in what she hoped was a positive response, as she considered the people with her. With the exception of Robert, her family in Twyford, and Sarah and Daniel at the manor, they were the most important people in her world. She'd do everything she could not to let them down; especially as they were risking their own safety by accompanying her on the journey through the fading night. Then she pictured Nicholas Coterel and his brothers, somewhere in Derbyshire, probably hungry and cold and definitely angry.

Turning her mind from the Coterels' flight, about which she could do nothing, Mathilda thought instead of Justice

Willoughby. Was he the Folvilles' prisoner yet?

The forester's hut, built as an occasional shelter for two men, was cramped with seven people inside. The minstrels, Bettrys, and Adam were all trying to keep a respectful distance from Thomas and Mathilda, but that meant them shivering by the broken doorway, which let in as much winter air as if they'd all sat on the frosted ground outside.

'Lord Thomas and I appreciate your deference, but please, come in properly and sit down.' Mathilda perched on the end of a rough pallet which clearly hadn't had its straw changed for months, if not a year.

'Lady Mathilda is right.' Thomas agreed. 'We should all rest as best we can. There is no knowing how long we'll be waiting before word arrives from Lord Eustace.'

Adam dipped his head in acknowledgement, but stayed next to the door. 'If you'll pardon me, my Lord, I think one of us should act as lookout and keep an eye on the horses. Seven mounts are not easy to conceal for long, even when the trees are as closely knitted together as they are in this part of Morkery Woods.'

'You're right.' Thomas got to his feet, ready to take first watch, but Adam stopped him.

'I'll do it, my Lord. With respect, you should rest while you can. Once this is done, you have a long ride home.'

Encouraging Bettrys to try and sleep as she curled into a pile of straw on the floor, Mathilda smiled at the minstrels, who'd sunk down onto the floor, resting their backs against the part-rotten walls. Their eyes shut as the rigours of riding through the night began to catch up with them.

Staring through a crack in the wooden wall, Mathilda watched as the day broke properly. Her whole body ached. She'd not had any sleep for over twenty-four hours and her fatigue, mixed with fear of what lay ahead and the jarring of riding for over five hours, was making its presence felt.

Thomas tapped her arm affectionately. 'Rest while you can. No need to talk. Save your energy for when you need it.'

Closing her eyes, Mathilda pictured herself back in her bed, with Robert, in Ashby Folville. They would get back there together. They would.

The shout that woke her sent Mathilda sitting bolt upright before consciousness had taken a firm hold. 'What was that?'

'Adam.'

Thomas was on his feet and out of the door, with the minstrels right behind him, before Mathilda had the chance to marvel at the fact she'd managed to sleep sitting up. Bettrys, her eyes unnaturally wide, pulled her cloak tighter around her as she shuffled into a sitting position. 'What's happening, my Lady?'

'I don't know.' Mathilda strained to listen, trying to work out how long she'd slept. 'We should wait here.'

A second later the door of the hut swung open on its damaged hinges and Aldus leant his head inside. Hs face was flushed and his voice breathless. 'Borin. He has the ring.'

Mathilda jumped to her feet. 'The justice is taken?'

'Just beyond Waltham-on-the-Wolds. They are bringing him here, moving from wood to wood. Lord Thomas is readying your horse. You must all leave. Now.'

Scrabbling up from the floor, Bettrys followed her mistress to where they'd hidden the horses. They arrived in time to see Borin's mount disappearing into the distance.

'He's gone already?' Mathilda marvelled at Eustace's

man's resilience. 'Didn't he want to rest?'

'No time.' Thomas lifted his sister-in-law into her saddle as he addressed everyone with haste. 'The justice is taken. According to Borin, he does not yet know who captured him, but he isn't a stupid man, and will work it out soon enough even if he has no proof.'

'The blindfold worked?'

'So far.' Thomas tightened the girth of Mathilda's saddle as he continued, 'Here's the seal. Maxeye,' he paused and spat on the ground, 'gave Lord Eustace this before pulling off Willoughby's other rings and disappearing into the night.'

'He ran off with the jewels just as we guessed he would?'

'He did.' Thomas growled, 'and I for one am not surprised. At least we know he won't turn us in, not if he intends to live off the proceeds of his theft.'

Mathilda turned the seal over in her fingers. It was smaller than she'd expected, but well made and clearly cut. The hollow, which would be filled with wax to make its mark, had a knight on a horse, wielding a sword, cut into it, with a tiny pair of scales beneath the horse's legs. There was no way it would be mistaken for anything other than what it was. The official seal of a Justice of England.

'You have very little time. Eustace is bringing Willoughby here; he'll demand a ransom only a few hours after that. Then they'll be a short delay before the money is found and the ransom is paid. It will take a day at least to move him safely, and possibly a night as well, but no longer.'

'Assuming the money can be found.' Adam didn't sound sure.

'Believe me, the ransom will be found very quickly. Willoughby is a rich man with a vast number of income sources, many of which he has no entitlement to in the strict letter of the law. There is no time to waste. You must leave for Wollaton now. Adam,' Thomas turned to his steward, 'I'm entrusting you with my brother's wife, and I in turn will do all I can to ensure Ashby Folville is safe and your wife protected.'

'Thank you, my Lord.' Adam bowed, 'Are you to stay and await Lord Eustace and his party?'

'I'll keep this place guarded and make sure no one compromises the hiding place until my brother arrives, and then I'll go back.'

'Alone, my Lord?' The steward was torn between offering to stay and going to Wollaton to guard Lady Mathilda.

'You're a good man, Adam, and I know what you're about to say, but I care more for my sister-in-law's safety than my own.' He switched his attention back to Mathilda. Lifting her hand, he kissed it. 'Do your best, Lady Mathilda, but if that doesn't include learning of Lady Isabel's fate, then we'll find another way to add evidence to our argument to convince the king of Willoughby's deceit.'

'Thank you, my Lord.' She lowered her head as she cupped the seal in her palm. 'Please stay safe.'

'Go now.' Thomas gave the palfrey a gentle push as the party of six walked back to the main road. A more respectable sight now they were travelling by day: a lady of the manor, her steward, a maid, and three minstrels who had kindly offered to ride as escort.

~ Chapter Twenty-seven ~

14th January 1332

Reaching the crossroads, they'd seen on their last visit to Wollaton, Mathilda, Bettrys and Adam reined in their horses next to the minstrels.

'Are you sure you don't want us to come up to the hall with you, Lady Mathilda?' Aldus circled his tired horse to face towards the town.

'You are very kind, but it would be good to know we have eyes and ears in the town. Not to mention friends within reach should we need them.'

Aldus spoke honestly. 'If we can't get work at the inn, I can't promise we can stay. There is only work for minstrels when they are wanted, and the fair here has passed for the season.'

Adam agreed. 'They do have a weekly market though. I don't think they have regular entertainers, perhaps you could gain permission to sing there?'

'Wouldn't permission have to come from the manor though?' Mathilda massaged her forehead. A headache had set in not long after they'd left Thomas, alone, behind them, with nothing to do but defend a tumbledown shack and wait.

'It would.' Aldus nodded. 'We'll try our luck at the inn.

If we are unsuccessful, we will endeavour to get word to you at the hall.'

Bettrys rubbed her tired eyes. 'Why can't you just come to the hall too? Surely they'll want entertainment?'

'Lord Willoughby is not kind to his minstrels.' Dicun stroked the bag strung across his mount's neck, which held his instrument

'But he isn't there.'

The minstrels exchanged glances before Aldus said, 'If we are unlucky at the inn, we'll try the hall, but I have to warn you, the chances of us being accepted are slim.'

Mathilda suffered a stab of guilt to think she'd been considering more or less forcing them to go to Wollaton Hall with her before their plans for entering the manor had been finalised. 'You go to the inn. Adam will keep you informed of our progress. I intend to be on my way again very soon. Tomorrow, hopefully.'

'But that won't be nearly enough time, will it, my Lady?' Aldus circled his restless horse.

'Probably not.' Mathilda, her heart thudding in her chest, turned her palfrey around to face the track that led to Wollaton Hall. 'Adam will come to the inn tomorrow morning to see if you've heard anything of interest.'

'Where did you get that cart from?'

Thomas could see that something, presumably the Lord Justice Richard de Willoughby, was wriggling beneath a number of blankets and old sacks.

Eustace and Robert drew their brother to one side after signalling Lovet, Helewell, and Savage to manoeuvre the cart to under the cover of the trees. 'My men are resourceful, Thomas, you know that.'

Having expected to see his brothers triumphant and

full of bravado, Thomas was concerned to see their drawn brows. 'Apart from Maxeye's flight, did all go to plan?'

'Almost,' Eustace watched the three men tuck the cart out of sight as he spoke, his voice hushed. 'Richard headed straight back to Teigh; as the man who manhandled Willoughby, it was wise to get rid of him as fast as possible, Walter and Laurence dealt with the two guards that travelled with Willoughby. The justice's clerk, however, got away.'

'Ah. So there's a chance word will get back to the authorities faster than expected.'

'Yes.' Eustace turned his attention to Robert. 'Your wife is the one who needs the extra time, it makes no difference to us, and to the Coterels the less time spent concluding this business the better. It is her I am uneasy for.'

Robert pictured Mathilda; was she still was trying to get into Wollaton? Had she arrived unhindered? 'My wife was in good spirits when she left here, Thomas?'

'Anxious but as determined as ever. She had the seal safe, and a sound plan to gain entry to the manor. I gauge she'll be there by now.' Thomas whispered as he stared at the cart. 'Did you send anyone in pursuit of the clerk?'

'Sort of.' Eustace shifted uneasily; Thomas could tell he was uncertain about the action they'd chosen to take on the spur of the moment. 'I sent Pykehose to follow him, but not to stop him.'

Knowing that Robert would be battling an urge to shout, ruing the loss of the clerk, Thomas asked, 'You instructed Pykehose to see where the clerk went and who he speaks to?'

'Precisely. He'll come here once he's found out the situation.'

'And if we're gone?'

'He's to go directly to Ashby Folville and report to you.

Talking of which, you should be on your way, Thomas.'

Walking towards his horse, Thomas asked, 'What news from Ingram, Robert? Had word reached Leicester of Willoughby's predicted next stop before you left?'

'It's to be Leicester itself. Although of course he won't be going there now; not for a while at least.'

Eustace snorted. 'Not at all, if he has any sense.'

Robert grimaced. 'He has no sense, but he does have greed and an overdeveloped desire for vengeance. Once Willoughby's free, this will continue until King Edward says stop. Be very wary in Ashby Folville, Thomas, the bailiffs and men-at-arms employed to arrest those suspected of helping the Coterels will still be operating, and they approach our home ground.'

Thomas's mount had only just disappeared through the trees when a sharp groan echoed through the late afternoon, coming from the direction of the cart.

Lovet and Helewell appeared through the trees, smug expressions on their faces.

'What was that noise? Where's Savage?' Robert strode forward with Eustace on his heels.

Roger Savage sat in the back of the cart, his weight centred firmly on top of the hidden justice. He was making a great play of shifting his position to try and get comfortable.

Eustace lunged, gripping Savage by the lapels of his cloak, hauling him bodily off the cart despite his six-foot frame, and dropping him against the hard forest floor. Kicking Savage sharply in the ribs, the older Folville pointedly glared from him to the hut, and back again, until the hired thug got the message and limped off to join his colleagues undercover.

Whispering, Robert worried, 'We should check he's not

hurt. Everything we've done will be a waste of time if Willoughby's been suffocated.'

Eustace moved behind the cart, so that, should his prisoner's blindfold have shifted in transit, he could instantly throw the covers over the man's face and so keep their anonymity. With Robert at his side, a dagger in his hand just in case, Eustace peeled back the covers.

As the fading daylight hit the justice's semi-covered face, he struggled. The curses which flew from his mouth were subdued by the sacking gag, but not contained.

Robert was filled with a sense of revulsion. Justice Willoughby was exactly as he remembered him from their unpleasant encounter in the months before he'd met Mathilda. A thick-set man in his prime, being no more than forty-two, if Robert judged correctly, and not of extraordinary height. Even the cloaking of his eyes couldn't disguise the avaricious curve of his mouth, and the contempt for his fellow man which lined his forehead.

Relieved to see their prisoner was breathing, Eustace quickly covered him back up, muffling the angry struggles and threats of reprisal beneath the layers that both hid him and stopped him dying of cold. Then, with a contemptuous grunt, they left him where he was, ensuring they were out of earshot before he spoke.

'Where did Walter and Laurence head to, do you know?' Robert moved away from the cart as he muttered, 'And Borin and his men?'

'Borin and his assistants are close. They're watching us and the forest. We'll see or hear from them if we need to. Walter has gone to report to Lord John in Huntingdon, while Laurence will be visiting Lady Joan. Her father is naturally keen to know how we've progressed.'

'Naturally.' Robert didn't add that, assuming Mathilda's

suspicions were correct, Lady Joan herself would probably be keen to know that her lover had survived so far.

A gruff rumble issued from Eustace's belly as they walked towards the hut, reminding him of how long it had been since Sarah's supplies had run out. 'I don't suppose you have any food left.'

'I wish I did.' Robert rubbed his belly. 'Would it be worth sending Lovet to the local church to ask for alms?'

'A churchman begging at a church.' Eustace savoured the irony. 'If only churchmen could be trusted to do more than they'd been paid for. No, we'd better sit tight for now.'

'How long before we send the ransom demand?'

Eustace pulled his dagger from his belt and toyed it between his fingers. 'Do you think Mathilda will be safely within Wollaton by now?'

'Thomas thought so. Assuming they didn't meet anyone unfriendly on the way. He said they left as soon as Borin delivered the seal.' Robert looked up at the sky. The winter's evening was already closing in. 'If Willoughby's clerk has alerted Sheriff Jort's deputy – assuming Jort remains out of the area or a bailiff about the abduction, we're already in trouble, and should send the ransom demand straight away.'

Eustace grunted under his breath. 'But if the clerk is too scared, or too sensible to have reported the attack, then we'll have longer.'

'I wish Pykehose would get here and tell us.'

'It's a long ride, and the man has been up as long as we have.'

'I know, but…' Robert ran a hand through his hair, ruffling it under the hood he wore. 'Mathilda's time to help us is short enough. If we could hold off making the demand for ransom just a little longer '

Eustace thumped the pallet Mathilda had sat on only

hours before. 'The demand will go out at dawn. It's a five-hour ride from here, four on a rested horse. Mathilda will have this evening, all night, and part of tomorrow. After that…'

'But she'll be exhausted, she'll need to sleep and…'

Eustace put his hand up to stem his brother's concern. 'Mathilda has to get inside the manor and gain their trust first, little brother. I'd be more worried about that, than how long she has once she's crossed Wollaton Hall's threshold, if I were you.'

Bettrys and Adam stood behind their mistress as they waited for the younger Richard de Willoughby to come and greet them.

They'd arrived in the courtyard just as the day had begun to merge into night, and while all courteousness had been granted to Mathilda when she'd introduced herself as Lady Ingram, she could feel the hostility radiating off the steward who'd rushed forward to meet them.

Trying not to fidget and relieved the groom she'd seen in Wollaton wasn't around, Mathilda pulled her shoulders back, reminding herself that she was there as the wife of a respected former sheriff of the shire.

As she waited, Mathilda battled to concentrate. She knew it was important to learn as much as they could as quickly as possible, in case they were denied a bed for the night.

Larger than Ashby Folville hall, Wollaton's main meeting point was focused around a central fireplace to the right-hand side. There was no one sat before it, but a female servant was bent to the hearth, sweeping soot spits from the floor and adding new logs to the fading crackle of flames.

Across the room, two regimented lines of oak tables and accompanying benches sat, running almost the full length of the hall. Beyond the fire, the hall was cold, and the draught that whistled down the stairs behind them, which led up to the entrance hall they'd been ushered through at speed, meant that anyone sitting at the end of the nearest bench would almost always be cold. Nearer the middle of the hall, some tapestries hung over the pale ancaster stone walls, providing an illusion of warmth.

Bettrys whispered, 'Where is everyone?'

'In their chambers perhaps.' Mathilda, who'd been expecting to see the remaining family eating their evening meal, said no more as the steward, his expression etched with displeasure, bustled through an arched doorway at the opposite end of the hall. He was following a far younger man of about nineteen, whose face showed caution rather than hostility.

Mathilda was already curtsying as Lord Willough-by-in-waiting reached her side. 'Forgive our interruption, my Lord.'

Richard bowed a curt response. 'Bennett tells me you're Lady Mathilda Ingram.'

'My Lord, may I introduce my steward, Adam, and my maid, Bettrys.'

Paying no regard to her companions, Richard focused firmly on Mathilda, 'You are welcome, but I'm afraid my father is not here. It is the Lord Justice you wanted an audience with?'

'In fact, I come from your father, my Lord, on a matter of some delicacy.' She glanced pointedly at the steward, who hovered close to the man's shoulder. 'He requested that I spoke to you in private.'

Richard's eyes narrowed. 'Forgive me, Lady Ingram, but I find that hard to believe. If my father wished to get word to me in private, he'd have sent a man; probably your husband himself.'

Having expected such a response, Mathilda agreed. 'In normal times that would have been his Lordship's prefer- ence, but Lord Ingram is very busy with Justice Lord Wil- loughby. He is helping with his mission to round up as many supporters of the Coterel family as possible.'

'That does make sense.' Richard turned to his steward. 'Bennett, arrange refreshment for Lady Ingram's servants in the kitchen. Then bring us some meat and wine. We will be in conversation by the fire. And inform Lady Marjory that we have female company.'

He turned to escort Mathilda towards the now raging blaze in the grate before adding, 'You'll stay the night, my Lady? The night already closes and as you'll know from your husband's work, the land is not safe once the darkness falls.'

Mathilda expressed her thanks as Bettrys and Adam were led towards the kitchen. Within the folds of her cloak, her fingers fiddled with the ring. Perhaps she wouldn't need to reveal she had it after all?

~ *Chapter Twenty-eight* ~

14th January 1332

Richard de Willoughby was not what Mathilda had been expecting. He wasn't much younger than she, and, unlike the picture that had been painted of his father, he was polite and lacked the air of impatience to get rid of her that she'd assumed he'd have. Whether that would remain the case when he learnt of her reason for being there was another matter.

The aroma of freshly cooked pork wafting off the platters a taciturn maid laid out before them was heavenly. It was all Mathilda could do not to pounce on the food after so long without any.

'This looks and smells delicious, my Lord. My thanks. Our journey has been long and our supplies ran out some time ago.'

'Then please, do eat.' He pushed a plate closer to his guest, smiling as hunger got the better of politeness, and she picked up a juicy morsel of meat. 'You mentioned a matter of delicacy concerning my father.' He stabbed a knifepoint into a piece of pork, 'I wonder, what could be so serious that he sends a former sheriff's wife to this door without so much as a token of his good intentions?'

'Oh but, my Lord,' Mathilda's hand came to her mouth

as she frantically chewed the piece of meat that had been dissolving in her mouth. 'Forgive me! In my haste to seek audience, and I have to say, my hunger, my propriety deserted me.'

Wiping her fingers, Mathilda produced the small velvet pouch she'd hung from her butterfly belt. 'Here, my Lord. I had it hidden for safe keeping. Your father gave me this as a gesture of his intent.'

Richard's forehead furrowed, knitting his black eyebrows together into a bat-like frown. 'I don't understand.'

'It is Lord Willoughby's, my Lord.'

'Indeed, it is. I'd know it everywhere.' Richard's voice grated with an abrupt fury that sent Mathilda shuffling back in her seat. 'He would never ever be parted from it.' A fist landed on the table, wobbling the goblets and causing a loose piece of pork to fall from the edge of the nearest platter.

'My Lord, I assure you…' Mathilda's mind raced. *The acorn didn't fall so far from the tree after all.*

'You can assure me all you like, woman!' He was on his feet now, holding the seal up the candlelight as if trying to find some way to prove it a fake.

'Please! My Lord Willoughby, will you let me speak? Let me explain how it is I come to have it. Time is against us, as I'm sure you'll appreciate. My man is to take the seal back to Lord Willoughby at first light. He'll need it at court, will he not?'

Richard froze for a second before lowering his arms and spinning on the balls of his feet to face her. His face instantly lost all traces of anger but for a faint glow of pink in his cheeks. Sitting back down, his gaze rested on Mathilda's clasped hands. A light of pleasure came into his eyes as he saw they were shaking.

A silent dread crept up Mathilda's spine as she watched the young master switch from calm to anger to calm again in less than a minute. *I wonder if we're chasing the right monster?*

Wanting to detract the unsettlingly open gaze of the man before her, wishing that Adam wasn't in the kitchen with Bettrys, Mathilda took a sip of her drink.

'Please explain how you came to have this seal, my Lady.'

'Lord Ingram,' She spoke faster as she saw Richard's brow begin to re-furrow, 'received word from the royal court, from King Edward, inviting many of the region's most trusted officials to London to be presented to himself and Queen Philippa.'

'An honour.' Richard picked up his cup and drank, without his eyes leaving Mathilda. 'My father will be delighted to attend.'

'He indicated as much to Lord Ingram, however, the invitation has raised a matter of concern which, in his dedication to duty, your father has not mentioned to the higher authorities. A matter which surely must concern you too, my Lord.'

'And what matter could possibly concern me beyond running Wollaton and its lands in my father's absence?

Mathilda gripped her hands together in her lap. 'Your mother's absence, my Lord.'

Having been careful to avoid the word 'disappearance,' Mathilda's body tensed as she waited for her host to erupt. Instead, he simply stared at her as though she was something increasingly unpleasant stuck to the sole of his boot.

'My mother is staying with her own mother, Lady Mortain. My father knows that.'

Hoping the panic that clutched at her chest didn't show

on her face, Mathilda kept talking. 'I regret to say that what your father told you was designed to keep you and your kin from worry. In truth, Lady Isabel's whereabouts are unknown, and her husband wishes to find her. Quickly, for Queen Philippa has specifically asked to meet the wife of her husband's most trusted Justice of the Peace.'

'The Queen has asked to meet my mother?'

Mentally sending up a prayer to Our Lady to help her and forgive her lie as an act of necessity, Mathilda nodded, 'Yes, my Lord. Your father bid me come here to help find her.'

'I do not believe that Father would conceal such a thing as my mother's disappearance from me.'

'From you, my Lord, no, but for the sake of your younger brothers and sisters perhaps? To save them worry? Would any father not adopt such a subterfuge to protect his children?' Hoping she was sounding plausible, Mathilda pressed on, 'I've been sent here to help you. A woman with connections to Lord Ingram is more likely, if you'll forgive me, to learn confidences from other women as to where Lady Isabel may have roamed, than an armed man.'

Whatever answer Willoughby had been about to give, it was halted on his tongue by the sound of a door being thrown open and footsteps running across the hall.

'Lady Marjory, how good to see you again.' Mathilda was on her feet, relief and a fresh wave of concern washing over her in a confused rush. She wasn't sure if she was closer to being believed, being thrown out, or worse, being removed to Wollaton's holding cell.

Almost tripping over her feet as she stopped to curtsey, Lady Marjory blinked as if unable to believe her supporter from Wollaton market was sat in the family home.

'Lady Ingram, an honour.'

'You know this woman, sister?'

'Of course. This is Lady Mathilda Ingram. She was so kind to me at the market when Anne and I were shopping for gifts before Christmas.'

It dawned on Mathilda that, until that moment, Master Richard hadn't believed her to be who she said she was. Privately thanking Our Lady for Marjory's timely arrival, Mathilda smiled at the new arrival. 'I trust you are well, my Lady.'

'As well as can be expected when one's mother is missing.' She took a seat next to their unexpected visitor, ignoring the grunt of disapproval from her brother. 'What brings you to Wollaton, Lady Ingram?'

'Your father has asked for help in locating your mother.'

'He has?' The colour drained from Marjory's face. 'Father said she was ill… mad; that she took bad after Hugh was sent into the cloister for his education. I didn't believe it when I saw you in the town, and I don't believe it still but Father was resolute. He said she'd gone to our grandmother for her own sake. Tell me, brother, was that a lie?'

Richard glared at his sister. He was clearly torn. Mathilda could feel him trying to decide if his sister was being honest with him about their guest, or if they were embroiled in some kind of mutual deception.

'Bennett!' The call for the steward was so loud and unexpected that both women started in their chairs. Seconds later, the steward was by his temporary master's side, his expression as unmoved as ever. 'Fetch Anne and Gilbert in here. Now.'

As Bennett strode from the room, Marjory, her voice wavering a little, asked, 'Why do you want them, my Lord?'

'They were with you in Wollaton, were they not? At a time when our father expressly forbade you to talk to anyone in case you unwittingly let slip his intentions for the court round ahead.'

Marjory paled further, and Mathilda felt compelled to speak on her behalf. 'My Lord, no word of your father's work was spoken. It was I who greeted Lady Marjory. I asked after your mother. I had no idea I was forcing your sister to break a promise in her obligation to be polite.'

'That's as may be, but, and I will be frank, you have nothing to prove that you are who you say you are. Anne and Gilbert can at least confirm that my sister has not sided with you as part of her ridiculous claim that Mother is not ill as Father said.'

'The news of Lady Isabel's supposed indisposition is widely known around the town. I am not one for gossip, but I am not deaf, and some voices are hard not to hear. As to me claiming to be other than I am, then perhaps you should call my steward, Adam, in here as well. He was also present in Wollaton and seen by Lady Marjory and her companions.'

With blotches of red on her cheeks, Lady Marjory rose to her feet as Anne hurried across the hall, followed by the slower clattering footfall of Gilbert's hobnailed boots. She hissed under her breath at her brother, 'How dare you treat a friend of Mother's as though she has ill intentions. Father would not be pleased, and rest assured I will tell him.' Marjory swung around to Mathilda, 'Forgive me, my Lady, you are welcome, despite my brother's actions to the contrary.'

Keen to calm the situation before it got out of control, Mathilda smiled at the girl and turned to Lord Richard. 'Perhaps we could begin again. I did meet your sister and her maid and groomsman in Wollaton before the winter solstice. The seal I gave you really does come from your father, and I am here to locate Lady Isabel.'

'What seal?' Marjory was on her feet in an instant, her

hands plastered to her hips. 'I think you should stop playing lord of the manor, Richard, and explain what's going on.'

Ignoring his sister, Willoughby turned to his servants. 'Do you know this woman? Speak.'

Anne nodded. 'Lady Ingram was kind enough to ask after Lady Isabel when we met her at the market in Wollaton.'

Gilbert grunted. 'She rode a fine palfrey. One you'd approve of, my Lord, with your love of horses. She had a man with her. Tall. Protective. I took him for a groom.'

'Indeed.' As Lord Richard flicked his hand at them in dismissal, Mathilda noted how relieved his servants looked at being sent away.

Remembering what she'd been told about Richard's memory for horseflesh, and wishing she'd had time to eat more of the meat that sat before her, knowing the twin perils of lack of sleep and hunger would dull her brain if she wasn't careful, Mathilda took a deep breath and tried again.

'Lord Willoughby, I am here as I stated. I have not lied to you. These are treacherous times, and I understand why you would feel the need to reassure yourself of my honesty. However, I have your father's seal. I am but a woman alone with two servants. How could I have got that seal without his consent? I was given it to show you as a symbol of trust. I'm unsure how else to convince you of my good intentions.'

~ *Chapter Twenty-nine* ~

15th January 1332

Bettrys looked pale and lost as a tight-lipped Anne ushered her into the chamber Richard de Willoughby had granted Mathilda for the night.

With a curt, 'Your maid, Lady Ingram,' Anne pointed towards a cot at the foot of a large wooden bed, and then shut the door behind her with an exaggerated bang.

Embracing Bettrys, Mathilda regarded the girl carefully. 'Are you hurt?'

'No, my Lady. No harm has come to Adam or me, but we're obviously not wanted here.'

'The same can be said for me. Although I have been treated courteously, their stunted level of good grace comes from duty alone.'

'We were treated with politeness in the kitchen, and we've been fed properly, but the atmosphere was brittle. There were four servants in there, including the cook, but no one spoke the entire time Adam and I were present. We were just sort of… watched.'

Mathilda hid her dismay. If they were going to be under constant surveillance and openly mistrusted, they'd never learn anything. 'Where is Adam? I need to speak with him urgently.'

'In the groom's lodgings above the stables. I don't think he's alone.' Bettrys yawned widely, 'Oh, I'm so sorry, my Lady!'

'You have no need to be sorry. We're all exhausted. Perhaps I'll talk to Adam in the morning, or should I say later today, for it has passed midnight already. Come on,' Mathilda pointed to the bed, 'share with me. It'll be warmer for both of us and although time is short, if we don't have some rest we'll lose the ability to reason.'

Bettrys blushed. 'Are you sure, my Lady?'

'Of course, you're my maid doing her duty by keeping healthy so you can look after me. A freezing, tired maid is of no use at all.' Mathilda grinned as she pulled back the sheets; they were icy to the touch.

'They could have at least put a fire in the grate for you.' Bettrys tutted in a manner that revealed how much time she had spent with Sarah. 'I'll see what I can do.'

Ten minutes later, both bundled in all their clothes, tucked under the meagre supply of blankets, the two women watched the tiny fire Bettrys had managed to get started with the few twigs of kindling on hand. The maid yawned again. 'Why did you want to talk to Adam, my Lady, if I may ask?'

Stifling a yawn of her own, Mathilda decided not to tell Bettrys she was going to have to send their male companion away until after she'd slept. 'Nothing that can't wait until dawn.'

Mathilda awoke with a start. Her head pounded as she sat up too quickly. She'd planned to allow herself three hours sleep, so she could make a good start on the day ahead, but immediately she knew she'd slept for longer.

Bettrys was still asleep as Mathilda crept from the covers, pulling her travelling cloak around her shoulders. Now she was seeing the chamber in the day, although the light was dim, she could tell they'd been housed in a low-status guest room although not as spartan as the one she'd locked Maxeye in at home.

Stoking the fire until a flame licked through the remaining fragments of wood, Mathilda wondered where to start. She had to get the seal to Adam, which meant she had to get it back from Richard, who'd hung on to it so tightly that she'd feared it would break in his grasp. She'd last seen it slip into the folds of his tunic.

'My Lady!' Bettrys abruptly jumped from the bed, 'you should have woken me, I'm so sorry. I meant to have a blaze going and have taken a trip to the kitchen for food before you stirred.'

'You are kind, but I think we'll both go to the kitchen. They'll be less dismissive of you if I'm there.'

Bettrys hesitated. 'Should you go into the kitchen, my Lady?'

'It won't be expected of me, but if we are to learn what happened to Lady Willoughby, then we need to go against what's expected.'

Bennett, his countenance troubled, strode across the hall as Mathilda and Bettrys descended the stairs. As soon as he saw them, the steward stopped and gave a brief bow. 'An early start, Lady Ingram?'

'I have much to do before I can leave Wollaton.'

'I have a message from Lord Willoughby the younger.'

'Indeed?'

'He asked me to convey his apologises for his absence. He has gone to Mortain House to find Lady Isabel, and has taken his brother, Lord Edmund, with him.'

Mathilda felt a prickle of relief that she wouldn't have to contend with Richard that morning. 'He has gone to see if his mother resides with his grandmother?'

Bennett didn't answer, but merely gestured to the table by the fire. 'The Ladies Marjory and Joan will rise to break their fast soon. If you would like to sit down, I'll inform the servants to bring you some food.'

Deciding this was too good an opportunity to miss, Mathilda inclined her head. 'You are most kind, Bennett. I thank you. Perhaps Bettrys here could be of assistance to you by helping in the kitchen.'

'You imagine a long stay, my Lady?' His brow furrowed further.

'I've been asked to find Lady Isabel. Lord Willoughby the younger has helped greatly by investigating the possibility that she has gone to her mother's home after all.' Mathilda took a seat by the fire, 'I hope to be gone before the end of today.' She saw Bennett sag with relief, before adding, 'I need to speak to my steward. Could you ask him to come here, please?'

'Certainly, my Lady.' Bennett's displeasure at being given an instruction by a stranger was etched on his face. He hesitated, as if deciding whether to carry out his master's next command or not. 'His Lordship bid me give you this.' Opening his palm, Bennett held up the seal. 'Your man is to take it back to Sir Richard right away. He'll need it at the next court session.'

Turning on his heels, Bennett had almost reached the far side of the hall, when he spun around and glared at Bettrys, 'Come on, girl, you can fetch your mistress' breakfast.'

'It's time. We can't wait any longer.'

Robert wished Eustace wasn't right, but they'd done well to keep their captive hidden for so long without discovery. Delaying any longer before demanding the ransom would be foolish.

'I don't understand why there haven't been any forester patrols since we set off. It's reasonable that we should've evaded some, but to see no officials, not a single soldier, since we left Ashby Folville? It's unsettling.' Robert got to his feet to stamp some warmth into his feet.

'Ingram.'

'Sorry?'

Eustace gestured around the thickset wood. 'I asked him if he could ensure our path was cleared.'

'That man is so useful. It's a shame he isn't still sheriff.'

'True, but as Jort is next to useless, and hardly ever in the county he runs, then Ingram is still looked to on many matters. But we can't ask too much of him, Robert, and there is little chance he can delay any patrol of this area for another whole day.'

Robert nodded, 'Should we move Willoughby?'

'We should. We'll take a circuit from wood to wood, navigating the forest before returning here. The hut will be a good point of exchange for the ransom money.'

'Who will you send?' Robert gestured to the hut where Savage, Lovet, and Helewell were asleep. 'I don't trust any of them to bring the money back once they have it.'

'Nor I.' Eustace pulled a roll of parchment from the folds of his cloak. 'So I'm going to ask them to deliver this instead.'

Robert unfolded the document and began to read. 'This was what was agreed with the Coterels?'

'Yes, a ransom of 1300 marks, of which we'll get a portion for our trouble; the rest will go to paying off the men and to help the Coterels pay their way under cover.'

'It's a great deal of money to most, but not to Willough-by. Should we have asked for more?'

'I was tempted, but we need this to be over as quickly as possible, and for that the ransom has to be paid with money that's readily available.'

Robert murmured his agreement as he read on. 'It says the money is to be delivered here by a trusted envoy, with the threat of Willoughby's death if force of arms accompanies him.'

'Yes.'

'Will you follow that threat through? It is unlikely the money will come unguarded. The chances of Willoughby's sons not trying to lay some sort of trap are slim.'

'I know. Why do you think I have men shadowing us?'

Robert's grin lacked humour. 'Of course, brother, of course.'

Eustace got up, his belly growling. 'We'll send Lovet and Helewell with the ransom demand, and Savage can find us some food. If he gets caught in the act I don't care, and although he has many faults, he's not stupid enough to tell anyone we're here.

Mathilda stared at the seal. Turning it this way and that in the firelight, she ran a fingertip over its carefully carved lines. The red clay had been beautifully fashioned. It was exquisite. She stared into the heat of the flames. It was too perfect. The seal she'd held yesterday had tiny residues of wax stuck to it, a sure sign of recent use. This one was spotless.

'Perhaps Bennett washed it.' She muttered under her breath, glad she'd yet to be joined by the Willoughby children.

A lump came to her throat as she saw a list of possibilities line up in her head, each as worrying as the next.

If this wasn't the real seal, if Lord Willoughby had two in case he broke one, then were Lords Richard and Edmund on their way, not to Mortain as claimed, but to their father to deliver the real seal to him? If so, they were bound to ask about the fake invitation from the Crown.

Or were Willoughby's heirs outside of Wollaton Hall right now; with armed guards, waiting for Adam to appear, so they could follow him to see who truly sent them to Wollaton Hall? Worse, would they waste no time, and kill Adam as soon as he set foot beyond Wollaton's boundary?

Nausea swam in Mathilda's stomach as the image of a grieving Sarah arrived in her head and refused to leave. If she sent Adam away now, it could kill him. Plus, if she didn't send him into Wollaton as planned, then the minstrels who'd been expecting Adam to visit them at the inn that morning, assuming they'd found accommodation there, would worry and come to the hall. Mathilda couldn't decide if that would be a good thing or not. The friendship of Aldus, Noll, and Dicun suddenly felt much needed, as did one of their Robyn Hode songs to keep her going.

'What would Robyn Hode do?'

'Probably something reckless and deal with the consequences later, my Lady.' Adam smiled as he arrived at Mathilda's side. 'Bennett said you wanted to see me.' Checking over his shoulder to make sure no one was listening, he mumbled, 'Should I go to the inn?'

'I don't think it's safe for that now.'

'My Lady?' Adam picked up the jug of small ale from the table and poured his mistress a drink while Mathilda explained about the seal and her suspicions about Willoughby the younger.

'Can I see it?'

Mathilda handed it over, muttering, 'Be quick, I'm expecting Willoughby's daughters to join me any minute.'

As she spoke, Bettrys reappeared from the back of the hall with a platter of food in her hands.

'You're right, this isn't the same seal.' There was no doubt in Adam's voice, and Mathilda's vestige of hope, that she'd been mistaken, evaporated.

'So, my Lady, what do we do now?'

'Something reckless, of course.'

~ *Chapter Thirty* ~

15th January 1332

Bettrys curtsied as Lady Marjory and a younger girl came into the hall.

Mathilda rose to her feet. 'Lady Marjory, my thanks for your family's hospitality.'

'I feel the thanks should be ours, Lady Ingram.' Marjory was beaming at Mathilda as if she was her saviour, 'May I present my younger sister, Lady Joan.'

Curtsying shyly, Joan stayed behind her sister, her petite frame and neat dark features echoes of her older sister.

'Lady Joan will join us for some food, and then Anne is to accompany her as far as Wollaton to exercise her pony. Apparently, the animal was a gift from Mother.'

'Was it?' Mathilda instantly regretted sounding so surprised.

'You are as amazed by this news as I was.' Marjory looked thoughtful, 'Perhaps we can speak on the matter as soon as we've eaten.'

Mathilda nodded, understanding that her hostess did not want to talk of her fears in front of her sister. 'Would you like Adam to accompany Anne and Lady Joan to Wollaton? An extra guard at this time would be wise, perhaps?'

Shrewdly regarding her visitor, Marjory spoke slowly, 'A good idea my Lady. I thank you for your forward thinking.'

Bettrys, who'd been waiting at her mistress's elbow, gave a silent nod and went to tell Adam that he was to go to Wollaton after all, hopefully in company that would ensure no harm would come to him.

'It will already have been noted that Willoughby has not arrived to hear his court in Leicester as planned this morning. It may even have been noted last night.' Eustace stared at Lovet and Helewell, who appeared equally serious as they awaited their instructions a few metres from their prisoner's cart.

'You will travel together to Wollaton Hall. On arrival you will deliver this message into the hands of the groom in the courtyard. Then leave. You will not wait for a response. Take separate routes to wherever it is you intend to go once you leave.'

'And our payment, Lord Folville?' Helewell lifted his hood over his greying hair as he took the parchment, stowing it into the folds of his cloak.

'It will be made one week from today. The innkeeper at Melton will either have the money itself or instructions for you on how to get to it, depending on the outcome of the next few days.'

Lovet opened his mouth, but Helewell nudged him sharply in the ribs, as if anticipating what he was about to ask. 'Lord Eustace has a reputation for honouring his word, if he says he'll have the money ready, then he will. Whatever the outcome.'

'Well said, cleric.' Eustace's countenance clouded as he regarded Lovet. 'Leave now. Stay safe.'

The men rounded on their heels. Unhooking their horses' bridles from the tree where they'd been tethered, they mounted and disappeared into the depths of the forest without another word.

Eustace could feel the weight of the words Robert hadn't spoken as they stared at the space where Lovet and Helewell had been. 'You wanted to ask them to get word of your wife.'

'Wouldn't you?'

'Possibly.'

The lack of an emphatic 'no' from Eustace surprised Robert, as his eyes landed on the cart containing Willoughby. It was quiet. There was no movement from the pile of covers. He wondered if the justice was asleep. Exhaustion must have overtaken his anger by now. But would it overtake his fear?

'We should move him.'

As Eustace went to fetch the horses, Robert heard a noise. Grabbing his brother, he pulled him back into the hut. Neither of them spoke as they waited, but both had their right hands on the hilts of their swords.

The sound was slight, as if someone was trying hard not to be heard, but failing. Eustace whispered, 'Whoever approaches can't be a threat, or Borin would have acted already.'

Ten seconds later they let out a communal sigh of relief. Eustace dived from the hut and grabbed Roger Savage by the throat.

'What the hell are you doing, man? You were making enough noise to summon the dead!'

Savage hiccupped, belching an ale-stench burp into Eustace's face, causing him to be dropped to the ground.

'Drunk!' Robert kicked the outlaw hard. 'Did you bring

anything for us, or have you eaten and drunk everything you stole?'

Savage grunted and pulled a loaf of bread and some bruised apples from his pack. 'Unguarded food store. Foolish people.'

As the outlaw swayed, Robert snatched the food, throwing an apple at Eustace. 'What the hell are we going to do with him? We can't leave him here. He'll spill his guts to the first person who asks what he's doing here.'

Heartily tempted to knock Savage permanently into the next world, Eustace growled, 'Throw him into the cart on top of Willoughby. I bet he'll be asleep before we get very far.'

Biting into his apple, Robert grunted. 'At least we have food.'

The conversation had stayed safely at the level of polite enquiries as to life at Wollaton until Anne had fetched Lady Joan to get ready for her outing. Now, as she sat with Mathilda, Lady Marjory played absentmindedly with her bread. Crumbs dotted the platter and hopped across the oak table. 'Are you really here to find my mother? Is that true?'

Hating lying to the earnest hopeful face before her, Mathilda knew at least this question could be replied to honestly. 'That is my intention. I can't promise I will succeed, for I must leave here this afternoon, or my husband will become concerned for my safety.'

'You are lucky to be wed to someone who cares, or even notices you exist, I fear that my father...' As if remembering her place, Lady Marjory stopped abruptly and sat up straight. 'It was kind of you to offer Adam as an extra escort to my sister.'

'It is the least I can do to show my thanks for your hospitality. When they return however, I must ask Adam to de-liver your father's seal to him. His court business cannot be concluded without his official stamp.'

For the briefest moment, Marjory looked as if she might cry, but then she pulled herself together. 'Then I must help you. The sooner we start searching for my mother, the bet-ter. I don't believe for a single second that she is ill. I told you before about their argument, did I not?

'You mentioned it.'

The girl leaned forward, her expression resolute. 'It can-not be a co-incidence that she disappeared only a day after that, can it?

'I don't know, but we can't discount it.' Mathilda rubbed her head. 'I am trying to think as my husband would in these matters.'

The words Mathilda had spoken were truth, but Marjory immediately said, 'You must learn so much being wed to a sheriff. And see so much.'

'Indeed.' Mathilda, conscious of the lack of time, prompted, 'The argument?'

'It was outside Mother's chamber. I do not know what had happened before they came out. They did not know I was there.' She sighed, 'Father was already shouting, but he often shouts, and I confess I took no notice. It makes me sad to hear him rail at Mother so. This time it was different though, because Mother argued back.'

'Perhaps something in her patience broke. Have they been married long?'

'Twenty-two years.'

'A lengthy time for so many one-sided arguments.' Mathilda was thankful her husband was not the kind of man she was afraid to argue with. 'I wonder why Lady Isabel spoke out that day of all days?'

'It would have been something to do with the Folvilles, I expect. It always seems to be their fault. In Father's eyes anyway.'

A cold chill froze Mathilda's spine. She averted her eyes to the fire, hoping the dance of the flames might calm her and keep her voice level. 'The Folvilles? Unless I'm mistaken, it is the Coterel brothers from Derbyshire he seeks so earnestly. Gossip on the matter is rife throughout the shire. I try not to listen, but it is hard to evade it when one's husband is so embroiled in the law of the land.'

Marjory took a nibble of her bread. 'Perhaps your man, Adam, will hear something about Mother while he is out in Wollaton.' She looked shyly up at Mathilda. 'That was your intention, was it not?'

'It was.' Mathilda hastily added, 'Although I would have offered his services anyway.'

'Of course.' Marjory shuffled her chair a little closer to her companion, her voice low. 'The argument was about where Father would be without Mother. I got the impression that he'd said something about wishing he'd never met her that set things off but I have no proof of that.'

'Can you remember what was said exactly?'

'Mother's voice sounded wrong. It wasn't louder than usual, but it was firm. Hard almost, as if every word was being deliberately bitten off so Father couldn't mistake her meaning.' She took a sip of her drink. 'If it hadn't been, I doubt I'd have taken any notice, but would have gone back into my chamber until the storm had died down. That's always the best thing to do when Father is angry. Keep your distance until the rage has passed.'

Mathilda smiled encouragingly as Lady Marjory went on, 'Mother said that he only had his lands because of her. Then she paused, and changed what she'd said, by saying, "No, you only have legally acquired lands from me, everything else you took wrongly."'

'That's what Lady Isabel said? Word for word?'

'Yes.' Lady Marjory blushed, 'I know I shouldn't have listened, but I knew something was wrong. I just felt it. Do you understand what I mean?'

'Very well indeed.' Mathilda was thinking fast now. 'You mentioned the Folvilles. Your father hates them because he thinks they murdered his friend, Roger Belers?'

The young Lady Willoughby was surprised, 'Yes, how did you…'

'I hear many things from my husband.' Swallowing, Mathilda went on, 'So why is he hunting the Coterels as he travels on his court, and not the family of men he regards as felons so much closer to home?'

'I think Father targeted the Coterels precisely because they live far away from here, and he knows the Folvilles are associated with them. Maybe he wants to hurt their friends as they hurt his.'

Saying nothing, Mathilda saw the logic in this.

'As you said, my Lady, the Folvilles are closer to home.' Marjory blushed, 'I am ashamed to say, on top of all his other faults, my father is a coward. He is afraid of them.'

'There are many who would say he is wise to be wary of that family. Lord Willoughby has, I am afraid to tell you, a reputation for not being the most law-abiding of officials. What I know of the Folville brothers tells me they would not like that. They will see a man of the law who breaks it to improve his own position.'

Marjory blanched, but she did not deny the statement. 'I have always ignored the rumours, dismissed them as jealousy from those who do not have our wealth or comfort, but now…'

The words "something reckless" echoed through Mathilda's mind as the minutes of the day draining away. 'You said you'd like to help me. Are you sure, my Lady?'

'Yes. I want to find my mother.'

'But on the way you may find out things about Lord Willoughby that you don't like. He is, whatever he may or may not have done, still your father.'

Lady Marjory sat as if in a trance. When she finally spoke, her voice was quiet but earnest. 'As you heard earlier, my sister was gifted a horse. Small and grey and perfect for her. It arrived the day after I questioned my mother's disappearance. Before I had summoned my courage to ask of her, there had been no word nothing had happened.'

'Yet the minute you questioned Lady Isabel's welfare, a present for your sister appears out of nowhere.'

'Yes.' Marjory pushed her plate away, her bread in tatters, but largely uneaten.

'Were there gifts for you, Richard, and Edmund?'

'There were not, but it wasn't yet Christmas, and so…'

'So that wouldn't have been so strange. A pony cannot be hidden until the day. When Christmas came, were there gifts for the rest of you from your mother?'

'There were not.'

'I will be bold, Lady Marjory, because time is short. I only ask that you forgive me if I offend you. I do not believe your mother to have gone to visit Lady Mortain. Nor do I think your brothers have gone to Lincolnshire to find her there. I think your father gave Joan the pony to delay an investigation he wasn't ready for. Something is wrong here, and I have promised my husband I will find out what.'

'So that Mother can be found and presented to the queen?'

'So that your mother can be found.' Mathilda got to her

feet. 'Come, we will fetch my maid and go to Lady Isabel's chamber.'

'It's kept locked.'

'Then we must persuade Bennett to unlock it.'

'He'll never agree. Father has Bennett well trained.' Lady Marjory trailed in Mathilda's wake. 'And he rules the servants here with a firm hand. No one would ever disobey him.'

'I will ask him politely. I'm sure he'll agree to help us.'

'But he'll tell Father when he gets back and then…'

'Are you afraid of your father, Lady Marjory, does he beat you?'

Her face crimson with embarrassment, the young woman mumbled, 'He makes Anne do it, and she is too afraid of him not to obey, although,' the young woman rubbed her arm as if in memory of past scoldings, 'she is gentler than she's meant to be. She always uses her hand and not the belt as instructed.'

'I see.' Mathilda hated Lord Willoughby more by the second.

~ *Chapter Thirty-one* ~

15th January 1332

Adam took Lady Joan's pony by the bridle and led it to the inn. He'd always marvelled at Lady Mathilda's ability to manoeuvre a situation to her advantage. As he headed towards the stables, having promised Anne he would groom and feed the beast while she and Joan enjoyed the market, he kept his eyes sharp and his ears open for any information his mistress might appreciate.

The journey from Wollaton Hall to the town had been uneventful. The small party looked precisely what it was; a young noblewoman and her maid with a groom and guard, out for a walk. Gilbert had remained as taciturn as ever, but Adam was glad of his presence. Not only was it less likely that the young Lord Willoughby would stage any sort of attack against him while in Lady Joan's presence, but should his master appear, Gilbert would be able to speak honestly about Adam's good behaviour.

There'd been no need to think of a ruse to go into the inn itself in search of the minstrels, for no sooner had Adam secured temporary shelter for the pony, named Heart, than Aldus dropped down from the hayloft.

'A sharp night for sleeping in the hayloft.'

Responding with an equal lack of familiarity, Aldus said, 'It was warm beneath the straw. My fellows and I were grateful of the shelter. Where we'll bed tonight is less certain. We may well be out in the open.'

Understanding this to mean that they had been turned down as entertainers at the inn, Adam took a brush from a nearby crate to groom Heart. 'These are harsh nights for travellers. You have fellows with you? Are you pedlars?'

'Some call us such, but music is our trade.'

'Minstrels? Where are you headed next?' Adam kept his eyes on the pony.

'We thought to try Leicester. There's often a welcome for a ballad or two around a fire in that city.'

Dicun and Noll jumped down from the hayloft, their instruments bundled safely in their arms, as Adam said, 'Perhaps I may offer your services to my mistress. She dwells at Wollaton Hall for the day, but later we journey to Leicestershire. I'm sure her husband would be glad of an enlarged company for her to travel with. The nights draw in so early, and you can never tell who lurks in the shadows.'

Aldus inclined his head. 'A kind offer. Would you truly request this of your mistress?'

'I will.' Adam laid down the brush and placed a pail of water by Heart's head. 'I have errands to run now, but if you come to Wollaton Hall for noon, I will have an answer for you. Who knows, they may even have a place for you there.'

Aldus bowed. 'Your kindness is appreciated.'

Adam smiled, and went to take his leave; as he did so, he leant into Aldus and whispered, 'Willoughby the younger is in the area, he claims to be hunting for his mother, but we think this is a lie. Go careful.'

Checking that no one was in earshot, Aldus replied, 'Rumours of Lady Isabel's madness have been replaced by those of her disappearance. The inn's scandalmongers cry murder.'

'Do they indeed?' Adam laid down the brush and made ready to return to Lady Joan and Anne. 'I will see you later, gentlemen.'

Lady Joan was grinning as she watched the fish swimming in the town's pond. They flashed beneath the thin layer of ice, occasionally nudging at the clear barrier that blocked them from the outside world.

Beckoning to Anne, hoping she'd listen to him, Adam muttered quietly. 'I've just heard tell that Lady Isabel is the subject of gossip you may not wish your young charge to hear.'

Anne gave a haughty sniff. 'We are used to harsh words against the family, steward. It's jealousy from the less fortunate. They'll suffer for such judgements when God calls them to him.'

'Are you used to people claiming your mistress has been murdered?'

Colouring crimson, Anne glared. 'You are mistaken. Or you have been told to say that to me by Lady Ingram. She brings trouble, I know she does, she '

Adam grabbed Anne's arm, which was flailing in her angst, drawing attention to their party. 'My mistress is good to the core. As I am sure yours is. Our masters have their own paths. Lady Ingram is afraid for Lady Isabel, but this rumour is new to us. Should we not return to the hall before such comments reach Lady Joan's ears?'

In a flurry of concern, her duty overcoming her indignation that she should be spoken to in such a way by an outsider, Anne agreed. 'Perhaps you could fetch Heart for us. We will wait here. I will tell Lady Joan that there is fever in the town, and we are concerned for her health.'

'I've news of the clerk, my Lord.' John Pykehose dropped down next to Eustace, his breath shallow and his face ruddy.

'He has reported Willoughby's kidnap?'

'Yes, my Lord.' The groomsman sat on the ground, glad to let Robert take his horse from him in an unusual reversal of roles. 'The clerk didn't delay, but rode straight to the sheriff.'

Eustace's lips curved upwards. 'The sheriff? Which sheriff?'

Pykehose laughed into the bread his master had passed him, 'Well, although Sheriff Jort has left some instructions concerning the rounding up of felons on Willoughby's behalf, he is out of the county again. The clerk had no choice but to defer to his deputy, who, uncertain what to do, deferred sideways to the former sheriff, my Lord.'

'Ingram?' Robert couldn't believe their luck. 'Are you sure, Pykehose? That seems rather convenient.'

'What would you have done in his shoes, Robert?' Eustace looked smug, 'He's a clerk, no power but to get blamed for everything his master decides is his fault. Wouldn't you go to the nearest authority, and if he wasn't there, then the next best thing? Our luck has only come through the combined good sense and ineptitude of Jort's choice of deputy.'

'It won't make much difference in the end,' Robert dropped his hood for a moment, 'but it will give us a few more hours before the hue and cry gets this far.'

Pykehose grunted. 'The authorities know the justice has been taken though, my Lords. The word is wide already. More men are being mustered. The foresters have been called to Leicester. Ingram had no choice. He must be seen to be doing something.'

Eustace grunted in begrudging agreement. 'He must. His loyalty to the law must not be questioned.'

Robert, his gaze firmly on the cart, asked, 'Does rumour say who took him?'

'Outlaws, my Lord.'

Robert and Eustace exchanged glances, before Robert spoke, 'Well, they're mostly wrong about that. At least, wrong for now.' From the cart, Savage could be heard snoring off his drink, and underneath that pig-like sound came the occasional faint groan of the justice below him. 'How did you find us, John?'

'I'm good at my job, my Lord.' Pykehose looked affronted, but Eustace laughed.

'You are, John. And now I must ask you to prove that to me once again.'

'Lord Folville?'

'Go back to Ashby Folville. Let them know we are well. Stay the night, and then return here, to the Morkery Woods. We will need you to help take the divided ransom money to where it's needed.'

'I have my orders, Lady Marjory.' Bennett was torn between outright refusal, and knowing that, for now at least, Lady Marjory was the senior Willoughby present.

'And Lady Mathilda has her orders, and they come, in a roundabout way, from the king himself!'

'My Lady?'

It was a masterstroke. Mathilda could only admire how the young woman got her way.

'Lady Mathilda is here, as you well know, because King Edward has requested both Father and Mother to attend him in London. For that, Father needs Mother found. It appears,' Marjory paused, and Mathilda wondered if the words she spoke were beginning to hit home, 'that Lord Willoughby only pretended Mother was with Lady Mortain to save us worry. In truth, her whereabouts are unknown. Lady Ingram is here to help us find her. So stop obstructing her, Bennett, and fetch the key to Mother's private chamber!'

With a reluctance which seemed to come from sorrow rather than defiance, Bennett produced a key from his belt.

'You had it with you all the time?' Lady Marjory frowned.

Bennett walked towards the room in question, the two women on his heels. As he slid the key into the lock, he turned to Lady Marjory, 'I'm sorry, my Lady. I didn't know what to do. Your father instructed me not to come in here. I did though. I came in the night Lord Willoughby told me Lady Isabel was going away for a while.'

Marjory was stunned. 'You disobeyed my father?'

'The only time I have done so. This,' he gestured to the key in the lock, 'will be the second time in all my years of service.'

Mathilda sensed that they might have an ally in Bennett after all. 'What made you come in here the night Lady Isabel went away?'

'I can't truly say. Perhaps it was the hour of night. Lord Willoughby returned late, saying he'd taken his wife to Lincolnshire, to Lady Mortain.'

'But?'

'He hadn't been gone long enough. He must have sensed my unease, for his Lordship quickly added that he'd passed his wife into the care of trusted friends.'

'You didn't believe him.' It wasn't a question. Lady Marjory stared at the thick wooden door before her as if at once eager to go inside and terrified to do so.

'I did not.' Bennett clicked the key and put his hand on the door. 'Twenty-three years I have been in your father's service. I was his servant before he married Lady Isabel and rose to the role of steward fifteen years past. In that time, I have come to know him. I know when he lies. He knows this and trusts me to remain loyal despite of that.'

'But you are fond of Lady Isabel.' Mathilda saw something in the steward's eyes she hadn't expected. A flash of emotion that could have been love. Controlled, held back, but there nonetheless.

'She is the best of women. A gentle soul. Like her daughters.'

Marjory gasped in surprise at hearing her father's man talk in such a way. 'I ask your forgiveness, Bennett. I fear I've misjudged you.'

'No forgiveness needs seeking, my Lady. You have not misjudged me. I have been the man I've always been required to be. But I will not stand by the removal of a wife in such an undignified manner, especially one as kind as my mistress.'

He pushed the door open and stood back to let the women in first. 'You will find something that may distress you, Lady Marjory. I'm sorry.'

Marjory stopped moving, the colour drained from her face. 'Mother isn't…'

'Oh no, my Lady,' Bennett realised his mistake. 'Your mother is not within. Should I have found her, I would have cared for her.'

Mathilda took the pale girl's hand and squeezed it gently. 'I need you to tell me what's missing, or if there's something here that shouldn't be.'

'I'll try.' Her voice was a whisper as Marjory added, 'but I have hardly been in this room. I won't know for certain what should or should not be there.'

The second they walked into the room, they were hit by

a blanket of cold. The fire hadn't been lit in the grate for some time, and a damp chill had invaded every nook and cranny. Spiders had made their homes in every corner, and the flat surfaces were covered in a layer of dust.

Mathilda took a deep breath as she surveyed the scene. Marjory however ran straight to the chest at the base of her mother's bed. It squeaked as she threw the lid open, before covering her mouth with her hand, stifling a cry.

'Lady Marjory?' Mathilda came to her side, seeing what had caused the girl's alarm.

The box was full. Wherever Lady Isabel had gone, she hadn't taken her clothes with her.

~ *Chapter Thirty-two* ~

15th January 1332

Helping Lady Joan onto Heart's back, Adam passed her the reins and took a deferential step back, so that Anne could hold one side of the bridle, and Gilbert the other.

After five minutes of silent walking, Adam asked, 'Does Lord Willoughby ever allow minstrels at Wollaton Hall?'

Surprised by the question, Anne regarded the visiting steward questioningly, 'Why do you ask?'

'There are three of them staying at the inn. They're heading towards Leicester later today. I invited them to accompany Lady Mathilda and myself as we'll be heading that way. I'm telling you so you're not alarmed when you see three men waiting outside Wollaton Hill around noon.'

'But you don't know them. They could be robbers!' Anne was scandalised at the notion of a steward making such a decision without his mistress's permission.

Hoping to calm her disquiet, Adam said, 'I should have explained. The minstrels are known to Lady Ingram. She is fond of their tunes. And I'm sure she will welcome an enlarged escort as we travel back to Leicester.'

'Father is mean to singers.' Lady Joan's voice was so soft that Adam almost missed it, but he didn't miss the daggered look the noblewoman got from her maid.

'He is no such thing. He just has more serious matters to consider than the frivolities of minstrels, my Lady.'

'Lady Ingram likes them.' Lady Joan presented the words with a note of triumph that caused Adam to bite back a laugh.

'Yes, well, she has more time on her hands than Lord Willoughby, I'm sure.'

Annoyed on Mathilda's behalf, Adam ignored Anne and spoke directly to Lady Joan, 'Do you like the ballads, my Lady?'

'I love them. They are stories and songs to lift the heart.' The young girl smiled, and Adam wondered how often anyone asked her opinion about anything. 'Adam Bell is my favourite one, but I like Gamelyn and Robyn Hode too.'

Gilbert grunted, and Adam had the distinct impression he was also trying not to laugh. Anne, on the other hand, was not impressed.

'When have you ever heard such things? Your father would not be happy. You know he hates his children to listen to anything that...'

Adam stepped in as Anne floundered for words. 'Songs that tell the truth about how our beautiful country has become corrupt?'

'How dare you imply that...?' Anne went beetroot, 'and in front of his daughter!'

Ignoring Anne, Adam smiled at Lady Joan. 'I was not implying anything about your father, my Lady, just that problems within the law are often sung about, that's all. Lord Robert Ingram is fond of such tales. He says they keep all men of law on their mettle.'

'I think I would like Lord Ingram.' Lady Joan blushed, 'Lady Ingram seems very nice. Does she truly like the songs too?'

'She does. Why don't you ask her about them when we get back?'

'Oh, I couldn't possibly presume to talk to Lady Ingram.'

'She is as kind a lady as you'll ever meet. She would welcome a conversation with the youngest Lady Willough-by, I'm quite sure.'

Anne said nothing but pursed her lips so tightly, that she looked as if she was about to break out into a whistle.

'I wonder if the minstrels would sing for us, Anne.' Lady Joan's tone was pleading, but her expression held no hope.

'What a lovely idea.' Adam jumped in; amazed he hadn't had to work any harder to get what he wanted. 'I'm sure they'd raise everyone's spirits while both Lord and Lady Willoughby are absent.'

'Lord Willoughby will be furious when he hears!' Anne was clearly getting worried.

'But Father isn't here, Anne. No one is.' Joan's eyes took on a sheen of tears, but despite her young age, her upbring-ing forced her to hold them back. 'Until our brothers get back it's just Marjory and me. So, if we want the minstrels to sing for us, then I say that is what will happen.'

Adam bowed towards Lady Joan. It was an effort not to give her a round of applause. 'Should I run back to the inn and summon them now, my Lady?'

'Do so. We will wait here.'

'Mother's dead, isn't she.'

Lady Marjory sat on the wooden chair before the empty fireplace, her hands clasped in her lap, her face drawn.

'I don't know.' Mathilda dismissed the urge to tell her companion that everything was going to be alright. Personal experience has taught her the cruelty of false hope. 'But I'm going to find out.'

'How can you? If you have to leave so soon and...'

Mathilda laid a hand on Marjory's shoulder and turned to the steward. 'Bennett, do you think we could have a fire in the grate?'

'Certainly, my Lady.' The change in the steward's attitude was marked now it appeared as if his mistress had gone beyond the realm of this world. 'Perhaps I could ask your girl, Bettrys, to see to that?'

There was something in his tone that made Mathilda agree. As he bustled off to fetch her trusted servant, Mathilda crouched before Marjory. 'I'm going to do my best to discover what's happened. Perhaps Lady Isabel left in such a hurry that there was simply no time to pack properly. Maybe she has been presented with new clothing? If she has gone to her mother's, do you know if she has gowns there that would prevent the need for carrying belongings with her?'

'I don't know.' Marjory wiped an angry fist over her eyes and stood up. 'But whatever the situation, Mother would never have left without some work of embroidery. It calmed her. I never saw her without some. Even when she travelled to nearby manors, she'd take a small bag with either a head linen or a square of silk to decorate. Her stitches are so neat, she...'

'Well, I see no embroidery here.' Seeing Marjory was in danger of bursting into tears, Mathilda added, 'So that is where we start.'

'We? You'll let me help you?'

'I'd welcome it,' Mathilda brushed her hands together, 'the more of us on the trail the better. Where could your mother have taken her sewing? It clearly isn't here, which has to mean it is either elsewhere within Wollaton Hall, or she's taken it with her.' Mathilda did not voice the thought that was going through her mind: *or the person who took her away has removed it in order to make us think Lady Isabel is safe somewhere else... But if they did that, surely they'd have taken her clothing too...*

'If Mother took her embroidery with her, then she's probably alright!' Lady Marjory grabbed the task like a life-line and headed to the door. 'I'll try the solar; but I hope I don't find it!'

The echo of Marjory's boots clattering along the stone corridor faded as Bettrys arrived to clean and restock the hearth. She spoke urgently, 'Bennett wants to talk to you, my Lady. He's in his master's room. The second door on the left, as you walk towards the hall.'

'Right.'

Muttering, careful to make sure she wasn't overheard, Bettrys added, 'My Lady, do you think Lady Isabel is beyond being found?'

'I don't know, but it's beginning to look that way. And yet...' She came to Bettrys' side, 'This is an unhappy household, maybe Lady Isabel has simply taken the chance for a fresh start and means to send for her children later. It could have been an instant decision when opportunity arose, with no time to gather her possessions.'

'You don't really believe that, do you, my Lady?'

Mathilda gave a sad laugh. 'No, I don't, Bettrys, but I'd like it to be true. Sometimes I think my life with the Folvilles has soured my optimism.'

'Do you want me to come to Lord Willoughby's chamber with you?'

'I'll be alright. Get that fire going, and then examine the room. Think about what you'd have expected to find in your mistress's chamber at Rockingham Castle. See if you can work out what is missing, or what, apart from the clothing, you'd have expected Lady Isabel not to leave without   assuming she went willingly.'

Bennett was adding another log to the fire in Lord Willoughby's chamber. Unlike his wife's, this bedroom was clean, tidy, and well cared for. Mathilda waited in the open doorway and observed the scene. The bed, a study oak-framed beast with thick curtains around it to block the draughts, was larger than Lady Isabel's. She was clearly expected to come here when the mood was upon her husband, rather than the other way around. The chamber had a masculine feel to it, and Mathilda couldn't help but speculate how often his wife had been allowed across the threshold. She shuddered, thankful for her more humble roots, and not having to live her whole childhood wondering if she'd be sold off to the highest bidder; never knowing if her life would be full of wealth and happiness or wealth and misery.

In the corner of the room sat a table covered in papers, quills, and a pot of ink. A thick church candle sat at its side. Evidence of regular burning displayed in the hardened wax rivulets that clung to it, from the top down to the saucer it sat in, which was so caked in wax it looked as if the candle wore a clergyman's smock.

'My Lady.' Bennett beckoned her within.

'Lord Willoughby uses his room as a study as well as a bed chamber?'

'He does. Most of his time is spent in here.' The steward gestured to the piles of rolled parchments that, now she was inside, she could see stored in a basket, stacked almost to the top of the desk's underside.

'Court rolls?'

'Yes.' The steward hesitated before saying, 'He only lets

me in here.'

'I can see why.' Mathilda was curious to see if her husband's name was amongst the papers under the desk. 'His Lordship must trust you a great deal.'

Bennett sighed, 'And here I am betraying that trust.'

'For a good cause.'

'Yes.' He wiped a hand over his forehead. 'As I said, I went into Lady Willoughby's chamber after I was told she'd been taken to Lincolnshire.'

'And saw that none of her clothing had gone with her.'

The steward nodded. 'I haven't been back in since, but someone has. Her embroidery was there. There was also a new gown on her bed. Both are missing.'

'A new gown? So, not something her daughter would note as missing?'

'No, although the sewing is a different matter. Lady Willoughby is known for her love of stitching.'

'I see.' Mathilda was thoughtful, 'There will be other items, of a more personal nature, that you wouldn't know were missing or not?'

'Correct.'

'So, Lady Isabel may have clothes with her after all, but not many.'

'No, my Lady. That's what I was trying to say. When I first went in, nothing was missing, but now the gown and sewing and - as you say - possibly some small items which wouldn't meet my eyes, are not there.'

'Items that disappeared from the room *after* Lady Isabel is alleged to have left Wollaton.'

'Yes. There's something else.' The steward gestured towards a large square of material draped over something in the corner of Lord Willoughby's chamber.

'What's under there?' Mathilda had a sudden dread she

was about to come face to face with Lady Isabel's corpse.

'A pile of linen.'

Mathilda exhaled in relief as she stared at the large square of rich blue material hiding the only sign of disorder in the room.

'Lord Willoughby's clothing awaiting washing?'

'Yes.' Bennett shifted uneasily. 'I collect it when instructed.'

'Not until you're asked to?'

'Lord Willoughby values his privacy.' Bennett stared at the offending corner. 'In the past I have offered to collect the linen every week, or every day, but his Lordship instructed me to wait until told to move it. The instruction came in such a way that it would be unwise to disobey.'

'Does a maid not come in each day to make up his bed and attend to the fire?

'As I said, only I come in here. I do those tasks.' He sighed, 'Until now I dismissed this as fierce privacy, and perhaps a slight eccentricity on his lordship's behalf. And, in truth, the maid who does our laundry likes the scheme. It means she can attend to the remaining household linen regularly and leave this pile for when his Lordship bids me deliver his bundle to her.'

'And that's always been his way?'

'Yes.'

'Bennett, what is it under there that you want me to see? I don't think you invited me to cross into this forbidden part of the house to explain his Lordship's unusual laundry habits.'

'This is the only other private space Lady Isabel ever occupied, albeit,' he coughed, 'only occasionally.'

Mathilda cleared her throat, unsure how to ask her next question delicately. 'How occasionally?'

'Rarely, to my knowledge. Once there were children…' Bennett's voice trailed off, and Mathilda let it go. Once an heir and a few spares had been produced, Lady Isabel was a necessary possession for the lord of the manor, and no more.

'And the linen pile?'

Pausing, Bennett said, 'What I'm going to show you must remain private, between us. Do you swear, Lady Ingram?'

'I will swear as far as I can within the law. If we find there has been foul play towards your mistress, then I reserve the right to withdraw that promise.'

The steward's fingers bunched into his palms, Mathilda saw him squeeze them hard before flexing his digits out again. 'Can I trust you, Lady Ingram?'

Mathilda's eyes landing on the bundle of court papers. 'I promise I am here to find Lady Isabel. I am not here to bring trouble to this family.'

Not commenting on her indirect answer to his question, Bennett said, 'I've served this family for so long, I don't know what I'd do if…'

'Lord Ingram would find a place for you with a good family.'

Bennett's proud head tilted upwards. 'I can't imagine it would come to that… but I thank you for that anyway.'

'On that, you can trust me.'

'But only that, my Lady?' Bennett smiled as he spoke. The change in his appearance was startling. His dark eyes lit with a gleam that turned him into a very attractive man.

'What's under the linen pile?'

Bennett strode forward. Now the decision had been made to help Lady Ingram, he was going to do so with his usual efficiency. Lifting the material, he pointed to the item lying on the top without a word.

A square of cloth sat on of a crumpled pile of hose, tunics, and other clothing. It had been stitched with a fine fold thread that shone in the firelight. As Mathilda knelt before it, she could see the pattern wasn't quite finished. It was going to be a tree, the trunk and a few branches stood proudly against the cream background. Three tiny silver leaves had been sewn over the top; one was half finished.

Had Lady Isabel been mid-stitch when she was disturbed? Had the cloth been ripped from her hands?

As she stared, her heart thumping in her chest, Mathilda noted that part of the linen was darker. Thinking it might be a trick of the light, she gently folded back the square, so they could see the underside.

There was no mistaking the pattern of what they saw. Blood dotted the reverse of the material.

'Bennett…' Mathilda stopped speaking, unsure what to say.

The steward, his voice uneven, whispered, 'Is there a needle? Any threads?'

Kneeling closer, Mathilda gently lifted the cloth clear, and searched through the dirty washing, her nose wrinkling at the smell of sweat and damp. 'There's nothing more.'

Taking the embroidery, she lifted it to the candlelight. 'Someone has tried to wash this out, see how it's dried here. It's stiff beyond the realm of the blood itself.'

'A cowardly act, to hide such a deed. Whatever that deed was.'

'I've heard much of Lord Willoughby, and in truth, I haven't liked what I've heard, but despite that, he never struck me as a fool.'

Bennett bristled. 'He most certainly is not.'

'He is arrogant though, yes?'

'He can be, my Lady.'

'Tell me honestly, Bennett, do you think your master is foolish enough to hide this in a place where he knows you will find it? Or is he arrogant enough to believe your loyalty to him would mean that if you found this, you'd remove it without a word?'

Bennett's shoulders stiffened as he stared at the exquisite sewing in Mathilda's hands. 'When Lord Willoughby said he was going to take his wife to Lincolnshire, he wasn't gone long enough. If he sent men, 'his friends', to transport her without him, then they might not have been gentle in their task… because if that's what he did, they would have been mercenaries. And if they were rougher than they should have been and cracked her head…'

'Why do you think he might employ mercenaries to remove his wife and not his own guards?'

'Because all his guards are out hunting the Coterels and their supporters.'

~ *Chapter Thirty-three* ~

15th January 1332

Sarah looked up as Lord Thomas stuck his head around the kitchen door, letting in a blast of cold outside air.

'My Lord?'

'It's Pykehose, Sarah. He has news.'

Dropping the dough she was forming into a loaf, Sarah scrubbed the sticky mixture from her palms and rushed into the courtyard as Eustace's man passed his tired, limping horse to Ulric. 'My horse is lame. He stumbled a mile back, and I've had to lead him since.'

'Poor beast.' Thomas stroked the animal's neck as it passed by. 'Come inside, John. Sarah, can you prepare food and a bed?'

Pykehose held up a hand to steady Sarah in her tracks. 'Thank you, my Lord, but I only have time for a quick meal and an exchange of information, then I must return. Is there a beast I could use? Mine would suffer greatly if I pushed him more.'

'There's Jep. I'm sure Lady Mathilda wouldn't mind you borrowing him.'

Lifting his hood from his face, Pykehose followed the Lord Folville into the kitchen. 'I'll waste no time if you'll forgive me withholding the formalities, Lord Thomas.'

'No forgiveness required, John. Tell us.' Thomas pushed a beaker of ale towards the groom as Sarah busied herself slicing some off the pork roasting on a small spit over the fire. She put some on a plate and gave it to John; the rest she wrapped in paper ready for his return journey.

'As you already know, Willoughby is taken. When I left Lords Eustace and Robert, they had the justice hogtied in a cart in Kesteven Forest. They are keeping ahead of the authorities thanks to Ingram delaying matters of a search in the area, not to mention their skill at carrying out this sort of manoeuvre.'

'Has the ransom demand been sent to Wollaton Hall yet?' Sarah took comfort in the familiar act of bread-making.

'Helewell and Lovet were on their way to deliver it. If they are not already there, they should be any time now.'

'Providing nothing has happened to them.' Thomas steepled his fingers together in a way that reminded Sarah of Robert Ingram. 'If they are delayed or intercepted…'

'Lord Eustace gave them firm instructions. Although arriving together, they are to leave apart and collect their personal spoils later. The route they are on is as sound as any that could be taken.'

'And Lady Mathilda and Adam…' Sarah floundered, unsure she wanted to the finish the sentence, but then she found she didn't have to.

'And Bettrys…' Daniel had appeared in the doorway, drying his hands, fresh from washing down the hall table in the maid's absence. 'Forgive the interruption, my Lord.' He blushed as he looked at Lord Thomas, realising his tone had given the personal nature of his enquiry away.

Taking no heed of the lad's discomfort, Pykehose chewed some meat. 'The party left to go Wollaton as planned. No word of any problems had come back to the forest between then and my time there.' He glanced towards the window. The light of the late afternoon was fading fast. 'If all is as it should be, then Lady Mathilda and her companions should be readying to leave Wollaton Hall in the next couple of hours.'

Daniel asked the question that had been on Sarah's lips. 'Before or after the ransom demand has been made?'

'I can't answer that. I wish I could.'

'But if…' Daniel took a calming breath before continuing, 'if they are still there when the ransom demand is made, won't Lord Willoughby's son think Lady Mathilda arriving with his father's seal, only hours before, is too much of a co-incidence for her not to have something to do with his kidnap?'

Sarah threw her dough onto the floured table with a thud, sending a cloud of white dust into the air. 'And if they've left, and then a ransom demand comes, it will look even more suspicious; as if Lady Mathilda was making sure she was long gone before the notice came.'

'But Bettrys and Adam are there too! Anything could happen to them. What if…' Daniel was already heading to the door when Lord Thomas leapt to his feet and barred it.

'Come on, lad, you rushing off to become another person in danger isn't going to help Bettrys, is it?'

Pykehose laid down the dagger he was about to stab into a piece of pork, his expression grim. 'Besides, you'll never get out of Ashby Folville. Not unless you're very skilled at moving through the woods without a sound or are very lucky.'

Lord Thomas sat back down, gently steering Daniel after him. 'What do you mean, John?'

'There are soldiers everywhere. They're combing Charnwood. It'll only be a matter of time before they get here.' He got to his feet, 'Which is why I must go. Now. Before they get here and there's no clear path back to Nottingham- shire.'

Mathilda clutched the bloodied cloth, trying to work out what it meant, as the steward searched his master's room for offending evidence concerning the removal of Lady Isabel.

'As much as it would be convenient to think so, Bennett, I don't think Lord Willoughby would hide evidence against himself in a place where he knew it would be found. It's all a little convenient. I arrive with a mission from my husband to locate Lady Isabel, and we find this.' She waved the cloth towards the steward.

'A mission from your husband, my Lady? You said you came from Lord Willoughby.'

Cursing her tongue, Mathilda took the embroidery clos- er to Bennett. 'I meant on orders from Lord Ingram because he couldn't carry out Lord Willoughby's request to search for his wife himself.'

'Which is also odd.'

'Odd?'

'That Lord Willoughby would send you here to search for his wife, if he knew she was not to be found.'

Quickly sifting the lies she'd told from the untruths of others, Mathilda found she agreed with Bennett, even if the root of the belief was rotten. 'He wouldn't. As we estab- lished, your master is not a foolish man.'

'So the cloth was put there for you to find.' Bennett scratched at his greying hair.

'More likely for you to find.' Mathilda's mind was afire with possibilities, none of them pleasant. 'I wonder if...'

'If it was put there to incriminate his Lordship?'

'Yes, and… and to test you in some way.'

'Me, my Lady?' Bennett paled, his head turning towards the doorway, as if he expected to see his master there, ready to scold him. 'I don't understand, my loyalty has never been questioned. I have always…'

'And yet you've allowed me into your lord's chamber and have begun to suspect the worst of him.' Knowing her words could be taken as an accusation, Mathilda softened her tone. 'I do not level any charges at you, Bennett, but think hard, have you displeased anyone of late?'

'No. No, I… I don't think so. Why?' He took a step backwards, shifting from side to side on his booted feet.

'Because by placing that bloodied cloth here, in this room, it isn't just Lord Willoughby who could be placed as suspect, but you too. You're the only one who tends this room, and you said yourself, you are the only one who is allowed to collect his soiled linen.'

Bennett gasped as his hand reached to the doorframe to support himself. 'Are you saying someone in this household wanted to implement *me* in the death of Lady Isabel?'

'*If* she's dead.' Mathilda murmured the words, more to herself than to the steward, but he leapt on the thought.

'You don't think she's dead?'

With a heavy sigh, Mathilda turned to the door. 'I don't know, but I'm certain this all feels contrived. That you were meant to find it, and whoever put it there, was waiting to see if you'd tell anyone, or if you'd quietly get rid of the evidence to maintain the good name of the Willoughby household.'

Bennett stood in the doorway, clearly unsure which direction to go in. Mathilda's suggestion seemed to have taken the very breath from his body.

Folding the soiled sewing into her cloak, Mathilda pointed along the corridor towards Lady Isabel's chamber. 'Bettrys should have finished by now. I think we should talk with her.'

'Forgive me for saying so, Lady Ingram, but you are an unusual mistress. Not many ladies of the manor would consult their staff.'

'I see no point in being usual, Bennett, it achieves nothing.' Mathilda paused as they passed a narrow window. 'It's almost noon, Adam will be back with Lady Joan soon.'

'And you will be leaving soon after that?' Bennett suddenly sounded far less keen for her to be gone.

'Our leaving was the arrangement with Lord Richard. I would not want to intrude on his hospitality. As it is, Adam's already tardy in taking the seal back to Lord Willoughby. I would not wish to incur his Lordship's wrath more than necessary.'

Bennett's lips parted as if he was about to speak, but no words came out. Instead he followed Mathilda towards Lady Isabel's chamber.

Back inside the room Lady Marjory was chatting excitedly with Bettrys. Her face looked lighter, as if her fears had been lifted. On seeing Mathilda and the steward she turned to them, gushing in relief. 'I've found nothing. No sign of Mother's sewing. Not even the frame for her larger works of embroidery. She must have gone somewhere after all.'

Feeling the weight of the hidden linen within her cloak double, Mathilda directed a warning glance at Bettrys. 'You have searched everywhere, Lady Marjory?'

'Everywhere! That means that when my brother returns from Lincolnshire, he should have good news. That Mother is with Lady Mortain after all.' She paused, 'I am rather ashamed that I doubted Father now. And thinking about it, Grandmother is most generous, she may well have gifted

Mother new clothes.'

'And the claim of madness?' Mathilda asked the question lightly, not wanting to ruin the girl's humour.

'I've been considering that.' She stilled, her colour darkening a fraction. 'It would be in character, I'm ashamed to say, for Father to overreact after Mother argued with him. Perhaps that was his punishment for her, to make people doubt her sanity. I don't believe it is true, but I can believe he would say such a thing. Father has a cruel streak.'

Mathilda, who'd been wondering how to take her leave without disappointing Lady Marjory, saw her chance. 'I'm heartened you think your mother to be safe. Perhaps, once Lord Willoughby the younger returns, then you will be reunited with Lady Isabel and all will be well.'

She turned to Bennett. 'Could I impose upon you to ask the cook for some food for our journey back to Leicester?'

Less sure of herself, Lady Marjory timidly asked, 'You're leaving?'

'I was granted a night's stay by your brother, my Lady, I would not like to impose longer, and, as it seems you are convinced of your mother's safety, I can tell Lord Ingram to inform Lord Willoughby that she is with Lady Mortain after all.'

Marjory looked from Mathilda to Bettrys to Bennett, her smile dissolving. 'But none of you believe that, do you?'

Adam stepped back to allow Gilbert and Anne to lead Lady Joan and Heart into the manor's courtyard first. Then, signalling to Aldus, Noll, and Dicun to follow him, he led them through the kitchen door, and on into the hall, where he expected to find Mathilda and Lady Marjory.

The ladies' absence was short as they, with Bettrys and Bennett, emerged through an archway on the far side of the room, Lady Marjory looking worried.

Lady Joan rushed forward, her face alight. 'Sister, I bring a gift, thanks to Master Calvin here. We have music. Minstrels to cheer our mood.'

'Lovely.' Mathilda's heart lifted at the unexpected arrival of her friends. 'How did this come about, Adam?'

'Lady Joan was kind enough to invite the minstrels to sing here before they accompany us to Leicester. I took it upon myself to ask them to add to our party. Forgive my presumption, but the nights draw in, and the roads are safer if we travel in numbers.'

'You are forgiven. A sensible suggestion. And who better to lift our spirits than some balladeers.'

Lady Joan shuffled forwards shyly. 'You truly enjoy the ballads, my Lady?'

'Very much.' Mathilda beamed at the minstrels, who bowed to the ladies with courteous smiles. 'Perhaps you'd be so good as to sing for Lady Joan and Lady Marjory while Adam, Bettrys, and I ready ourselves for the journey home.'

'Home?' Lady Marjory stepped forward, her hand outstretched, 'Please, please don't go yet. You said you'd find Mother. You promised… and I know you're not convinced she's with Grandmother.'

Mathilda close her eyes for a second. She *had* promised, but unless something had gone wrong, the ransom request for Justice Willoughby would arrive any minute. She'd also promised Robert she'd be away from Wollaton by now. If she was here when the demand arrived, she had no doubt the trust she'd brokered with Bennett would dissolve in seconds.

As Aldus broke into song, she looked at Bettrys. Her maid's eyes were on Marjory; they shone with pity. Then Mathilda thought about the square of embroidery, and how far they were from understanding what that truth of Lady

Willoughby's disappearance.

Had someone killed Lady Isabel and tried to frame her husband for the crime?

Was Bennett implicated as the killer, by the placing of the linen in a place only he would go?

Was her Ladyship even dead? The amount of blood on the cloth was not huge, and while it wasn't the spray of a nosebleed, there was nowhere near enough to suggest a cut throat or open wound...

As she thought, the soft strains of Aldus singing 'Robin and Gandeleyn' reverberated off the walls, each lyric under-lined by the skilful playing of Noll and Dicun.

I heard a carping of a clerk
All at yon woodës end,
Of good Robin and Gandeleyn,
Was there none other thing.
Robin lieth in greenwood bounden.

Strong thievës wern tho children none,
But bowmen good and hend;
They wenten to wood to getten them flesh
If God would it them send.

All day wenten tho children two,
And flesh founden they none,
Till it were again even,
The children would gone home...

Mathilda sighed. Whatever happened, she couldn't go home yet.

~ *Chapter Thirty-four* ~

15th January 1332

As the ballad ended, a silence cloaked the hall that was louder than the song. The tale of hope against the dark left a space in the air which Mathilda felt could be picked up and moulded into something sinister. It was telling her to act. To do something; but what was the right thing to do?

She was conscious of Lady Marjory looking at her expectantly, her wide eyes child-like despite her blooming womanhood. Robert would be worried if she stayed, but he wouldn't be surprised.

Robert. She'd tried so hard not to think about him; to stop her overactive imagination picturing him cold, hungry, and about to spend another winter's night outside. Shutting her eyes, banishing the vision of Robert sprawled across the forest floor, a gloating soldier stood over him, Mathilda made herself to concentrate on Lady Isabel and the other missing members of the Willoughby family.

Neither the younger Richard, nor Edmund Willoughby, had returned to Wollaton Hall. Had they gone to Lincoln-shire after all, or were they out in the forest, biding their time, watching the hall's entrance? If they were, what would happen when she failed to leave at the appointed time, a time which was approaching with increasing speed? Had they already noted that Adam had not yet left with the seal? She frowned. *Who swapped the seal and who has the real one now? It has to be Richard - doesn't it?*

Mathilda glanced towards the main entrance to the hall. She'd been expecting someone to rush through it and deliver the ransom demand ever since the noon bell, but that was four hours ago now, and no messenger had come.

Surely Eustace's men must be on their way - unless...

She shook her head. If it had gone wrong, then it was more important than ever that she uncovered evidence against Lord Willoughby here. The material hidden in her cloak mocked her: *You have evidence. The linen alone is enough to speak against him. But what if he's innocent? What if it wasn't him who bloodied his wife's sewing?* She could imagine Eustace's expression if she even suggested the justice had been framed for murder.

Feeling the eyes of every person in the hall on her, waiting for her to speak, Mathilda hid a sigh. Anne's chin was jutted towards her in defiance. The maid would never believe her master capable of murdering anyone.

A fresh notion arrived in Mathilda's head. *I wonder...*

'I will stay to help find Lady Isabel, but my steward, Adam, must leave with Lord Willoughby's seal. He'll need it, and, should Lord Richard the younger return and find that I have taken advantage of his home and failed to discharge his request of returning the seal to his father, then I'd be ashamed indeed.'

'But you'd be keeping your promise to my father to find Mother.' Lady Marjory's voice remained small, but it was growing with determination. 'That's the most important promise to keep.'

Lady Joan, her mouth open, whispered, 'But Mother is

with Lady Mortain. She sent my pony.'

Marjory took her sister's hand. 'It seems all may not be as appeared. Mother may not be where we thought.'

'But she sent Heart and '

'Of course she did.' Anne cut in. 'Enough of this nonsense. Lady Isabel is well and with her mother as she should be. Lords Richard and Edmund will be home soon to confirm all is well, and then this charade can end. So, it's fine for you to leave, Lady Ingram.'

Bennett caught Anne's eye and glared. His silence was sending her a message Mathilda wished she could read.

Anne, her cheeks redder than before, spoke more hastily, 'Obviously, it would be sensible to offer Lady Ingram a room for the night, as it's already getting dark. But,' she tuned to Adam, 'you should go. That seal needs delivering. Lord Willoughby, you can be assured, will not be amused at having had to wait so long for it.'

Mathilda, keen for Adam to get back to Ashby Folville, agreed. 'I am concerned however that you should not travel alone, Adam. The night already falls, and you had scant little rest before today broke.'

Adam dipped his head in respect. 'I'll go faster alone, my Lady, and the roads are known to me. My horse is rested, even if I'm not. If I leave now, I'll be in Leicester by the toll of the abbey's midnight bell.'

Bennett called to the maid tending the fire. 'Fetch some food for Adam to take on his journey and inform Gilbert that his horse needs saddling.'

Gesturing to the steward, Adam said, 'Your kindness is appreciated,' before turning to the minstrels, 'I charge you with the care of my mistress. You will escort her home on the morrow.'

'Most willingly,' Aldus and his friends agreed as Adam

dipped his head to Bettrys, who sent silent good wishes in his direction.

'We did not,' Anne snapped, 'offer a refuge to the minstrels. Just to Lady Ingram - for *one* more night.'

'And yet they'll stay.' Lady Marjory was on her feet, sixteen years of anger at being beaten, and told what to do, by her maid rising up and rushing out of her mouth in a confusion of frustration and concern. 'You forget your station! Lady Joan and I run this house in the absence of our elders. Once Richard, Edmund, and Father return, their rule will override ours, but here and now it is just us. And we say they stay to chaperone Lady Ingram home when she is ready to leave. And not a moment before.'

Mathilda watched with private satisfaction as Anne froze to the spot. She looked as if she'd been struck.

'If that is your wish, my Lady.'

'It is.' Lady Marjory turned to the minstrels, who'd wisely distanced themselves from the discussion over their immediate future. Mathilda however was confident they'd been listening hard and hadn't missed a word as Marjory asked, 'Aldus, isn't it?'

'My Lady.' The lead balladeer bowed.

'Please could we impose upon you to play for us while we eat this evening? The mood needs lifting, and you've already proved yourselves more than capable of raising our spirits.'

'We would be delighted.' Aldus bowed again, 'Perhaps you and Lady Joan have favourite ballads you'd like to hear?'

Marjory was about to reply, but Joan got in first. 'Lady Ingram loves the Robyn Hode stories; let's have one of those with dinner.'

Adam took the parcel of food from the kitchen maid and stared up at the sky. The air was clear and crisp without a cloud to be seen. There was over an hour until Vespers, but the frost was already starting to coat the roof of the stables.

'Sarah will warm you when you get home.' Mathilda pulled her cloak around her shoulders as she passed Adam the velvet pouch holding the seal.

'I'm banking on it.' Adam gave her a brief smile before becoming more serious. 'Is there anything new I need to know?'

Checking they weren't being overheard, Mathilda muttered, 'I found some blood-stained linen. It was Lady Isabel's. It was in Willoughby's chamber, but it was too obvious…'

'It was put there to be found?' Adam looked worried.

'I suspect so.'

'Then I can't go.' He lowered his leg from where he'd been about to leap into the saddle. 'If there's a murderer at Wollaton Hall, then I'm not leaving you here alone.'

'You must. Sarah will be worried. I have the minstrels.' Mathilda stared in the direction of the exit. 'Why hasn't it come?'

There was no need to explain what she meant.

'I wish I knew.' Adam, uneasy about leaving, readjusted the nearest stirrup. 'It can't be long now.'

'Maybe Robert wanted to give me more time, and so they delayed.'

Adam could tell she didn't believe that, but he agreed anyway. 'In that case, I suspect it will arrive tonight. Do you want me to stay until the demand is met?'

'Better you're not here. I have a feeling Anne would delight in twisting events, so it sounds like you had the demand with you the whole time.'

'She's a poisonous piece for sure.'

'I'm beginning to wonder about her. She's very loyal to Willoughby.'

'So is Bennett.'

'True, but with Bennett it feels more as if it's loyalty to the household and his position within it, with Anne…'

Understanding shone in Adam's eyes. 'You think Anne is closer to his Lordship than perhaps she ought to be?'

'It had crossed my mind.'

'A reciprocated arrangement or a lusting in her imagination?'

Mathilda shrugged. 'As yet I can't say. I have no evidence, just a notion.'

Climbing into the saddle, Adam whispered, 'Watch out for her anyway. If she is loyal to a fault, then you could suffer for it.'

Bettrys and Bennett emerged through the kitchen door as Adam fastened his cloak over his shoulders, unfurling its tail so it helped warm his mount as well as himself.

'You have the seal safe, Adam?' Bennett passed him a pouch of water.

'I do.' Adam gestured to the women. 'You will take care of them while they're here?'

'On my life.' Bennett promised as Adam turned his horse to face the gates and the fast closing evening light.

'My Lady,' Bettrys stood close to her mistress as they stared at the space that Adam had left behind him. 'We should go inside.'

'Yes.' Mathilda peered into the twilight.

Bettrys shuffled from foot to foot, keen to go inside, but not willing to leave her mistress alone in the cold. 'Are you alright, my Lady?'

'I was thinking.'

'About Lord Robert?' As soon as she'd asked the question, Bettrys blushed. 'Forgive me, I shouldn't have asked such a personal question.'

Smiling, Mathilda steered her maid towards the hall. 'I was considering Bennett. Tell me, do you believe we can trust him?'

As they reached the edge of the stable block, Bettrys paused. 'I think it would be unwise to trust anyone here too much, but I don't think he's a threat to us.'

'I would say that's sound reasoning.' Mathilda paused by her palfrey, stroking its mane, muttering 'We'll be home soon.'

'Your horse could do with some exercise, my Lady.' Gilbert's arrival made the women jump, 'Would you like me to walk her out for you?'

Failing to hide her surprise, Mathilda thanked the groom. 'That would be kind. A few circles of the courtyard perhaps, I would not want you riding abroad so late on my account.'

'And yet you send your steward out?'

Mathilda looked at Gilbert more closely. 'As a debt to your master and to keep a promise.'

'Just as you say, my Lady, I'm sure.' The groom unhooked the palfrey's tether and stroked her nose with calm reverence.

'You know why I'm here, Gilbert.'

'To find Lady Isabel, my Lady.'

'Do you know where she is?'

He kept stroking the horse, his eyes only on its fine equine features. 'I do not. I hope you find her though.'

'May I ask why?'

'Daughters need a mother.' Gilbert finally turned to face Mathilda. 'Lady Isabel is a good soul. Bennett will surely have told you what a gentle woman she is.'

'He did.' Mathilda was glad Bettrys was with her as the usually taciturn groom spoke, so they could discuss his words later. 'And her daughters miss her.'

'A man such as Lord Willoughby is a tough master and a tougher husband. If Lady Isabel did decide to leave, I for one would not hold it against her, but…'

'But you don't think she'd leave her children.'

'I do not.'

'The pony,' Bettrys looked to Mathilda for permission before she asked, 'do you know where it came from?'

Gilbert started to tease out some knots in the palfrey's mane. Each firm swipe of the brush took a little longer as he considered how to answer the question. 'There's a horse fair at Stow in Lincolnshire. It's been held there by permission of the Prior of Sempringham for one hundred years come next year.'

'The Prior of Sempringham!'

Mathilda immediately regretted her outburst of surprise on hearing the name of one of the Folvilles' greatest supporters, but Gilbert took no heed as he carried on. 'The pony came from there.'

'You're sure?'

'I chose her and led her here.'

Mathilda held her breath. 'And Lady Isabel?'

'Would approve, I'm sure, but I doubt she has knowledge of the pony. Unless someone here got a message to wherever she is.'

'Lord Willoughby sent you to buy the pony?'

'He did.' Gilbert put down the brush, 'I didn't ask him why. If you work for a man like Justice Willoughby, you don't ask questions, you don't speak unless spoken to, and you get on with your work.'

'Safer, I'm sure.' Mathilda felt the cold engulf her. There

was something about the way Gilbert was looking at her, and in an instant she realised he knew who she was. 'You must also get to know far more than most. Those who rarely speak are often forgotten, people speak without guard in their presence. They learn things.'

'That they do, my Lady.'

Bettrys' teeth chattered and she gave a violent shiver, which woke Mathilda to her surroundings. 'If you have anything to say about Lady Isabel, Gilbert, it would be kind of you to tell me. The sooner I find her, the sooner you'll be relieved of our presence.'

'All I know is that she isn't here. Not in the hall or the grounds.'

'You've searched for her?'

A rapid thundering of hooves, followed by a cry from the two guards on the gates, cut off any answer Gilbert may have been prepared to give. Instinct took over, and he thrust the women behind him, shouting the alarm as two horses cantered across the threshold, the gateway still open from when Adam had departed.

As the manor's few remaining guards ran forward, swords drawn, three servants rushed from the house. Anne and the minstrels were on their heels as the unexpected arrivals, their heads hooded, their features swathed in scarves, swerved their horses in a dust cloud of skittering hooves, before one of them threw a roll of parchment to the floor.

Two seconds later they were gone. The guards, who hadn't been able to get anywhere near the intruders for fear of being trampled under their horses' hooves, leapt onto the nearest mounts and headed into the dark in pursuit.

The quiet left behind was eerie and unnaturally still, until a fuming Anne strode forwards, intending to retrieve the parchment.

'Who dares to enter this household in such a manner?'

'Anne, no.' Gilbert, his eyes narrowed, held up a hand to halt the maid. 'I will fetch it.'

No one moved as he walked across the frosted ground. Mathilda's heart was beating so fast she feared it might explode from her body. All her effort was going into not betraying that she knew what it was she'd just witnessed. She grabbed Bettrys' hand and held it tight.

Gilbert passed the unrolled document to Bennett, his face solemn. 'You should read to us all inside. We should also bar the gates.'

Bennett nodded, and as the servants were sent scurrying forwards to secure the manor, he took the roll inside, with Anne at his shoulder. Bettrys, Mathilda, and the minstrels trailed anxiously behind them.

~ *Chapter Thirty-five* ~

15th January 1332

'It was the steward! Adam is guilty of this!' Anne spat the accusation. 'No sooner does he leave, than this abomination arrives. Who is to say he was not one of the men who came, hidden and secret?'

Bettrys' gasp of shock echoed around the hall as Lady Marjory gripped the ransom demand, her knuckles white, her face whiter.

'I assure you, Lady Marjory, Lady Joan, Adam would never…' Mathilda's defence of her steward was cut short by Gilbert as he walked across the hall, his hobnailed boots scratching against the stone floor.

'It was not Adam. He is not of the right build to match either of the men who invaded the manor.'

'You are certain, Gilbert?' Lady Marjory threw Mathilda an apologetic look, 'I have to be certain, I have to know who… First my mother and now Father…'

Guilt lodged in Mathilda's chest. They'd been so set on their task to teach one of the most corrupt men in England a lesson, that not one of the Folvilles, not even she, had stopped to think that they had just robbed, albeit tempo-rarily, his children of a father while their other parent was missing. *Is a bad father better than no father?* The question was knocked aside in favour of a more pertinent one.

'May I ask, what does the message say?'

'It is none of your business.' Anne stood behind the Willoughby children, her hands on the backs of their chairs. 'Your coming here has done this. I know it!'

'Anne!' Marjory was on her feet, her cheeks were blotched scarlet as she flourished the paper, but her tone was steady. 'I have had to warn you once today about overstepping your station. Do it again and you will be confined to your chamber until both my parents return. And as it is looking unlikely that will ever happen, you'd be talking yourself into a life away from here with no references. Lady Ingram is here to help us. Do you understand?'

Too stunned to reply, Anne clamped her lips together.

The uneasy silence was broken by a distraught Lady Joan, who whispered, 'Mother isn't coming home, is she?'

'I don't know.' Marjory reached out to her little sister. 'I'm afraid she may not.'

'This,' Lady Marjory passed the roll to Mathilda, 'is about money. We have money. Bennett, I will ask you to deal with the request here. Father trusted you with our coffers. He would wish it paid and dealt with quickly and quietly.'

'How much do the greedy wretches ask for?' Bennett's voice boiled with fury.

Unsure how she was managing to stay outwardly calm, Mathilda answered as the numbers, written in a hand she recognised so well, leapt out at her. 'One thousand three hundred marks.'

The intake of breath was communal. It was a fortune, but it was a fortune Mathilda knew could be found and was easily replaceable to someone like Willoughby. In fact, she'd put money on his petitioning the king for compensation for having to pay such a sum. She rather hoped he would, as soon as he was free.

'It says,' Mathilda read slowly, her letters being adequate for the task, but not efficient, 'that the amount should be paid in money or chattels before midnight tomorrow. It is to be taken to,' she paused, squinting at Eustace's appalling script, 'the ruined forester's hut in Morkery Woods. Does anyone know it?'

'I do.' Gilbert leant against the cream wall near the fire, taking advantage of a rare chance to warm his bones away from his over-stable lodgings. 'The wood at least, the hut I could find. It's about five hours' ride from here. Through Kesteven Forest.'

'Are there any clues as to who sent it?' Bennett was giving Lady Mathilda a look that was making her uncomfortable.

Knowing it was reasonable they should suspect her, she replied steadily, 'There are no clues that I can see.' Mathilda levelled her gaze on Bennett, 'I am not a fool. My man leaves and this arrives. Bettrys and I are truly here to help. We have been sent by my husband to find Lady Isabel on his behalf, or, at least, to get to the bottom of where she is. I can only promise we mean you no harm, but I can't prove that.'

Lady Marjory waved her guest's words away. 'You are trusted, I regret I even wavered.'

'I would have thought it too, should I be in your shoes.' Mathilda, keen not to dwell on the point, spoke to Bennett. 'You can find the money your master needs?'

'Largely. Some will have to be made up in jewels.'

Gilbert pulled a dagger from his belt and polished it on his tunic. 'I will take it.'

'Thank you, Gilbert.' Lady Marjory paled further.

'You'll take care, won't you? We can't lose you too.'

'Shouldn't we wait for our brothers to come home, sister?' Lady Joan asked the question that had been playing in Mathilda's mind.

'I don't think we should delay.' Marjory took back the parchment, holding it as if it was about to spark into flames. 'Who knows what Father is going through?'

Knowing that the worst that could be happening to Lord Willoughby was humiliation and the experience of real hunger for the first time in his life, Mathilda nonetheless agreed with her hostess. 'I think swift action would be wise. I do wonder what Lord Richard would do if he was here though. Forgive the question, but how long does it take to get to Lady Mortain's residence and back?'

Lady Marjory pursed her lips, but rather than reply, she turned to Anne. 'Perhaps you would escort Lady Joan to her chamber. We've had a long and difficult day. It would be wise for her to rest.'

Dismayed, Joan pleaded, 'But, sister, you promised I should hear the minstrels.'

'So I did.' Marjory sighed, 'Then, perhaps...'

'If I may?' Aldus stepped forward, and suddenly Mathilda realised what he meant by people not seeing them. She'd known he was there, and yet he and his fellows had merged into the background so well, that they'd become absent from her mind.

Lady Marjory nodded at the minstrel, encouraging him to proceed.

'We could play for Lady Joan in her quarters, in Anne's presence of course. It might soothe her while she takes her supper and aid a peaceful sleep.'

'Such kindness.' Marjory smiled at her sister. 'Would you like that?'

'I would, but Father would never allow…'

Marjory got to her feet, and brushed down her skirts, 'Father isn't here, and has more important worries. You go with Anne; the minstrels will follow once your supper is ready.' The temporary lady of the manor turned to Bettrys, 'Would you be so kind as to visit the kitchen and ask one of the maids to arrange refreshment for my sister in her room?'

As Lady Joan rose to leave, she asked, 'Father will be alright, won't he?'

Mathilda gestured towards the ransom note. 'They want money, there's no hint here of ill intent to his life. No one would get away with the murder of a justice. Even the risks these people have taken so far are huge.'

Consoled for now, Lady Joan allowed herself to be bustled away by a seething Anne.

No one spoke until they were both out of earshot, then Gilbert, his face solemn, gave a bow and asked for permission to speak.

'The guards chasing the felons returned before I came inside. They could tell me nothing other than each man rode in a different direction, before being swallowed up by the forest.' He rubbed his short beard as he continued, 'Lady Mathilda said there was no threat of violence stated in the missive towards his lordship. Was a threat attached to the safe delivery of the ransom?'

Wishing Adam had been there when the demand came, so he could have passed word to her family not to harm Gilbert when the ransom arrived, Mathilda watched the groom carefully as Lady Marjory spoke.

'We are instructed to send one man with the ransom. However, this would be foolish. My father and, indeed my brothers, would never forgive me if I did not make some attempt to capture these villains, or at least find a way to identify them, so that the weight of the law can be applied later.'

Glad Bettrys wasn't there, Mathilda agreed 'While it would be wise to be seen to be complying with the demand, it would be wrong to send one man into the forest carrying so much wealth.'

'You think I should be accompanied by force of arms, my Lady?' Gilbert fixed his eyes on Mathilda's in such a way that made her wonder for a second time whether he knew her secret.

She held his gaze. 'I think you should have capable company to ensure your safety. This family has lost enough of the people it loves, and you are clearly cared for here.'

Gilbert was clearly taken aback, as Lady Marjory concurred. 'I agree with Lady Ingram. As I said, you are too important to this household to go alone. The gate guards will accompany you. They need to redeem themselves after failing to apprehend the felons who delivered this.'

'Three men may not be enough.' Mathilda glanced around the manor. 'Your home is not well guarded, if you'll forgive my saying so. Are there no others watching over you?'

'Father thinks his reputation should be enough to protect him.'

Mathilda remembered hearing Eustace once saying something similar about the Folville family. That had also been an arrogance too far and proven wrong in the past. It struck her that he and Willoughby were more alike than her brother-in-law would ever wish to admit.

'There must be other guards, though?' Mathilda asked. 'Gilbert can't take all your protection with him.'

Bennett nodded, 'There are, but Lord Willoughby likes his protection to be invisible.'

'There are men in the forest watching the house? Skilled

men?' Mathilda was again reminded of Eustace's tactics and wondered if Adam had been followed home.

'Indeed.'

'So, one of those men, if not more, could have seen your unwanted visitors arrive and leave, and also know which direction Lords Richard and Edmund went in? I ask this because they seem to have been gone a long time for people simply seeking to reassure themselves of their mother's whereabouts.'

Marjory's mouth dropped open, her face etched with a new fear as Mathilda hastily added, 'I did not wish to imply that ill has befallen them too. I don't believe that for a minute. Your father has value to these felons because of who he is, that's why he's been taken and why he will be returned. He is too dangerous to kill. Your mother's disappearance…' She paused, unsure how to continue, glad to see Bettrys returning, her arms full of a tray of ale and wine. 'That is a different situation. One that I will get to the bottom of.'

'You don't think someone is targeting my family, removing us one at a time?' Lady Marjory peered over her shoulder as if expecting to see a hooded figure lurking in the corner, a crossbow loaded and ready to shoot.

'No, my Lady, I don't.' Shaking her head, Mathilda gave a gentle smile. 'I suspect that, on discovering your mother was not with Lady Mortain, Lords Richard and Edmund travelled further afield looking for her. Would that be in character?'

Lady Marjory picked up the cup of small ale Bettrys had poured for her. 'My brother favours my father in many ways. He cares for Mother, but…'

Seeing his charge struggle to finish her sentence without speaking ill of the heir of the manor, Bennett relieved Lady Marjory of the burden. 'If Lord Richard believed finding his mother would bring him favour from his father, then he would certainly endeavour to find her.'

Mathilda stared into the fire. Sparks of orange vied for position with flecks of gold as the log pile shifted, and a spatter of charcoal smuts dotted the stone floor. She needed to think. And quickly. As soon as Gilbert left, she had to act and find out the truth of Lady Isabel's situation. Once he was back, the suspicions Mathilda was sure Gilbert held about her identity would be confirmed.

But where do I even begin to look for answers?

~ *Chapter Thirty-six* ~

16th January 1332

The moon had obligingly gone behind a cloud, helping to disguise their identities.

Hooded, with a scarf obscuring his face, Robert de Folville held their captive's arms behind his back. He signalled to Roger Savage to pull down Willoughby's gag.

An outpouring of coughing and cursing rage erupted from Willoughby's lips, until Savage clamped a grubby gloved hand over his mouth.

'If you want a drink of water, *Justice*, I suggest you cease your whining.' Savage spoke with a hatred that shone in his slate eyes. He shoved the water pouch against Willoughby's lips as Robert pulled their prisoner's head back.

Water ran down the justice's chin. He spluttered and choked in his eagerness to consume as much liquid as he could down his parched throat.

Savage eyed the man with disgust, taking in the patch where he'd soiled his trousers. The stench of urine, sweat, and fear filled the night air as he shoved the thick cloth gag back between the justice's teeth. Uncaring that the man had turned bright red and was struggling for breath, he pulled a sack over Willoughby's head, and shoved him into the base of the cart.

Stepping away, Robert brushed his hands against his

cloak. He glanced to where Eustace was standing, a loaded crossbow to hand, and a satisfied expression on his face. Whatever else they'd achieved, Lord Richard de Willoughby was suffering, albeit only from lack of food and dignity. Robert hoped the lesson would be one he learnt from. But he doubted it.

'Adam!'

Sarah's relief at seeing her husband arrive through their bedroom door was instantly overwhelmed by fear as she looked past him, expecting to see Mathilda and Bettrys, and seeing neither.

'Don't worry,' engulfing her in his arms, Adam held Sarah close, 'they are safe. I'm here alone due to circumstances that could not be prevented.' He stood back, keeping his wife in his arms, his eyes running over her. 'And you, you're well? Nothing has happened here?'

Sarah shook her head. 'Nothing.' Her face creased back into concern, 'but that isn't likely to remain so. You've missed Pykehose by only hours, and he warned of approaching search parties.'

'Ulric told me when he took my horse. I was sorry to wake the boy, but glad to see him whole.' Adam slumped onto the bed next to his wife. 'John took Jep?'

'His own horse was lame. It seemed the right thing to do.'

'It was. Jep is a swift one, and Pykehose is no man for dawdling. The mount will suit him far more than it would Lady Mathilda.' Adam's belly gurgled as he hugged Sarah close. 'It seems my stomach has missed your cooking as much as I've missed you!'

'Then I shall feed you.'

In the kitchen, moments later, Sarah and Adam were busily preparing food and drink when Lord Thomas arrived, closely followed by Daniel.

'I thought I heard voices.' Lord Thomas beamed, 'I'm heartened to see you, Adam. You have news?'

'Bettrys?' Daniel, uneasy that Pykehose's visit had yielded so little information about the situation at Wollaton Hall, regarded the steward with more concern than relief.

'Well and capable. She's a fine maid for Lady Mathilda.'

Pouring a drink for Lord Thomas, Daniel ventured a half-smile as his master asked, 'What news brings you back to the manor so soon   and alone?'

Fetching the velvet pouch from his tunic, Adam placed it on the table. 'That.'

Thomas emptied the bag, sending the seal rocking onto the table. 'Willoughby's?'

'Yes.' Adam scratched his hands through his hair; the fatigue he'd been trying to ignore from the last forty-eight hours was beginning to dull his senses. 'It isn't the one that Eustace delivered to Lady Mathilda.'

Sarah's brow furrowed. 'Then why…'

'It was the only way to keep up the pretence of Lady Mathilda being seen as Lady Ingram in the eyes of the Willoughby household.'

'But if you have that seal, and Mathilda had the one taken from Willoughby, then someone there, at Wollaton manor, knows you've been transporting the wrong seal… I assume they argued it should be returned to his lordship with urgency so that he could continue with his legal work?'

'Yes.'

'But this isn't, it is it? This is a spare.'

Daniel's countenance was a concerned furrow. 'How do you know this isn't the one taken from Lord Willoughby,

Adam?'

'It's clean. The one Lady Mathilda was presented by Lord Eustace was worn from use and it had tiny streaks of red wax in the engraving. This,' Adam gestured to the seal Lord Thomas was holding up to the light, 'is spotless and perfect. It's a spare.'

'Where is the original? Lord Thomas scrubbed at his beard.

'Lord Richard, Willoughby's heir, he has it. At least, we think he does. He left Wollaton Hall shortly after our arrival. He was determined to prove Lady Isabel was at her mother's, as claimed.'

'Is that where he went, or is that where just said he was going?' Daniel threw another log on the fire with more energy than necessary, sending sparks shooting up the chimney in a crackle of flames.

'Lady Mathilda thinks he's watching the hall, but she isn't sure why. There's more.'

'More?' Lord Thomas continued to roll the seal in his palm as the steward explained.

'There are precious few guards at Wollaton. I thought it odd from the start, but then we learnt from Gilbert, that's the groom there, that Willoughby favours tactics of a more private nature.'

'Meaning?' Thomas's eyes narrowed as he began to see what Adam was alluding to.

'He uses mercenaries, my Lord. They too watch the hall, but in secret.'

'Like Lord Eustace does?' Sarah didn't bother containing her groan. 'Does this mean that everything Lady Mathilda has done, everywhere she has been, has been watched since her arrival at Wollaton?'

'I imagine so.'

'And your departure too?'

Adam shrugged. 'I saw no one, but then, I pass by Borin and his men every day, and unless they want to be seen, I don't see them.' He shifted in his seat, stifling a yawn. 'When I left, the ransom demand hadn't been delivered. I waited as long as possible, but if I'd delayed longer there was a danger of Lady Mathilda's true identity being discovered. The manor is under the writ of the eldest daughter, Lady Marjory, a lass of sixteen. She is kind and trusts Mathilda, but her maid, Anne, is another matter. She is loyal to Willoughby to the bone.'

'Now you have brought this seal here, or in their minds returned it to Willoughby, will you ride back?' Daniel shifted from foot to foot; he looked ready to bolt for the door again.

'If his Lordship wishes me to return,' Adam turned towards Lord Thomas, 'then of course I will. But Lady Mathilda wanted me to stay here. She intends to be back tomorrow.'

'But in the meantime, you've left her alone!' Daniel raised his voice, forgetting his place in his fear.

'Daniel!' Sarah snapped before Lord Thomas had the chance to open his mouth.

Adam raised a hand, 'I haven't left them alone. As if you could think I would? They are being cared for by Aldus, Noll, and Dicun.'

'The minstrels are there?' Lord Thomas leant forward. 'In Wollaton?'

'Yes.' Adam gulped down some ale, 'Let me start from the beginning.'

Mathilda threw her gown over the chair and climbed into bed. Her limbs ached with the twin weight of lack of sleep and responsibility, but it hardly seemed worth sleeping when dawn was already on its way. She'd tried not to wonder if Adam was still riding through the dark, or about Robert waiting for the ransom demand to be met.

Bettrys poked the fire one last time, putting a name to the fear that was foremost in Mathilda's mind. 'Where do you think they are, my Lady?' She pulled herself into the bed, her body swaddled in the clothes she'd worn all day, 'Lord Richard the younger and his brother?'

'I wish I knew.' Tucking her knees up and resting her chin on them, Mathilda in a protective huddle, 'I'm sure they didn't go to Lincolnshire. The more I think, the more I wonder if Richard knew where his mother was all along. If Lord Willoughby was going to trust anyone with his secrets, surely it would be his son and heir?'

'But Lord Richard took his younger brother with him, Lord Edmund. Would he be privy to his father's disposing of his wife too? If that is what's happened?'

Mathilda sighed. 'He took Edmund with him, but did he keep him with him?'

'What do you mean, my Lady?'

'There is another brother, Lord Hugh. He's the youngest and is in Lenton Priory.'

'Younger than Lady Joan, and cast into a priory already?'

'It happens. The child is six.' Mathilda swallowed hard. She knew well how damaging that life could be to a child thrust into clerical life so young. You only had to spend ten minutes with Richard de Folville to see that.

'You think Lord Richard took Edmund to join Hugh in Lenton, and then went on somewhere?'

'Perhaps.' Mathilda frowned, 'unless… could it be so simple?'

'My Lady?'

'Lady Isabel. One of the facts that feels so wrong in this puzzle is that she left her children behind without saying goodbye. So, maybe she didn't. Not all of them at least…'

'She went to one of them, and asked Richard to bring the others to her when he could!' Bettrys' eyes shone, 'You think she's at Lenton Priory, and that Richard is helping her?'

'No one's mentioned Hugh or Edmund very much, come to think of it. They may be younger sons, but they are still sons.' Mathilda thrust her legs forward and lay back. 'The women have been left here, and Lord Richard the younger abandoned the place he'll inherit, just as I arrived with a plausible reason for his father and mother to appear together. Before the King and Queen of England no less… and then I find the damaged embroidery, and a gown goes missing from her chamber.'

'But if Lady Isabel is at Lenton, then she isn't dead, so…' Bettrys stifled a yawn.

'What if she faked her death? What if Lady Isabel was so unhappy here that she chose to leave, but wanted to do so in a way that would make life as difficult as possible for her husband?'

Bettrys felt sad for the life Lady Willoughby had led. 'I meant to say, my Lady, I think Bennett must have spoken for us in the kitchen. The maids and cook are less wary now. They don't speak much, but that's how it has to be here apparently. Everyone sees little, hears little, and says less.'

'Not unusual in such households.'

'But in truth, my Lady, they see and hear plenty, they are just wise enough to keep their mouths closed and their ears open.'

'What have you learnt from them?'

'That Lady Marjory spoke the truth about the argument

between her mother and Lord Willoughby. It was the talk of the kitchen because it was so rare. The only row Cook can remember between man and wife, and she's been at Wollaton since before they married.'

Mathilda nodded. 'And the subject of the argument, that was her Ladyship commenting on his Lordship's greed for land?'

'Yes, my Lady.'

Mathilda lapsed into a thoughtful silence before saying, 'Adam should be at home by now.'

Bettrys didn't say anything, not wanting to voice her fear that anything could have happened to Adam between there and Ashby Folville. Instead she said, 'Do you think there are Wollaton men watching the hall from the forest road?'

'I did, but now I'm not sure.' Mathilda started to undo her plaits as she spoke, the action calming her mind. 'When the ransom demand arrived, the messengers were chased by the guards on the gate, but, no hue and cry was raised, no armed men suddenly appeared. Nothing happened.'

'Because the household knows help is already out there hiding in the woods?'

'I thought that to start with, but now I'm wondering if it's because someone here doesn't want help to come and has been very careful to make sure it does not.'

~ *Chapter Thirty-seven* ~

16th January 1332

Daniel looked down at Ulric's sleeping body. The stable lad was wrapped in two thick blankets as well as the straw from the hayloft. Lord Thomas had invited him to sleep inside, but he'd refused, saying he needed to be outside in case someone raided the manor in the night.

Guilty for the trouble his friend might get into when the household woke to find a horse missing and their servant gone, Daniel glanced back at the kitchen door. Nothing stirred. No one had followed him.

Checking his knife was secured to his belt, Daniel led his mount to the side gate as quietly as he could. He knew there would be men watching the main entrance. He hoped if any of them were paying attention to the lesser-used side entrance, they'd be Lord Eustace's men, and that they'd assume he was on a mission for Lord Thomas, and be allowed to pass unchallenged. Stopping by the single-barred door, Daniel hoped Sarah, Lord Thomas, and Adam would understand he couldn't leave Bettrys alone in the hands of a bunch of minstrels. Anything could happen to her. With a sharp shove, he lifted the barring plank, holding his breath as a splintering creak broke the hush of the frosty night.

Still no one came to prevent his flight. Nothing moved but for the pricking of his horse's ears.

Leading his mount through the gap, Daniel eased the door shut behind them, wishing he could bolt it from the other side. Heading along the narrow path that shadowed the back of manor, Daniel disappeared into the dark.

Ten steps later, a hand landed on his shoulder. It spun Daniel around so fast that there was no time for him to draw a blade.

Dawn was still fresh but Mathilda was wide awake. Leaving Bettrys to sleep, she made her way to the hall. Instinct told her that, despite the hour, Bennett would be up. She doubted he'd even gone to sleep.

The steward was sat with Gilbert; an exhausted maid hovered at their elbow. The table was heaped with gold marks. A small pile of jewelled rings sat on a folded velvet pouch next to them.

'Is that all of it?' Guilt lodged in Mathilda's throat before she sharply reminded herself why Willoughby was being treated this way. This money had been extorted from so many people. He deserved what was happening to him. She just wished that Bennett and the servants of the manor didn't have to suffer as a result.

The steward didn't seem surprised to see her. 'Gilbert will leave within the hour.'

Mathilda thought fast. She had until he returned to find out what happened to Lady Willoughby. She did not want to be here when Sir Richard returned to his home. Her pulse raced as if to underline the tick of each second of precious time.

'You have provisions with you beyond the ransom?'

The men looked blank, so she elaborated, 'We do not

know how Justice Willoughby has been treated. He is likely to be hungry, thirsty, and tired. He may be hurt. Perhaps he'll be unable to ride… he may not want to be seen.'

Bennett viewed Mathilda with renewed respect. 'You are suggesting Gilbert takes a cart?'

'Not all the way. It would slow him down, but, if he was followed by men with a cart, perhaps one containing a change of clothes and victuals; trusted men who would never speak of it again if they saw their lord the worse for his experience, then I suspect his Lordship would be grateful to be able to hide from view. The accounts of your master I've heard describe him as a proud man.'

'He is that.' Bennett was rueful. 'He would wish to preserve his dignity.'

Gilbert gave Mathilda his shrewd stare, before getting to his feet. 'I will prepare the litter. His Lordship can choose to sit or lie down then.'

As the groom left, Bennett issued orders to the maid to gather food and drink for the return journey.

As the maid scurried off, Mathilda felt for the girl. She looked ready to drop. 'Will you let her sleep in?'

'Certainly not. Everyone will be needed once Justice Willoughby is back.' The steward had returned to the cool demeanour he'd displayed on Mathilda's arrival, and her spirits dipped. She needed Bennett on her side if she had any chance of finding out the truth behind Lady Isabel's disappearance before the justice returned.

Not commenting on the luckless maid, Mathilda gestured for the steward to sit with her. He paused before agreeing. 'Bennett, I wish to be away from here before your master returns. He will be in no mood for outsiders, and I have encroached on your hospitality enough.'

'But?'

'But I promised Lady Marjory I would find out what happened to her mother, and I intend to keep that promise.'

'A promise that happens to match one you made your husband.' Bennett was sceptical.

'I would keep my promise to the young Lady Willough-by even if it wasn't to my advantage   and indeed, to my husband's and Lord Willoughby's himself, if he is to please the king.'

The steward looked at her without a word, his features softening.

'The linen. I have it hidden,' Mathilda tapped her cloak. 'If I have no reason to reveal its finding, I will not speak of it. It is not evidence of anything except spilt blood.'

Relieved, Bennett said, 'It occurred to me that it could be the result of a nosebleed?'

'No,' Mathilda gave a reluctant shrug. 'The pattern of blood is wrong. It could be from a cut head or hand. A nicked ear maybe; that produces a lot of blood.'

'How do you know this?'

'My husband's work.'

'Of course.' Bennett started to count the marks into the velvet bag. 'You are unusual, my Lady. Not many wives take such an interest in their husband's work. Even fewer are allowed to show they are interested.'

'I was lucky in my choice of husband.'

'You had a choice?' He looked stunned.

Mathilda decided to leave that enquiry unanswered in case it gave her away. 'I think the embroidery was left there for me to find. For all we know the blood may not have been Lady Isabel's at all. Tell me, Bennett, did you put it there?'

'You scared me half to death!'

Daniel sank back against the nearest tree, his stomach

churning as John Pykehose stood before him, grinning widely. 'I knew you'd head to Wollaton. Honestly, boy, you're see-through.'

'I'm not going back. I…'

'Save your breath, lad. I've heard it all before. Stay close, stay quiet, and stay alert. We'll go to your girl together.'

Robert led the horse pulling the cart containing Willoughby along a route they'd walked before. The dark was thinning now as dawn faded into a haze of pink and grey sky. It was set to be a bright, cold day. Eustace walked ahead, his head turning this way and that, his ears and eyes alert for danger as they edged their captive back to the forester's hut to await the arrival of ransom.

Savage was already near the hut, keeping watch from high in a tree. As much as Robert disliked the outlaw, he didn't envy him the task of sitting high and unsheltered in the cold. His stomach growled as he walked on, his mind on Mathilda. He hoped she was out of Wollaton and had found and earned the trust of Lady Isabel. If they were going to escape a noose after this, they'd need her to vouch for her husband's corruption.

Robert stopped and listened. There was a rustle in the fallen leaves ahead. Was it Eustace… or was it someone else?

Bennett hadn't dignified Mathilda's question about him being responsible for hiding the linen with an answer. Instead he bluntly asked, 'Do you think Lady Isabel is dead?'

'I have a number of theories concerning the fate of your mistress.' Mathilda held his gaze.

Lifting the filled money pouch and weighing it in his palm, Bennett took a careful look around the hall, as if willing the walls to speak to them. 'Which are?'

'Theories.' She leant forward. 'One of them is that you were fond of your mistress. May I ask how much? What would you do for her?'

A red hue infused his cheeks as Bennett rounded on her in a flash of anger, only to hiss out his words quietly rather than shout as Mathilda had expected. 'I told you before, she is the best of mistresses, but if you are suggesting what I think you are, then you are a disgrace. You think like a woman who can be hired by the hour!'

Unmoved, Mathilda pointed to the bag of money. 'I think like someone trying to work out if the man you are gathering that money together to save is the sort of man who would kill his wife, or more likely given his reputation, arrange for someone to kill his wife for him.'

Bennett sagged into a chair. 'So, you do think she's dead.'

Playing him at his own game, and not giving a direct answer to his question, Mathilda said, 'She could have been removed to safety. Someone who cared for Lady Isabel could have got wind of what his Lordship planned and removed her from harm's way, without time to do more than hustle her out of Wollaton. This person could have had her best interests at heart.'

Bennett's eyes flared with hope. 'If that happened, it was not I who took her.' The hope in his eyes died again as he said, 'But I saw Lord Willoughby, remember? He told me his wife had been escorted away.'

'So he did.' Mathilda sipped from her small ale. 'I wonder if that was the truth?'

'I'm sure it wasn't, but...'

'Perhaps it was a half-truth. He took her away, but not to where he claimed. If I'm right about that, where might he have had her taken?'

Bennett glared into the flames. 'I truly don't know. Not somewhere local, Lady Isabel is too well known, and Lord Willoughby has eyes everywhere.'

'The mercenaries in the forest?'

'Indeed.' The steward glanced towards the kitchen as the maid re-emerged, her arms heavy with linen. He remained quiet until she'd scuttled away, and they could no longer hear her boots echoing down the stone corridor. 'If that is what happened, she would have been taken far away, or at least somewhere where she could be safely out of sight.'

'Lenton Priory?'

'The priory, that's where Master Hugh is… Ah, a sensible suggestion, Lady Ingram.'

Mathilda leant forward, 'How far is it to Lenton from here?'

'An hour on horseback.'

'We need to check. If only Adam was still here.'

'I would send Gilbert in normal circumstances, but…'

'Quite.' Mathilda nodded, 'I had wondered if young Lord Richard would have gone to Lenton and left Master Edmund there.'

Bennett's eyebrows rose. 'I doubt he'd have been that considerate.'

'Unless he wanted to go on to visit Lady Mortain alone. Assuming that was where he was heading.'

'You remain in doubt of that?'

'The mercenaries that Lord Willoughby uses   I understand that the majority are helping him hunt for those who follow the Coterel family, leaving only a few to watch Wollaton.'

'How did you know that?' An edge of suspicion tainted Bennett's voice as he stood up straighter.

'I overheard a conversation in Leicester.' Mathilda's mind raced; she was on the edge of understanding what had happened, but the final answer was frustratingly out of reach. 'Then I wondered how none of those mercenaries had come here to tell you or Lord Willoughby where his wife had been taken. One at least must have seen her go, because '

'Because Lady Isabel left here *before* he went away to court.'

'Precisely.'

'A lot of the paid soldiers had already gone; Lord Willoughby sent them to Derbyshire to hunt felons, as you said, but there were still men here; more than there are now.'

'That means the chances of those mercenaries seeing Lady Isabel leaving were high. Which also means she was taken by someone they wouldn't be concerned about seeing her with.'

The steward was about to respond when the clatter of Gilbert's boots alerted them to his return.

'It's time.'

~ *Chapter Thirty-eight* ~

16th January 1332

The three armed men sat together, blocking the only track wide enough for them to pass along with their horses. As Daniel watched, he saw them pass around a pouch of ale, something they clearly didn't need, for they were already the worse for drink. If they hadn't been, they'd never have been making so much noise in the middle of the forest so early in the morning.

Pykehose held up a warning hand. It wasn't safe to move forwards or back.

Praying the horses kept quiet, sweat trickled down Daniel's neck. For the first time in three hours he was frightened. Until that moment, all he'd been thinking about was getting to Bettrys, now all he wanted was to be still alive at noon.

Following John's silent instructions, he eased his knife from his belt. Pykehose pulled the bow from his back, and with a skill Daniel could only envy, notched an arrow onto the string.

Peering back the way they'd come, desperately praying for an alternative way out to appear from nowhere, Daniel was afraid his heartbeat had become so loud that the mercenaries would hear it.

As they watched, the laughter ahead became more raucous. The men drew daggers from their belts and took it in turns to throw them at the nearest tree trunk.

Pykehose whispered into his companion's ear, 'They're betting on how high they can get the knives. The winner will get a swig of whatever drink they have left.'

Opening his mouth to reply, Daniel's lips were clamped back into silence by Pykehose's sharp shake of the head. Instead they watched as the victor of the competition glugged back more ale and the contest began again.

The second winner shouted his victory to exaggerated shushing from his comrades. 'Willoughby's finest are coming your way, Coterels!'

Pykehose's eyes narrowed as the victor mentioned the Folvilles' allies. 'The more they drink, the safer we are, but we still need to be lucky.'

Too afraid to speak, Daniel simply inclined his head as he listened to his companion.

'We can't afford to wait. When I say ride, then ride as fast as you can to Wollaton. My path is different from yours beyond the fork in the road ahead. You must continue, while I'll find Lord Eustace off to the right.'

'But how?' Daniel mouthed the words, his palm sweating against the knife handle, making his grip slippery.

'By riding as fast as we can and hoping they're too drunk to get up and throw knives in our direction.' Pykehose smiled as he pointed to their horses. 'You go ahead. I'll follow and cover you with my bow.'

'From your horse?'

'I work for Lord Eustace; I can fire my bow from anything.'

Keeping his eyes fixed on the mercenaries, trying not to

consider how accurate they were even when they were blind drunk, Daniel smoothed his horse's neck. Willing him not to whinny, stamp, or even move until they were ready, he leapt into the saddle, wincing as the leather gave the tiniest of creaks under his weight.

An hour had passed. It had gone so fast, yet so slowly, that Daniel felt it wasn't real. It couldn't be real. His horse was galloping, heading forwards as if it knew where to go.

Daniel's head thudded with pain, guilt and incomprehension. He didn't know if he should stop, go back or turn right and head towards Lord Eustace. It didn't matter, because his horse was racing, on and on, and Daniel couldn't stop it. He had to get to Bettrys now, if he didn't then… then…

The galloping horse was heard before it was seen. Mathilda and Bettrys looked up in alarm as they crossed the courtyard, carrying armfuls of linen towards the cart waiting to head into Kesteven Forest.

Seconds later they were fleeing for cover as a horse they recognised thundered towards them, the rider out of control.

Bettrys ran forward before Mathilda could stop her, and without registering that she could have been trampled to death, grabbed the bridle and staggered backwards as the horse careered to a halt.

Winded as she was knocked back against the wooden post holding up the stable roof, Bettrys gasped as Daniel slid from the saddle to the ground.

A stable lad ran forward, taking the horse as Mathilda and a shaking Bettrys dashed to where Daniel lay.

'Please, no…' Bettrys' words came out as a whisper as she put her hand to his chest, desperate to make sure he was breathing. A second later, the maid fell back in relief. Daniel was alive, even if he wasn't alright.

Doing her best to stay calm, her own relief overwhelming, Mathilda knelt to her servant. 'Daniel, you're at Wollaton. Bettrys is here. Do you know who I am?'

The lad frowned; his eyes were having trouble focusing through the tears he'd been crying. 'Lady Mathilda?'

'That's right.'

'Wollaton?' Daniel winced as he tried to sit up, his back bruised from the fall. 'Bettrys?'

'I'm here. Let me help you sit up.' Placing a hand in his, Bettrys stared at Mathilda in bewilderment as she asked him, 'Are you hurt?'

'Hurt?' Suddenly registering he was sitting on the ground, Daniel clambered to his feet, but he swayed as he stood. Holding onto Bettrys, he heaved and then, turning fast, emptied his guts across the gravel.

Leaving Bettrys with Daniel, Mathilda rushed to the house, her heart thudding. If Daniel wasn't thinking straight, there was a chance he'd give her away as a Folville. She needed to think. And fast.

Running into the kitchen, she asked a startled maid for a clean cloth and some cool water, before returning to her fallen servant.

'He didn't follow me.'

'Who didn't?' Bettrys looked from Daniel's shaking body to Lady Mathilda.

'John, John was behind me, and they… they got up, and I tried to throw the knife, but my hand…' He glared at his right hand. He didn't deserve to have it.

'John?' Bettrys took the cloth from her mistress and dabbed his brow. 'Lord John?' She checked over her should before whispering, 'Lord John Folville?'

'My hand,' Daniel held it out before him like it was repulsive; diseased. 'Useless!'

Bettrys took the proffered hand, examining it front and back. 'It's fine. No breaks, not even a bruise.'

'Exactly! Nothing. It did nothing to save him. It dropped my knife. Too afraid.'

'Save who, Daniel? And who from?' A trickle of apprehension ran down Mathilda's spine as an unwelcome thought came to mind. 'Pykehose? John Pykehose?'

The tiny amount of blood that remained in Daniel's face drained away, his reply bleak. 'I didn't even see him fall. I was in front, you see. I heard though. I heard him scream. I'll never forget.'

'Pykehose.' Mathilda muttered the name. The man was undefeatable. That's what Eustace had always said. 'Daniel, are you telling us he's dead?'

'I…'

'Please, Daniel, I know you're shaken, but it's important. If he's gone, we need to know.'

'Shot. I heard a crossbow. We didn't even know they had them.'

'Who are they?'

'Mercenaries. Willoughby's men. Hunting Coterel followers.'

A movement to their right alerted Mathilda to the arrival of Gilbert and Bennett in the courtyard. Three other men also stepped forward. Two climbed onto the front of a cart, the third mounted a horse and waited beside his colleagues for Gilbert to join them.

Seeing Bennett's displeasure at another unknown face within Wollaton's walls, Mathilda got to her feet, tapping Bettrys on her shoulder, as if telling her to stay where she was. 'Are you ready, Gilbert?'

'Yes, my Lady.' He patted his cloak over where the ransom was hidden as he dipped his head in Daniel's direction. 'We have a visitor?'

'My kitchen hand. I don't know what message he is bringing yet. It seems he met a man on the road and they travelled together, then they ran into some mercenaries.' She paused, 'Lord Willoughby's men. Something happened and the other man was killed. The lad is badly shaken and guilt-ridden for not preventing what, I have no doubt, he couldn't possibly have prevented anyway.'

The steward and groom exchanged a knowing look as Gilbert asked, 'The fallen man, did the lad get his name?'

'I think he said Pykehorse, Pykehouse maybe… Daniel is very distressed.'

'Pykehose.' Gilbert glanced to where the boy and maid huddled, their arms around each other. 'Those two are close.'

'Yes.'

Gilbert stared hard at the boy, before twisting around to face Bennett. 'The fallen man's horse will be loose in the forest.'

Bennett agreed. 'Only bring it here if you see it. Your mission is to bring his Lordship home safely. Don't go searching for the mount beyond your given path.'

'It could be hurt.'

'Nonetheless; his Lordship first.'

'I should go.' Gilbert inclined his head. He took two steps before stopping. 'Look after them, Bennett. All of them.'

~ *Chapter Thirty-nine* ~

16th January 1332

'Why did Gilbert want to fetch John's horse?'

Daniel was still shaking, but he'd reclaimed command of his speech. Grateful to be warming himself by the hall fire, the lad clutched a bowl of stew in his hands; a beaker of ale waited by his side.

'Apparently Lord Richard, that's Lord Willoughby's eldest son, has a passion for horses. If he's seen the horse before, he'll know it again.' Mathilda was worried. 'If he finds the horse and makes a connection to…'

Relieved he was able to give at least one piece of comforting news, Daniel said, 'John rode Jep. His own horse was lame. They won't know the animal.'

'Thank Heaven for Lady Joan la Zouche!' Mathilda exhaled as Bettrys crouched in front of Daniel, refilling his beaker with small ale.

'We don't have long before Bennett rejoins us, and I can't imagine Lady Marjory will sleep for much longer. I'd like us to be out of here before Gilbert gets back. That gives us until about five o'clock to be gone from here.' Mathilda looked over her shoulder towards the kitchen door. 'I wonder now if I should have mentioned John's full name.

If Gilbert has heard of Pykehose's name in relation to the Folvilles before…' She sighed. 'Oh well, too late now. I just hope my instinct to trust Gilbert was sound.'

Mathilda was relieved when she saw that Daniel or Bettrys had been too wrapped up in their own fears to hear hers. 'How is it you're here, Daniel, what news do you bring?'

'News?' The lad coloured and lowered his gaze to the floor. A fresh wave of guilt filled him as the knowledge that Pykehose would be alive if he hadn't crept out of Ashby Folville overwhelmed him.

'Is it Adam? Has something happened to him?' Mathilda voiced the question that had been nagging at her since Daniel galloped through the gates of Wollaton Hall.

'Adam's fine. He is with Sarah, Ulric, and Lord Thomas. I…' Daniel suddenly looked up, holding Bettrys' eyes, his whole being pleading with her to understand, to forgive what he'd done. 'I have no message, I'm here because…' He licked his lips, 'because I didn't like the idea of you and Lady Mathilda being here alone, with no protection. Without Adam to watch over you, so I… I…'

Bettrys tucked a strand of hair that had flopped over Daniel's eyes behind his ear. 'But we aren't alone. Didn't Adam tell you we were with Aldus, Noll, and Dicun?'

Daniel's shoulders quaked as he battled the instinct to cry again. 'Adam told me, but they're just balladeers, what training do they have in arms? What if '

Understanding the burden Daniel's good intentions had brought upon him, Mathilda got to her feet. 'So you snuck away from Ashby Folville and bumped into Pykehose as he travelled on whatever mission Lord Eustace sent him. A good man, John Pykehose, he wouldn't have wanted you to journey alone along roads that he knew to be teeming with men-at-arms. So, he took it upon himself to protect you.' Mathilda watched the fire dance in the hearth as she whispered, 'and he did protect you, didn't he, Daniel. Right to the very end.'

Daniel did cry then. Silent racking sobs into Bettrys' shoulder that were so violent they made the bench shake with his guilt-ridden grief.

Sarah's greying hair hung around her shoulders. Wrapped in a blanket, blurred from sleep after her disturbed night, she ran to answer the early morning summons of an urgent hammering on the manor's front door.

Right behind her, Adam dashed through the manor, through the kitchen, and out through the door to the courtyard, so he could approach whoever it was demanding entrance from the outside.

The first person Adam saw was Ulric. He had his back to the stable block; two soldiers, wearing the livery of Sheriff Jort, stood either side of him. Their swords were drawn but lowered. It was clear they intended the lad to stay where he was.

At the front door, with his fist propelling back and forth against the oak as if he was attempting to knock through the wood, the Captain of the Guard waited with growing impatience.

'What's the meaning of this?' Lord Thomas de Folville bellowed across the courtyard as he appeared behind Adam, before whispering quietly to his steward, 'I've sent Sarah back to the kitchen to make breakfast.'

Acknowledging his master with a minute dip of the head, Adam strode to Ulric and pointedly took the boy by the shoulder and escorted him away from the armed men. 'Are you alright?'

'Yes.' Ulric muttered nervously, 'Daniel isn't here.'

Adam said nothing. His eyes strayed to the stall which usually held Daniel's horse. It was empty.

Lord Thomas glared at the men-at-arms, 'Put those swords away. While you are in my family's home you will conduct yourselves with some decorum.'

'That's rich, coming from one of the most notorious men in England!' the captain snarled, but he waved for his men to do as requested.

Keeping his gaze fixed on the captain, Lord Thomas addressed his stable boy, 'Go and tell Sarah we have guests, please, Ulric.'

'Call that an order?' Scoffing, the captain glared at the temporary lord of the manor with contempt. 'No wonder you are so little respected if you treat your servants as if they are equals.'

'First you say I'm notorious, and then I'm too polite to my fellow man. Make your mind up! Then you can tell me what you want so early in the morning,' Lord Thomas pointed to the gates, 'and then you can leave us in peace.'

'It's long past dawn. You should be up and about your business.'

'In your opinion.' Lord Thomas pulled his dagger from his belt and examined the blade. 'I repeat, state your business.'

Peering around him, as if only just registering that no other Folville brothers had come forth from the manor, the captain stood a little straighter, his tone regaining its authority. 'We've been ordered to search the manors and lands of all Folville family members.'

'For servants who have been granted an extra hour abed for good service, so you can turf them out of their slumber?'

'Don't be facetious!'

'Bold words for so few men on Folville land.'

The captain's Adam's apple wobbled, but he stood his ground. 'I have my orders, I would advise you to not to dispute them.'

'I wouldn't dream of it. Perhaps you could tell us what you are searching for?'

'You know full well.' The captain of the guard beckoned to his men, who stepped forward.

'Three of you, hunting for Coterels? You must be braver, or more stupid, than you look.' Lord Thomas waved a hand towards the kitchen door, 'Adam, would you like to escort our guest inside. He is welcome to poke his nose into any room he likes. His men, however,' he twisted on the balls of his boots so fast that the waiting soldiers automatically took a step backwards, 'will stand as guards, preventing their master's work from being interrupted.'

The captain opened his mouth to argue, but then closed it as he followed Adam towards the kitchen. He had almost reached the door when he turned back. 'You are alone here, Lord Thomas?'

'I have six brothers, Captain. Just because you can't see them, doesn't mean they aren't here, or aren't close enough to be here in an instant if I so much as snap my fingers.' Thomas gave a humourless laugh. 'Whereas you, Captain, would need a three-day window to get Sheriff Jort to your side, should you need him.'

Having left Daniel resting on the cot at the end of her bed, Lady Mathilda instructed Bettrys to pack up their few belongings and went in search of Bennett. Finding the steward in the doorway to his master's chamber, looking unsure whether he should go in or not, Mathilda called out softly, 'Are you alright?'

'No. Are you, my Lady?'

'Not really,' she regarded the interior through the open door before them. 'You are unsure how to prepare for Justice Willoughby's arrival.'

'I am not even sure he will arrive.'

Mathilda felt unable to put the steward out of his misery without giving away her role in what had happened. Once the silence began to get uncomfortable, she said, 'We are almost ready to leave.'

'Leave? Before you've located Lady Isabel?'

'His Lordship will be in no mood for house guests. Anne is perfectly capable of nursing him, and she has made it clear our assistance in that matter is not welcome.'

'It is not.' Appearing behind them, Anne more or less elbowed Bennett out of the way as she pushed into the chamber, her arms full of clean linens, bandages, and all manner of other things that might be required once her master returned. 'Now that Lord Willoughby is coming back, he can retrieve Lady Willoughby from Lincolnshire himself and make preparations for her to see the Queen. You are not required. I'm sure Lord Ingram will be glad of your safe return. I hear he is a kind man, so perhaps he won't punish you too much for failing in your mission.'

'Anne!' Bennett was furious, 'How dare you speak to Lady Ingram in such a manner? Put that lot down and get back to attending their Ladyships. It's my place to care for the master, not yours.'

Ignoring the steward, Anne placed her load on top of the wooden chest at the foot of the bed before swinging round. 'If I thought I could trust you to tend to his Lordship's needs I would, but clearly I can't.' Ignoring the steward, she pulled off the top layer of bed linen and, marching over to the discarded linen pile, threw back its cover and added the soiled bedding to it.

Bennett, his face red, spoke with a calm command that Mathilda would not have liked to have been on the receiving end of. 'You will put that down and go and care for your charges. I will inform you when his Lordship is back. *If* he requires any medical attention that I am unable to administer, I shall inform you.' Then, stepping forward, he took the maid by the elbow and escorted her from the chamber.

'His Lordship will hear about this!' Anne almost spat as she spoke.

'He most certainly will.' Bennett, taking hold of Anne's elbow, pointed along the corridor to where Lady Joan resided. 'I'm sure he will be particularly interested to know how you were happy to leave his daughters alone in the company of three grown men. Three minstrels! Wasn't it you who reminded us in what low regard Justice Willoughby holds such men?'

'I, I…' Anne spluttered as she ripped arm out of Bennett's grip. 'You will never suggest I am derelict in my duty ever again. Do you hear! Never!'

'Who was that shouting?' Daniel stood with Bettrys, holding open their pack roll as she folded up Lady Mathilda's spare gown. 'I swear I've heard that voice before.'

'Anne, the girl's maid,' Bettrys tutted, 'she is a bully. I can see why Lord Willoughby holds her in such high regard. Right in his mould she is.'

'Willoughby… Lady Willoughby. It was her! Her voice.'

'No, Daniel.' Bettrys spoke gently; she was beginning to wonder if he'd suffered a bang on the head as he fled from Pykehose's murder. 'That was Anne shouting.'

The lad shook his head. 'I meant the voice at the church at Willoughby-on-the-Wolds, remember. There was a woman talking to the reverend about whether he thought Lady

Isabel was mad, or not.'

'Of course!' Bettrys dropped the gown. 'We have to tell Lady Mathilda. Now.'

~ *Chapter Forty* ~

16th January 1332

'Someone's coming.' Robert braced himself behind a wide oak as he signalled to Eustace.

He knew Savage was close, but where, and how capable he was after all the ale he'd drunk, Robert wasn't sure. He was sure however that Borin and at least two of his mercenaries were nearby. He hoped that he wouldn't have to see any of them before this day was done.

As the footsteps got closer, Robert pulled his hood over his head, and checked his scarf was covering his face. Unsure if the footsteps approaching belonged to the messenger they'd been waiting for, Robert squeezed the handle of his knife and murmured a prayer to Our Lady. Asking her to care for Mathilda if what was to follow went wrong.

Robert peered around the tree. It was a man alone. Tall, well built; not a man of noble birth, yet he carried himself with pride and confidence. He carried a sword at his side, but it wasn't drawn. His hands were empty and open, as if to show he was not a threat to anyone.

It's him. The ransom carrier from Wollaton.

Feeling, rather than seeing or hearing, Eustace tense as he reached the same conclusion, Robert made ready to confront their visitor, who'd stopped abruptly a few feet from the forester's hut where Justice Willoughby was currently bundled.

'I have come from Wollaton Hall as instructed.' The man's voice rang through the trees. 'I know this to be Morkery Woods. I have come alone, but I will own to three men waiting with my horse and a cart some few lengths back so I can take his Lordship home in comfort.'

Robert tensed as Eustace's voice rang out just as clearly.

'State your name, messenger.'

'If you will state yours.'

'I hardly think that's necessary.' Eustace's voice was firm, but Robert had the strangest feeling that his brother was trying not to laugh.

The messenger took another step towards the forester's hut. 'I trust Lord Willoughby is alive and well cared for.'

'He is alive.' Eustace grunted, 'You have the ransom?'

'I do.' The messenger reached inside his cloak, pulled out a velvet bag, and raised it high above his head so that whoever was watching him could see it. 'How would you like the exchange to be made?'

Expecting Eustace to order the man to lay the bag on the ground, having emptied it out first, so they could make sure it contained what they'd requested rather than a load of stones, Robert was stunned when his brother strode casually out of trees, greeting their visitor in person.

'Gilbert.' He clapped the man on the back, his voice muted for fear of being overheard by the messenger's associates. 'It's been a long time.'

'My Lord.' The groom bowed and held out the ransom. 'You didn't ask much for him. Is this on principle rather than a need for money? Or do you see Willoughby as being as worthless as I do?'

Eustace answered with a grin, 'Principle, but I agree the man is worth little. Less than this.' He slid the bag into his pocket and beckoned for Robert to come forward. 'Brother, let me introduce you to Gilbert Ward, head groom to Wollaton Hall and a fine horseman.'

Emerging from his hiding place, Robert came forward, keeping his hood up and his dagger to hand.

'My Lords,' Gilbert lowered his voice, 'I'm glad to see you, but I bring grave news.'

'Mathilda?' Robert had breathed out his wife's name before he remembered she was posing as Ingram's wife at Wollaton.

'Ah, so she *is* the Lady Folville I've heard so much about. I wondered. A clever woman, my Lord.'

'And well, I trust?' Robert gritted his teeth.

'Well, and playing the role of Lady Ingram to perfection. No one has connected her to your family. Her servants are also well, although…' Gilbert paused; checking over his shoulder to make sure his colleagues hadn't disobeyed him and come further forward to check he was alright. 'The lad that's just arrived at Wollaton, Daniel. He's shaken up.'

'Daniel?' Robert looked at Eustace. 'What's he doing there?'

'It appears he was disturbed by the idea of Lady Mathilda and her maid being at Wollaton alone.'

'Alone? But Adam '

Gilbert turned again, this time to see his colleagues approaching. He switched his manner in a second. 'You will let me see his Lordship now!'

Robert and Eustace stepped backwards, both pointing silently at the hut.

Gilbert turned to his colleagues and yelled, 'Bring the cart!' Taking his chance, he spoke fast under his breath,

'Adam was forced to return to Ashby Folville to protect Lady Mathilda's identity. And the ill news… John Pykehose is dead.'

The sound of the men moving with their cart sent Gilbert running towards the hut as Eustace disappeared into the cover of the trees. Following his brother, Robert felt his heart thud in his chest. Mathilda was alive, but she was still there. Still at Wollaton. And Pykehose was gone from the world.

She should have left by now. She promised she wouldn't stay, even if she hadn't found Lady Isabel by the time the ransom was demanded. Robert ducked under some low hanging branches. *When will I learn that my wife never does as she's told?*

Aldus smiled as Lady Joan clapped, her young face beaming as the final line of the ballad came to an end.

'I don't think we've ever had such a kind audience. We thank you both.'

Lady Marjory grinned at her sister. 'And we thank you. We've had little to take joy in lately. Music to brighten our morning was just what we needed.' She rose to her feet. 'Perhaps you would like to take some refreshment in the hall. I will instruct the maids to bring you some food.'

The three men bowed gratefully, as Aldus said, 'Again we thank you. I feel we should check on Lady Mathilda, however. We promised Adam that we'd ensure her welfare while we are here.'

'I will ask Anne to attend Lady Joan, and then I'll join you in the hall.'

Cradling his instrument close to his chest, Dicun looked around as they walked, 'This establishment has changed since our last visit. Could his Lordship's absence really cause so much difference to the atmosphere of the place?'

'All the men of the house are missing, not just Lord Willoughby. It is telling.' Aldus lowered his voice, 'We've been gone from Lady Mathilda's side longer than I planned. We must find her.'

The stone walls were giving out a chill that added an extra air of despondency to the chamber.

Bennett hadn't said anything, but Mathilda knew he'd noticed what Anne had done. Or more precisely, where she'd done it.

'You told me this room normally locked, and that only you and his Lordship had a key?'

Bennett was grave. 'I believed I had spoken honestly.'

'Could his lordship have left Anne his key?'

'I suppose so, but why would he? Anne is...' The steward was shaking his head before he'd reached the end of his sentence. 'No, I won't believe that of her, or his Lordship. I've never seen any evidence to suggest such a... liaison.'

'Yet Anne knew where the soiled linen was hidden. You said only you knew that.'

'Yes,' he frowned, 'his Lordship made a point of it only being me that came in here. He laboured it, even. I was told it was because of the documents in here, the important legal papers I...' Bennett's shoulders sagged. 'I was foolish enough to believe that after all my years of service, it was only me he trusted.'

Mathilda knelt by the linen pile and rolled off the top linen, 'He flattered you into thinking you were special to him. I'm sorry to say that ties in with all I've heard about your master being a cruel man.'

'What are you searching for?' Suddenly remembering his station, Bennett beckoned for Mathilda to stand. 'I should be doing that, your Ladyship. It's not seemly for you to be sat in such a manner.'

A cough from outside the door caused them both to turn, as the three minstrels stopped on their way from Lady Joan's quarters to the hall.

Scrambling to her feet, Mathilda asked, 'Did Lady Joan enjoy your music again this morning?'

'She was good enough to say so.' Aldus bowed, 'Forgive our intrusion, but we promised Adam we'd check on your welfare.'

'Forgiveness is not required.' Mathilda turned to Bennett, 'I must speak to my friends, please excuse me.'

Leaving Bennett searching through the linen pile for a second time, she followed her friends into the corridor.

'Lady Marjory wishes to talk to you.' Aldus checked over his shoulder, 'She is searching for the woman, Anne, to look after her sister.'

Mathilda spun round and called back to Bennett, who was by her side in seconds. 'My Lady?'

'Anne didn't go back to Lady Joan's room after we spoke to her.'

'She didn't?' Bennett automatically looked along the corridor. 'So where is she?'

The minstrels exchanged glances, 'Anne left after the first ballad some two hours ago. We were going to stop, but Lady Joan begged for another and then another.'

Mathilda spoke fast. 'Aldus, go to the stables. See if anyone has seen Anne leave. Dicun, Noll, place your instruments here, on the bed, I will ensure they are untouched by others. Go to the kitchens. See if she is there. It's a big place; Anne might be hiding in any of the nooks and crannies.'

The minstrels were already disappearing into the distance when Mathilda called after them, 'The ballad, the one Anne stayed for, which one was it?'

'Adam Bell,' Dicun, paused, 'she wasn't happy though. Restless all the time we sang. At the time I thought she hated music as much as her master does, but now I'm wondering if she was just impatient to be off.'

'Not a long ballad, but long enough to sit through if you're impatient to be somewhere. When she did leave, what excuse did Anne give for abandoning her charges?'

'Just before noon.' Dicun blushed, 'She asked Lady Marjory to forgive her indisposition and left. I rather assumed that she needed to… well…'

'Thank you, Dicun, I understand what she intended to imply.'

As the minstrels dashed off to carry out their tasks, Bennett muttered, 'She was searching for the bloodied linen when she came in here, wasn't she.'

'I think so.' Mathilda stared at the dislodged pile of discarded tunics and blankets, 'No wonder she was so agitated to find us here.'

'You think bringing in new linen was an excuse to be in here should she be discovered?'

'Possibly.' Mathilda surveyed the chamber as a whole, hoping to see something that would tell her its secrets. 'The bigger question is, did she put the bloodied cloth there in the first place? And if she did, was it because she wanted to frame his Lordship or because he, or someone else, told her to?'

'But if she put it there, why come back for it?'

Mathilda sighed. 'I wish I knew.'

~ *Chapter Forty-one* ~

16th January 1332

If Mathilda's reckoning was correct, then Gilbert would have delivered the ransom by now. Even if Eustace and Robert had contrived to delay him as long as possible, it was likely that the justice would be on his way home.

The need to leave Wollaton was like an urgent tug in her chest, but she'd promised Lady Marjory she'd find her mother. And Lord Richard the younger had not returned.

Having agreed with Bennett that they'd say nothing about Anne's presence in Lord Willoughby's chamber for now, Mathilda hurried to the hall. The sound of footsteps in the stone corridor behind her slowed her pace.

'Lady Ingram, what is happening to my home?' Lady Marjory was distraught, 'First Mother, then Father, then my brother Richard takes off with Edmund, and now I can't find Anne.'

'Your father will be home soon, my Lady, of that I am sure.' Mathilda took the girl's elbow and guided her along the hall. 'Your sister, Lady Joan, she is attended?'

'There is a most able maid from the kitchen who Mother had tipped for advancement. I have left her to care for my sister.'

'Excellent.' Mathilda kept walking, 'You'll make a fine lady of the manor one day. Does your father have marriage plans for you?'

Shuddering, Marjory shrugged. 'He has been so consumed with his vendetta against the Folvilles and his ambitions for power that my future is unspoken. After all, he has Richard and Edmund to consider above me and Joan. Hugh was married off to Lenton Priory from birth.'

'The Folvilles,' Mathilda's pulse quickened as she asked, 'have you met any of them, my Lady?'

'No.' The young woman looked horrified. 'Father says they are so evil they'd not hesitate to eat any one of us.'

Mathilda couldn't stop the laugh that shot out of her mouth, which she covered with a hasty palm. 'Oh, I'm so sorry, my Lady, but Lord Willoughby appears to be given to exaggeration.'

'He does get impassioned about that family, as I told you before; he is too much of a coward to approach them directly. He attacks from the sidelines, hits out at their friends…'

'The Coterels of Derbyshire.' Mathilda nodded. 'And when he can't win, he makes up lies of convenience…' The last words were spoken more to herself than her companion, but Lady Marjory caught on to them at once.

'Mother's illness. He really did make it up, didn't he?'

'I think so.'

Marjory was quiet as they entered the hall. She stopped on the final step and whispered, 'Was it them, do you think, who took my father?'

'Them?' Nausea rose in Mathilda's throat as she braced herself to hear what Lady Marjory de Willoughby was about to say.

'The Folvilles. In revenge for my father attacking their friends?'

Knowing it would be foolish to lie, Mathilda said, 'I wouldn't be at all surprised, but if it was them, then at least you know Lord Willoughby will not be hurt.'

'But they are notorious, they…'

'Keep their word.' Mathilda smiled, 'I have met them, and so has Lord Ingram. The Folvilles don't always do the right thing, and some of the brothers are less stable than the others, but what they do is always done for the right reasons. Does that make sense?'

The young woman's mouth dropped open as she uttered in awe and confusion, 'You respect them?'

'Their principles, yes. Their methods, not so much.' Steering her young companion towards the fireplace, Mathilda said, 'Whatever the case, your father is on his way home, and when he gets here, I think we can agree that his mood will be bleak.'

Bettrys filled everyone's cups with small ale and passed around chunks of fresh bread, as, with permission from Lady Marjory, Mathilda invited Bennett to take a seat with them rather than standing on ceremony.

The steward was grave. 'Wollaton Hall has been searched from top to bottom. If Anne is here, her hiding place is secure.'

'Are there any horses missing?'

Mathilda took hold of Lady Marjory's hand and gave it a reassuring squeeze as Bennett replied, 'One pony. Heart.

'She's taken my sister's pony?' Lady Marjory was back on her feet. 'How dare she? I cannot believe this!'

'Please sit down, my Lady.' Mathilda coaxed, 'I think I'm beginning to see what may have happened, although how is unclear.'

Bennett frowned. 'But you know why?'

'Possibly.'

Feeling everyone looking at her expectantly, Mathilda closed her eyes for a second. *What would Robyn Hode do?* She heard Robert answer, his eyes shining, his tone mischievous. *Something reckless.*

It was Daniel's voice that pulled her from her pondering.

'My Lady, I know something about the missing maid, Anne.'

'Tell us.'

'When Bettrys and I went to Willoughby-on-the-Wolds we went into the church there. While we were praying, a woman came in.'

'The one you took to be discussing Lady Isabel?'

'Discussing my mother?' Lady Marjory switched her attention to Daniel, 'Why would Father Reynard be talking about Mother?'

'It was more the other way about. I believe that woman to have been Anne. She was asking the reverend if he believed the rumours concerning Lady Isabel's state of mind.'

Mathilda frowned. 'You're sure it was Anne you heard?'

'Yes, my Lady.'

'I remember you saying that the reverend sounded convinced of Lady Willoughby's indisposition.'

Daniel sipped some ale. 'It was more that he was convinced of Lord Willoughby's honesty rather than Lady Isabel's affliction. He would not consider his patron a liar. It would not be in his interests, after all.'

'Why would she go there though?' Mathilda mused. 'So far Anne has been a staunch supporter of Justice Willoughby, why would she suddenly question his actions?'

'And why with that churchman?' Bettrys added, 'There are clerics closer to here. The church of St Leonard's is but a short walk away, whereas Willoughby-on-the-Wolds is a decent ride.'

Bennett looked up from where he'd been staring into his ale. 'I know why. Reynard is Anne's kin. Her cousin.'

Mathilda's palms tingled. 'Would that be where she's gone now?'

'It's possible.' The steward banged his beaker against the table in frustration, 'If only I had men to send but I daren't dismiss any more guards from their duty with his Lordship on his way home.'

'I can't understand why she's gone!' Marjory's forehead puckered in concern and confusion, 'I know she's been acting oddly of late, but I thought it was anxiety about my parents' situations.'

'When you say oddly,' Mathilda leant forward, 'do you mean her manner had become strange, even before our arrival in your home?'

'I suppose it had. She has always had an abrupt manner. Mother was never taken with her. It was more that she tolerated her because Father liked her efficiency. But lately Anne has been openly resentful of the tasks she's been asked to do.'

Mathilda exchanged glances with Bennett. She was sure the steward has reached the same conclusion she had. Anne was resentful of her servile status because Lord Willoughby had led her to believe she would be replacing Lady Isabel, not waiting on her daughters.

'Something else that's odd,' Lady Marjory laid her hands on the table. 'I don't understand why Anne was so insistent that your man Adam leave with the seal. She knows Father carries a spare. He has three, you know. One he leaves here, and two that he takes on his court rounds. Just in case one breaks.'

'What on earth was that about?'

Robert slammed the church door behind them and listened to the sound of his heart screaming in his chest.

'Gilbert Ward, you mean?'

'Damn right I mean Gilbert Ward. You could have told me you had a man undercover in Wollaton! I've been worried sick about Mathilda and '

Eustace rushed forward and clamped a firm hand over his brother's mouth, hissing, 'It echoes in here!'

Giving the tiniest inclination of his head, Robert took a steadying breath as Eustace dropped his hand. The small church was as cold as ice. The few pews were placed so close together that the congregation would have been virtually sitting on top of each other as the Almighty peered down upon them.

'Gilbert worked for me some years ago. He was good at his job.'

'You sent him to spy on Willoughby?'

'No, his employment there was a lucky happenstance.' Eustace cleared a table, sweeping the candlesticks, Bibles, and associated religious artefacts to the floor with no regard for their spiritual value. Emptying out the velvet bag, he divided the contents into haphazard piles.

'Gilbert fell in love. Unwisely, as it turned out. He asked to leave my service to marry, and I granted his request. I was reluctant though; Ward is a good horseman and an excellent watchman.'

'Yet you let him go,' Robert started to divide the coin from the jewels.

'I told Gilbert he could be excused my service if he found a replacement worthy of his position.'

'John Pykehose?'

'Yes.' Eustace paused, his fingertips dancing over the

pile of coins. 'I am going to miss that man.'

Robert looked up from his work in surprise. His brother admitting to any sort of emotional loss was unheard of. 'We ought to recover his body.'

Eustace grunted. 'As we're on the run and have no idea where young Daniel last saw John, then the chances of locating him are slim.'

'I know. Still.'

'Yes.' Eustace pulled a fist full of money pouches from his tunic. 'The Coterels are to have 700 marks, that thief Maxeye has taken his own, so the hundred marks he was due are now ours. Helewell, Lovet, and Savage will be at the inn in Melton to collect their share. And you can bet your life our brother, Rector Richard, will be after an extra portion for carrying out the actual kidnap before skulking back to the safety of his church.'

'How will we get the money to the Coterels?'

'Wennesley. The innkeeper at Melton will know where I can find him.'

'Right.' Robert filled the nearest pouch with a hundred marks. 'We can't stay here tonight, we'd freeze to death.'

'Agreed.' Eustace pointed to a curtain drawn across behind the altar. 'Go and see if there's any food hidden back there; we'll leave some coins to pay for it. Then we'll get this lot divided up and head to Melton.'

'We could be seen.'

'It doesn't matter if we are.' Eustace stuffed the leather bags into his cloak. 'We haven't done anything wrong, and we will be in an inn we are known to protect. Willoughby won't have got back to Wollaton quite yet, and even then, he'll wish to rest an hour or two while before he acts against us. We might as well benefit from one night in a proper bed before we disappear for a while.'

Robert smiled. 'Well, when you put it like that…'

~ *Chapter Forty-two* ~

16th January 1332

Sarah poked at the kitchen fire, watching as it sent orange sparks flying up the chimney. It was the only sound she could hear. Ashby Folville Manor was unnaturally quiet. Nothing moved. With the kitchen door firmly shut and bolted, she couldn't even hear the horses shuffling in the stalls.

Sheriff Jort's men and been and gone, their hands empty, their mission a failure, but they hadn't gone far. Adam had told her the two guards that had accompanied the captain were stationed beyond the main gates, and they weren't alone.

Pulling herself upright, Sarah looked at the makings of tomorrow's bread dough on the kitchen table. She normally delighted in the daily routine, but today she was too distracted to concentrate.

Lord Thomas was in his chamber. He said he needed to think, she hadn't liked to ask about what. He only claimed to be thinking when he was worried. Adam was chopping wood in the courtyard, and Ulric was grooming the horses before he came in for his evening meal.

Daniel, where are you?

'Evening will soon be upon us.' Mathilda stood by the door to the courtyard. Cold air danced on her face and she could taste ice on her tongue. 'If we don't leave soon, there'll be no light left.'

Bennett nodded. 'It's not safe to go far. Will you head to the tavern in Wollaton?'

'My husband has friends there, so they'll make room for us. I've sent Aldus, Dicun, and Noll ahead to let them know I'm on my way.'

'Wise as ever, Lady Mathilda.' Bennett smiled, but she could see anxiety in his eyes nonetheless.

'Not wise enough.' She tugged her hood over her head, 'I have failed to find your mistress, and I promised my husband I'd be home by now.'

'Won't Adam have informed him you're safe?'

'If he got home.' Mathilda hated herself for maintaining the lie, and being less than truthful to the steward. 'Adam left here before we'd heard of Justice Willoughby's capture. He could still be travelling from the court to our home   if the court wasn't disbanded after Lord Willoughby's disappearance. Plus, if there are men out hunting the Coterels' followers, as well as soldiers hunting for the justice, it is not unreasonable to assume that, if Adam turned up to return your master's seal, then he could have been delayed by all manner of obstacles.'

'You mean they could have arrested him?'

'It's possible. I may be required to vouch for his good name.'

The sound of Daniel and Bettrys' feet crunching against the courtyard gravel sent Mathilda scurrying towards her horse.

'Please reassure Lady Marjory that I have not given up on her mother. I promised I'd help find her, and I will.'

'Certainly, my Lady.' Bennett whispered, 'I would come with you to the inn, to help protect you, but…'

'But your duty is here. I understand. Your master will be home soon, and with Anne missing as well as his sons and wife…'

Bennett sighed. 'I don't understand why the young Lordships haven't come back. Lord Richard in particular, he enjoys running the manor when his father is away on court matters.'

'I can imagine.' Mathilda mounted her horse. 'Thank you for your hospitality. I hope his Lordship is not too angry when he gets here.'

'That, my Lady, could be wishful thinking, but I thank you for it anyway.' He placed a hand on the palfrey's mane, 'Will you get word to me, if you succeed in your mission, whether the news is good or bad?'

'I promise.'

The only free chamber the inn had was small but warm. Mathilda wouldn't have cared if it was freezing, she was just glad to be away from Wollaton Hall. There was something unsettling about that place. It was so rich, held such a statement of wealth and success about it, and yet it was cold despite its many lit hearths, and soulless despite the occupants.

Daniel had hardly spoken since he'd told them about hearing Anne talk to her cousin. She could feel the weight of his guilt over Pykehose's death as he watched Bettrys tend the fire.

Mathilda knew she had to give the lad a task, something to keep his mind occupied and help ease his conscience. There were two places she wanted to visit, but each lay in an opposite direction to the other, and both might lead to little more than a wasted ride in the countryside.

The church of the Reverend Reynard ought to be checked to make sure Anne was there, as Bennett suspected, and then there was Lenton Priory… Mathilda sat at the end of her bed, watching the newly encouraged flames dance up the chimney.

'Would you like some food, my Lady?' Bettrys broke through Mathilda's indecision.

'Please.' She stood up decisively, 'Make sure you and Daniel have food too. Bring it up here. Once we've eaten, we have work to do and little time in which to do it.'

'Yes, my Lady.'

'While you fetch supper, I will go and speak to our minstrel friends.' Mathilda brushed her hands down her front as she got to her feet, 'I think it's time I released them from my service.'

Bettrys exchanged surprised looks with Daniel as she said, 'But won't we need them, my Lady?'

'Possibly, but they have their living to make. And besides, Lord Robert would never forgive me if I put them in danger and anything happened to his favourite balladeers.'

Robert checked his horse's hooves, and then those of Eustace's mount. They were clean but would soon need to be re-shod. Melton's inn stables were quiet for the time of year, and he was grateful for the relative peace. Just as he was grateful for the few hours sleep and substantial meal they'd eaten, hidden away in a chamber at the back of the tavern.

Walking to the road, Robert stared as far into the distance as he could. There were people going about their business, but no soldiers that he could see. His eyes narrowed. Just because he couldn't see them, didn't mean they weren't there.

'Anything?' Eustace spoke in a murmur.

'Nothing visible.' Robert accompanied his brother back to the horses. 'You've left our payments as arranged?'

'All debts settled. The innkeeper is aware of his role in the ransom distribution and has been rewarded for the risk he takes in holding such funds ready for collection.'

Relieved to have made it this far, Robert blurted out, 'I'm not going into the Peaks with you. I'm going home.'

Eustace's eyebrows rose in surprise. 'That is not wise.'

'No, it isn't, but there is no proof we've done wrong. We've merely been away for a while.'

'If Jort's men are rounding up supporters of the Coterels that will make no difference. Just being a Folville puts you in peril.'

'Which means Thomas, plus Adam, Sarah, and young Ulric, are in peril at home.' Robert glanced around again. 'Even staying here is not safe, although I grant you the protection we have within is reassuring.'

'Protection the innkeeper pays for. It cuts both ways. He will be released from retaining payments for a while, as well as getting his cut of the ransom.'

Robert was pleased with Eustace's decision. The county's innkeepers were powerful friends. They saw and heard everything that happened across all quarters of society. 'I am still going to Ashby Folville. If I encounter difficulties, then I will rethink my plans.'

'And Mathilda should be home by now.' Eustace spoke plainly.

Robert swung up into his saddle. 'I may get there and simply reassure myself of her safety, or I may stay; it will depend on my findings.'

'They will be watching the house.'

'I know.' Robert tugged on the reins and turned to face

the courtyard's exit. 'I will accompany you to find Roger Wennesley on my way. Where in Leicester did the innkeeper say he was to be found?'

'The tannery nearest the city's southern gate.' Eustace gave a half-smile. 'I'll go alone. If you're heading to Ashby Folville, you should go now.'

'What?' Robert was beginning to wonder if Eustace had suffered a blow to the head. 'But if you're caught with that money on you…'

'Wennesley isn't going to find me in Leicester; he's going to meet me at Lady Joan la Zouche's home.'

'But you said…'

'We had an agreement   if Wennesley said the tannery it meant he was going to the home of Lady Joan. I did not want the innkeeper to know my business.' Eustace looked away as he spoke, 'I will stay with Lady Joan once Wennesley has headed into the Peaks to find his masters. And while I want the ransom to reach the Coterels, I care not one jot what happens to the miserable excuse for a human being they use as messenger.'

Robert would have grunted his agreement, but he was too busy remembering what Mathilda had told him she suspected about Eustace and Lady Joan. 'Her Ladyship will not thank you for bringing trouble to her door. Don't forget, her father was embroiled up to his neck in Belers' death and that's at the root of this. Her father killed Belers. Willoughby's mercenaries or Jort's guards will be keeping an eye on her too.'

'I have ways of getting into Lady Joan's home unseen.'

Robert bit back the urge to say 'I bet you do' as he slapped Eustace upon the back. 'Then I will bid you safe travels, brother. I look forward to us all being under one roof again.'

'As do I. We have always worked best with strength in numbers. Keep your eyes and ears open, Robert.' Eustace stared along the road. 'If you need to leave Ashby Folville, or find the road to it blocked with soldiers, go to Lichfield Cathedral or Polesworth Abbey. The Coterels have agents at both places in case of news. They will let me know where you are.'

Daniel had begged to go to Willoughby-on-the-Wolds to search for Anne. Mathilda, understanding his need to redeem himself, granted his request, on the understanding that he kept to the shadows. Even if he saw Anne, he was to do nothing, but travel on to Lenton Priory as fast as he could.

Now, as she and Bettrys rode through the gateway of Lenton Priory after a sleepless night. Mathilda was glad of her decision. Providing Daniel did exactly what he was told – and she was sure he would, having so recently learnt a harsh lesson about not listening to his friends – then at least she'd know if Anne was hiding out with her cousin or not.

'Do you think they'll let us see Lord Hugh?' Bettrys whispered to Mathilda as a sour-faced porter went to request an audience with the Prior.

'I'm not sure. Did you see the expression on the porter's face when I asked to speak to Lady Isabel or her sons?'

'He went puce.' Bettrys looked around at the spotless yellow brickwork. There wasn't a soul in sight. 'Where are the monks? It's the wrong time of day for prayers.'

'At work, I suspect. It's late, but I suppose the children could be in lessons.'

Bettrys shivered. 'I can't think God so cruel as to want us to keep children in a place like this.'

Mathilda didn't argue as they waited for the porter to

return

At last a shuffling of sandaled feet came towards them. Mathilda tilted her chin. Having expected the porter, and perhaps the monk in charge of the novices, she was surprised to see the prior himself bearing down on her, his face set in a criss-cross of wrinkled suspicion.

'I am William de Pinnebury. What brings you to Lenton Priory, my Lady?'

'Your porter did not repeat my request to you, Prior William?'

She knew from the expressions on their faces that he had. Mathilda savoured the moment's disquiet that flashed through the pompous doorkeeper's eyes.

'He did, but I am of a mind that he must have misheard you, for Lady Willoughby does not reside within these walls. Only her youngest son, Hugh lives here. He is at his last lesson of the day and should not be disturbed.'

'Most commendable.' Mathilda tilted her chin even further upwards, 'and Lord Edmund, is he joining his brother in lessons, or is he residing elsewhere for the duration of his stay?'

The Prior glared down his thick nose. Mathilda could almost hear the conflicting voices in his head as he decided how to respond.

'I think we should talk privately, if you would be so kind as to join me in my office, Lady Folville.'

Mathilda felt Bettrys stiffen behind her, as she said, 'And now you are mistaken, Prior. I presented myself as Lady Ingram.'

'You may well have done so, young woman, but I have known Lord Ingram for a long time, and consequently I know with absolute certainty that he is not married.'

Daniel patted his horse's neck, muttering an apology for the lack of rest it had received since his abrupt departure from Wollaton's inn. The ride to Willoughby-on-the-Wolds had been mercifully uneventful. Nonetheless, Daniel's entire body was stiff with tension as he surveyed his surroundings, his eyes and ears alert for signs of trouble.

He wasn't sure if he was relieved or disappointed that Anne hadn't been at the church when he'd arrived, nor was she hiding at Reverend Reynard's home, which Willoughby's startled innkeeper had pointed out to him.

Anne's cousin had sworn on his life that he hadn't seen her since she came to the church enquiring about Lady Willoughby. Daniel hoped his instinct that the churchman had been telling the truth was correct. He smiled grimly to himself as he recalled the cleric's terrified expression when he'd questioned him as to Anne's possible whereabouts and his real feelings as to Lady Willoughby's state of mind.

The man's a maggot. Claiming he has a duty to believe whatever his master tells him. A coward, to afraid to have an opinion of his own!

'We can rest as soon as we get to Lenton. Once we've made sure Bettrys and Lady Mathilda are alright,' Daniel murmured, 'At least, thanks to that excuse for a cleric, we know where Anne is likely to be.'

~ *Chapter Forty-three* ~

16th January 1332

Prior William's study was opulent, matching his personal appearance which, with the rich fabric of his habit, and heavily jewelled hands, belied any sense of charity. Mathilda felt sick as she thought of the stark surroundings in the rest of the priory and the many hungry and homeless people that roamed the land between here and her home. How well they could live off the proceeds of just one of the four rings he wore on his podgy fingers.

'You know me, my Lord Prior?'

'I do. The tales of Mathilda, the potter's daughter who tamed a Folville, have spun far and wide.'

Mathilda folded her hands in her lap. 'Is that so? As much as the tales of cruelty and greed which go hand in jewelled glove with the deeds of Lord Justice Willoughby of Wollaton Hall?'

Rather than explode into a storm of temper, start quoting defiant scripture, or dismiss her as impudent, the prior held her stare. Then, very slowly, his face broke into a broad grin. 'I don't think anyone could be said to outdo Lord Willoughby on that front, do you?'

Mathilda perched on the edge of her seat, holding the

prior's gaze. She wasn't entirely sure she could believe what she was seeing. His tiny eyes, sunken within his round face, were twinkling.

'Prior, I ask once more; are Lord Edmund, Lord Richard, and Lady Isabel de Willoughby here? If not, have you seen them in recent days? This is not a casual enquiry. I have every reason to be concerned for their safety.'

'But not for Lord Willoughby's safety?'

'You are well informed about my circumstances, so I suspect you are informed in that regard as well. Will you tell me in what manner you know my family, my Lord Prior?'

'You ask a lot of questions. Have you any preference in which order you receive the answers?'

Mathilda found herself getting angry. It was a relief that she wasn't endangered by this man, but she was tired and worried that time was running out.

'Lord Prior, a woman's life is in danger. Are they here or have you seen them?'

Immediately the clergyman dropped his levity. 'You are in earnest about their lack of safety?'

'I am.' Mathilda spoke quickly, filling her host in on the events of the past three days. 'Lords Richard and Edmund have not yet returned from Lincolnshire.'

'It's not a short journey, Lady Folville.' The prior passed her a goblet full of crimson-coloured liquid.

'I know, but the errand was urgent and Richard at least is an accomplished horseman.' Mathilda took a sip of the strong wine, 'and I understand, from the steward at Wollaton Hall, that it is Lord Richard the younger's habit to use the time his father is away at court as practice for being the future lord of the manor.'

The prior laughed. 'Delicately put, my Lady.'

'Thank you.' She took more wine; it was thick and red

and slipped down her throat like velvet. A warm and welcome change from the small ale of Wollaton Hall.

'You are beginning to wonder if young Willoughby has knowledge of his mother's disappearance, and only pretended to go to Lincolnshire?'

'Amongst other theories, yes. I would be happy to be wrong. He could just have a lame horse, or his grandmother may have asked him and Edmund to stay a while.'

'Or perhaps Lady Isabel is there all along and her sons are keeping her company, should she really be ill.'

'You believe that she is unwell, Prior?'

The churchman paused, savouring his wine. Mathilda tried not to flinch in disgust as he rolled the red liquid around his slightly open mouth. As she watched, she knew she'd never want to make an enemy of this man, and she vowed to thank whichever Folville it was who had tamed him.

Eventually he spoke. 'I do not believe she is mad, but she is troubled and possibly afraid.' He put down his goblet and spoke more earnestly. 'Lady Willoughby is an intelligent woman. She knows her position in that family, and she knows her duty as a provider of children has ended.'

Mathilda's eyes narrowed as she remembered Anne. 'Are you suggesting his Lordship was planning to dispose of his wife so he could replace her with someone more of his choosing now that his duty to provide heirs with an acceptable background has been fulfilled?'

'I said no such thing.' The prior tried and failed to hide a grin.

'But your thoughts were loud.'

'Then I should be more careful with my thoughts in your presence. I'd heard the Lady Mathilda had gifts to find the truth.'

'I have no such thing. I do however have knowledge of two young women at Wollaton Hall worried sick for their mother, brothers, and father.'

'And it occurred to you that if Lord Hugh was here, the others might be too.'

'Are they, Prior?'

Standing up, the Prior of Lenton rang a bell that sat on his desk, and his door opened. 'Brother Mark, please escort Lord Edmund de Willoughby to the warming house. I'm sure the lad could do with something to thaw out his bones after a few hours in the school room.'

When the door closed again, Mathilda asked, 'Just Lord Edmund?'

The prior gestured for his guest to rise. 'I'll let him tell his own story. Perhaps your companions would like to join us. You will take some soup and bread before you leave?'

'Thank you, Prior.'

The cleric bowed. 'And don't worry, I'll refer to you as Lady Ingram in company.'

The room lived up to its name. As soon as the three visitors pushed open the double wooden doors, the heat of the roaring fire to their left worked its magic, relaxing their tense muscles and warming their bones.

Edmund de Willoughby was already in place, seated on a wooden bench next to Brother Mark. His face was lined with concern as he held his palms to the flames.

'My Lord Prior, Lady Ingram?' Rising as the guests arrived, Edmund clearly didn't know whether to sound honoured, surprised, or worried by their combined presence.

Blessing the space as he approached the young man, Prior William gestured for him to sit and then perched his own palatial backside by the blaze. 'Lady Ingram needs to ask you some questions, Lord Edmund. I would encourage you to speak openly.'

Without giving Edmund the chance to respond, Mathilda began, 'Please forgive my bluntness. This is not lack of courtesy but a requirement for speed. How do you come to be here, Lord Edmund, at Lenton Priory, and have you recently seen your mother or brother Richard?'

'I…' Edmund faltered. He turned to the prior, as if to seek reassurance.

'You are safe to talk to Lady Ingram, Edmund. Please be honest with her, even if, perhaps, your brother has instructed you to be otherwise.'

The lad stared at his clasped hands for a while, before Prior William prompted him further. 'This is the House of God, he is listening.'

'I am worried for my family.' Edmund's eyes flicked up at Mathilda, before he drew them back to his lap. 'My father seems convinced of my mother's insanity, but we… their children… we are not so sure. Father has no time for anything unnecessary in his life, and over the past year it's been as if Mother has been cast into that category.'

'In what way?'

'We saw her less and less. She was kept more to her chamber. Father dismissed her from the hall whenever we had callers to the manor, as if…'

'You wondered if he was ashamed of her?'

'An appalling thing to admit, but … yes.'

'How did Lady Isabel take this?'

'Calmly. Mother always takes things calmly. She was not keen on Father's company anyway, so more time alone or with her children was welcome to her.'

'Until recently?'

'There was a row. I don't know how it began.'

'I know of the argument.' Mathilda glanced at Bettrys sat to her side. 'Was that the day you last saw Lady Isabel? The day of the row?'

Edmund shook his head. 'At Wollaton I saw her the day before, not that day, although I heard about the argument soon enough. But I have seen her since.'

'Here?'

'Yes, my Lady.' Edmund raised his eyes and again the prior gestured for him to keep going. 'I came here with my brother, Lord Richard. I thought… I thought we were going to travel to Lady Mortain, but only a few miles into our ride, Richard told me he knew my mother was here with Hugh.'

'Did you travel alone or with an escort?'

The young man swallowed. 'Richard took all the remaining mercenaries from the forest around Wollaton.'

'All of them? He left Wollaton unguarded?' Prior William sat up in alarm, realising that Mathilda's claims of the shortness of time were in earnest.

'The basic household guard remained, but those our father employs unofficially, who hadn't gone on the court tour with him, came with us.'

Mathilda was beginning to wish she had more of the prior's wine. 'What happened when you got here?'

'Mother was here, in this room.' Edmund patted the bench next to him. 'She was tired but in good spirits. She was not mad. Not at all.'

'Then?'

'The good prior granted us refreshment. Hugh joined us for a while, and Mother said her goodbyes. She was going to Lady Mortain, she said, but hadn't wanted to leave without saying farewell to her youngest son.'

'She didn't say goodbye to her daughters.' Mathilda frowned, 'and unless I've been labouring under a misapprehension, Lord Willoughby took your mother away some days before his court session was due to start?'

Edmund was bleak. 'I have since learnt that Father only rode with my mother as far as the border with Lincolnshire. There he instructed his men to take her on into Lincolnshire without him.'

Mathilda was confused. 'But that isn't what happened.'

'My mother has money of her own.'

'She bribed them to turn around once her husband had gone and asked them to bring her here?'

'Yes.' Edmund looked proud for a split second, before his expression faded, 'but one of the mercenaries is loyal to my father always; money or no money. When he returned to the hall, he let it be known to Richard that Mother had come here instead.'

'The assumption being that Richard would tell Lord Willoughby?'

'Yes.'

Mathilda listened to the crackle of the fire as Brother Mark fetched bowls of soup for everyone. 'I don't think your brother told Lord Willoughby.'

Edmund suddenly sat up straight. 'He told me he had as we travelled here.'

'Even so.' Cupping her wooden bowl, Mathilda inhaled the delicious aroma, 'What else did Richard tell you?'

'As I said, that Mother wanted to see me and Hugh before she went on to Lady Mortain.'

'How long was Lady Isabel here?'

'An hour, maybe. It was brief. Richard said…'

'Richard said what?'

'That he would escort her safely to Lincolnshire and then come back. We were to return to Wollaton together from here.'

'Did he tell Lady Isabel of her invitation to the King's Court?'

Edmund's eyes widened in surprise. 'I was unaware of such an invitation.'

Mathilda crossed her fingers beneath her cloak against the lie she was about to tell on Holy Ground. 'You didn't know that's why your brother decided to search for your mother after my arrival at Wollaton, because I carried a message saying King Edward wanted to meet her and your father?'

'I did not.'

Mathilda's brow creased. 'Just so I'm sure, may I ask again, did you believe Lady Isabel to be leaving her home due to insanity?'

'No.' Edmund shifted uncomfortably. 'I believed Father to be bored with her and angry at her outburst. She was being sent away before she caused disgrace to the family and embarrassment to him.'

'I see.' Mathilda got up, her head teaming with conflicting ideas. 'If Lady Isabel and Lord Richard went on to Lincolnshire after all, then all could be well. The rumours of her disappearance nothing more than idle gossip, and yet...' Lowering her soup bowl to the table, Mathilda faced her host. 'I thank you for your hospitality, Prior William, I wonder if I may impose upon you further?'

'Anything.'

'Could you send a messenger to Wollaton Hall to reassure Ladies Marjory and Joan that their younger brothers are safe?'

'Consider it done.'

Edmund got to his feet, 'Lady Ingram, what does all this mean?'

'Hopefully, that our fears for your mother are unfounded, and that the rumour of her illness is nought but sourness from a husband who wanted an excuse to be rid of an unwanted wife.'

Unflinching on hearing his father described in such a way, Edmund returned his gaze to the fire. 'I think you're right. We will miss Mother at Wollaton though, especially Richard.'

'Richard? I got the impression they were not that close.'

'Oh, they are. Very. He's her first-born after all. He had plans to take her to a hut in the forest on the way to Lady Mortain's for old time's sake. We used to play there as children.'

~ *Chapter Forty-four* ~

16th January 1332

Despite the encroaching dark of evening, the previously quiet priory was now a place of activity. Three monks, who Mathilda could easily have pictured being at home on the battlefield, had gathered in the courtyard, ready to act as either messengers or guards.

Prior William gave a brief smile as he saw her regarding his brothers. 'Not all men come here from birth. Some take the long route around. Those fine gentlemen came via the Holy Land.'

'Crusaders?'

'Once upon a time.'

'Their horses are noble indeed.' Mathilda watched as the clerics mounted beasts of such stature and grace that she was sure Richard Willoughby the younger would have envied them.

'I have a friend in the Prior of Sempringham. I believe you are familiar with him. He has horse-dealing connections.'

'The name is familiar to me, although our paths have never crossed.' Mathilda thought of Gilbert and his acquiring of Lady Joan's pony. 'Prior, may I ask a direct question?'

'No harm in trying.'

'Do you know the groom, Gilbert Ward?'

'Very well.'

'And were you, and perhaps the Prior of Sempringham, privy to his purchase of a pony for Lady Joan de Willoughby?'

Prior William said nothing as two of his mounted monks left for Wollaton, to deliver the message Mathilda had requested. As soon as they had disappeared through the porter's gate, he turned to his companion. 'I heard you were clever.'

'You may have heard wrong. Can you tell me why Lord Willoughby arranged for the pony to be sent to Lady Joan as a Christmas gift from her mother?'

'I cannot. My only guess would be that he was trying to reassure the child that Lady Isabel had not forgotten her.'

'And yet Lord Willoughby did not arrange for any such tokens to arrive for his other children.'

'That I cannot explain. Perhaps he intended for other gifts to come, but had no time to implement his plans before he was indisposed. Or, perhaps he believed that Lady Joan, as a young female, was the only one to require reassurance.'

Mathilda nodded. 'Maybe it is as simple as that.'

Prior William took a pouch of wine from the ever-hovering Brother Mark, and passed it to Mathilda. 'You have to remember that Lord Willoughby has his own ideas on what should or should not be. Beyond the Crown, he doesn't conform to any rules but his own, and if he has judged that his other offspring no longer have need of their mother, then there will be no shifting that opinion.'

Not liking what the prior was saying, but suspecting he was right, Mathilda turned her attention to more pressing needs as Lord Edmund approached. The prior beckoned to the remaining mounted monk. 'This is Brother Peter, our librarian.'

Resisting the urge to ask if the prior was sure about that, because she couldn't imagine such big hands turning the pages of priceless parchment, Matilda inclined her head as her host added, 'He will accompany you to the hut in question and act as either messenger or protector, or both.'

'You are kind, my Lord Prior.'

'It's my job to be kind.' He gave a squashed wink as Mathilda mounted her palfrey.

'Will you care for Daniel when he returns?'

'Of course.' The prior nodded.

'Thank you. We will return Lord Edmund to you here once he has shown us the place.'

The prior lowered his voice so the young Lord Willoughby would not hear, 'I pray you do not find what you expect to, my Lady.'

Robert changed direction for the second time. He wasn't far off course, but this additional loop through the thinnest tracks of the forest was beginning to spook his horse and add to his frustration.

He hadn't been surprised that the main roads towards Ashby Folville were guarded. But when the lesser-used track into the town was also picketed by two guards wearing the livery of Sheriff Jort, crossbows in their hands, he'd sworn as he'd doubled back into the forest.

Urging his horse forward under a low-hanging set of branches, his back bent, his cheek brushing his mount's mane, Robert was grateful for the fast failing light. At least it would help hide him if he had to dive into the heart of the forest completely.

Words from Robyn Hode flitted through his mind as he

wove onwards; taking a hidden path towards Teigh, which he knew would - eventually - bring him around to Ashby Folville from the opposite direction. Even as he paced, he doubted it was worth it. If this side of the town was guarded, surely the other side would be as well?

Wondering how Eustace was faring, Robert smiled. His brother would be fine, because it wouldn't occur to him that he wouldn't be. His smile faded however as he thought of Mathilda and the trouble his wife might have got herself into this time. Gilbert had said she was still at Wollaton, but that was hours ago. Surely Mathilda would be home with Sarah by now.

If she could get there.

The obvious thought landed loudly in Robert's mind. If he had to circumnavigate the pathways of Charnwood to get home, Mathilda would have had to as well. She was a Folville, and if everyone suspected of association with the Coterels was being rounded up, that would include her.

Robert pulled his mount to a stop. He'd been so hell bent on getting to Mathilda he hadn't taken the time to think about what he was doing. He could hear her voice, telling him for the umpteenth time that if the Folville men stopped to think before they acted, their lives would be much easier. A rueful smile formed on Robert's lips. If he knew his wife at all, she wouldn't return to Ashby Folville until she'd located Lady Isabel. He was risking arrest to get home to his wife, yet the chances of her being anywhere near their manor were slim.

Swinging his horse around, Robert set off again, certain he'd been riding in completely the wrong direction.

At the last minute, Prior William had tried to stop them; asking if they wouldn't be better to wait until first light before they acted, but Mathilda declined. She was convinced their quest could not wait. It might already be too late.

Daniel, breathless but determined, had clattered into Lenton's courtyard just as they were leaving. A swift change of mount later, and he was riding with them, explaining that Anne had not been seen in Willoughby-on-the-Wolds, and that her cousin suspected she'd be with her brother in Nottingham.

Lord Edmund sat erect in the saddle as he led the way to his childhood hideaway, with Daniel by his side. As Mathilda watched Daniel chatting to Edmund, she realised they were of an age. They could be friends but for the divisions placed on them by birth.

Mathilda felt it was a shame that Edmund should be the second son. He'd have made a good Lord Willoughby, much fairer than his father and, she suspected, more rational than his elder brother.

With each stride closer to their destination, which Edmund claimed to be just over an hour from Lenton, Mathilda's thoughts ran faster. Now certain that Lord Willoughby had chosen to remove his wife from Wollaton because he'd tired of her, and that he'd leapt upon her one and only step out of line as an excuse to pack her off to her mother, Mathilda could feel the stirrings of an idea forming in her mind.

Lord Willoughby hadn't been the only one who could benefit from his wife's outburst.

'Lord Edmund, Daniel! We must go faster.'

Robert tugged sharply on his reins. There was someone lurking in the trees off to his right. He could hear another horse shifting from hoof to hoof.

Dismounting quietly, Robert took the dagger from his

belt and tethered his horse to the nearest tree. The sound had stopped; as if whoever was there was listening for him too.

Robert took a step forward, keeping to the shadows. All he could hear was the brush of naked branches as they blew in the light evening breeze, overlaid with the soft huff of a horse breathing.

A riderless horse?

Stepping closer to the thicket, Robert's blood raced. Holding his breath, he stepped forward, only to exhale softly as he was greeted by the silhouette of a horse, but no rider.

Keeping quiet in case there was someone hiding nearby, Robert crept forward. 'Jep?' The horse pricked up its ears and lifted its head.

'Mathilda?' The word came out as a whisper as Robert dived forward and grabbed the bridle. 'Our Lady, where is Mathilda?'

Lord Edmund and Daniel came to a halt as they reached a large gap in the trees. A small hut faced into the clearing, its rear nestled against the bulk of the forest. The distant exchange of two owls sent shivers through Mathilda, their calls adding to the eerie atmosphere they seemed to be carrying with them.

Mathilda glanced at Bettrys. She wondered if the maid was reminded of a similar location they'd visited when hunting for a missing woman near Rockingham Castle. Mathilda hoped the outcome would be far happier this time around.

Brother Peter rode forward. 'I should go inside the hut first.'

Lord Edmund's proud carriage sagged. 'You believe someone dangerous resides within?' He didn't add that the person could be his mother or brother.

'I have no belief in this matter, but I know a man wearing monk's garb is less likely to cause alarm than an armed nobleman and his squire.' Brother Peter turned to Mathilda, 'Wouldn't you agree, Lady Ingram?'

'I would.' She slipped from her horse and stood next to him, 'Nor would a monk and an unarmed noblewoman be seen as a threat.'

Daniel and Bettrys exchanged glances as they observed the monk's surprised face.

'I don't think you should come within, my Lady, not until I've ensured all is well.'

'And I thank you for your concern, but I've faced worse nightmares than anything we might find in there.'

The monk's eyebrows rose, but he said no more, as with a nod to a yawning Daniel, who'd been briefed not to let Lord Edmund inside, Mathilda stood on the threshold of the Willoughby boy's childhood haunt.

She listened hard. There was no sound. If there was anyone within, they were being extremely quiet.

Placing the flat of her palm on the door, Mathilda pushed at the weather-softened wood. The hinges swung freely, as if well maintained, and rather than being hit with the musty damp aroma of neglect she'd experienced in Morkery Woods, Mathilda found herself stepping into a cared-for space.

There was an embroidery stand in the middle of the floor.

~ *Chapter Forty-five* ~

16th January 1332

The chair next to the stand was on its side. But had someone knocked it over by accident or kicked it over? Beyond that the hut was clean and tidy. It was only its location that gave it any resemblance to a traditional forester's hut.

A small cot in the corner was covered in a clean blanket. There was a collection of gowns laid across it; presumably, for want of anywhere else to put them.

Brother Peter broke the silence. 'Lady Isabel has been living here.'

'It would seem so.'

'Seem so?'

Mathilda let out a long-held breath, but kept her eyes on the fallen chair. 'I meant, yes, she has been living here. Or at least, someone female has. It should be easy to establish from Lord Edmund if the woman in question is Lady Isabel from the gowns. What concerns me most is that it's late. If you were staying here, a woman alone, would you stray outside with night fast drawing in?'

The monk headed towards the embroidery frame. The canvas on it was tightly fastened, the view from the back neatly knotted. 'This is fine work.'

Mathilda examined the sewing. The picture under construction was a golden tree. 'She started again.'

'I'm sorry?'

'There was another linen with this tree on it. This one is more advanced however.' She ran her fingers over the stitching, admiring the skill. There were tiny letters added here and there. Mathilda realised she was looking at the makings of a family tree. 'I found the original in Wollaton Hall. Hidden and covered in blood.'

'Lady Isabel's blood?'

'I cannot say.' Mathilda searched the confined space. It appeared Lady Isabel had done her best to make herself at home. A bowl and jug sat on a table in the corner. A wooden pail for water was near the door, and a basket of scraps of material and threads was placed at the foot of the bed. There was a pile of apples on another makeshift table, and a fire warmed a pot of stew.

'The fire is low, but hasn't been left so long that it's died out.' Mathilda was about to call for Bettrys and Daniel to bring Edmund inside when she saw what she hadn't realised she'd been looking for.

What she had taken as a blanket across the bed, was a thick winter cloak.

Why would Lady Isabel leave here, late on a cold January night, without her cloak on?

Robert struggled against the urge to throw up. Jep. Mathilda's new horse.

He'd already made a frantic search of the undergrowth, but there was no sign of his wife. Not so much as a torn strip of cloak or a fallen shoe. Nothing.

There was no sign of anyone.

Think, think....

He sat on a fallen trunk, keeping hold of Jep's reins.

There is no sign of a struggle, therefore there was no struggle.

He breath calmed as his panic eased.

If Mathilda fell, Bettrys would be here looking for her.

Getting back to his feet, it occurred to Robert that he wasn't sure where he was. His bearings had gone astray at least a mile back, although he knew he was skirting the boundaries of Kesteven Forest once more.

Taking back the reins of his own mount and leading Jep with him, Robert changed tracks again, heading in the direction of where he knew Morkery Woods to be. If he was right, then he was about two miles from the crossroads that led to either Wollaton or Ashby Folville and Leicester. When he got there, he'd decide which way to go.

Thankful that he appeared to be beyond the scope of Jort and Ingram's guards for the time being, Robert found it far harder to keep quiet with two horses to lead, but he no longer cared. His wife was out here somewhere, without her horse.

My Mathilda would never let a fall from a horse stop her.

'I bet she fell and you ran, didn't you, Jep?' Robert cursed himself for encouraging her to use a horse she wasn't used to and had no affinity with. 'She'll have been with Bettrys, and they will be sharing a horse now. She is not injured. She is not dead. She's too stubborn, for a start.'

Mathilda whispered instructions into Daniel's ear as Brother Peter led Lord Edmund inside the hut.

Paling, the lad gave Bettrys' hand a quick squeeze, left his horse tethered to a tree, and disappeared into the forest behind the hut.

Before the maid could ask questions, Mathilda said,

'Come and have a look at the embroidery. Tell me your initial thoughts when you see it.'

Bettrys followed her mistress, only to take a sharp intake of surprise when she saw the comforts within. 'Lady Isabel has been living here?'

'It appears so, but how long that arrangement was meant to last, we can't be sure. Everything appears to be settled, and yet I can't stop feeling this scene's been staged.' She tapped Bettrys' shoulder and pointed to the sewing. Edmund was standing in front of it, his angular face blotched red with either anger or fear or both.

'Who dared keep my mother in this way?'

'It is Lady Isabel's stitching?'

'I would know my mother's fine hand anywhere.' He twisted on the spot, taking in the whole hut. 'And that is her cloak, and that's her new gown.' Edmund stopped talking as he registered the significance of his mother being absent without her cloak. 'Where is she?'

Keeping her voice level, not mentioning she had sent Daniel to scout the area in case Lady Isabel had gone for firewood and had a fall, or worse, Mathilda said, 'Could Lord Richard have taken her on to Lady Mortain?'

The young man shrugged. He radiated confusion. 'They were coming here to take a look, he said. To relive happier times on the way to our grandmother's lands. I imagined a short stop; a moment to share a drink of water and exchange reminiscences.' Edmund peered around him again. 'I had no idea about this.'

'Well, it was clearly planned, because… When did all this get here? Planned - it *was* planned.' Mathilda stopped talking and turned to Edmund. 'When your father, Lord Willoughby, first left with Lady Isabel, did you see them leave?'

'No.'

'And when you and your brother left Wollaton, did Richard have any possessions with him? Things that he was taking for your mother?'

'A roll of clothing,' Edmund pointed to the gowns, 'those, I suspect.'

'And the cloak?'

He shrugged. 'I don't think so. The roll wasn't big enough. Anyway, she'd have worn her cloak.' He pointed at the garment on the bed, 'Father bought her that cloak as a Christmas gift from the market in Leicester.'

Mathilda's eyes widened in surprise. 'He did?'

'Well, it was from Father officially, but Richard got it on his behalf in early November. There's a silk and fine fabric merchant that travels Europe. From Picardy originally; his work is exquisite. Richard picked that one because it was lined well. It was good quality and had space for Mother to embroider her own design onto it. She loves making her outfits unique.'

Mathilda nodded slowly. 'Did your father know about the gift? I mean, did he instruct Richard to buy it, or did your brother see the cloak and take it upon himself to buy it anyway? And when was the gift presented? Straight away, or was it to be saved until Christmas?'

'I don't know. Why?'

'Because your mother left Wollaton before Christmas, my Lord, remember? Her usual cloak remains in her chamber at home.'

Brother Peter, understanding what Mathilda was saying, spoke calmly, 'Perhaps Lord Edmund and I would be better employed helping Daniel search for signs of Lady Isabel outside?'

Edmund asserted, 'Anything is better than staying in

here. It isn't real. My mother is a high-born lady. She would not - could not - live like a pig woman in the forest!'

Waiting until the monk had ushered the boy outside, Bettrys turned to her mistress, 'Who planned this, my Lady?'

'Not Lord Willoughby, I'm sure of that. He is too proud to risk his wife being discovered living here. I can believe he'd pack her off to her mother's, but to a peasant's home in the middle of nowhere? No, that isn't his style.'

'Lord Richard the younger then?' Bettrys scratched her head, 'But why did *she* allow it? This looks comfortable. Her Ladyship has made it her own.'

'There is a third option?'

'There is?'

'Lord Edmund said this was a place of happy memories. Could it have been Lady Isabel's idea to stay here, even if only for a while? Maybe she wanted to disappear, not forever, but for long enough to worry a thoughtless husband.'

'I hope that's the truth.' Bettrys ran a hand over the cloak on the bed, 'This is an expensive garment. I wonder when the merchant was in Leicester?'

'That at least, is something we can find out.'

'Ask the minstrels, you mean?'

Mathilda smiled. 'I hadn't thought of that. They would probably know. I was considering Alice of Picardy, daughter of the merchant in question without a doubt, and soon to be Matthew's wife and my sister-in-law.'

'Your brother is to wed?' Bettrys' eyes lit up as she turned her attention back to the embroidery on the frame. 'That is good news in this dark time. I wonder if ' She paused, her fingers hovering over the material. 'Some of this has been unpicked.'

'Where? Show me.' Mathilda observed her maid travel light fingertips over a tiny area of linen that had no stitches. Looking harder, Mathilda could make out tiny puncture marks, where a needle had passed through the fabric, but no stitches remained.

Moving to the rear of the frame, Bettrys examined the same patch of material. 'There was originally a line of stitches here; not thickly sewn. And perhaps something else, something small, sat at the end.'

'Like the branch of a tree and an initial?'

'Maybe.' Bettrys looked worried as she straightened up. 'Someone has been taken off the family tree.'

'But who?' Mathilda frowned, 'the tree looks balanced, so we can assume all the branches are in place, and only three letters have been added so far for each branch. R, I, C... the beginning of her husband or her son's name presumably, M, A, R... her daughter Marjory, and so on it's as if she'd been planning her spaces, and was intending to add the end of each name later.'

Bettrys scanned the dwelling. 'I wish Daniel would come back. He's so tired and...'

Mathilda held out a hand to her maid. 'He hasn't gone far. I asked him to search for Lady Isabel's horse. If it was her decision to stay here, it's unlikely that she'd have allowed herself to be cut off without a means of leaving should the need arise.'

Bettrys shuddered. 'Should I put more wood on the fire, my Lady?'

'Good idea.' Mathilda continued to examine the embroidery, counting up the golden branches as she went. Assuming the tree was for Lady Isabel's family, there was one for each of the Willoughby children, one for her husband, and higher up, branches that reached outwards, presumably for her parents.

'I think it was her.'

'My Lady?' Bettrys poked at the tiny blaze, coaxing some heat back into the hut.

'The stitching that's missing. I think it once said *Isabel*. She's part of the family. The children's mother, no less. Yet her name is missing.'

~ *Chapter Forty-six* ~

16th January 1332

The crossbow bolt had gone right through the body.

Robert wouldn't have spotted the fallen figure if he hadn't been paying attention for signs of travellers having passed that way.

No effort had been made to conceal the body. Only the shadows of the trees and the gloom of early evening had stopped him seeing it straight away.

Bending to the man at his feet, Robert's throat constricted. John Pykehose had deserved better than this.

A whinny from Jep caused Robert to look up sharply. 'John rode you, not Mathilda.'

Breathing deeply, Robert was conflicted with grief, revulsion at the careless way in which John had been left, and relief that Mathilda hadn't been thrown after all.

Whatever made me think Mathilda would have done what she was told and ridden Jep? Of course she took her palfrey.

Mathilda would go her own way, whatever he said. In that moment he loved her more than ever.

Closing John's eyes, Robert took a blanket from his pack roll and wrapped it around his friend, before lifting him over Jep's saddle.

Robert glanced around. Moving towards Wollaton with a dead body on his horse didn't feel like a welcome option.

'Well, I'm not leaving John here.' Robert steered the horses towards the road. Sitting straight in the saddle he tilted his chin high. 'Enough indecision. I'm a Folville and I am going home.'

Daniel froze. He'd gone further into the forest than he'd intended, but now he knew he'd found what he'd been hunting for.

Bile rose in this throat. His legs buckled and his feet refused to move forward. Disgust at his cowardice filled him as Daniel willed his friends to join him. He knew he should call for help, but his tongue had dried in his mouth.

You let John Pykehose down. You are not going to be that sort of coward ever again. You work for the Folvilles.

Forcing his legs forward, feeling as if they were made of lead, Daniel approached the figure that lay before him. All he could see was the person's back. Their legs and head were shrouded by shadows.

What if the killer is here? Watching?

Forcing some moisture into his throat, Daniel huskily shouted for help. The volume was so feeble that Daniel was amazed when Brother Peter and Lord Edmund appeared almost immediately.

On seeing what had alarmed Daniel, Brother Peter gave a resigned grunt. Stepping forward, he gestured for the lads to stay where they were, but Edmund had other ideas.

'Richard!'

As the cart rumbled into the courtyard Bennett's stomach constricted. Only a few days ago he'd have known exactly what to expect when his master returned home from wherever he'd been; this time felt very different   and not just because of the manner of his coming.

At the head of the mini procession, Gilbert looked set and grim. There wasn't even the glimmer of a smile in his eyes as he hailed the steward. Nor was there any sign of his master, who presumably, lay inside the cart, which was guarded on all sides Bennett muttered silent thanks for Lady Ingram's cool thinking in suggesting they took the cart with them. It was not like Lord Willoughby to hide away. Whatever he'd gone through, he clearly wanted it to remain hidden.

Hurrying forward, he came to the groom's side. 'He is alive?' The words were whispered for fear of his master overhearing.

'And spitting all hell.' Gilbert turned so the steward could see the growing bruise that enflamed the right side of his face.

Bennett took a step backwards. 'His Lordship did that?'

'Apparently it was my fault he was taken.'

'Your fault?

'If you'd found him, it would have been your fault. Believe me!'

'But we were all told to stay here.' Bennett's forehead furrowed as he approached the cart. He was about to yank back the thick leather sides, when a hand shot out and grabbed him by the throat.

'Get the sheriff and the bailiff here now. Now!'

Mathilda was as relieved as she was confused. Lord Richard Willoughby the younger was the last person she'd expected to find near the hut. It explained why he hadn't returned to Wollaton, but left a string of brand new questions to add to those already unanswered.

Moving Lady Isabel's gowns and the cloak, they laid him on the cot. Bettrys busied herself with warming water on the hearth to clean the wound that ran across the side of his head. It was a miracle the man was breathing.

'How long do you think he's been like this, my Lady?' Bettrys' stomach churned as she examined the twisted state of the man's leg. It was broken below the knee, the bone sticking out at a gut-wrenching angle.

'I don't know.' Mathilda grabbed one of Lady Isabel's gowns and wrapped it around the wound, trying not to be sick as she manoeuvred the bone gently nearer to its original home.

Brother Peter, having left Edmund in Daniel's care outside the hut, tapped Mathilda on the shoulder, 'Let me. I've done this before.'

Glad to relinquish the grisly task, Mathilda recalled what Prior William had said about Brother Peter serving in the Holy Land.

'He can't have been here like this too long. It is a mercy the winter has been mild, or he could have died of exposure if we hadn't found him.'

'Did he fall from his horse, Brother?' Bettrys squeezed the crusted blood from her cloth and gently worked on cleaning the next section of the head wound.

'That would explain the broken leg, but not that.' He pointed to Lord Richard's head. 'Stone fragments.'

'He could have hit his head as he fell.'

'He could, and probably did. That's what would have knocked him out and be thankful to God that it did, for the body can do incredible things with healing when it sleeps. But if you look closely, you can see another wound beneath the fragments, He suffered a blow delivered with impact.'

Mathilda closed her eyes as the monk clicked the bone into place and the first cry of pain shot from Lord Richard Willoughby's lips. 'Quickly, Bettrys, find water.'

As her maid dabbed cold water on the heir of Wollaton's lips, Mathilda looked from the head wound to the broken leg. 'Did you see hoofprints out there, Brother?'

'One set leading to where we found his Lordship. It must have been his horse.'

'Which isn't here anymore.'

'No.' The monk pointed towards the gown. 'Rip it into strips, please. I need bandages to bind this in place before we can get him back to Lenton.'

Hastily destroying the gown, Mathilda's mind raced. 'So either Lady Isabel got to the horse and rode away, or someone else did.'

'Couldn't it have simply bolted?' Bettrys watched as her patient curved his lips, sucking in the moisture in his semi-conscious state.

'By all accounts Lord Richard chooses his horses carefully. I don't think any mount of his would have left him willingly.'

'Unless it was frightened.' The monk straightened up. 'We need a litter to get him back to Lenton. He will be tended well in the hospital there.'

'You think he'll return to us properly?' Mathilda examined the damage to Richard's head. The more she looked, the more she saw what Brother Peter meant. There were two wounds there. A lump and small scar, where he'd hit the floor, overlaid a jagged wound that had clearly come first.

'Lord Richard was here, probably with his mother, and someone set upon him outside.'

'Outside?' Bettrys asked.

'There's no sign of blood in here, no struggle apart from

the fallen chair.'

Brother Peter agreed. 'That could have happened if the occupant got up too fast, startled by a sound that frightened them.'

Mathilda turned to the embroidery. 'Let's assume Lady Isabel was sitting here working on her sewing. She hears a noise that frightens her, and she runs outside. What does she find? Her son's horse perhaps, and then her son, who she presumes is dead. So, afraid for her life, she leaps onto the horse and rides for the place everyone thought she'd been all along.'

'To Lady Mortain's manor?' Bettrys dropped the cloth into the bucket of water and dabbed the wound dry.

Mathilda turned to Brother Peter. 'Unless Lady Isabel attacked her son.'

'You think that a possibility?'

'I think we need him to wake up.'

Accompanied by a trembling Lord Edmund, Brother Peter got ready to return to the priory, intending to bring a litter back for Lord Richard.

As he mounted his horse, the monk addressed Daniel. 'The women are your responsibility. Time to prove you are the good soul I take you to be.'

Daniel inclined his head as he watched the men leave. He'd been given a chance to atone for his rash actions in leaving Ashby Folville in the first place. He would protect Bettrys, Lady Mathilda, and the fallen lord with his last breath if he had to. Sitting on the step of the hut, wrapping his cloak about him, he pulled his dagger. This time his hands did not tremble.

Robert saw the two armed guards waiting in the road ahead,

but he kept going anyway. There were only two miles between him and his home and he was not going to let anything stand in his way.

Pressing on, he ensured his sword was visible, but made no attempt to draw it. The last thing he needed was to be accused of provocation by Sheriff Jort's men.

Before they had chance to comment, he called out, 'I am Lord Robert de Folville. I am returning home with a fallen friend. An escort would be appreciated.'

Taken by surprise, the guard's expressions declared that each wished they'd be put on duty far away from the Folville manor as Robert went on. 'There is no time for debate. This man, groom to my brother, Lord Eustace de Folville, has been murdered. It is your duty to report his death to your master and allow me to take him home to prepare for burial.'

'Murdered, you say, my Lord?' The nearest guard glared at Robert with open suspicion. 'But he was a follower of the Folvilles?'

'This does not make him invincible. He was a good man. Loyal. Kind. You may not know such men considering you work for Sheriff Jort, but if you have been around a while, then you will have worked for Sheriff Ingram before him. I'd consider what he would say before you prevent me proceeding towards my home.'

The guards jumped to the side of the road, the elder saying, 'We cannot escort you, my Lord. Our duty is to watch for Coterel sympathisers, but a fallen colleague needs his home.'

'Sensible.' Robert kicked the horse forward, calling after him, 'Wiser men would already have worked out that a Coterel supporter could have been my man's killer. Thus the death of John Pykehose should be reported to Lord Ingram, in Sheriff Jort's absence, with extreme speed.'

He smiled as the guards disappeared into the forest, almost tripping over each other to get the message to Lord Ingram. 'Saves me a job.'

~ *Chapter Forty-seven* ~

17th January 1332

'Adam!'

Sarah shouted so loud the guards outside the open gates to Ashby Folville jumped, as Robert pushed past them, ignoring their enquiries about how he'd got so close to the manor without being captured.

The steward was at his wife's side in seconds. 'Lord Robert. You are a sight for sore eyes, and… Oh no…' His words trailed off as his eyes fell on the body thrown over Jep's saddle.

Robert patted Adam gently on the shoulder. 'Take John inside, while I speak to our friends here.'

Sarah, her face drawn, ran to find Lord Thomas, as her husband led Jep and his burden under the cover of the stalls.

Mathilda couldn't remember what a full night's sleep felt like. She and Bettrys were taking it in turns to watch over Lord Willoughby the younger. Although his lips seemed to respond to water and his eyelids fluttered, he hadn't yet fully returned to the land of the living. There was a chance he wouldn't. Whoever had done this too him had almost certainly believed him to be dead.

Bettrys was curled asleep on the rug before the fire. *Lady Isabel even had a rug by the fire. Maybe she wasn't intending to leave here.* The more she looked, the more details Mathilda noticed. There was enough of everything in the hut to keep one person healthy and warm for at least a week or two, even in the depths of winter.

Daniel had reported finding a stack of firewood behind the hut, and a makeshift shelter holding a few sacks of vegetables.

'But why would Lady Isabel go to all the trouble of stitching her name into her embroidery, and then unpick it?' She sighed, 'Perhaps she made a mistake, or simply wasn't happy with her stitching?'

Unfolding her legs from the chair next to Lord Richard, Mathilda went to check on Daniel. The lad was wide awake, staring into the clearing before them.

'Is he back with us, my Lady?'

'Not yet.' She sat next to her guard. 'Are you alright, Daniel? I haven't had the chance to talk to you properly since you arrived at Wollaton.'

The lad blanched. 'I wish I'd never come. If I hadn't '

'Then we wouldn't know that Anne had fled to her brother in Nottingham and Bettrys and I would be alone in a forest with a victim of attempted murder and a killer on the loose. John wouldn't have wanted that.'

Daniel said nothing as he stared into the dark.

'Once the litter for Lord Willoughby arrives, we'll all go back to Lenton. The Willoughby children need to know what happened to their family.'

'Bettrys told me Prior William knows you. What if he tells them who you really are?'

'He won't, but if circumstances call for it, then I might tell them myself.'

'But…'

'The Folville family are hardly likely to have kidnapped the Lord Willoughby with one hand, while catching his wife's killer with the other.'

'Killer?' He looked around. 'But we haven't found Lady Isabel's body. She's with Lady Mortain, isn't she?'

'I hope so, Daniel.'

'You don't think she is though, do you. You think she's dead.'

Prior William regarded the two guards on the gate of Ashby Folville manor. He could tell that, despite it being only just past dawn, they were having a very bad day. A day he was about to make worse. He smiled. This was going to be fun.

With Brother Mark at his heels, the Prior knocked hard on the gates, completely ignoring the sheriff's men who rushed towards him. As the gate opened, the Prior turned to the guards, 'You might want to report to Lord Ingram that a matter of delicacy and urgency has arisen at Lenton Priory. He would be advised to go there at his earliest convenience.'

'Why should we?' The nearest guard had had enough of being shunned by the local nobility, who seemed to regard the law as a thing to be ignored when it didn't suit their needs.

'Because it concerns Lord Willoughby. The justice so recently kidnapped. I'd move fairly fast if I was you.' The Prior then turned to Lord Thomas de Folville, who'd arrived at the gate and was regarding him with some surprise. 'Lord Thomas, a pleasure. Shall we go inside?'

Brother Peter, accompanied by four of his brothers, including the Infirmerer, arrived at the forester's hut two hour's past dawn; a litter between them.

'Any news, Lady Mathilda?'

'The young Lord Willoughby regained consciousness an hour since. He is confused and in pain.'

'Has he spoken of what happened?'

'Of one thing only, Brother Peter.'

The monk's grave expression intensified into dark furrows, 'Of what has happened to his mother?'

'Yes.' Mathilda pointed to the forest on the opposite side of the clearing. 'We didn't search in that direction yesterday, but we did at first light.'

Brother Peter sighed. 'You found her?'

'As did Lord Willoughby's heir, before we arrived.' Mathilda led the way across the clearing towards the tightly packed ash trees opposite. 'I should have asked you to bring a bigger litter.'

'Enough room for mother and son?'

'Enough room for three.'

Two of the monks had already been sent back to Lenton to fetch another litter, to transport the dead to Holy ground for the attention of the sheriff and bailiff.

Daniel, with the help of a shaken Bettrys, collected up Lady Isabel de Willoughby's belongings, wrapping them in the bed linen before dousing the fire.

Minutes later Mathilda was staring at the only item left in the hut. The embroidery stand. 'That needs to come with us, It's important.' She looked at her loyal servants, 'Brother Peter has news from Prior William. We are to return to Lenton. Sarah and Adam will be there too.'

'They are leaving Ashby Folville?' Bettrys was scandalised.

'Justice Willoughby got word to Sheriff Jort. He'll already be on his way from Buckinghamshire towards the counties he's supposed to manage. It is only a matter of time before our home is overrun in his zeal to show King Edward that he isn't neglectful of his position.'

Daniel was alarmed. 'But our Lordships wouldn't have shown their faces when they took Willoughby. There is no proof, and…'

Mathilda gave a sad smile, 'It was bound to happen. Come on, let's get to safety. At least we'll be with our friends and, unlike these poor souls, we are alive. Mathilda's stomach growled, 'even if we are hungry and tired.'

Robert and Thomas glanced back over their shoulders as they cantered away from their home.

Sarah, Adam, and Ulric were ahead of them on their way to Lenton in the company of Prior William and Brother Mark.

'We'll yet return, Robert.' Thomas spoke without a trace of speculation.

'I know,' Robert kept his eyes on the road, not allowing himself another backwards glance, 'but when will depend on how much trouble Willoughby is intent on bringing us.'

'This situation is not a surprise though, brother. Mathilda was counting on such a reaction from the justice. We need this; his overreaction, to highlight why he was taken in the first place.'

'Let's just hope Mathilda has found Lady Isabel. I have a feeling we'll need her testimony against her husband if we are going to get through this without at least some of our necks being stretched.'

~ *Chapter Forty-eight* ~

17th January 1332

The bodies of Lady Isabel de Willoughby and her maid, Anne, had been laid out in the chapel.

If only you'd gone to Nottingham like your cousin assumed, Anne.

Mathilda knew the Infirmerer hadn't approved of her request to examine them properly, but Prior William had allowed her the privilege.

Her findings had confirmed her suspicions, but she was keeping them to herself for now. The women's wounds, both fatal, were so similar – and yet poles apart.

Meanwhile, tucked into a bed in the infirmary, Lord Richard the younger had taken a morsel of food and, although he was shocked after his experiences, he was going to survive.

His conversation with Mathilda had been stilted, his words painful to him as he explained through cracked lips what he'd seen and done.

Leaving him in the capable hands of the monks, Mathilda headed to Prior William's study. Ushered inside by Brother Mark, Mathilda stooped dead as her feet crossed the threshold.

'Robert?'

Was her husband really stood there with the prior, or was lack of sleep playing tricks on her?

A few minutes later, making the excuse of preparing the warming room for a meeting of the Folville family, Prior William left Lord and Lady Folville alone to reassure each other they were both in one piece.

Thanks to the prior's visit to Ashby Folville, and a series of messengers, within four hours of the bodies arriving at Lenton, only the Rector of Teigh, too far away in his church in Rutland to reach them in time, and Lord Eustace, who was travelling to Lichfield with the Coterels' portion of the ransom, were absent.

Mathilda, with Robert at her side, looked across the room to Sarah and Adam, her heart swelling with love for her friends. It was comforting to see them, but odd too. Whenever she pictured them, it was always within the walls of Ashby Folville manor. In fact, now she thought about it, she didn't think the housekeeper had strayed beyond the town for years. It saddened her that Robert had judged it too dangerous to leave them in the manor.

'In the early hours of this morning, word reached me that Lord Justice Willoughby has summoned the sheriff against the entire Folville family. On receiving this information, I visited Lords Robert and Thomas at Ashby Folville, and bid them join us here.' The Prior took a draught of wine, his countenance solemn. 'Information has also reached me, saying the justice is intending to petition King Edward for compensation against the ransom he was compelled to pay.'

Laurence de Folville growled into his cup, 'The man has no evidence it was anything to do with us. All assumption.'

'Accurate assumption.' Prior William cleared his throat.

'After consultation with Lord Robert, I thought it wise to gather you here for the time being. At least, until we have listened to Lady Mathilda's news concerning another branch of the Willoughby family.'

Robert looked at his wife. 'You disobeyed me again, then?'

'Naturally. Although I'd like to have been prevented from having to.'

Lord John de Folville, newly arrived at the priory from Huntingdon, bought the meeting to order. 'We must converse quickly. It can only be a matter of time before those deemed to be involved in Willoughby's needful humiliation are declared outlaw.'

Mathilda's mouth had gone dry. She had been so caught up in the unthreading of the knots of the disappearances at Wollaton Hall that she'd temporarily forgotten that the result of their attempt to curb Willoughby's injustices would come with a heavy price.

Lord John addressed the prior. 'I had assumed Ingram would be here.'

'He was invited, and knows you are all here. His exact words were, "I trust Lady Mathilda to deal with the matter of the murder, and I hope I proved a useful husband to her." He went on to explain that it would be better for all concerned if he stayed away from you all, until he has no choice but to search for you.'

Blushing, feeling the weight of responsibility on her shoulders double at Ingram's trust in her abilities, Mathilda swallowed as Lord John coughed, 'Lady Mathilda?'

'My Lord?'

'As I understand it,' John poured himself some of the Prior's wine, 'Lady Isabel was believed to have gone to her mother's because she was mad. A fiction of Lord Willoughby's making?'

Mathilda scowled. 'A tried and tested way to remove an unwanted wife from her home.'

Telling the gathered Folvilles and Prior William all that had happened while she was at Wollaton Hall, Mathilda explained how Bennett had found the linen in his master's room. 'It was Anne, Lady Isabel's maid, who put that there. I think, on the instruction of Lady Willoughby herself.'

John leant forward. 'Lady Willoughby wished to frame her husband for her murder, even though she was alive?'

'I'm guessing of course, but I think it was to frighten him into thinking that she could if she chose to. Revenge for years of ill-treatment. I don't think there was ever any intention to do more than disappear for a while. He'd told the world she was suffering from madness; an act of cruelty she was not going to easily forgive.'

The elder Folville fixed his shrewd eyes on Lady Mathilda. 'This maid, Anne, she was given the key to Lord Willoughby's chamber by his wife so the bloodied linen could be planted there?'

'I don't believe Lady Isabel had a key, but rather instructed Anne to find one.' Mathilda squeezed Robert's hand under the table, 'I was not convinced anyone had been hurt when I saw the linen; the blood was wrong. An animal's, I expect, perhaps from the kitchen. Initially, I believed Bennett, the steward, had planted it there, but later, I understood the truth of the situation.'

'And Anne agreed to help her mistress because they were close,' Lord John stated. 'My wife and her lady are inseparable.'

'In this case the opposite was true. Lady Isabel was a clever woman, she suspected   or possibly knew for sure that her husband was making private use of her maid. She may even have known that Anne possessed a key to the chamber and had no need to hunt for one. What I doubt she realised was that Anne had fallen in love with her lord. An emotion which was to prove fatal for both of them.

'At first, I assumed Anne had gone to her cousin after she disappeared from Wollaton Hall; the reverend of Willoughby-on-the-Wolds. It seemed logical that she would flee to his sanctuary. Daniel went there in search of her, but Anne was not with her cousin. He, however, thought she'd be with a brother in Nottingham. I thought that likely until we found Richard the younger. That's when I began to wonder if the maid had followed her mistress. I should have seen that Anne had started to believe in the fairytale Lord Willoughby had weaved around her far sooner than I did. If I had, then perhaps

Sarah winced at the maid's naivety. 'She truly thought a man as powerful as Lord Willoughby would take her as his wife?'

'She did.'

Mathilda could feel everyone's eyes on her as Lord John asked, 'And you are convinced of the order of events? That Richard the younger killed his mother and then Anne?'

Taking a sip of her wine, Mathilda spoke quickly, 'I know time is short, my Lords, but we get ahead of ourselves. All is not as it immediately appears.

'I have spoken with Richard. The heir to Wollaton has been repeatedly told by his father that his mother was unstable; suffering with a growing level of madness. I don't think Richard believed his father, although he'd never say so openly. He was devoted to his mother   as his actions in helping her get away have shown   but he is also in awe of his father. After Lady Isabel directed Richard to the hut in the forest '

Daniel cut in, 'Forgive me, my Lady, but wasn't it Lord Richard's suggestion that they go there?'

'Edmund thought so, perhaps even Richard did. But I'm convinced it was Lady Isabel's plan all the time. She manipulated her son into thinking it was his idea. Maybe with Anne's help.'

'Anne's help again?' John's eyebrows rose.

'They were in this together. Or so Lady Isabel believed. Perhaps Anne thought that too, in the beginning. But when she discovered she would never get what she wanted, Lord Willoughby himself, her plans changed.'

'Jealousy.' Robert said the word without judgement. 'Who was it that ended Anne's dream?'

'The younger Richard Willoughby.' Mathilda gripped the stem of her goblet, 'and that was the point at which everything changed.'

The serving of warm bread and bowls of stew gave Mathilda the chance to think. To consider what she'd said and what still needed saying. Looking to where Bettrys and Daniel sat, their growing closeness no longer hidden, she muttered, 'I feel so sad for Ladies Marjory and Joan, not to mention Lords Edmund and Hugh.'

'What will happen to them now?' Bettrys dipped some bread into her stew.

'Very little, I imagine.' Mathilda sighed, 'Lord Willoughby is back in Wollaton swearing vengeance. The only mercy in him suspecting this family of kidnap, is that he can't blame us for collusion in his wife's murder.'

Robert grunted. 'And he, of course, will take no responsibility for that. Yet it does not take a fool to work out that if he hadn't been using Lady Isabel's maid as his whore, they'd both be alive and his son would not be facing the noose.'

Lord John gave a pointed cough. 'We digress. Lady Mathilda, you were telling us that Lord Richard Willoughby killed his mother?'

Laying down her bowl, Mathilda shook her head. 'An examination of Lady Willoughby's body shows that she was stabbed in the back with a knife or dagger. Her son wouldn't have done that.'

'He *didn't* murder his mother?' Laurence was becoming restless. 'You confuse me, Lady Mathilda.'

'After Richard had escorted Edmund here, to Lenton, to visit Lady Isabel and Hugh, he thought he'd then be taking his mother to visit the hut in the forest for old time's sakes. The possessions he had for her, he believed to be going all the way to Mortain. I can only imagine his surprise on learning that his mother intended to go no further than the hut, and to find many of the home comforts we witnessed there, already in place.'

Robert frowned, 'Placed there by whom?'

'I have to assume it was some of the mercenaries who were happy to be paid to transport them without asking questions.' Mathilda rubbed at her forehead, 'You will understand that some of my thinking is superstition as we can ask neither Anne nor her mistress about their actions.'

'Hold on,' Lord Thomas raised a hand, 'was the maid, Anne, at the hut when Richard and his mother arrived there?'

'No, but assuming she travelled straight there from Wollaton Hall, after going missing from Lady Joan's chamber around noon yesterday, Anne would have arrived only hours after them.

'According to Richard, the younger, when Anne reached the hut, she found him and his mother arguing. He was aghast that she was choosing to live like a peasant, while his mother was telling him he could learn a lot from peasants.'

Robert ran a hand through his hair. 'I think I'd have liked Lady Isabel.'

'And I.' Mathilda turned to the Prior, 'My Lord, how long was Lady Isabel resident here before she headed off with Richard? It was for longer than you suggested, I believe?'

Prior William's eyes narrowed. 'And what makes you say that?'

'Gut instinct.'

The churchman burst out laughing. 'I will never wager against you, Lady Folville, the gamble would never pay off.'

'You could answer my wife, Prior.'

'A pleasure, Lord Robert.' He poured more wine into his goblet, 'Lady Isabel has been my guest since she bribed her husband's men to bring her here, after he left her with them on the road to Lincolnshire to be escorted to her mother's estate.'

'Several weeks, then.'

'Since the end of November.'

'And the pony for Lady Joan?'

'Was from Lady Isabel, as Lord Willoughby declared.'

'How did Lord Willoughby come to receive the pony?'

'Gilbert and my colleague at Sempringham arranged delivery. It wasn't hard making his Lordship think it was his idea.' The prior snorted into his wine. 'Willoughby is blind beyond his thoughts for himself. He jumped on the gift as a ruse to bring him favour with one of his children.'

'Why didn't Lady Isabel send such tokens to her other children?'

'Ah,' The Prior placed his palms together in a clattering of jewelled rings, 'you must understand that Lady Willoughby was not without a ruthless streak of her own. She wanted her children to wonder at the truth of her absence. An uncharacteristic purchase of one gift, rather than five, that would raise suspicions against her husband. That, along with the bloodied linen you mentioned would '

The press of time caused Mathilda to interrupt, 'And you aided her in the endeavour?'

'Believing I was helping. There were to be other ponies for the remaining offspring later. We had no way of knowing that she would be killed before that happened.'

'Gilbert could have told me.' Mathilda sighed, 'He knew who I was from the start I think.'

'He'd promised to say nothing.'

Robert raked a hand through his hair. 'Are you telling us that Lady Isabel was using her exile to teach her husband a lesson?'

'Lady Mathilda is not the only intelligent woman in the region, Lord Folville.'

Mathilda was about to respond, when Brother Mark ran into the room, a bluster of apologies on his lips.

'What is this imposition, Brother?' The Prior was on his feet as fast as the Folville brothers. However, he was the only one who hadn't magically produced a dagger from his sleeve.

'A messenger from Lord Ingram, my Lord Prior.' He gazed helplessly around him, 'All the Folville men, bar Lord John, have been declared outlaw.'

~ *Chapter Forty-Nine* ~

17th January 1332

The uproar was contained by Lord John's fist slamming down on the table, as with increasing haste he asked Brother Mark to clarify the situation.

'Lord Willoughby has instructed the bailiff and the sheriff of his belief in your guilt as kidnappers. Arrest warrants have been issued and your outlawry declared.'

Mathilda gripped her husband's hand. 'So soon.'

'Are the soldiers already nearby, Brother?' Robert asked.

'Lord Ingram has not sent them out yet. But he warns that Sheriff Jort will be the man in control. He's been on the road to Leicester for some days already. You have a day, maybe two, until he reaches here.'

Lord John got to his feet. 'Thank you for your prompt word, Brother.' He turned to the Prior, 'We will leave your enclave shortly. You do not deserve such trouble at your door.'

The prior bowed. 'I am thankful for your consideration, but I have Lord Richard the younger in my infirmary. Is he a fugitive or a victim, my Lord? Do I see his wounds tended, or do I allow the bailiff to arrest him?'

All eyes returned to Mathilda as Robert beseeched,

'Speak quickly.'

Gripping her husband's hand, her words left her tongue as if chased by the Devil himself.

'Richard told me that his mother's decision to stay in the hut made him start to wonder if his father had been right all along. That Lady Isabel was indeed suffering from some insanity. A situation which, on her arrival, Anne used to her advantage. Rather than siding with her, as Lady Isabel had expected, the maid spoke plainly to Richard about her fears for her mistress's condition. That she, Anne, believed Lord Willoughby to only ever speak the truth.

'It was then that Lady Isabel snapped, revealing that she knew of her maid's affection for her husband.

'Lord Richard the younger told me how he'd watched in horror as the women screamed like shrews from either side of the embroidery stand. Unable to stand the folly of what he was hearing from Anne's lips, he told the maid squarely that his father would never tolerate her as anything other than a distraction.'

'Anne ran from the hut into the forest sobbing and yelling threats in anger. He tried to follow her, but Lady Isabel beseeched him to stay where he was. Then, to calm herself, she had picked up her needle and thread ready to sew the family tree she'd been working on. The action, as I came to learn from Lady Marjory, was the manner in which Lady Isabel always steadied herself. Embroidery was her passion.'

Lord Walter shifted uneasily in his chair. 'Is this relevant, my Lady? Time passes.'

'Very relevant.' Mathilda licked her lips. 'This was the first time Lady Isabel had been to the hut since her plan to reside there for a week or two. Anne had been entrusted with getting it in order after the mercenaries had got everything to the hut. It was the first time her Ladyship had looked properly at her embroidery for a while. It was a family tree.'

'I thought she always had some sewing with her ' Bettrys bit back the comment, as she remembered the press of time.

The Prior smiled. 'Lady Isabel has been working on a small, hand-held piece for the church. It's most beautiful. Please, Lady Mathilda, do go on.'

'It was Bettrys who noticed that there was some stitching missing. That a name had been removed from the family tree. The name of Lady Isabel herself had been unstitched. But not by her. Whether Anne intended to leave the space blank or add in her name instead '

'Surely she wouldn't have done such a wicked thing?' Sarah looked to Adam, who shrugged.

'We will never know.' Mathilda moved closer to the fire. 'Either way, Lady Isabel bid her son stay where he was and went after her maid herself. The fact Richard didn't follow her will be a regret he has to live with forever.'

'Are you saying,' the Prior lowered his goblet, 'that Lady Isabel herself killed her maid?'

'No, my Lord. I am saying that Anne knifed her mistress in the back.'

'Just like that?' Lord John leant forward, 'are you sure?'

'We'll never know whether more words were exchanged between the women, but the position of the wound shows that the stabbing was delivered at speed, possibly without Lady Isabel ever knowing what was coming.'

'Why did the maid have a knife with her?' Robert asked.

'A woman alone in the forest, setting up an isolated dwelling in secret for her mistress? I'd have a knife handy to defend myself, just as you would.'

A second of silence coated the room before Lord John moved the proceedings on. 'So, the maid killed her mistress. And then the maid died by Richard's hand.'

'Whereas the death of Lady Isabel was intentional   it may even have been Anne's plan to remove her mistress all along, although in a less abrupt manner   Anne's death was never meant to happen.'

Daniel raised a hand. 'Forgive the interruption, but I discovered Lord Richard behind the hut, whereas Anne was next to her mistress, on the opposite side of the clearing. How did his Lordship come to be found out of his wits where he was?'

'After a few minutes in the hut, Richard disobeyed his mother and ran outside. He ran forwards, thus stumbling upon her body straight away. One glance would have been enough for him to know his mother was dead. Drawing his sword, Richard dived into the trees. An accomplished soldier, it took him no time to follow the short trail of destruction Anne had made through the undergrowth to the place she hid.'

'He admitted as much?' Lord Thomas lifted his head from where he'd been staring into his wine,

'He did. The death that followed was an accident. Self-defence at worst.'

'Such things happen.' Thomas gave a sad smile. 'Anne tarried? Why, I wonder? I'd have been away on my heels if I'd been her.'

'I imagine she intended to live in the hut until Lord Willoughby returned to Wollaton so he could claim her as his wife.'

'The woman was delusional!' Lord John shook his head, 'And Willoughby had the nerve to claim it was his wife who was insane!'

Returning to her thread, Mathilda said, 'Lord Richard the younger had no plan other than to haul the maid to justice. But when Anne saw him approach, she picked up a large stone and threw it at him.' Mathilda winced as she remembered the wounds on Richard's head. 'It must have landed with some power.

'About events after that, Richard is hazy. It all happened so fast. He recalls Anne wielding her knife as he stumbled towards her. He says he lashed out, knocking the weapon from her hands and picking it up. He thinks she ran at him, impaling herself on the open blade in the process. Richard's description is of confusion and shouting and then a terrifying silence. The maid, he said, fell to the ground, her expression pure shock as she saw her own knife in her belly, before falling next to her mistress.'

Daniel swallowed. 'I will not forget the sight of them as long as I live.'

Bettrys took Daniel's hand as Mathilda went on. 'Intending to fetch help, Richard blundered across the clearing towards his horse. He mounted, but the blood was pouring from him now, and he was getting dizzy. He dropped the reins and fell as the horse broke into a canter, breaking his leg in the process and compounding the injury he'd already received to his head. We have to assume the horse bolted. After that, Richard recalls nothing until he woke in Lenton.'

Lord John fixed his eyes on Robert. 'Your wife was embroiled in this enterprise because she was hoping Lady Isabel would speak on our family's behalf against her husband?'

Robert exhaled slowly and nodded. 'That had been our intention.'

'And now we have no one to speak for us, how do you suggest we proceed? It seems we are in no different a position than if we had simply lopped Willoughby's head off.'

A low grumbling of agreement from Walter and Laurence was interrupted by Brother Mark returning to the warming room. This time his pink cheeks were flushed a worried scarlet.

'My Lords, my Lady, soldiers approach the priory. You must leave. Now.'

Robert wrapped his arms around his wife and held her fast. 'Look after our friends. Go home. You are not out-lawed, so you can go there safely. I will get word to you soon.'

'But…'

'Please, my love.' He kissed her head, his hands on the leather girdle he'd given her after they first met. 'This will be soon become a hollow outlawry, but until the dust has settled, we have to play their games.'

As the other members of her family, bar Lord John, has-tened to leave, each unaware of where they were going, Robert grasped Mathilda's hand. 'Before I leave, will you take me to Lord Richard?'

'Of course, but why?'

'Because Lord John is right. Without Lady Isabel to talk for us, we are more vulnerable than we already are. But we have her eldest son   and we know he has just killed his mother's maid…'

Mathilda decided that she wasn't going to think. She wouldn't allow herself the luxury until later. Much later, when she was home with Sarah and her household staff. Suddenly, they were to be her responsibility alone. That was something else she didn't want to consider   not yet.

A whispered word to the Brother Infirmerer, and she and Robert were alone with Lord Richard. He looked small in the bed; his head wound in bandages, his leg propped up, his face a waxy yellow.

'Lady Ingram?' Richard's voice cracked with the effort of speaking, his lips dry.

Mathilda glanced at Robert, uncertain whether to answer to her false name or not. The matter was taken out of her hands by her husband.

'I'm relieved to see you recovering from recent events, Master Willoughby.'

Richard gripped his sheet, his pallor whitening as he peered into the eyes of one of his father's demons.

'I have not come to hurt you. Despite the lies your father has woven about me and my family, I take no joy in killing and no pleasure in death.'

The injured man said nothing, but his eyes remained wide with fear.

'Thanks to your father, my family has to go into hiding. He accuses us of a crime without evidence. Again. We tire of his cruelty, his easy accusation of others if he has an eye on their goods or lands. When you are well, Master Richard, I would urge you in the strongest terms to give him a message from the Folvilles.'

Mathilda's blood chilled as she watched, unsure what her husband was about to say.

'Lord Folville?' Richard's eyes darted to Mathilda, his expression beseeched her for help.

'My companion here promised your sisters that she would find Lady Isabel. She has kept her promise. I am sorrier than you would ever understand that Lady Isabel died before she was located. An act that, like so many other crimes in this region, would not have happened if it weren't for your father's need to own everything, including his wife's maid.'

Richard's flesh blanched further, making him appear almost translucent.

'When you return to Wollaton, you will inform your father that the eyes of the Crown are on him as a result of his bleating about his kidnap – which was, let's face it, inevitable. There are so many he has wronged; the list of suspects as perpetrators of that endeavour is lengthy. King Edward will be informed of all of them. Every single complaint that has reached our ears with accompanying evidence will be sent to London.

'As it happens, we know who inconvenienced Justice Willoughby. I would, if you value your continued existence, steer your father away from us, and towards one Geoffrey de Maxeye.

'You will also refrain from telling anyone that the Lady Mathilda had your father's seal, because if you do, you won't live to be the next lord of Wollaton Hall and the death of the maid Anne will, miraculously, be known far and wide *not* to have been an act of self defence, but one of cold hard murder. A hanging crime. An extreme embarrassment to a family such as yours, as well as life ending for yourself.

'Think of your brothers and sisters. Think of how they'd have to cope with your father's rage if you were to be accused of murder... Even if he paid everyone off and you walked free, he'd always be the justice with the son who killed his mother's maid - and maybe even his mother... '

'But my Lord, Anne killed Mother, I...'

'We know that, but the truth can be rearranged if necessary. Adjusted. Manipulated to meet particular needs. You should know that. Your father does it all the time.'

'I...'

'One more thing...' Robert picked up Mathilda's hand and held it fast, 'Lord Ingram is not married.'

~ *Chapter Fifty* ~

15th March 1332

'Do you think Lady Marjory and her sister are alright?'

Bettrys wrapped a clean apron around her waist, 'I know their father is back, and Lord John was kind enough to send word that Lady Isabel had been buried with all reverence, while Anne was thrown into an appropriately unmarked grave, along with other criminals, but I fear the matter won't be closed for them for some time.'

'At least Prior William saw Master Richard nursed back to health. He's been left with a slight limp apparently, but nothing too bad.' Mathilda took up her vigil by the open door to her father's pottery. 'I'm sure he will care for his siblings. The manner of the loss of his mother will never leave him. Perhaps, in a strange way, it did him good.'

Bettrys rolled up her sleeves ready to scrub the excess clay splatter from the pottery. 'I still can't imagine why Lord Eustace allowed himself to get caught. It's not like him. Daniel tells me he all but walked into the sheriff's waiting arms.'

Mathilda laughed. 'I can think of a very good reason.'

'My Lady?'

Mathilda peered along the empty road beyond the workshop. 'Wasn't it convenient for Lord Eustace, to have been given the choice by Sheriff Jort between serving King Edward by fighting the Scots, or being arrested, just when Lady Joan's husband returned from his tour as Sheriff of Yorkshire?'

'Ah. I see.' Bettrys smiled. 'How came he to have the choice, though?'

'Ingram intervened, I believe.'

The maid relaxed into her work. 'Lord Eustace will be fine, won't he?'

'He's probably enjoying every second. Unlike the poor Scotsmen he meets on his travels.' Mathilda's eyes strayed from their vigil of staring along the road, as she glanced over her shoulder at her maid. 'I can hear a horse. Once the pottery floor is clean, Bettrys, then rest yourself until I return. I must move into the house. My husband approaches.'

'You are well?'

'Sarah and Adam cosset me, and Bettrys and Daniel cluck like hens at my heels.'

'Their kindness is driving you mad?' Robert ran a hand over the butterfly girdle that circled his wife's waist.

'It is well intentioned. You can be sure they will interview me closely as to your welfare when Bettrys and I return to Ashby Folville.'

'You may tell our friends I am in good spirits, but missing my wife and Sarah's cooking.'

Mathilda allowed herself to be held close. 'My father and Oswin are with Matthew, making plans for his wedding next month.'

'So this house is empty?'

'Bettrys is in the workshop, but otherwise, it's just us.'

'Come then, wife, let us remind ourselves of some of the

home comforts we are missing out on while our king deliberates the results of our meddling in his justice system.'

Wiping a stray red hair from his wife's eyes, Robert tucked her under his arm as they lay together, squashed in the cot Mathilda had slept in when she'd lived at the pottery.

'Now we've said hello, I have some news that will interest you.'

'Are you going to tell me where you've been staying?'

'No. And with good reason, but I am going to tell you that, at long last, King Edward has seen fit to listen to the messages we sent for his attention concerning Lord Willoughby's lawless activities.'

'You did send them, then, just as you warned the young Willoughby you would?'

'It wasn't I. It was the Coterels' man, Roger Wennesley, who penned them in the end. I'm given to believe he was cheeky enough to adopt the Royal Style of warrant in his missives.' Robert grinned, 'Either way, the list of charges, complete with witness evidence, have ruffled a lot of feathers.'

Mathilda sat up, clutching the sheet to her chest. 'And? Did King Edward believe it?'

'It wouldn't be wise for him to say if he did. We've been outlawed, so he can't be seen to agree with or condone anything associated with us. What he has done, however, is call the three most senior judges in England to his side. They are to travel across our region on a commissioning investigation, sparked by the aforementioned missive Wennesley sent the king detailing Lord de Willoughby's offences, as well as complaints against us from other quarters – Willoughby I suppose.'

Mathilda nodded, 'Will that mean they'll come to our

home, these three judges? Will it mean an increase in the hunt for you and your brothers?'

'Maybe, but now the King has finally taken note of the complaints against Willoughby, the investigators he is sending aren't just going to look at the region's crimes, but also at the men trying them. It won't be long before I can come home.'

'You think they'll allow that?' Mathilda, suddenly tired of being strong, of living without her husband, rested her head on his shoulder.

'I think, once the judges set out, their first visit will be to Willoughby, and that will be a most rewarding interview, I'm sure.'

'Because Richard de Willoughby the younger will remember what you said. Ummm...' Mathilda tucked her knees under her chin as Robert got out of bed. 'So, has it worked, do you think? What we tried to do in curbing the Justice of the Peace's power?'

'Too soon to say, but it has made the Crown sit up and think. Let's hope King Edward isn't distracted by another war with France before this matter is concluded.' Robert fastened his belt around his waist. 'In our favour also is the arrest of that thieving bastard Maxeye. He was found with some of Willoughby's rings on his person   stupid dolt.' Robert's smile morphed into a reluctant sigh. 'I must leave. I wish I did not.'

'Will Maxeye tell the bailiff about our role in the kidnap?'

'Would you, if you were him?'

'No.' Sounding braver than she felt, Mathilda gave a stout smile. 'You will be away longer this time?'

'Probably. While the king's judges see for themselves what passes for law enforcement here, I should continue to be absent.'

'Then take care, my Lord.'

'And you, my Lady.' Robert bowed, before pulling on his cloak. 'The second I have word it is safe to return to you, I will.'

There was a brief silence, before Mathilda asked the question which had been nagging her since she'd returned to Ashby Folville without her husband, two months ago.

'I asked you, before all this began, if you thought Roger Belers' death worth it, and you said it was.' She licked her lips, knowing she had to go on, but not wanting to ruin her precious time with her husband with an argument. 'Even now, so many years since he fell to Lady Joan's father's hand, the ripples of the pond tremble. Is it over now? Is the matter of his death closed?'

'I still hold that Belers' death was necessary, but the long-running consequences...' Robert sat back on the side of the cot they'd just vacated. 'I would never have guessed the shadow he cast would be so long.'

'And now Willoughby, his chief supporter and friend, has had a taste of what it means to be a corrupt justice in a place where there are men brave enough to act against him. How long, do you think, before he forgets that lesson and slips back to his old ways?'

Robert kissed her. 'Word from Wollaton inn speaks of a more subdued lord of the manor. Only time will tell if, at last, he'll let the matter of his corrupt colleague's death rest, or if he'll stick to the rules for long. But one thing is for certain: in time the younger Richard will become Lord of Willoughby. He will take over any duties his father is allowed to keep, and our family will be watching him.'

'And he has more reason than his father to keep his mouth closed against us.'

'Precisely.'

Holding Robert close, Mathilda nodded; there were no promises he could make when it came to the spectre of Belers' murder, but at least her discovery of Lady Isabel's body and saving Richard's life would count for something in the long term.

'Should I continue to liaise with Gilbert, if I have urgent word for you?'

'Do so.' Robert nodded, 'John Pykehose's loss is keenly felt, but there is no question that Gilbert Ward is a good replacement. When he is back from plaguing the Scots, Eustace will approve of his return to our family's service.'

'It's odd to think he worked for Eustace in the past.' Mathilda smoothed her girdle back into place around her waist. 'Gilbert has been rather amusing on occasions, when retelling some old Folville adventures.'

'I can imagine!'

~ *Epilogue* ~

November 1332

Gilbert Ward had delivered the parchment into his hands with such a flourish that Robert had immediately known the news was good.

On Gilbert's heels, he'd left the Abbey of Polesworth at a gallop, riding hard into the oncoming of winter.

Abandoning his mount to a delighted but startled Ulric, Robert was off his horse and running into the kitchen, before he'd even attempted to catch his breath.

The flagon of ale in a startled Sarah's hands hit the floor and shattered into a shower of soaking shards. Taking no notice whatsoever, Robert engulfed his housekeeper in a hug as, running towards the sound of the broken pottery, Mathilda and Adam came into the kitchen.

Hardly daring to hope, but speaking the words she'd long to say for so long, Mathilda whispered, 'The outlawry is lifted?'

'It is.'

Leaving the sticky, fragmented mess on the floor, Sarah ushered Adam from the kitchen as Robert pulled his wife into his arms as he called, 'Gather in the hall, my friends. We will join you soon.'

'Are you really home?' Murmuring into his shoulder, unbidden tears ran down Mathilda's cheeks.

'I'm really home.'

Moments later, gathered around the hall fire, wrapped in his travelling cloak, Robert unrolled the crumpled parchment.

'As we already knew, in March of this year, King Edward called upon the three most senior judges in England, Geoffrey le Scrope, William de Herle, and John Stonor, to tour the region investigating criminal claims. These eminent men have taken their time, visiting Stamford in Lincolnshire, much of Leicestershire, including Melton Mowbray and Leicester itself, as well as Nottingham, Derby, Oakham, and Northampton.'

'But not here, my Lord.' Adam exchanged looks with Sarah, who had yet to lose the suspicious expression on her face, choosing to hear the whole of it before she dared celebrate.

'They are clever men, Adam. Why walk into a hornets' nest when there are so many wasps to swat elsewhere?'

Mathilda gestured to the manuscript. 'Can you get to the bit where it says our family are no longer outlawed and the Coterel brothers need not remain on the run?'

'We are no longer outlawed, nor are our associates on the run.' Robert's smile widened as he returned his gaze to the manuscript. 'It'll be nice not to have to skulk about amongst a heap of nuns.'

'Nuns, my Lord?' Adam's eyebrows rose.

'The good sisters of Polesworth Abbey have been our friends for many a year. They have looked after me handsomely, but I tire of their wittering prayers.' Sitting down, pulling Mathilda closer as they warmed by the fire, Robert went on, 'Gilbert is on his way to Bakewell to get word to Roger Wennesley, who can presumably get word to the Coterels that it's safe to go home. Lord Eustace will be released from service in Scotland in June.'

Although relieved to have her youngest charge accounted for, Sarah remained cautious, 'May I enquire, my Lord, have the sacrifices of the last year been worth it?'

'You mean, did our attempt to show the Crown how corrupt Justice Willoughby had become, work?'

'That is precisely what I meant.'

'It did.' Robert raised his mug of ale, 'How about we drink a toast to the successful curbing of Willoughby's powers? There were too many rumours, too much evidence of corruption, for the travelling judges to overlook while they were in the region. Consequently, he is no longer a Justice of the Peace. In fact, the role of Justice of the Peace itself is to be disbanded in favour of the new Keepers of the Peace. As yet, Willoughby hasn't been appointed as such.'

'You mean, we won?' Sarah finally allowed herself to smile.

'The Lord of Wollaton remains a powerful man, but one whose greed has dug him into a hole, seen him humiliated before the king, cost him a wife and a mistress, as well the respect of his children and the region as a whole. A lifetime's punishment.'

Mathilda beamed. 'I hardly dared for such an outcome after all this time.'

Clearing his throat, Robert gave the manuscript a shake. 'Listen to how this message ends, *"With regard then to the misuse of power by certain justices; popular opinion tells of one Lord Eustace de Folville and his family enforcing God's law and social stability, fighting a blow against a corrupt local authority, and thus bringing attention of this troubling matter to those in power."'*

'For corrupt local authority, we can read Lord Richard de Willoughby?'

'We can, wife. We can.'

Mathilda laid a hand on her husband's arm. 'Robyn Hode would be proud, my Lord.'

'I'd like to think so.' Robert smiled, 'his approval would be praise indeed.'

Historical Notes and References

Those readers who have enjoyed the previous novels in *The Folville Chronicles* will recognise the kidnap and ransom of the justice Sir Richard de Willoughby, in 1332, as the felony alluded to as the 'future crime' Mathilda becomes aware the brothers have been plotting for some years.

Eustace, Robert, and Thomas de Folville (and others) were all indicted for this kidnap and ransom in the official Assize Rolls, *Just 1/141b*.

Despite his obvious corruption, Willoughby eventually returned to power within the legal system. However, he was removed from the King's Bench in 1340 after being accused of having "perverted the laws of England and sold them as though they were oxen or cows." He was tried in the court of King's Bench because of "the clamour of the people."

Roger Belers was murdered in 1326 in the field of Brokesby, Leicestershire. The incident was recorded in the Assize Rolls – *Just1/470*

Sir Robert Ingram was sheriff of Nottinghamshire and Derbyshire on four occasions between 1322 and 1334. Lists of Sheriffs for England and Wales from the earliest times to AD 1831 Preserved in the Public Record Office (List and Index Society 9, New York, 1963) p.102

***

The ballads and political songs within this story can be found within:

Dobson & Taylor, <u>Rymes of Robyn Hood: An Introduction to the English Outlaw</u> (Gloucester, 1989)

If you are interested in learning more about Robin Hood and the historical felons of the English Middle Ages, there are many excellent references available. Here a few of my personal favourites.

Books

Bellamy, J. G. (1973), <u>Crime and Public Order in England in the Later Middle Ages</u>, (London, 1973)

Hanawalt, B.A.,' <u>Crime and Conflict in the English Communities 1330-1348</u> (London, 1979)

Holt, J., <u>Robin Hood</u> (London, 1982)

Keen, M., <u>The Outlaws of Medieval Legend</u> (London, 1987)

Knight, S., Robin Hood: <u>A Complete Study of the English Outlaw</u> (Oxford, 1994)

Langland, W., <u>The Vision of Piers the Plowman: A Complete Edition of the B-Text</u> (London,1987)

Leyser, H., <u>Medieval Women: A Social History of Women in England 450-1500</u>, (London 1995)

Pollard, A.J., <u>Imaging Robin Hood</u> (London, 2004)

Prestwich, M., <u>The Three Edwards: War and State in England 1272-1377</u> (London, 1980)

Periodicals

Bellamy, J., '*The Coterel Gang: An Anatomy of a Band of Fourteenth Century Crime*', English Historical Review Vol. 79, (1964)

Kaeuper, R., '*Law and Order in Fourteenth-Century England: The Evidence of Special Commissions of Oyer and Terminer*,' Speculum, Vol. 54, No. 4, (University of Chicago, 1979)

Lloyd, P., '*The Corners of Leicestershire in the early fourteenth century*,' LAH, Vol 56, (University of Leicester, 1980-1)